SF
STAR W
HIGH

Into the Dark
Star Wars: The High Republic ;

DISCARDED
from Public Library

P9-CFI-520

# INTO <u>the</u> DARK

## CLAUDIA GRAY

P R E S S

LOS ANGELES·NEW YORK

HURON PUBLIC LIBRARY
521 DAKOTA AVE S
HURON, SD 57350-2797

© & TM 2021 Lucasfilm Ltd.

All rights reserved. Published by Disney • Lucasfilm Press, an imprint of Buena Vista Books, Inc. No part of this book may be reproduced or transmitted in any form or by any means, electronic or mechanical, including photocopying, recording, or by any information storage and retrieval system, without written permission from the publisher. For information address Disney • Lucasfilm Press, 1200 Grand Central Avenue, Glendale, California 91201.

Printed in the United States of America

First Edition, February 2021

10 9 8 7 6 5 4 3 2 1

FAC-020093-20353

ISBN 978-1-368-05728-8

Library of Congress Control Number on file

Design by Soyoung Kim and Scott Piehl

Visit the official *Star Wars* website at: www.starwars.com

SUSTAINABLE FORESTRY INITIATIVE
Certified Sourcing
www.sfiprogram.org
SFI-00993
Logo Applies to Text Stock Only

# STAR WARS
## THE HIGH REPUBLIC

The galaxy is at peace, ruled by the glorious REPUBLIC and protected by the noble and wise JEDI KNIGHTS.

As a symbol of all that is good, the Republic is about to launch STARLIGHT BEACON into the far reaches of the Outer Rim. This new space station will serve as a ray of hope for all to see.

But just as a magnificent renaissance spreads throughout the Republic, so does a frightening new adversary. Now the guardians of peace and justice must face a threat to themselves, the galaxy, and the Force itself....

# STAR WARS TIMELINE

### THE HIGH
### REPUBLIC

### FALL OF
### THE JEDI

### REIGN OF
### THE EMPIRE

THE
PHANTOM
MENACE

ATTACK OF
THE CLONES

THE
CLONE WARS

REVENGE OF
THE SITH

THE
BAD BATCH

SOLO:
A STAR WARS
STORY

## AGE OF REBELLION

## THE NEW REPUBLIC

## RISE OF THE FIRST ORDER

REBELS

ROGUE ONE:
A STAR WARS
STORY

A NEW HOPE

THE EMPIRE
STRIKES BACK

RETURN OF
THE JEDI

THE
MANDALORIAN

RESISTANCE

THE FORCE
AWAKENS

THE LAST JEDI

THE RISE OF
SKYWALKER

# PROLOGUE

"**A**h, pirates." Jora Malli shook her head almost fondly. "They never learn."

The Togruta Jedi Master sat beside her Padawan in their PI-R airspeeder as it swooped through the massive constructions that covered a good third of Coruscant, in pursuit of a pirate skiff. In the decades since the latest building boom had begun on the planet, valuable ores and materials had been shipped and stored there. Tempting stuff, for a pirate. And for many years, stealing a haul and getting away had been far from impossible. Yes, Coruscant was the central world of the Republic, one with a vast security force. But *everything* about the planet was vast—including its opportunities for concealment and escape.

However, Coruscant was becoming a more ordered place. An even more important place. And already home to the largest of all the Jedi temples in the galaxy.

Which meant Coruscant would be safer than ever before. About time the pirates learned that.

Jora opened her mouth to tell her Padawan what she sensed—that the pirates were going to try to surprise them by swooping upward—but Reath was already guiding the airspeeder up and over the spiderweb of construction beams, toward the brilliant sky.

*His strength in the Force isn't remarkable, not among the Jedi,* she thought as she studied her young human apprentice. The wind blew his dark brown hair into even more of a nest than usual. *But Reath works harder than almost any Padawan I've ever known. He tuned in to my thoughts not through his natural gifts but through effort of will—and he did it faster than the naturally gifted ever manage. He'll go farther than many of them ... perhaps in ways he doesn't yet understand.*

Their airspeeder crested the ridge of construction, and for a brief moment, Jora and Reath were treated to a panoramic view of the glittering structures of Coruscant—many of them crowned with silvery scaffolding but more of them complete, whole and shining. Sunlight streamed through the wispy clouds in the pale sky, painting everything pink and gold. Most beautiful of all, to Jora's eyes, were the five spires of the Jedi Temple on the horizon.

Then the pirate skiff surfaced from the maze of buildings, its pilot realizing the mistake too late. Reath immediately fired a tow cable. Its magnetic clamp shot out and seized the skiff's hull.

Calmly, Jora said, "Do you know the engine specs for that skiff?"

"I don't, Master Jora." Reath looked puzzled, then dismayed as realization set in. "Oh, n—"

His last word was cut off as the skiff dove desperately toward the ground level, easily overwhelming the airspeeder's engines and dragging the Jedi down with it.

Reath's hand went to the control to release the clamp and remained in place, ready to act. He already sensed what Jora had planned, then. She smiled as she braced herself, the rushing wind sending her striped montrals streaming behind her. Her eyes focused on the skiff's cockpit, on the just-visible silhouette of the pilot so frantic to get away that he might kill them all in the process.

"This is not how it will be," Jora whispered to herself, and then jumped.

Her leap took her from the airspeeder to the skiff itself; Jora's boots slammed hard against the cockpit as she ignited her lightsaber. Its blue blade slashed through the air, through the cockpit, slicing a hole. A faint shudder told her Reath had released the cable—*perfect timing,* she thought. The Force strengthened her grip, allowing her to hang on even as the skiff swerved violently in an effort to throw her free. Reath kept the airspeeder just behind them; what had begun as an accident was now breathtakingly close pursuit.

Jora punched through what remained of the cockpit opening and leapt inside. The pirates were so cowed by her attack—or, perhaps, by her lightsaber—that none of them insulted her by even pulling a blaster. However, the skiff continued plummeting toward the fast-approaching surface. In less than two minutes, they'd be killed in a pulverizing crash.

"Please take the ship out of this dive," she said, "and report to the nearest docking station for arrest."

The Rodian pilot hesitated. In that split second, she sensed the anger within him. Did it burn hot enough to make him sacrifice his own life, and that of his comrades, just to take her along?

Maybe.

Jora waved her free hand through the air, a casual gesture. "You want to report to the nearest docking station."

"We want to report to the nearest docking station," the pirates intoned in unison, and the pilot obediently took the ship out of its dive. Jora looked over her shoulder to see Reath falling in behind them, his grin as bright as the sunlight above them.

*A pity, to take away that smile for a time,* Jora thought. *But I can't put this announcement off much longer.*

She was able to put it off another hour. It took that long to get the pirates arrested and processed by the appropriate authorities, and to check out the PI-R airspeeder to make sure it hadn't been damaged. Reath had flown it well in challenging conditions.

He, however, remained focused on his one mistake. "I'll start on an in-depth study of engine specs tomorrow," he promised as the two of them strolled away from the station, through the myriad booths and kiosks that made up a kind of permanent street market in the area. A group of Bith, all the way in from the Outer Rim, mumbled over their mugs of Port in a Storm as the Jedi passed. "I've already come up with a list of ship models I should concentrate on, if you want to look it over."

"That's not our highest priority at the moment." Jora clasped her hands behind her back. "We've spent a great deal of time on Coruscant, you and I. You've traveled much less than most other Padawans your age."

"But we *have* traveled," Reath said. "Enough for me to know that the whole galaxy isn't like Coruscant, and for me to know that I like it here best. Besides, I understood that when you chose me, Master Jora. Not many Padawans are lucky enough to learn from a member of the Jedi Council. Traveling a little less as a result—it's not that big a sacrifice to make."

Jora wasn't letting him get away with that. "It's no sacrifice at all for you. It would take a gravity well to pull you out of the Archives, some days."

Reath grinned as he ducked his head. "Okay, fair enough. That's one of the reasons I've always thought we were well matched."

"I, too. Yet the time has come for each of us to expand our horizons. I've taken on a new assignment, one that will lead us far from Coruscant for many years to come. We'll be traveling to the frontier."

As Jora had anticipated, Reath's first reaction was dismay. He half stumbled over the curb in front of the Bilbringi food kiosk. "But—the Council—"

"I'll soon be leaving the Council for the foreseeable future," she explained. "This assignment is important enough to justify long-term involvement, and I have volunteered. It's work that plays to my diplomatic strengths. Still, I wouldn't have taken this on if I didn't think it was important for you, too."

"Why?" Reath blurted out. "How could it be important to leave Coruscant for a—a place in the middle of nowhere—"

"A place where Jedi once gave their lives to protect the people of that area of space," Jora said. "That is not nowhere. That is worthy of any honor we can give it."

"Of course. I didn't mean any disrespect." His face had paled, which made the freckles on his nose and cheeks stand out. Jora liked it when humans had some face markings of their own. "I only meant that I've been working as an archivist, trying to be a good one, and it doesn't seem like the frontier would need many of those."

She tilted her head, considering. "You might be surprised. But I intend for you to be more than an archivist, Reath." More gently, Jora added, "You prefer to concentrate on those areas where you believe effort counts more than talent. But you have more than enough talent for anything you set your mind to—and effort *always* counts. For any task, in any place."

"Doesn't it count more here? Where it does the most good?"

Jora shook her head in fond disbelief. "My first Padawan craved endless adventure. My second one would happily avoid it. What both of you actually needed was the same thing: balance. I found it for him, and I've found it for you."

(At least, she hoped she'd helped Dez find it. Sometimes, hearing of his exploits on Zeitooine and Christophsis, she wondered.)

The depth of Reath's dismay would've been comical if it hadn't been so heartfelt. That was one thing they never told you about being a master—that sometimes teaching a hard lesson hurt more than learning it. She said, "Tell me, Reath, why can you not cross the Kyber Arch by yourself?"

Reath frowned. "Do I need to?"

Jora didn't reply. The Kyber Arch stood within one of the vast meditation chambers of the Coruscant temple. Each crystal in the arch was a kyber crystal, one retrieved from the damaged lightsaber of a Jedi fallen in battle. As beautifully as it sparkled in the light, it was a reminder of the price their fellow Jedi had paid in the pursuit of justice over the past millennia. Thick at the bases, the very topmost curve of the arch had deliberately been left extremely narrow, as a representation of the perils the fallen had faced.

Scaling and crossing the Kyber Arch was an advanced meditation technique. Most Jedi never attempted it—only those who felt called to do so by the Force. So if Reath insisted on taking her question literally, he would never have an answer.

Literal he remained. "I mean, I think I could cross it. We've made our way across ropes and tethers skinnier than that. Do you want me to try?" Reath looked hopeful again. "If I make it alone, does that mean we don't have to go to the frontier?"

"Neither you nor any other Jedi has ever crossed the Kyber Arch alone," Jora said. "Nor will anyone ever do so. When you know the answer why, I believe you'll understand why we're headed to the frontier."

Reath sighed. Frustration practically radiated from him, but he maintained control admirably. He managed to ask, "Where are we going? Specifically, I mean."

Jora raised her head and looked into the sky as if she could see the stars beyond the sunset. "To the beacon of the Republic," she said. "To Starlight."

# ONE

Reath Silas was about to leave the Jedi Temple on Coruscant for his impressive new assignment on the frontier, and he was miserable about it.

"Cheer up!" Kym insisted, clapping him on the shoulder and nearly making him spill the contents of his cup. Her face was flushed with the excitement of the farewell party that percolated around them. "You're about to have an amazing adventure!"

"'Adventure' is usually a euphemism for 'going places that have lots of bugs,'" Reath said. "I mean, I know bugs have their place in the Force and are living beings in their own right . . . but that doesn't mean I want them in my socks."

Kym laughed at him. A couple of the colorful streamers decorating the Padawans' common area had gotten snagged on her lethorns. "You realize at least half of the apprentices here would do almost anything for a placement on the frontier, right?"

In Reath's opinion, "frontier" was usually a euphemism for "the middle of nowhere." But he didn't have the heart to debate with Kym any longer. It was hard enough pretending to be grateful for the big goodbye party his friends were throwing him.

No. He *was* grateful. It could never be a bad thing to know that others cared about you and would miss you when you were gone. But Reath was in no mood for a party when all he felt was melancholy and the absolute certainty that he was being taken from the best place in the galaxy to one of the worst.

Coruscant was the center of the known galaxy, literally and figuratively. Reath had always been grateful that was the temple he'd been sent to, that he'd had the privilege of growing up there, of learning directly from the members of the Jedi Council. His luck had continued when he'd been chosen as the Padawan of Jora Malli, one of the most renowned Knights of the age and a Council member herself. This meant Reath had served on a handful of the most significant missions of the past few years. What he lacked in natural strength in the Force (which he'd been keenly aware of since he was hardly more than a toddler) he made up for by working hard, being trustworthy, and taking responsibility. The majority of apprentices were still hoping for a measure of independence when they turned twenty; at only seventeen, Reath had already been trusted with tasks that his master said would've proved a challenge for even a full Jedi.

But most of all—*best* of all—he'd had access to the Jedi Archives.

Reath loved stories. He loved histories. He loved digging through records, learning what people had thought, said, and done in ages gone by. While the other Padawans were practicing their acrobatics or dueling with lightsabers, he'd been sitting up late with his digital texts.

This made him the odd one out, most of the time. Rather than conform, Reath embraced his bookish ways. He didn't see why anybody should think *he* was weird; really, it was weird of *them* to expect that every youngling would turn out to have the same personality. When the searchers went around looking for Force-sensitive infants, they only checked for potential ability. Not temperament, and certainly not preferences. Nobody ever asked the younglings, "Would you *like* to become a swashbuckling heroic Knight? Or would you rather stay at home and read?" Some people—however courageous and capable they might be—still preferred reading stories to living them, and Reath was among that number.

Until recently, Master Jora had been more than understanding. She'd always said the Order needed academics as much as it needed adventurers, and there were usually too many candidates for the latter, not enough for the former. She said she found it refreshing that Reath went against the grain. So his assignments had always included plenty of time in the Archives. Other Jedi based on Coruscant had even begun to leave open a particular carrel, with the silent understanding that it was Reath's spot.

Then, when no one ever would have expected it, Master Jora took an assignment in the *middle of nowhere.*

He'd protested. Respectfully, of course—but he'd made his feelings known, not that it did any good. "It will be healthy for you to stretch," Master Jora had said with a smile, "to test your abilities in other ways."

But Reath *had* tested himself. He'd pushed himself to excel in every field, not just his favorites. Who was always near the top of the lightsaber duelist rankings, Padawan class, despite not liking dueling much at all? Reath Silas. Who had aced every single one of his exams, except that time when he'd been sick to his stomach? Also Reath. Who was the only apprentice in decades to master Gatalentan meditation practices before his twentieth year?

*You're falling prey to pride,* Reath reminded himself. *Too much pride in yourself is proof that such pride is unwarranted.*

It wasn't like this was all his master's idea. After his protests, she had admitted as much: Master Jora had been selected by her peers to lead the Jedi mission on this new edge of the frontier. She'd be the Jedi Master in charge of Starlight Beacon, which would become fully operational any day now, to serve as a source of unity and allegiance throughout the newest sector of the Republic. His master deserved every honor she could be granted and any duty she chose. Master Jora would've turned down the assignment if she didn't want it. Clearly she did. And where the master went, the apprentice followed.

Master Jora had left for Starlight weeks before, going on ahead of him so he could finish exams in the historiography course he'd undertaken. But they were done. His time on Coruscant was over.

(He'd considered flunking something on purpose but couldn't quite bring himself to do it.)

*Why can no Jedi cross the Kyber Arch alone?* he asked himself for the umpteenth time. Reath strongly wanted to have the answer ready for Master Jora when he arrived at Starlight. Preparing for exams meant he hadn't had much time to meditate upon her question. He'd gone to study the arch itself, hoping that would spark some insight; instead, he'd watched a Jedi cross the arch entirely solo and with no apparent difficulty. But he knew telling Master Jora this wouldn't get him anywhere.

He had a mission. Time to focus on it.

Reath told Kym, "I shouldn't complain about this assignment. About any assignment, ever."

Kym managed to shrug and dance to the music simultaneously. "Hey. It's not like everybody's equally ready to take on every possible assignment. That's why they're called assignments instead of, I don't know, 'volunteering opportunities.'"

"I'm treating this like it was just a job." By then Reath was talking to himself as much as to Kym. "Being a Jedi is a calling. We're blessed with these abilities—these gifts—that we're meant to use for the good of all living things. That's just as true on the frontier as it is here on Coruscant."

It just didn't *feel* as true.

Rolling her eyes, Kym said, "Thanks for the lecture, Master Yoda. Now will you loosen up and have some fun already?"

Reath tried. It was good to see everyone again. (A handful of apprentices had gone on already; he was looking forward to reuniting with Imri in particular. And Vernestra had somehow gotten herself knighted already, which was *amazing*, so she'd be able to show them the ropes around Starlight.) The amateur band a few apprentices had put together had actually practiced, for once, which meant they sounded pretty good. He smiled, he danced, he drank certain beverages that, while not technically forbidden, were frowned upon for Padawans his age. A small measure of indulgence wasn't necessarily a bad thing, his master had said. Such celebrations could be embraced when they brought people together in communion and harmony.

But his gaze kept being drawn toward the one broad viewport in the room. Through its wide transparent stretch he could see the vibrant swirl of Coruscant: ships and speeders

zipping by at various heights and angles, the spires of buildings, walkways so numerous they crisscrossed his view like
an arachnid's web. As long as he could remember, Reath had
loved this buzz of energy—the sense that the galaxy itself
had a beating heart and that he could feel its pulse all around
him, every single day.

"Look within, my Padawan." That was what Master Jora
had said when Reath tried expressing this to her. "You're just
reluctant to leave the only home you've ever known."

That wasn't all of it . . . but it was part of it. A small part,
but still. Knowing that changed nothing. Reath still wanted
to be there, and nowhere else.

His chrono beeped, and his heart sank. Time to leave the
party, the Archives, the Temple, the planet, and, effectively,
civilization itself.

⚜

Reath didn't manage to disentangle himself from his friends'
affectionate farewells for some time, which meant he left late
for the spaceport. He dashed in, bag slung across his back,
only minutes before their scheduled departure—yet somehow
was the first person to show up at the designated berth. None
of the other Jedi was there, nor was the ship itself.

Did he have the wrong berth number? Reath was already
frantically double-checking when he heard a voice he recognized: "I was hoping I'd run into you!"

Reath turned to see a young Jedi Knight approaching—Dez

Rydan, striding closer with a bag over the shoulder of his traveling robes. It didn't look like he'd come to the spaceport to tell Reath goodbye. "Dez? What are you doing here?"

Dez grinned as he said, "Looks like we're on the same transport to the frontier."

"I didn't know you were assigned out there," Reath said. A young Knight as illustrious as Dez could go anywhere he wished.

"Just came through." Dez shrugged. "Actually, I requested this assignment only a few days ago. Lucky it got approved in time, huh?"

Reath nodded, which was easier and more tactful than saying, *Why does* anybody *in their right mind want to leave the known galaxy for the back end of beyond? Much less Dez Rydan?*

Probably it had to do with what Master Jora had said about her second Padawan not wanting enough adventure while her first craved adventure too much.

Dez had been Master Jora Malli's apprentice before she took on Reath. Sometimes younger Knights became mentors and close friends to their former masters' next charges. While Reath and Dez didn't have as tight a relationship as that, due to Dez's missions farther away in the galaxy, they were friendly and had practiced dueling together. This made Reath the envy of many Padawans, several of whom had chosen Dez as a role model.

Despite Reath's more academic bent, he admired Dez

as much as any of the others. Handsome, driven, tall, with golden skin and thick black hair, Dez made friends readily. Though he had passed his Knighthood trials only eight years previously, he'd already distinguished himself in both diplomacy and battle.

"Where's the transport?" Reath said through the blur of those beverages he'd drunk, hoping Dez wouldn't notice his condition. (He didn't fear a lecture, in any case. Reath had it on good authority that Master Jora had once caught Dez after a party at which far, far more beverages had been consumed, and that she didn't let him entirely off the hook until after he'd passed his Knighthood trials.)

If Dez did notice the state Reath was in, he apparently saw no reason to point it out. "It seems our original transport has a blown subalternator," said Dez. "Obviously there's not much to be done with that. They claimed to have arranged a substitute for us, but even the substitute is running late."

"What if they don't show?" Reath asked, half hoping the answer would be, *You get a whole new assignment and start over!*

Dez shrugged. "We'll find another ship. Surely somebody's headed out there in another day or two."

"A day or two? Forget *that*." Orla Jareni folded her arms across her chest as she leaned against one of the nearby struts. She seemed to have appeared out of nowhere, almost luminous in the dark gray mundanity of the spaceport. While Reath and Dez wore common mission attire, she had on snowy robes that were uniquely hers. "I'm ready to get out there. Trust me, there's at least one ship in this spaceport that wants our money badly enough to take us straight through the Maw, if need be."

Reath only knew Orla Jareni by reputation, but that reputation was a memorable one. Orla had recently declared herself a Wayseeker—a Jedi who would operate independently of the dictates of the Jedi Council. Some Jedi, from time to time, found themselves drawn to a period of solitary action, whether that meant meditation on a mountaintop, helping revolutionaries on a tyrant-ruled world, or even, in one legendary instance, becoming a minor singing sensation on Alderaan. All paths could lead to a deeper understanding of the Force, Reath had heard. Personally he didn't buy it. Still, if the Jedi Council respected Orla's decision, so would he. It seemed she felt her path led to the frontier.

Her appearance was as strikingly individual as her choices. She was an Umbaran, with the stark pale skin and high cheekbones common to that species. Her white robes were so pristine that they made her skin appear to have some small measure of color by comparison. Her hair, drawn back into a smooth knot, was a silver nearly as dark as black. Everything about Orla was angular, from the joints of her double-bladed lightsaber down to the corners of her knowing smile.

Which she was giving Reath right then, because he'd been caught staring. He ducked his head and hoped he wasn't blushing.

"I wouldn't be so sure," said Master Cohmac Vitus as he walked up to join the waiting group. His resonant voice beneath the hood of his golden robe made each word sound like a judge's weighty pronouncement. "Hardly any commercial traffic is headed toward Starlight—at least, so far."

Reath didn't know Master Cohmac well, though he would've liked to. The human man was renowned as both scholar and mystic. He seemed to have footnotes in half the books Reath read, on topics as diverse as ancient Force rituals and high-crisis hostage negotiations. None of that fully explained the mystique that hung about him. Master Cohmac stood at average height for a male of human or near-human species, but seemed taller because of his slender, angular build, the thick black hair he wore almost to his shoulders, and the gravitas of his presence.

Until recently, Reath had often seen Master Cohmac in the Archives. He'd spent many hours seated not far away while both of them dove into holocron after holocron. So why would Master Cohmac have requested a distant duty posting on the frontier? Then it hit Reath: *Oh, right, he's also a folklorist. He'll be collecting the local histories and legends, probably.*

He wondered whether that might be dangerous for Master Cohmac, who was known to be highly sensitive to the Force. Going someplace so wild would surely expose them all to influences none of them had yet dreamed of.

Only then did Reath realize that Orla Jareni and Cohmac Vitus were walking toward each other, gazes locked, half smiles on their faces. "Now, see, I could've sworn," Orla said, "that I once heard you say you'd never return to that patch of the galaxy again."

"It doesn't matter how far we run, or in what direction," Master Cohmac replied. "In the end, we always come back to the beginning."

Slowly, Orla nodded. "Yes. It's time for me to bring things full circle."

What could that mean? Reath and Dez exchanged glances that suggested they were equally curious, but equally unwilling to pry.

At that moment, Reath's attention—and everyone else's— was distracted by a ship flying through the spaceport, rather low, then landing squarely on the pad where their transport ought to have been. It was an unusual ship, at least to Reath: its plating was dark blue, and its cockpit and engines both rounded to the point of being bulbous. Either it had been built a very long time before, or the beings who built it didn't bother keeping up with technological developments—which was a troubling thought. As it settled onto the pad, the Jedi all exchanged glances.

"Looks more like a transport ship than a passenger craft," Master Cohmac said.

"Who cares? It can make hyperspace, can't it?" Dez grinned as displaced air ruffled their hair and robes with a hiss.

Reath frowned. "Maybe?"

No sooner had the ship settled onto the platform with a heavy metallic clunk than the hatch popped open. From it emerged a young girl—possibly Reath's age, no more than a year or two older, with tan skin. Her long brown hair hung free as she strode toward them wearing a normal pilot's coverall, an unusually neat, pressed one, in the same distinctive shade of blue as the ship itself. On the sleeve was stitched a star-shaped crest in dark orange. She put her hands on her hips and studied them all as though disappointed. "You're the passengers for Starlight? I thought we were picking up a bunch of monks or something. You look . . . normal."

"We are your passengers, and could be called monks of a sort," said Master Cohmac without any sign of surprise and only a slight pause before asking, "Are you the pilot?"

She grinned and pointed her thumb at the door. "Of course not. I'm the copilot, Affie Hollow. *He's* the pilot."

A teenage copilot seemed questionable to Reath, but when he looked in the direction she was pointing, all those questions vanished, replaced by far more pressing ones. Questions like: *Is that man's shirt open to the waist? Is he holding out his arms to us like he wants a group hug? Does he want a group hug? Is that guy on spice?*

*No—how much spice is that guy on?*

"Beautiful children," said the pilot, with a laconic drawl and a huge grin. "I'm Leox Gyasi, and I hereby welcome you to the vessel."

There was a brief pause, which made Reath feel better;

even experienced Jedi weren't totally sure how to approach this guy. Dez finally stepped forward with his usual charm. "Dez Rydan. A pleasure to know you. What's the name of your ship?"

Leox and Affie shared a glance, clearly in on a joke that was about to be sprung. "Already told ya," Leox said. He was a tall, tan, and rangy human, and his wavy dark blond hair looked as though it might not have been combed recently. Possibly ever. "Our vessel is called . . . the *Vessel*. I named it not for the container itself, but the space within the container that gives it its value and purpose. To remind me to look beyond the obvious, you know?"

*That sounds like Master Yoda on spice,* Reath thought. Which was either a very good sign or a very, very bad one.

"*Love* it," Orla said with apparently genuine relish. "So, can we see our bunks?"

Affie made a face. "About that. We're really more of a transport ship"—Master Cohmac gave Dez a look that seemed to say, *Just our luck*—"but we'll set up some partitions and cots for you." Affie's narrow face lit up when she smiled. "Just because we're a last-minute substitution doesn't mean we can't make it comfortable."

Leox cut in: "That is, if you're not super particular about your personal definition of 'comfort.'"

Orla was the first to head toward the gangway. "We are Jedi, Mr. Gyasi. We don't require pampering."

Affie wrinkled her nose. "So, are the Jedi monks or not?"

That stopped Reath short before he realized what this must mean. If they didn't even really understand what the Jedi were . . . "You guys have to be from out on the frontier, huh?"

"To us, it's not a frontier, son." Leox led them all after Orla into the *Vessel*. "It's home. But if you mean we're not used to this stretch of the galaxy, that's the truth. Never been this close to the Core before, not by a long shot."

"The Byne Guild handles shipping throughout the sector." Affie sounded proud. "We're just one of the Byne Guild's ships—one of the smaller ones, honestly—but Scover Byne still gave us the first-ever mission to Coruscant."

Reath, embarrassed by his tactlessness about "the frontier," was eager to move the conversation forward. He felt sure that this was his opening to ask more about Leox and Affie, their ship, and why they'd earned this particular honor. He also found himself eager to explain the Jedi Order to people who somehow had *never heard* of it.

But all conversation came to an end as Leox and Affie stopped their group at the edge of the cockpit. "And this here," Leox said with a grin, "is our ship's navigator, Geode."

Standing in one corner of the cockpit was a rock.

About as tall as and slightly wider than Reath himself, dark gray, with rounded edges and a flinty, flaky surface. Impressive, as rocks went. But still, it was just a rock, wasn't it? Reath frowned, sure this was some kind of weird joke.

"He's a Vintian, from Vint." Leox lazily wrapped an arm

HURON PUBLIC LIBRARY
521 DAKOTA AVE S
HURON, SD 57350-2797

around the rock's "shoulders," just like anyone would with a friend. "Geode's a nickname, by the way. Turns out you can't pronounce his name correctly unless you don't have a mouth."

Reath tried to parse that, and failed. His main consolation was that Dez and Master Cohmac looked as confused as he felt. Orla Jareni, however, wore another of her knowing grins.

"Geode, huh?" she said. "Pleased to know you."

Affie briefly patted Geode's side. "He's a little shy at first, but just wait until he gets to know you."

Leox cackled as he began leading them from the cockpit into the ship. "Yeah, you just wait. But I don't want to give you fellas the wrong idea. Geode's a wild man, for sure, but when it comes to steering the ship, he's all business."

"Solid, you might say." Orla raised an eyebrow. "Very well. Let's get a look at our bunks."

"Well, we sort of have to create your bunks before you can see them," Affie admitted. "Might as well get started."

*Great,* Reath thought as he turned to follow the others. *Not only am I headed to the back end of the galaxy, but the job of getting us through hyperspace belongs to a rock.*

Sometimes the Force had a sense of humor.

⚜

Within the half hour, their temporary quarters had all been built and assigned, and both passengers and crew had strapped in for takeoff. From where Reath sat, he could just glimpse the cockpit window, framed by control panels on one side and the outline of Geode (still motionless) in what must have been the navigator's position. He had to crane his neck for that look, but it was worth it. This was the last time he would see Coruscant for many months, maybe a year; Reath refused to consider the possibility of his assignment lasting any longer than that.

*Home,* he thought. The word pierced him like an arrow. The Jedi were not taught to think of their temples as home, nor the planets where they'd been born. Yet the longing for a home was something that no sentient being could ever completely be free of. Reath didn't want to be free of it. He wanted to remember Coruscant just like this—glittering, prosperous, ascendant.

*Do you resist your duty, my Padawan?* Master Jora's voice echoed within Reath's memory, gently amused but pointed, too. *Surely that is unworthy of a Jedi.*

*I want to do my duty,* Reath replied in his own head, more clearly than he'd managed to express himself to Master Jora when they'd last spoken. *But I feel that my duty is here, on Coruscant, in the Archives.*

He reminded himself that if something was telling him he shouldn't change his life at all, not even a tiny bit, that might not be the Force.

But it *might* be.

Reath scrunched down in his seat, clinging to his trust in the instincts that told him this entire trip was a bad idea, at least for him. The other three Jedi all looked steady, even serene. He envied them their certainty, their steadfast connection to the Force.

*When I've passed my trials,* Reath mused, *I'll be like them. Steady and sure. With purpose. Without any conflicts or doubts.*

✦

Orla Jareni braced her hands on the thickly padded straps of her safety harness. This was rougher transit than she was used to—the kind of thing she'd hoped to find on the frontier and had found even closer to home. She wanted to see it as a good sign, but it was always a mistake to carve omens out of hope, or dread. True omens created themselves and could not be mistaken when they came.

No signs had yet appeared to prove that she'd made the right decision.

*Should I take it all back?* Orla wondered. *The Council wouldn't begrudge me that. If I tell them I was wrong, then—*

*Then you'll break faith with yourself. At least begin. Go back to the origins of it all. Then you'll know whether you've made the right decision.*

*Or not.*

✦

The hood of a cloak could serve many purposes: warmth, disguise, muffling of excess noise, and so on. At the moment of their departure, Cohmac Vitus had his pulled up as a shield. He was working too hard at mastering his emotions to worry about controlling every flicker of feeling that might appear on his face. The turmoil within had to be quieted before he undertook his responsibilities on the frontier.

Volunteering for this had felt like the right move, at the time. Not only was it important work, but it also took Cohmac back to the place where—in his mind—he had ceased to be a student and become a Jedi in truth. The Knighthood trials had been only a formality after the Eiram–E'ronoh crisis.

But whenever Cohmac thought about those events, he had to fight back emotions no Jedi was supposed to experience.

*Going back will give you peace,* he told himself. *You will finally be able to set those feelings aside for all time.*

When Cohmac had told himself that on Coruscant, he'd believed it.

Now he wasn't as sure.

❧

Dez Rydan's long legs stretched out in front of him, crossed at the ankles, and he'd leaned his jump seat far enough back that he thought he had a chance of dozing off once they were underway. He'd expected this moment to feel more fraught, but instead he was invigorated. The mere making of a decision sometimes had as much power as any action. Purpose clarified every move, every thought.

27

Master Jora would no doubt say that he should be more careful. That craving adventure as he did could lead to other cravings less compatible with the role of a Jedi.

But resigning from the Zeitooine mission as suddenly as he had—questions had been asked and would be asked again.

*You did what you had to do,* Dez thought. *If you'd stayed any longer, your frustration would've ripened into anger. Aren't you done second-guessing yourself yet?*

He'd thought he was. For the moment that was true. But only time would tell how long his resolution would hold.

In the cockpit, Leox nodded as the coordinates came up on their screen. A few strands of his meditation beads, draped over the landing-strut lever, swayed and clicked as Affie eased the *Vessel* off the landing pad and beyond the spaceport's confines into the rush of Coruscant. "Good job, Geode," Leox said. "I'm about ready to get off this crazy planet. It's so built-up and busy, being outside still feels like being inside."

"I wasn't impressed, either," Affie said. "We didn't get to go around a whole lot, but still, Scover made it sound like this was the greatest place in the galaxy."

"Great in terms of scale." Leox nodded toward the surface of the planet as they soared away from it. "Not so much in charm, if you ask me."

Affie couldn't help feeling disappointed. She'd hoped to come back to Scover Byne with some insight or impression that would prove her worthiness to be one of the first members of the Guild to travel to the Galactic Core. There had to be something significant and fantastic about Coruscant, or it wouldn't be the most important of the Core Worlds, would it? Whatever that was, Affie had missed it. Maybe their passengers would be interesting; if this "Jedi" thing meant much, at least she'd be able to tell Scover about that.

*I just want to make you proud,* she thought to the Guild's owner, and her foster mother.

The atmosphere thinned. The sky darkened. The *Vessel* escaped Coruscant and slipped into space. Leox grabbed the hyperdrive levers and said, "Can't wait to get away from civilization."

With that he pulled them into hyperspace, away from the Galactic Core, into the wild.

# TWO

The makeshift bunks aboard the *Vessel* weren't luxurious, but then again, neither were the Padawans' quarters in the Temple. Reath noted the small cot, the thin partitions, and the bare-bones 'fresher without complaint.

Nor could he complain about the *Vessel* itself. All right, its crew was . . . eccentric, and maybe it was more ramshackle than the average ship that landed on Coruscant. However, the engines hummed along easily. The internal temperature remained within a range comfortable for humans and most near-human species. The Jedi had plenty of room to relax, either in solitude or with others in the mess.

Was there any information center? Any way to access histories or fiction? Of course not. It would be silly to expect anything like that on a small transport. But Reath noted it anyway, as the first sign of the deprivations he'd no doubt face on the frontier. Probably it was better to go ahead and get his sulking done now, before he made it to Master Jora and had work to do. Reath still had hopes of changing her mind, but he would rule out that faint possibility before he'd even started if he showed up at Starlight at anything less than his best.

So he wasn't in the mood for company. However, he *was* in the mood to eat, as usual. Growing as fast as he was— twelve centimeters the past year alone—sometimes it seemed as if it were physically impossible to stuff in as much food as he actually needed.

To Reath's relief, the *Vessel*'s mess was completely silent. He could have privacy *and* lunch. Under his breath he muttered, "The best of both—*gahh!*"

At the far end of the mess stood Geode. Had he moved from the cockpit? Had Leox and Affie moved him? Did he walk, or crawl, or roll, or teleport? Reath squinted at the rock, trying to determine whether the being was friendly, irritated, or even awake. Trying, and failing.

"Sorry," Reath began. "You, uh, you startled me there."

Geode made no response. Reath felt silly for expecting one.

"Oh, hey," said Affie Hollow as she trooped into the mess. "So, how do you like her? The *Vessel*, I mean."

"She's perfect for what we need," Reath admitted.

The word *perfect* made Affie's face light up like a Naboo lantern. "I love this ship. It's my favorite in the whole fleet."

"What fleet?"

"The Byne Guild," she said, opening up a packet of pale pink powder and tapping it into a small bowl. "Scover Byne is the owner, and she says she's grooming me to help take over someday. If I take on just a little more responsibility, she'll give me a ship of my own—I just know it. And I'd pick the *Vessel.*"

Reath silently downgraded his thoughts about the size and influence of the Byne Guild. The *Vessel* was serviceable, sure, but if this was the pick of the fleet, he had questions about that fleet.

His expression must've betrayed his thoughts too clearly, because Affie laughed. "Scover doesn't get why this is my favorite, either. But I feel like certain ships . . . they have an energy, you know? Maybe even a little bit of a soul. The *Vessel* has more of a soul than any other ship I've encountered. And that's what I want to travel the galaxy in."

"I understand that," Reath offered. Maybe the ship grew on you, after a while. "It does have, um, personality."

Affie stirred a little water into the bowl, and the pinkish powder puffed up into a sticky bun. "So, okay, tell me what the Jedi are in two sentences or less."

For the first time in what felt like days, Reath smiled. "Those two sentences might be pretty long."

"We've got nothing but hyperspace and time." She settled herself into a chair and took a big bite of the sticky bun, through which she mumbled, "Ready for this, Geode?"

Geode said nothing and did nothing.

Reath sighed. Best to begin at the absolute beginning. "Do you know what the Force is?"

Affie gave him a withering look. "*Everybody* knows about the Force, come *on*."

"All right, all right." He held up his hands in mock surrender. "Sorry. Just making sure. So, the Jedi are Force users united in our quest to understand the mysteries of the Force and to serve as guardians of peace and justice throughout the galaxy."

"I've heard of Force users before," she said. "But why does that make you monks?"

"I still have one sentence to go. Um, we ground ourselves in a spiritual existence and give up individual attachments in order to focus entirely on greater concerns."

Affie chewed thoughtfully on her sticky bun for a moment before saying, "So, that means no sex."

Should he give her Master Jora's whole speech about the difference between celibacy of the body and true purity of the heart? It was a *very* long speech. Reath decided to skip it. "Basically."

She nodded. "Definitely monks."

"Now, see, that I just don't get," Leox said later, when Affie and Geode tried to explain the Jedi to him. "How are you supposed to prove love to the galaxy at large if you don't know how to love any one individual person?"

Affie shrugged as she double-checked their readings. The wavering blue light of hyperspace glinted off every bit of metal in the cockpit, making it look beautifully electrified. Even Geode sparkled slightly. She said, "You don't have to have sex with someone to love them. You should know that if anyone does."

"Indeed I do. But other beings seem to value copulation as a form of bonding." Leox then made a face and swore. "Not appropriate. Sorry."

He meant well, she knew, but Affie *hated* it when he treated her like a kid instead of as an equal. Fortunately, he didn't do that much. "It's okay. I think I heard of sex once already."

That made Leox laugh. "Just make sure your mom knows I'm not the first person who talked to you about it."

Every time someone described Scover Byne as Affie's mom, it warmed her through. "You know, it would be easy to get Scover to like you more. If you'd just wear the Guild coverall once in a while—"

"Up with that I cannot put." Leox shook his head. "A man's gotta have standards. And since I lack the financial wherewithal to declare my independence from the Guild, my personhood must be asserted sartorially. In other words, you can take my beads from my cold dead body."

Affie suppressed a smile. "You know, the Jedi would probably say you were putting too much emphasis on worldly things."

"My relationship to the metaphysical is my own to judge, Little Bit."

"Don't call me that!"

⁂

Cohmac Vitus was a man of reason and logic. While he did not deny he possessed emotions, he never allowed them to cloud his judgment—or so he hoped. His precise, mathematical mind preferred the tangible to the nebulous, the quantifiable to the mysterious. More than one of his fellow Jedi had pointed out that this was an unusual frame of mind for a mystic. However, that was part of what Cohmac felt he brought to the Order: steadiness and rationality.

So why did that mindset now feel less like a gift and more like a defense?

*Because you are traveling to the place where you first learned the harm that arises from imprecision. From emotion. All that was born between Eiram and E'ronoh.*

For a moment he was back in the caverns, Orla shivering at his side, staring in fear at the shapes in the frigid dark. . . .

Cohmac shook his head, as though he could physically

rid it of the memory. The best way to get out of the mind was to exercise the body. Options were limited on a ship that size, but a brisk walk through the corridors would do. He made his way through the *Vessel*, hoping for privacy. The hope was in vain, as he almost immediately came across Dez rapt in conversation with Reath Silas. "I mean," Reath was saying, "would you call us monks?"

"Not exactly," Dez said. "I see you haven't been able to talk Master Jora out of the Padawan braid."

"No such luck." Reath gestured vaguely at the back of his head. In olden days, the braid had been mandatory, at least among apprentices from species that grew hair on their heads. These days, not every master required them; Cohmac had no intention of doing so, if he ever took another Padawan. Master Jora Malli clearly felt otherwise.

Cohmac intended to absent himself, but before he drew away, Reath turned to him. "Excuse me, Master Vitus? May I ask how you go about discovering and recording new legends? As a folklorist, I mean. Just find the local wisewoman, ask for a story?"

"Sometimes." Cohmac gazed out of one of the *Vessel*'s very few, small windows at the brilliant, eerie blue of hyperspace. "Often it is more complicated. There are always the stories a people *want* to tell about themselves . . . and then there are the other stories. The secret ones, the dark ones, the ones whose meanings are more difficult to comprehend. Those aren't the ones they offer to outsiders. Of course, those are generally the most important of all."

They were the stories that would have done the most good, between Eiram and E'ronoh.

Dez grinned as he set about restrapping his boots. "How do you get them to open up about those?"

"It varies," Cohmac said. "There are species who respect outsiders who push them hard, demand the facts. There are also species who eat outsiders like that. It's best not to pry until you know which kind of culture you're dealing with. While you're waiting"—he shrugged—"you study their art. Paintings, tapestries, literature. Symbolism and allegory can reveal a lot. Then you ask about the art, and the legends come up naturally."

"Crafty," said Reath. "But also ingenious."

"Thank you." Cohmac inclined his head.

Dez said, "That's got to be a challenge for you, doing something so completely new. To go off the map."

"Literally," Reath joked.

Cohmac could've said that he'd been to that area of space before. Specifically, to the lost moon between the twin planets that served as hosts for the new Starlight Beacon.

But there was no need to speak of it, and Cohmac had learned to limit his words. It was far too easy to say too much.

In the cockpit of the *Vessel*, Leox Gyasi chewed on a spice stick and considered the navicomputer readings.

(The spice stick was legal in Republic space. For now. Mostly because they hadn't had time to get around to outlawing everything yet. Maybe the sticks would make the cut and remain legal. But maybe not. Leox had laid away a stash just in case.)

*Oughta see signs of other traffic,* he mused. *Clearer signs than this. Are the readouts blurry? If so, why?*

"Geode, buddy," Leox said, "you seeing what I'm seeing?"

Geode's ominous silence told the whole story. Something was genuinely wrong with hyperspace traffic. Deeply wrong. The few traffic patterns he could make out were moving in directions that didn't make any sense.

Leox muttered. "Not liking this. Not liking it *at all.*"

The ship was still moving forward, under no more than the usual stresses, so they might as well keep going. The problem might be local, he figured—something they'd fly right by.

Orla Jareni hoped to spend at least part of their voyage to Starlight Beacon talking with the *Vessel*'s crew. She'd be buying a ship of her own soon, something she'd never done before. As much as she'd studied specs and models, she still thought there might be valuable tips to glean from people who spent their whole lives navigating the stars.

(Some Jedi fell into the trap of thinking that non-Jedi

didn't have anything to teach them. Orla, however, always remembered that every single being in the galaxy knew at least one thing she didn't.)

Affie Hollow seemed the likelier candidate for the conversation, Orla decided, if only because Affie seemed to have a greater commitment to sobriety.

Yet Orla found herself putting off the chat. Actually talking about purchasing her ship would mean talking about her decision to become a Wayseeker. As little as Affie knew about the Jedi, she would surely ask the most obvious question: *Why?*

At the moment, Orla didn't feel confident of her answer.

She could simply say instinct. That was true, but unlikely to satisfy Affie's curiosity. It was more likely to pique it.

Or she might say, *The Jedi Order and I no longer . . . see eye to eye.*

Also true. Also likely to get her into trouble if anybody from the Council ever heard of it.

Probably the best answer would be, *I needed to come to know the Force in a deeper, even more meaningful sense.* Also true, and both long and dull enough to discourage further questions.

*Wayseeker,* her mind had whispered, and there she was: Walking away from the Order to navigate an unknown region of the galaxy all by herself. Hoping that out there she would find the purpose her recent missions had lacked.

"Am I deluding myself?" she muttered as she stood in the mess, making herself some Chandrilan tea. "If I can't find the answers at the Temple, what makes me think I'll find them out here? What would my master say if she could see me?"

Then she paused, hoping no one had overheard that. Probably not, but on a ship so small, you could never be certain. She resolved to keep her musings internal for the duration of the voyage.

Orla took a moment to center herself—but found she couldn't. The energies on the ship were becoming muddled. Even frenzied.

Orla murmured, "What's happening?"

That was when Leox Gyasi's voice came over the ship's comms: *"Everybody who wants to stay alive, strap yourselves in now!"*

✺

Reath ran for the jump seats, reaching them just as all the other Jedi scrambled in. As they hurriedly fastened their safety harness straps, Orla called out, "What's happening?"

Leox answered, "Near as I can figure, hyperspace is broken."

"*What?*" Dez looked as bewildered as Reath felt. "How is that possible?"

"Tons of debris, the kind of thing you usually never find in hyperspace? It's *all over* hyperspace." The spice stick gripped between Leox's teeth was getting a grinding. "As in, littering every route out there."

Reath could barely put the thought into words. "But that would mean a disaster on—on a galactic scale."

"That's pretty much the size of it," Leox said. "Now everybody *hang on.*"

# THREE

Affie had seen a lot more than most seventeen-year-olds. Had boarded and served as crew on ships traveling the length of the sector, now across the galaxy, all the way from Kennerla to Coruscant. Had helped steer a ship through a hyperspace vortex once.

But she'd never seen Leox Gyasi so close to losing his nerve.

His hands remained fixed on the controls as he attempted to hold steady. "So," she said, "what do we do now?"

"We try to check whether our path is clear." Leox would've looked almost relaxed to anyone who didn't know him as well as Affie did. Only she and Geode could detect the tension coiled inside. "If we get hit by so much as a splinter of metal, we're looking at explosive ejection from hyperspace, followed by your favorite and mine, a hull breach."

*Hull breach.* Every space traveler's worst nightmare. A breach meant being blown out into the frigid void of space—which would kill you within two or three minutes. Within only seconds if you had any breath in your lungs, which would immediately expand and burst.

Even worse: the electric blue of hyperspace was changing color. Shifting more violet, all the way to red. Affie had no idea why that was happening, but it couldn't be good.

The navicomputer began blinking fast, sending staccato crimson light across the bridge. "We're picking up debris," she managed to report. "Something *huge.*"

Leox said what she was really thinking: "That thing's got a bull's-eye on us."

"Can we evade?"

"We're gonna find out."

Steering in hyperspace was no mean feat. Generally, there was no need to do so, since the navicomputer calculated and modified the jump at inhuman speeds. Today was an exception. Experienced pilots formed a kind of intuition about hyperspace—an instinct—that worked better than any droid or machinery. Leox had better instincts than any other pilot Affie had ever encountered. He could save them if anyone could.

She just wished she didn't know how big an *if* that was.

❦

"*Hang on!*" Leox's voice rang through the shuddering *Vessel*. Reath, who was already hanging on as tightly as possible, felt his gut drop. The other Jedi maintained their calm, or seemed to, but Reath could only manage the appearance of it. Not the reality. His jittery mind kept talking: *We should've held out for a better ship or a bigger ship or a ship with a more credible crew or basically any other ship except this one—*

*WHAM!* A bone-shaking jolt struck the ship, jarring Reath so hard he jerked against his safety straps and bit his tongue. Strange vibrations began rippling through the *Vessel*, more ominous than the crash had been. Was their ship about to fall apart?

Over the intercom came Leox's voice, lazy as ever. "*Okay, so, there's good news and bad news.*"

Master Cohmac and Orla shared a glance, which Reath caught out of the corner of his eye. He wasn't the only one having doubts.

"*The good news is that instead of space debris smashing us into so much scrap metal, it only winged us,*" Leox continued. "*The bad news, as the astute among you have already perceived, is that we've taken some damage. Affie's gonna check that out.*"

Already Affie was dashing past the jump seats, catching herself against the wall every time the ship lurched in a new direction, as it did constantly. Dez said, "Does anyone here have any expertise in starcraft repairs?"

"I just finished the basic course," Reath said, then waited for the other Jedi to chime in with their superior knowledge.

Nobody did. "Your experience is more recent than any of ours, then," Master Cohmac said. "See if you can help." He winced, as if in pain, but said nothing more.

Thinking that *he* might be the repair expert on board was almost as unnerving to Reath as the collision had been. But he immediately unfastened his straps and followed Affie.

The ship lurched from side to side; Reath stumbled into one wall, then another, but managed to stay on his feet until he finally got to the ladder that led belowdecks. He grabbed the rungs firmly before venturing a foot down.

"What are you waiting for?" Affie called. "Hurry!"

Reath let go of caution, and of the ladder, dropping down into the inner workings of the ship. Affie was already hip-deep in machinery, tools in hand. He asked, "What's going on?"

Then he saw for himself what was going on—which was that the coaxium regulator had come completely unhitched from its station. Affie had grabbed the regulator with her bare hands, which were already turning blue with the severe cold. Shaking, trembling, she was managing to hold the regulator in place, directing its cool green beam of energy into the engines where it belonged.

If she lost her grip, the beam would slide sideways and tear the *Vessel* in two.

Affie didn't look up. "We also need someone to reset the regulator station, if you think you can manage it."

Reath grabbed a tool packet and jumped down into the workings beside her. "I can do it. But if you'd rather I held the regulator while you did the repairs—"

"No. If the ship lurches during handoff, we're done for." Affie shivered from the cold but kept hanging on. "Just be quick about it, okay?"

He worked as fast as he could, welding the station frame firmly enough that the worst turbulence shouldn't shake it. The ship continued bucking and shaking, and once Affie seemed on the verge of losing her balance. Reath reached out with the Force to steady her as best he could. He didn't have the finesse necessary to hold the regulator exactly in place, but he could keep her upright.

"Whoa," Affie said. "What is that? Do you—is that a third hand or something?"

"It's the Force."

"Seriously? You can *feel* it!" She laughed out loud with surprise, and maybe even delight. "You're not a monk. You're a *wizard*."

"Yes! Monk-wizards. That's us." Reath checked what he'd done; it looked right, but a more experienced eye was called for. "Are you able to see my work? Do we have it?"

Affie glanced over her shoulder. "Yeah. That should do it. Help me lift this."

Reath put his hands on the regulator, too, and nearly cried out. It was freezing, so much so he could feel stabbing pain in every bone of his arms. Affie had to be in agony.

But she did no more than wince as they carefully, carefully pushed it upward. The metallic click of the regulator snapping back into position was one of the best sounds he'd ever heard.

Groaning, Affie stumbled back from the machinery. Her hands remained blue, and blisters had formed on her palms. "A stim stabilizer," she gasped. "The medpac's in that orange emergency box—"

Reath had it before she could finish talking. Quickly he pressed it to her neck until he heard the *hiss-click* of medication being dispensed. In only seconds, her hands began to return to their normal color, and the blisters flaked away.

"Great," he said. "We made it."

"We're not out of this yet," Affie said. Already shaking off the earlier pain, she climbed the ladder.

"What do you mean? More repairs?" Reath looked around for any sign of further damage, but nothing seemed apparent.

"Please think about this—*something in hyperspace hit us.* And I thought I saw . . ." Her voice trailed off, and she dashed back toward the bridge.

<br>

"If we had to get hit, I wish it would've been by anything else. Any damn rock out there in space," Leox said. "No offense."

Geode's amiable silence indicated that none was taken.

Affie hurried back into the cockpit, breathless. "Are we all right?"

"We are for now. Good job on the repairs, by the way."

"The kid monk helped me. But, that freighter—Leox, that looked like a fragment of a passenger craft."

Leox sighed. So much for breaking it to her gently. "Yeah, it was."

"There would've been hundreds of people aboard. Maybe even thousands." Her face was stricken; moments like these reminded him how young Affie really was.

"Horrible way to die," Leox agreed. Might as well hit her with all of it up front—even if she was still a kid, she could handle the truth better than she would any lie. "Listen, I can't be sure, but going over the readouts . . . that looked a hell of a lot like wreckage of the *Legacy Run* to me."

Affie's dark eyes widened. "But—the *Legacy Run* is a Byne Guild ship. Scover travels on it sometimes."

"I didn't say it *was* the *Legacy Run*. They're similar. Maybe not the same. Just—you oughta brace yourself. All right?"

She nodded, already attempting to focus herself back on the matters at hand despite the febrile reddish light of disturbed hyperspace all around them. His heart went out to her. Not every girl could throw herself into her work when she'd just found out her momma might've died.

※

*Scover is fine. Scover is absolutely fine.*

Affie repeated this to herself as she settled back into the copilot's seat. Scover Byne rarely traveled on Guild runs; she preferred to remain on their hub planets, overseeing their fleet in its entirety. She hadn't mentioned any recent plans to do otherwise. So Affie refused to panic.

Even if Scover wasn't on board (and she *wasn't*), the destruction of the *Legacy Run* was bad enough. The Republic's arrival in their sector had driven shipping to feverish levels of activity; everyone wanted to move cargo before it could be taxed, tariffed, or outlawed. Settlers wanted to reach the frontier badly and paid for transport by the thousands every day. Every single ship went out packed with as much living and inert freight as it could possibly contain. Even the *Vessel* had traveled to Coruscant with so many crates of denta beans that Geode hadn't been able to get through the corridors. Any loss would be a major loss. And the *Legacy Run* . . . there would've been hundreds of families aboard, thousands of people, even small children. . . .

"The ship's still acting weird," she said, both to snap herself out of worrying and because it was true.

"That's because hyperspace is still acting weird, though now I think it's got more to do with the freighter wreck throwing absolutely everything outta whack. I mean, look at this." Leox gestured at the readings. "Debris is flying all over hyperspace. Navicomputer's shutting down lanes faster than we can count them." He shook his head. "We're changing course."

Affie went cold, as though the coaxium regulator had been dropped back into her arms. "In hyperspace?"

"Yeah, I know—and don't even start, Geode. Thing is, we gotta drop out of hyperspace as fast as possible. We can't do that *and* get where we're going. So now we're going someplace else. Hopefully someplace safe."

She braced herself as preset coordinates began scrolling down the nav screen. Whatever preset would get them into realspace fastest was their new destination. She'd have to trust that the *Vessel* wouldn't be preprogrammed with coordinates that led to, say, the center of a dwarf star.

The final preset clicked in. Leox said, "Kid monk back in his jump seat?"

"If not," Affie said, "it's on him. By the way, he's actually a wizard."

Leox raised his eyebrows as though to say, *Not bad.* "Hang on!" he called out over the intercom, and then—

They were in realspace. No bounce, no jostling, as sweet a reentry as anybody could hope for. Affie and Leox shared a grin as she called, "Good pick, Geode."

"Now we can figure out what the hell went wrong out there," Leox said, "and then we can get on our way."

Relief washed over Affie as she looked out at the largely empty sector of space surrounding them. They weren't facing hostile ships, or intruding into a war zone, or anywhere near the heart of a star. They were . . . pretty much nowhere.

Despite the giddiness of their escape, she couldn't help wondering, *Why would the ship be programmed to take us* here?

"What happened?" Orla Jareni whispered. Her white face had gone even paler. "The voices crying out—"

"Many have died," Master Cohmac said. "You felt it, too, Reath?"

Reath had sensed something was terribly wrong far beyond the *Vessel* itself—and that it was tied to the disaster—but he felt nothing like the kind of shock reflected in both Orla and Master Cohmac's expressions. It occurred to him for the first time that there might be certain advantages to not being as acutely Force-sensitive as the average Jedi. "Can you tell what happened exactly?"

Unsurprisingly, Master Cohmac pulled himself together first. "No. We should contact Starlight Beacon immediately. We need more information, and we wouldn't want our delay to cause alarm."

Reath agreed. Well, mostly he agreed. A small, unworthy part of him wanted Master Jora to feel a *little* alarm—just enough to make her say, *You know, the frontier's a needlessly dangerous place for us to be. We should return to Coruscant right away.*

Still, he rose and went with Master Cohmac to the *Vessel*'s comm station. It was unlikely that Cohmac would need help sending their messages, but it was the role of the Padawan to be prepared to offer assistance to any Jedi, at any moment.

The comm station was a small area with a curved ceiling,

hardly big enough for even one adult humanoid. Two were already crammed inside: Leox and Affie, the former of whom was holding an amp unit to his ear. Apparently Geode was alone on the bridge, which Reath didn't find reassuring. Master Cohmac knelt at the door, as smoothly as though that was what he'd prepared to do all along, and said, "I realize your ship has urgent communications to make, Captain Gyasi, but—"

Leox held up one hand. "Hang on."

If Master Cohmac felt impatience, he showed no sign, merely nodded. But Reath could sense tension building within Leox and Affie—a tension that was catching. He blurted out, "What's wrong?"

"Everything, from the sound of it." Leox put down the amp unit and flipped a switch, projecting into the room instead.

Immediately they were inundated with noise, more than a dozen signals trying to break through at once, overlapping and blurring one another:

"—lost all power, stranded in the Bespin system, signaling any craft within—"

"—at least one thousand souls lost, possibly more—"

"—littered with the stuff, like someone mined hyperspace—"

"—can't even begin to assess the damage until we can get through to—"

"What sector are these messages coming from?" Master Cohmac asked quietly.

Affie's expression was grim. "All of them."

"So many fragments of the truth," Master Cohmac said. "No complete picture. Which of course is more frightening than the whole truth could ever be."

"We *hope*," Affie retorted.

Orla Jareni appeared in the doorway behind Reath and murmured, "Any news?"

He whispered back, "It sounds like—like this is a pretty epic disaster. Many people have already been killed."

*Killed.* The word was so final, so absolute. Reath suddenly felt ashamed to have been unhappy about his frontier assignment, to have been unhappy about his future when so many beings had lost their futures entirely.

Then a new transmission came through, louder than the rest:

*"All hyperspace lanes should be considered closed until further notice. For travelers beyond the boundaries of the Republic, through to the Outer Rim, we reiterate that hyperspace is currently unnavigable and extremely hazardous. All traffic is advised that hyperspace travel should be avoided at all costs."*

"Well, that's that." Leox shut the transmissions off. "You heard the lady. Looks like we're sticking around here for a while."

"Where is here?" Reath asked.

Affie replied, "Pretty much nowhere."

They were in a near-empty corner of space, unable to either move forward or get back home. For now, and for an unknowable amount of time to come, they were stranded.

"Listen," Leox said. "Sure, we can look at this as being marooned in deep space. But when you think about it, it's all just space, really."

Reath was uncomforted. He went to the bridge, which at least felt potentially useful, and for one moment was alone with Geode, who still sat—stood?—at the navigator's station. "Um," Reath began. "Hi. This is terrible, huh?"

"Please," Affie whispered as she entered the bridge just after him. "Don't try to talk to him about it yet. Geode's incredibly sensitive."

"Of course," Reath said. "But—I thought you said he was a wild man?"

Leox, who was passing by, interjected, "His is a capricious nature, one of many moods and climes." After that, and a fond glance at Geode, he continued on his way. Reath studied Geode for a few seconds, wondering what exactly he was missing, because it was *just a big rock sitting there.*

Affie settled into the copilot's seat, apparently to kill time, but then frowned at a blinking sensor. "What's that?"

"Is it more damage to the ship? Something else we need to repair?" Reath was only beginning to realize how badly he needed something to do, to make him feel less helpless.

Affie shook her head. "It's a beacon. A signal beacon. Not an actual message, but an indicator from a ship nearby that needs help."

"Nearby?" Reath asked. "How near does that mean?"

"Within this system, reachable by sublight," Affie said slowly. "We're not alone. Somebody's out there."

"Don't answer!" Orla called. She'd been walking by the bridge, apparently, but had halted at their words. "You don't know who's out there." Her gaze had gone distant. "You never know."

*— Twenty-Five Years Earlier —*

## PART ONE

Padawans Orla Jareni and Cohmac Vitus were steering the T-1 shuttle through hyperspace, and Orla couldn't believe her luck. To judge by the grin on Cohmac's face, he was equally pleased.

It was the role of a Padawan to do whatever task a Master required help with. Yes, sometimes this included thrilling acts of heroism, but it could also involve mending robes or cleaning the floors. Piloting a ship counted as a high-quality assignment, particularly when that meant bringing them closer to another, even more exciting task: rescuing two kidnapped rulers from the system of Eiram and E'ronoh.

This system lay far beyond the Republic's borders, in an area that had long resisted Republic membership or help—which the residents labeled "interference." While Jedi occasionally traveled into this zone of space, such voyages were rare, and the citizens seemed determined to keep it that way. This was, they proclaimed, independent space.

So the fact that these two worlds had called for the Jedi's assistance was hugely promising. A successful mission might finally bridge the gap between this area and the Republic.

(Master Laret had pointed out that if these planets were willing to ask for help from within the Republic, the situation was undoubtedly a thorny one. But Orla was undaunted.)

Probably this hostage crisis could've been resolved by the two worlds working together—something neither planet was willing to do. Eiram and E'ronoh occupied a system that served as a waypoint through hyperspace; they held a gateway, one that had long remained closed to the rest of the galaxy. This could've led to immense power for both worlds, had they been willing to share it. Instead, they competed for control of the region, belligerently dealing with those who dared to violate their space, each limiting traffic almost to nothing. Eiram and E'ronoh weren't actively fighting a war against each other, but intelligence suggested a bitter standoff between the two, one that had lasted for more than a century. Its origins were obscure and, by then, beside the point. Eiram hated E'ronoh. E'ronoh hated Eiram. The end.

Until royalty from each planet had been kidnapped and ransomed.

"It is both a great honor and a great opportunity that these people have called to the Jedi for help," Master Laret had said when she briefed Orla on the way to the spaceport. "We can do more than save these two rulers. We can prevent a war. We may even be able to open another part of the galaxy."

Orla had never had an assignment so significant before. Very few Jedi ever had. She didn't intend to let her master down.

Not again.

Of late, Orla had been asking too many questions. Challenging the decisions of the Jedi Council—only to Master

Laret, of course, but still. At first Master Laret had heard her out and even gently debated her, but her patience was being tested.

"To be a Jedi is to *serve*," Master Laret had said. "How do you intend to serve if you keep questioning every command?"

The rare rebuke from her master still stung. So this time, Orla would prove how willing she was to serve the Order. She wasn't going to question a single thing.

※

Nobody knew whether the moon had once orbited Eiram or E'ronoh, only that it had, at some point countless millennia past, drifted from its orbit and come to rest in dead space between the two worlds. The moon was so devoid of any value that Eiram and E'ronoh didn't even bother fighting over it. It just hung there, obscure and ignored.

Which was why almost nobody knew about the caves and tunnels deep within the lunar salt flats, and why the caves were a perfect hideout for those who did not wish to be found.

It was the only element of the kidnapping plan that could be called "perfect." The rest of it left much to be desired.

"Fools!" Isamer growled. The bulky Lasat threw the nearest thing he could reach at his lieutenants; it turned out to be a heavy chair, so they were lucky to dodge it. "How could you kidnap the *wrong queen*?"

At the far end of the cavern huddled two hostages, each

bound with metal cuffs, each wearing finery that had been stained and torn during their abduction. Monarch Cassel of E'ronoh, a bright blue Pantoran, looked extremely nervous about his situation, which indicated more intelligence than Cassel was generally credited with. Next to him sat the tawny-skinned human Queen Thandeka of Eiram, who looked *furious*. Isamer could crush most humans without even trying, and Thandeka was a small woman—but he was grateful she had no blaster.

One of the lieutenants pointed toward Thandeka, specifically to the silvery coronet woven through her thick black braids. "She wears their crown—the manifest reported the queen was on board—"

"Yes." Isamer folded his massive arms in front of his chest. "The *queen consort* was on board. The queen consort is the one who's married to the ruler. On Eiram, the ruler is Queen Dima—the *queen regnant*. In other words, the useful one!"

"Oh, bosh," said Monarch Cassel, amiably enough. "I'm certain the queen regnant wants her consort back. That'll do, won't it, for, ah, leverage?"

Under her breath, Thandeka muttered, "What are you playing at? Do you think you can team up with them?"

"Goodness, no." Cassel seemed appalled at the thought. "But—hearing them describe you as useless, it's rather impolite—"

"You're trying to *spare my feelings*?" Thandeka looked

toward the cave ceiling in what might have been either disbelief or despair. "Trust me, right now my ego is the least of our problems."

Isamer had ignored all this. "We will discuss it no further," he said. There would be time to punish these lieutenants—and find smarter replacements—after this was done. For now he could only stay the course.

The Hutts would expect no less.

They had approached Isamer, as one of the leaders of the Directorate. The mighty Hutts had come to *him*! With the Directorate's greater local knowledge, they explained, he was in a better position to destabilize the local governments. That destabilization would play to the Hutts' long-term advantage—an advantage they would share with those who had helped them.

Isamer could see it: the Directorate, empowered as partner to the Hutts, eclipsing every other criminal organization in that part of the galaxy. It was worth more than a little risk.

"Lord Isamer!" one of the sensor jockeys called. "A T-1 shuttlecraft has emerged from hyperspace, seventy radii distance."

Isamer's fur stood on end in anticipation. His fanged smile widened as he said, "Call to them from Cassel's ship." The wreckage of that ship lay broken across the planetoid's surface, but his lieutenants had managed to salvage the communications array. At least they got one thing right. "Plead for their help. Lure them in."

Cohmac pulled himself from a daydream, mentally repeating, *Focus.*

It hadn't been a bad daydream—just one in which he was dueling brilliantly with his lightsaber, the kind of detailed imagining that could actually improve real performance. But that was a practice for meditation. He had to improve his ability to live wholly in the present, as Master Simmix constantly reminded him.

At first he thought he'd done well to pull himself from his reverie, but then he realized it had been the comm panel lighting up with an incoming signal.

Orla and Cohmac exchanged glances as the voice came through: "Monarch Cassel—in distress, attempted abduction—systems failing—"

The code signature of the signal confirmed that it was Cassel's ship. Orla responded immediately. "The Jedi are on our way. Hold on!"

Should they have double-checked the signal first? That seemed like a minor detail, one Cohmac didn't dwell upon. He simply steered in the direction of the signal. "So at least one of the hostages got away. Does that make our mission easier or more complicated?"

"I guess we'll see," Orla replied. They exchanged smiles. As different in temperament as they were—Cohmac always turning within, Orla always leaping ahead—they'd been friendly since the creche and were equally eager to begin their mission in earnest.

Within moments, some sort of planetoid appeared in the distance—one so small and remote it didn't even have a name. Cohmac punched in the shuttle's approach vectors without a second thought.

Then Master Laret hurried onto the bridge. She, like Master Simmix, had been deep in meditative trance; Cohmac had expected to go rouse them both. But something had brought Master Laret to awareness, and then to alarm. "What's happening?" she said.

"Monarch Cassel must have escaped," Orla began. "We got a confirmed signal from his ship—"

"From his ship," Master Laret said grimly. "Not from Monarch Cassel."

Cohmac and Orla exchanged uncertain glances. Too late, Cohmac felt a shiver in the Force—the eerie dissonance that meant not all was as it seemed—

And then outer space itself seemed to blaze with light, and the ship shook and twisted, and there was no up or down anymore, no way to stop, no way out.

# FOUR

Reath wouldn't have been concerned for even a moment if they'd been stranded in space in the Republic. Longbeams always flew stocked with surplus fuel and provisions for journeys two or three times as long as scheduled. The surpluses were unnecessary, of course. Abundant hyperspace traffic and a subspace transceiver meant that a potential rescue ship was rarely more than a few hours away.

Out on the frontier, however . . . it seemed possible to be stranded for very long periods of time. Maybe permanently.

So Affie's announcement had at first sent a wave of grateful relief washing over Reath. Someone needed help. They might be able to give it, which would lend this strange detour some meaning.

But Orla's words had stopped him, hand halfway to the holo-transceiver switch. He couldn't believe he'd been on the verge of *trusting* the frontier.

Affie had obviously gotten there even before Orla's warning. "What if they're pirates? What if they're Nihil? What if they're just desperate people who'd raid us for food?"

"I'm sorry," Reath said, apologizing for the mistake he'd nearly made. "These aren't risks we have to deal with very often in the Republic."

Leox Gyasi eased around Orla and strolled back onto the bridge, clearly having overheard much of this. "That's about the first good thing I've heard about our joining the Republic," he said. "Makes me reconsider my reservations, and I sincerely appreciate any chance to look within. But this ain't the Republic yet, my man. Not by a long shot."

Master Jora's voice echoed in Reath's head: *Whenever you feel foolish, remember that you have been given an opportunity to learn. The truly foolish act is to refuse that opportunity.* "All right. Pirates I know about. But the Nihil? Who are they?"

"Good question," Orla said. She remained still and quiet at the door, though the tension Reath sensed within her seemed to arise from something other than their current situation.

Leox and Affie shared a glance that somehow seemed to include Geode, despite Geode's notable lack of eyes. "They rose up a few years ago," Affie said. "I mean, they've been around longer, but they just recently became dangerous. Nobody's sure where they're from."

"Nor can we determine their ethos," Leox added. "A confounding people. But we know three things for sure: they're raiders, they're brutal, and they're not out there right now."

It was Affie and Reath's turn to share a glance. Reath said, "How do you know it's not them out there?"

"I know it because we're still alive." Leox took his seat. "Doesn't mean we couldn't have some trouble, though. Tell you what. You pull the head monk or whatever in here, and we'll go through the signals together. See if we've got help, or need to give help, or should absent ourselves posthaste."

"We'll go get Cohmac," Orla said, already turning to leave.

Reath scrambled to catch up with her, thinking, *Master Jora couldn't have known about any of this, or she'd never have brought us out here.*

As soon as Reath and Orla were gone, Affie turned to Leox. "Since when do we need Jedi to help us decide what's dangerous and what's not? Especially since they've never even heard of the Nihil."

"We don't need 'em for that," Leox said. "But we three need to have a quick talk without any Republic types present."

Affie realized what he had to be referring to almost

instantly. She leaned in as Leox put one arm around her shoulders and one around Geode.

"Here's the situation," Leox said. "We would of course never want our Jedi to think that they might be aboard a ship carrying some cargo that is not, in the strictest sense, legal in the Republic."

"Never," Affie said, straight-faced. "That would *never* happen. The Jedi don't know anything that would make them think that."

Leox nodded. "We'd be prudent to keep it that way. Which is why no matter who's out there, or what they want, or what they might pay, we continue to present ourselves as an absolutely open ship, a hauler turned passenger transport just for the one ride."

Affie added, "No matter who comes on board, or where they want to search, certain compartments should continue not to exist."

"So very true." Leox pulled back. "Remember, everybody, our perceptions define the reality of the universe. Nothing is even *a thing* until our thinking makes it so."

"Not thinking about those compartments," Affie said. "The ones that aren't there."

"Scover's gonna be so proud of you." Leox smiled at her. Affie could've hugged him—not for the praise but for his casual assumption that her mother was still alive.

There was, of course, no "head monk" among the Jedi party. However, Cohmac Vitus had the most field experience of the group, and he could tell that Orla was shaken. They would need to talk about it soon—the parallels between this mission and the first they ever undertook together—but there would be time for that later. The distress call demanded his attention. So he went with Reath back to the bridge to help sort through the various signals. "Why not in the comm center?" Cohmac said, instead of hello. Leox Gyasi did not seem the sort to stand on ceremony.

"First, because we're not talking back just yet," Leox replied. "So we only need to isolate and analyze the signals right now. Second, because we can get a much better bead on each signal's origin from up here."

"Logical," Cohmac said approvingly. How rare to find a freelance pilot who operated on a rational basis—even if he looked and talked like this one. How steadying to have a problem that demanded concrete solutions, one that required him to search beyond their ship for answers instead of looking within. "How many are we picking up in the immediate sector?"

"Looks like—eleven," Affie said, gesturing to various red blinking dots on a green grid. "Of those, six are standard cargo haulers, not that different from us, except none is Guild-registered. Another two are standard passenger haulers, ranging in size from five-person skiffs to"—she whistled—"to at least one with two hundred sentients aboard."

Many people needed help, then. Possibly soon. Cohmac felt reenergized with purpose. Already he'd been itching to do something, anything, of use; it appeared that he would be called upon even sooner than he'd hoped. The Jedi's mission at the frontier would begin with both mercy and strength. First, however— "What about the others?"

"What about that one?" Reath asked, pointing over Affie's shoulder. "The bigger one? Some of those readings—those are high radiation levels, right?"

Leox nodded, but his lack of concern was so complete that it nearly operated as a tranquilizer. "Looks like Mizi to me. They're not as susceptible to radiation as most sentient species, so they haul cargo a lot of other ships can't. And that one there"—he pointed to the next-to-last dot on the screen— "that looks Orincan, which is bad news. Their lack of outer beauty is perfectly matched by their lack of inner beauty. I hate to be disparaging of an entire species, but if there are any Orincans overflowing with wit, charm, and kindness, I've yet to make their acquaintance."

Cohmac asked, "What about the final ship?"

"That's the one that bothers me." Leox zoomed in until the specs for that particular ship—the farthest out—became clear. "Smallest of the lot. The one that sent the original signal we intercepted. But I can't make heads or tails of it."

Cohmac could see the difficulty. "The engines of a racer— the plating of a transport—sensor strength almost akin to a research vessel—and yet some of the components are weak."

"Old, to judge by the readings," Affie said. "So they've souped up some of their systems but ignored the others until they're almost falling apart. Which is weird, right?"

"Yes. But hardly unique." Cohmac considered the possibilities. No armaments showed up on scans. Armaments could be shielded with certain plating. However, the engines didn't seem powerful enough to support that kind of shielding. He weighed the possibilities and decided. "Let's contact them directly."

"But if they're pirates—" Affie began, then stopped when Leox shook his head.

"You saw their scanners," he said. "They know we're here. They know what we're about. If they want to attack, they're gonna. So far they haven't. It's worth a shot. You want to make the call, Pawaman?"

It took Reath a moment to make the connection. Cohmac concealed his amusement. "Oh, uh, it's Padawan, actually. But I can make the call." He stepped closer to the comms and flipped the toggle. "This is the vessel—ah, *Vessel*. What's your designation? Can you transmit a visual signal? Over."

The screen fuzzed, then clarified into the image of a young girl—younger, even, than Reath Silas and Affie Hollow, though Cohmac thought only by a year or so. Her shining dark hair was pulled back into a neat tail, and her rounded cheeks blushed as she smiled. *"Oh, thank goodness! We were so scared you might be pirates. But you don't look like pirates. Wait. Are you pirates?"*

Reath was smiling, too, as were most of the other people on the bridge. "Not pirates. Travelers bound for Starlight Beacon, and now stranded here."

"*At least we're not the only ones,*" said the young girl. "*I'm called Nan. It's just me and my guardian out here, and we don't have much.*"

Cohmac interjected, "Some of us, including Reath here and myself, are Jedi, sworn to protect and defend the peoples of the Republic." All peoples, really, but he wanted them to understand the good that the Republic could bring to their lives. "We'll contact all the ships in short order, work on organizing together. Sharing resources will be the best way to survive this crisis." Nan beamed. Perhaps the Jedi had made their first friend in the sector. "Hold on. We'll be back in touch shortly." She nodded as the visual signal faded out.

No pirate attack was imminent. However, a vague feeling tugged at Cohmac—a barely conscious sense that something important remained undiscovered. "Captain Gyasi," he said, "can you expand your scanner perimeters?"

Leox nodded. "Just so long as you know when we gain reach, we lose clarity. As with so much in life."

"An acceptable trade." Cohmac leaned closer to analyze any scraps of information they might receive.

Instead of scraps, the screen suddenly filled with data. Leox's eyes widened as he scrolled in closer. "Whoa, whoa, whoa. What the heck have we got here?"

"A space station?" Reath said, making the leap faster

than Cohmac would've guessed. "But—it's nowhere near the system's star, and the energy levels are low—"

"Doesn't look like anybody's aboard," Affie said while bent over her own readings. "Though at this distance we can't tell for sure."

"We've heard nothing from the station, despite the unexpected arrival of eleven ships in this system," Cohmac said. "Energy readouts are fairly low. The likeliest conclusion is that the station's abandoned."

"Abandoned?" Reath asked. "Why? Simply gone derelict? Or has it become dangerous for some reason?"

Cohmac shrugged. "Maybe. Or could be this area was once a prosperous shipping route, and now is less so. Or it could simply have gotten old. Regardless, we should search it."

"I'll add to that," Leox said. "We need to search it soon. As in, right around now. And so should every other ship in the area. Because the local star isn't happy."

A quick scan showed the danger; the star of that blank, empty system was a volatile one, not yet ready to go supernova but beginning the final millennia leading up to that cataclysm. As such it would be prone to solar flares of dangerous scale and intensity. Their readings indicated it was about to flare up, sending out plumes of superhot matter that would be a million kilometers in length. When that happened—as it would within the day, if not the hour—the individual ships would be at risk of immolation.

"We have to put the space station between our ships and

the star," Cohmac said. "Obviously the station has shielding that allows it to endure in this system. If we anchor ourselves on the far side, we have a chance."

Leox nodded. "Sending out the alert right now."

*Thank the Force,* Cohmac thought, *for problems with simpler solutions.* They allowed the illusion that the universe could be controlled—an illusion everyone needed from time to time.

✺

For the first time since Master Jora had told him of their assignment to Starlight Beacon, Reath felt excited. An abandoned space station seemed likely to offer adventure *without* bugs, and some stories to tell his friends—whenever he got to see them again.

But Reath wasn't going to think about that just yet. Finally, he could get back to living in the present moment, as a Jedi should. It had been too long.

Every second they traveled closer to the station, his fascination grew. The design was one he'd never seen before: Its center was a large sphere made of hexagonal plates of some transparent material. Heavy metal rings clustered on square-shaped tethers at its poles, with another metal ring stretching around its equator, which he estimated at roughly five hundred meters in diameter. One airlock was part of the sphere itself, but was unusable, mostly because it was both enormous and highly irregularly shaped, built to welcome some kind of ship none of them had ever seen before, perhaps because it had ceased to exist. Master Cohmac's theory about the station's abandonment seemed to be accurate, because signs of damage and wear were apparent—missing panels, a small chunk of one ring broken away. However, its power core must have remained strong, because light still shone from the transparent central globe. Their readings confirmed this as the *Vessel* got closer.

"Gravity, check," Affie said. "Life systems, check. Atmosphere's an oxygen/hydrogen mix, so we can go on board if we want to."

Reath wanted to. "How long do you think that place has been abandoned? Decades? Centuries?"

"More like millennia, to judge by the tech," Leox said, squinting as he studied the station. "That looks . . . familiar, but I can't place why."

"The Amaxines." A thrill of recognition swept through Reath, bringing a smile to his face as he placed the familiar curved shapes and patterns of the metal. "That's Amaxine technology!"

"Amaxine?" Affie wrinkled her nose. "Who are they?"

Reath loved nothing more than a chance to explain. "They were ancient warriors—from really long ago, even before the Republic. Their fierceness in battle was supposedly unmatched. There are all these legends of how their scouts would appear almost out of thin air, signaling the troops to sweep in for attack."

"What happened to them?" Affie asked.

"Apparently, when the Republic unified so much of the galaxy, the Amaxines weren't willing to accept the peace. So they left the galaxy and flew into empty space, in search of another great war to fight." Which didn't make much sense, in Reath's opinion, but he didn't waste time judging a people who'd died out thousands of years before. Besides, the sheer thrill of this moment—seeing something that had once been only myth and legend suddenly come vividly alive—eclipsed everything else.

Leox drawled, "Now that you mention it, I believe I've heard some stories about the Amaxines, how they took off so long ago. But people have been here way more recently than that."

Frowning, Affie asked, "How do you know?" Reath was glad she had, because that meant he didn't have to.

"Preprogrammed coordinates." Leox thumped the dash. "This system was in our navicomputer. I don't know why, and neither does Geode, and neither do you—which is why I want you to ask your momma about this as soon as we get back to her. You're the only one who might get a straight answer as to why Byne Guild ships all come programmed with a map that leads us out of hyperspace, straight to here."

Reath turned his head, as though studying the readouts more thoroughly, so he couldn't see Affie's face. The explanation was obvious: some kind of illegal trade, maybe something the Guild did on the side. It wouldn't be easy for Affie to hear that, surely.

But there were other possibilities. The Guild might monitor illegal trade rather than engage in it—or even work against it, in an effort to eliminate corrupt competition. They didn't have enough information to know.

For Reath, information had always been as vital as air, something he felt he could never accumulate enough of. However, he was realizing that not knowing everything created a certain . . . exhilaration.

Which was probably going to be brief. And wasn't as good as actually being informed and prepared. Still, he'd take what enjoyment he could get.

A red light appeared on the *Vessel*'s console. Then another. Then all of them almost at once, glaring scarlet. Every single alert on the ship was sounding.

"Uh-oh," Leox said. His usual calm was finally shaken. "We've got a solar flare incoming."

Reath stared in the rough direction of the star, but it wasn't visible at that angle. "When?"

Affie's face had gone pale. "Four minutes."

# FIVE

**N**ormally an apprentice was to wait for a Master's approval before taking any dramatic action.

Nothing about this situation was normal.

Reath went for the comms. "All vessels! Approach the station for immediate docking. You have four minutes to get on the safe side of the station, away from the star. We'll send boarding orders shortly, after we've checked the station out. Just get there now!"

Coordinates came up on Leox's panel, and he nodded. "Thanks, Geode. Heading in."

The ship shifted so swiftly the gravity didn't have time

to compensate, sending Reath sliding to the far side of the bridge; apparently the senior Jedi had been caught off guard also, to judge by the thumps and a muttered *oof* he heard from within the main cabin.

Within seconds, the other ships came into view, all of them headed for the one small sliver of safety to be found behind the station—until one, the smallest one, slowed.

"That's Nan's ship, right?" When Affie nodded, Reath took the comm again. "Nan, you guys need to hurry."

*"Our engine's given out! We need repairs—and there's no time."*

Reath turned toward Leox. "Does the *Vessel* have a tractor beam?"

"Negatory." Leox wore a thoughtful look. "What we do have is a towline."

"Head for Nan's ship," Reath said.

Affie shot him a look, and it occurred to him that while the Jedi were ready to risk their lives for others, civilians weren't necessarily as committed. Nor was it fair to expect that of them. People had the right to guard their own survival. Before he could speak, though, she'd already flipped the toggle to ready the towline, and Leox turned them sharply toward Nan's ship.

More thuds sounded from the back, and a harried Orla Jareni appeared in the doorway, bracing herself against the jamb. "What in the seven hells is going on?"

"We're evading a solar flare," Reath said. "Another ship needs help to get to safety."

"Got it." Orla had instantly snapped out of her mood. "What can I do?"

Leox answered her. "Solar radiation's about to soak this whole system. For everybody except the Mizi, that station's the only safe place to be. So we need exosuits at the ready."

Affie chimed in, "And an order of boarding for all the ships, so not everybody's trying to hitch themselves to an airlock at once."

Immediately Orla got to work. Reath could only hang on and watch as they drew nearer to the pitifully small ship belonging to Nan and her guardian. It looked even more slapdash up close, obviously pieced together from other ship fragments. *Like a rainy-day craft project for Ugnaughts,* Reath thought, then mentally took it back. These people were doing the best they could with what they had. They deserved respect for their ingenuity.

He asked, "How close do we have to get for the towline?"

"Not too close," Leox said, then proved it by firing the tow. It lanced through empty space before colliding with the hull of Nan's ship. With a shimmer of energy, the electromagnetic clamp kicked in. "All righty. Now we just have to get to the station before being incinerated to atoms."

Reath tried not to let his reaction show, but he must not have done a good job, because Affie said, "Don't scare the landlubbers."

"We've only got forty-five seconds left," Leox said, and

Affie's jaw dropped. Apparently the situation was just as scary as Reath had thought.

But Leox (and, possibly, Geode?) took them around the curve of the spherical station a full two seconds before outer space filled with a flash of brilliant white light. Reath shielded his eyes with his arm and was still nearly blinded for a moment.

When he could sort of see again, he said, "That means we made it, right?"

Leox put his hands behind his head. "Am I good or what?"

* * *

Before anyone could board the station, a landing party had to make certain the interior was safe. Dez had asked to lead the way; Affie agreed to go on behalf of the *Vessel* crew.

Reath volunteered readily, though he had questions. "Should we conduct more scans first? There could be dimensions to this station we don't understand. Risks we haven't guessed."

"That's why they call it adventure." Dez was already double-checking settings on his wristband equipment, pacing near the airlock. "We already checked the atmosphere, so we know we can breathe. Anything else, we'll handle as it comes."

As Leox carefully maneuvered the *Vessel* into docking position on the central ring, Reath asked Affie, "Have you explored lots of abandoned old places? Are there tons of things like this out here?"

"First time," she said brightly, like there was zero chance they were about to die.

Maybe that was true. *Look at it this way,* he told himself. *You're doing research with primary sources. Getting the information straight from the source, to share with others later.* It helped, thinking that the last phase of this task would be simply writing it all down.

Their airlock spun open. Light streamed in, almost blinding at first, and Reath momentarily feared another solar flare. His eyes must have adjusted to the light more slowly than Dez's, because he whispered, "Would you look at *that*?"

An instant later, Reath could see it, too: a tunnel leading from the boxy, utilitarian ring straight into the central globe of the station itself. As the three of them walked through the tunnel, he realized it was transparent, creating the illusion that they were suspended in the blackness of space. He'd never experienced anything like it, strolling through a sea of stars. Vertigo threatened him for a moment, but it soon vanished in sheer fascination. Reath was drawn by both the spectacular view around him and what he saw ahead—an abundance of green.

They emerged into the central globe, which included booths and kiosks on multiple layers of walkways. They might've once been shops, laboratories, all open to the glassy sphere that formed the body of the station—and all covered in vines.

And ferns. And moss. Even a couple of trees. Plant life

spilled over every beam, climbed up every wall. This was more flora than Reath saw in a year on Coruscant.

"How—" Reath murmured as they stepped out, stems crunching beneath their feet. "How is this possible?"

Dez gestured toward the blazing light at the core—a small array of supercharged hexagonal power banks, suspended in energy fields. "Self-generating light and heat, fueling the station. The plants took care of the rest themselves."

"It's beautiful," Affie breathed, walking forward with her face turned up to the light.

Reath couldn't disagree. Instead of something menacing and diabolical, he'd strolled into an orbiting garden. "I bet the station had an arboretum," he mused as they walked forward. "To supply oxygen and food, and help travelers relax—all those things—and after the station was abandoned, the plants took it over."

"Sounds about right to me," Dez said, then inhaled deeply and smiled. The air was not only breathable but also smelled wonderful—fresh, sweet. "Look there. Turns out the plants have had some help."

Following Dez's pointing finger, Reath glimpsed movement within the greenery. A small droid emerged—an antique 8-T gardening model, which looked a lot like the "head" dome of an astromech let loose on its own. The thin metal instruments protruding from one of its panels appeared to be busy pollinating some bell-shaped flowers in shades of orange and violet. Another 8-T appeared, closer by, busy at the same task. They took no notice of intruders; their programming was solely about taking care of plants. It appeared the droids had done their job admirably.

"Should we do a botanical survey?" Reath asked. "Catalog all the life-forms here, find out if any are unknown to us at present?"

"Eh, that's droid work," Dez said. "And not particularly urgent. Personally, I'd like to get a better look at the other things sentients left behind . . . starting with *that*."

He gestured toward a particularly thick patch of fronds, revealing a shape that had been almost obscured behind them: a statue of a figure, human or at least humanoid, carved of some kind of stone and gilded with something dully golden that reflected the light. The vaguely feminine figure wore an elaborately carved headdress set with either colored glass or actual jewels, and it held its arms crossed over its chest. It resembled no mythological deity or folkloric hero Reath knew of, but he felt a thrill anyway. This was a window into history—into legend.

But behind that thrill lurked a shiver. A shadow.

Staring at the statue, he said, "Do you feel that?"

"Yes," Dez said. His voice had grown more thoughtful. "The shadow. It might not mean anything."

*Or it might,* Reath couldn't help thinking.

Affie Hollow neither understood what "shadow" Dez and Reath were talking about (which made no sense, since they were all bathed in light) nor cared. Whatever mysticism this brand of wizard-monk peddled was only mildly interesting to her. The station, however, was fascinating.

Not because of the antiquities the Jedi were already fawning over.

Because of objects far more recent than that.

Affie's sharp eyes picked out the spanner first, then the anx. A handful of spacer's tools, strewn in one corner—obviously abandoned for a while but not long enough for any vines to grow over them. The moss beneath them still seemed healthy and green, so they couldn't have been there longer than—a few months. A couple of years? She wasn't exactly an expert on moss. Maybe Geode would know. However, she was certain that it hadn't been very long since other travelers had come through the station.

Probably some of them had been Byne Guild pilots. Why else would this system's coordinates be preprogrammed into the *Vessel's* computer? Definitely nothing else remotely interesting was to be found around there; even by the standards of open space, that area was bleak. So this station had to have been of some use to the Guild, sometime, or it wouldn't be one of the places in their navicomputer.

*Hundreds of places,* she reminded herself. *Maybe even thousands. We never counted them all—what's the point? Some of that data might be old, out of use. Obsolete to how the Guild runs today. Scover built everything off preexisting navicomputers, back when she was first creating the Guild.*

Then she remembered that Scover might at that moment be dead or injured because of a disaster far larger than anything they'd ever encountered before, and her heart ached anew. For the Jedi this disaster was of great but abstract concern; for her it was intensely personal. Remembering how hard her foster mother had worked to build her shipping fleet made Affie even more fiercely hopeful that Scover had lived. She *deserved* to live, to reap the benefits of all that effort.

But the others killed in the disaster had probably deserved to live, too. Chance was too cruel to pay attention to what people deserved.

Dez was studying the inscription on the sandstone statue. Reath asked, "Can you read it?"

"No, it's not written in Aurebesh, and the glyph groupings don't look like Basic," Dez said. "But it's not wholly unfamiliar, either. Reminds me of a couple of ancient languages we studied. An actual scholar might be able to translate. Luckily we've got one on board."

Affie wondered whether she should mention the tools or not. The Jedi didn't seem to care one way or the other about who might've used the station recently, so she decided she'd keep that information to herself for the moment. When she had a chance to talk with Leox or Geode alone, they could discuss this and decide what the Jedi did—and didn't—need to know.

⚜

When Cohmac got his first good look at the small ship approaching them at one-tenth power, he felt a moment of empathy—almost tenderness. It had been literally patched together from at least four or five other ships, none of which appeared even vaguely similar in design. What poverty must have inspired this? At least desperate need had been matched with determined innovation. Where most would've considered themselves planet-bound and trapped, these people had found their own way to the stars.

As soon as they had confirmation that all species aboard could breathe inside the station, Cohmac indicated that the ragtag ship could dock at the nearest airlock and went out to meet them, Orla at his side. The initial exploration trio returned to stand beside them as the second airlock spun open.

"Oh, look," Nan whispered as she walked forward. She was even tinier than she'd appeared on the screen—a girl hardly more than a meter and a half tall, dressed in a shabby but colorful dress. Her dark hair was vividly painted with blue streaks, a flash of vivacity and life. "It's like my terrarium, but big enough to walk in!"

"Yes, just like your terrarium," said the elderly Zabrak

hobbling out after her, chuckling. His clothes were a match for hers, and his walking stick had countless notches carved into it as a record of some measure of a life Cohmac could hardly imagine. "Hello, there. I'm Hague, and apparently you've met my ward, Nan."

"Cohmac Vitus, Jedi Knight." He held out his hand to shake, a custom that fortunately seemed to be as familiar on the frontier as at home. "Welcome. Let me introduce my compatriots, Dez Rydan, Orla Jareni, Reath Silas, and Affie Hollow. We hope to turn this station into a place of refuge for those stranded by the hyperspace closure."

"You're the ones in charge, eh? Good, good. I don't mind saying that we're grateful to see you. Hardly enough provisions on board to last us three days. I don't need so much, but the little one—"

"I believe the larger transports will offer adequate food for us all," Cohmac said. *Assuming they're willing to share, and that the hyperspace lanes aren't closed for too long. No point in worrying these people about it.* "For now, get yourselves settled."

Orla nodded her greetings but moved past Cohmac, back into the *Vessel* for reasons of her own. The travelers weren't offended by her departure; Nan, in particular, looked delighted to have found people her own age. No wonder— Cohmac wasn't familiar with Zabrak life spans, but Hague was at a minimum several decades older. Looking back and forth between Reath and Affie, Nan asked, "Are you both Jedi Knights, too?"

Affie made a sound that Cohmac decided not to interpret as rude. "Hardly. I'm the copilot on the *Vessel*."

"I *will* be a Jedi Knight someday," Reath said, "but for now I'm still a Padawan. A student in the ways of the Force."

Nan lit up. "I've heard tales of the Jedi. Can you tell me more about your Order? How you learn to do the things you do?"

Curiosity about the Jedi was great in the frontier region, in ways both good and bad. Cohmac hoped they would make a good impression starting from this moment on. However, he suspected Nan's interest had as much to do with Reath's pleasant face as it did with the Jedi. Probably far more.

As older Jedi always did when observing such inter-actions between younger ones and outsiders to the Order, Cohmac mused, *I fear someone will have to break it to her that the Jedi don't—*

Well. Let Reath deal with that if and when it arose.

Orla came to his side. "Listen, I know you have plenty to think about at the moment. Leading the group, organizing the refugees as they come on board—"

"Your point?" Cohmac asked.

Orla arched an eyebrow so sharply it could have cut. "My point is, you can delegate your other roles. You can't delegate your knowledge of ancient artifacts. Dez has pointed out that this place is chock-full of ancient tech and even more ancient statues. With *inscriptions*. In *unknown languages*." Orla pro-nounced all this in the same tone of voice she might've told a racing enthusiast about the Neutrino Angler in the hangar next door, or described holiday sweets to an excited child.

Even though Cohmac was usually more moderate in his enthusiasms . . . Orla *had* caught his attention. "Totally unknown languages?"

"One of them, at least, reminds Dez a little bit of Old Alderaanian. He could be wrong, though. An expert's eyes would see much more."

"Then I leave it to Dez and Reath to handle the station boarding for now." He put one hand on Orla's shoulder. "Lead the way."

After they had walked several steps away, Orla said, more quietly, "It threw me, at first. An accident in this area of space, a ship we didn't know well—"

"I thought of it, too," Cohmac replied. This chapter of his past was one he rarely reflected on. The parallels between this mission and the first one he and Orla had undertaken together—he'd hoped to put them aside and ignore them for the duration of the disaster.

Apparently Orla didn't intend to let him. He should have expected no less. Cohmac could practically see the words hovering on her lips. However, before she could delve into the subject, she halted in her tracks and said, "Do you feel that? The . . . shadow? The chill? Reath and Dez sensed it as well."

"It's darkness," Cohmac said. "I've felt it, too. Something on this station is bound to the dark side."

# SIX

**S**ome people were awestruck by Jedi, unable to relate to them; others could be hostile, afraid of what they didn't understand, afraid of power they couldn't possess. Sheltered as he'd been within the Temple, Reath often wasn't sure how to bridge the gap and connect with regular people as, well, *people.*

With Nan, there was no gap at all.

"Are the Jedi soldiers? Sworn to the Republic?" She glanced down shyly as they stood beneath the canopy of leaves that sheltered the station docks. "Or do you fight only for yourselves?"

Reath shook his head. "Neither. I mean, we defend the

Republic, but we work *with* them. Not *for* them. And that's not all we do. We try to help and protect all those in need, when we can."

This didn't seem to make sense to Nan. "Do you accept payment?"

"We're not mercenaries." He had to laugh. "Is it so unimaginable that a group of people might try to do the right thing just because it *is* the right thing?"

"It is around here," she said, her expression grim. Despite her youth, Nan had evidently witnessed some terrible things. "What's that at your belt? Is it the sword we've heard of? The fire saber?"

He grinned. "It's called a lightsaber. And yeah, this one's mine."

"Will you light it?" Nan asked, anticipation sparkling in her dark eyes.

"Not unless I have a good reason." (It wasn't forbidden— but if he did that, he'd draw too much attention. Master Cohmac might even think they were flirting. Actually, Reath thought Nan probably was flirting, but he was just *explaining*.)

"Please?" Nan's expression could've melted ice. "I'd love to know how it works."

Before Reath could figure out how vulnerable he might be to that expression, Leox's voice came over the comms. *"The final ships are boarding all passengers to the station. You guys ready out there?"*

"Absolutely," Reath said. The moment was broken; he

could focus on his duty again. "Come on, Nan. Let's greet the guests."

She made a face. "Mizi? Orincans? You can call them whatever you want . . . but they're not going to act like guests."

"What will they act like?" Reath asked.

Nan had a mischievous smile. "Wait and see."

❧

*Good thing the bracing joints held on this station,* thought Affie Hollow as she made her way along the walkway, through a tangle of vines. *Otherwise this thing would've imploded, and who knows where we'd have wound up?*

(Somewhere else preprogrammed into the computer. Some other location Scover had downloaded, not knowing what traps might have been set for her in old navicomputers.)

Affie had chosen to wander upward, along the lone spiral walkway that traveled along the central globe of the Amaxine station, leading toward the topmost rings. From her vantage point, she could survey the layout almost completely. Outer ring: several metal arches separating the various segments, each of which had an airlock of its own. Central sphere: several enclosures set up along the walkway, but otherwise completely an arboretum. (She would've thought it was always intended to be one, if it weren't for the fact that the Amaxines had built this. The legends suggested they weren't the "tranquil gardener" type.) Through the transparent plates, she could see some of the other ships coming in to dock.

*They put the Orincan ship next to the Mizi? Oh, that's going to be a huge mess.* These Jedi might be brilliant monk-wizards, but they were also completely uninformed about this part of the galaxy, especially which species within it hated each other. As she passed the one large, irregular airlock in the sphere, Affie was tempted to head back to the bridge to help Leox and Geode sort through the resulting squabbles—and to witness the poleaxed expressions on the Jedi's faces.

(She didn't dislike any of the Republic types, actually, but it was verrry obvious how much they thought they were the ones bringing wisdom and knowledge. About time they learned better.)

But while plenty of the ships would be crewed by beings that loathed each other, none of them seemed likely to make war. It would be a mess, not a disaster.

Probably.

So that meant Affie was free to explore on her own.

Lower rings? She still didn't know. Upper rings?

Affie looked up; by then she was within meters of the tunnel that would lead up and out. Time to discover just what else this station had to offer.

From one corridor she heard Orla Jareni and Cohmac Vitus saying something indistinct, no doubt about the antiquities that seemed to practically litter the decks. They'd be distracted by that for a while and would pay no attention to where Affie went or what she did. This was ideal.

She pushed aside a curtain of vines and made her way

into the tunnel that led "upward." Gravity adjusted with her as she went, an unusual and ingenious modification; apparently all those ancient station mechanisms remained in perfect working order. Affie had no intention of touching anything inside, because any tech so old that was still running would be best left alone. Any other space traveler would know that, too.

Other space travelers would also know that the top and bottom rings were the likeliest places for storage bays, and for the cargo others had left behind. If she was any judge, this station's storage was at the top.

Sure enough, as Affie stepped from the tunnel into the shadowy topmost rings, she could make out long lines of storage bays—some locker-sized, some bigger—stretching into the central dark. Larger storage might be located on the lower rings. The larger bays could hold potentially dangerous substances, so she'd go through those later, maybe with Leox's help. For now she would just rummage around . . .

Then she cocked her head. Was there *writing* on the lockers?

Affie turned on her glow rod as she crept forward. Across the lockers and other bay doors were scrawled some symbols—not labeling but actual handwriting or painting, with the same kind of grease pencil pilots used to mark wires for repair. Affie had never handwritten anything in her life, which was hardly unique. Probably she'd never even met someone who wrote something down.

Nor was this writing Aurebesh. It was . . . symbols. Little

pictures instead of letters. Different lines were written at different heights, in different styles. Then she spotted, at the very ends of the lines, much smaller numbers—

*Dates!* Affie realized. *Those are dates; that tells us when they were here!*

As she'd suspected, it hadn't been that long before. One line was from just six years back. Another was from earlier, but still only about thirty-two years prior. All the writing seemed to come from the recent era, a very long time after this station would've been abandoned.

There was no making sense of the lines without knowing their language—or, more likely, their code. The pictographs were fairly crude. Affie ran one finger beneath a line drawing of a crested wave with a diagonal streak through it; that looked like the readouts that indicated a gravitational disturbance. And there was one shaped like a Y—that suggested a potential fork in the hyperspace lanes, or some other diversion. She began to smile as she realized that this was a place where wayfarers left messages for each other, warnings about the path ahead.

But why leave important messages in code? Why not make them easy for everyone to read?

Affie kept picking out new symbols, trying to guess what each might mean, trailing her finger beneath each line. Then her finger came to a stop and her smile faded. This symbol was a four-pointed star—a distinctive, stylized one, a symbol

Affie knew by heart. Which was fitting, because she wore it over her heart every day she wore her uniform coverall.

It was the crest of the Byne Guild.

"It's muggy in here," Orla said. "Almost steamy. Gotta give the biome credit—the best-seeded arboretums rarely last anything close to this long. This one not only survived, it's got *humidity*."

"Lucky us," Cohmac said wryly.

They stood in the central sphere, within what Orla could see had been a kind of ceremonial area, one marked with a stone-carved seat—or, perhaps, a throne. A total of four statues stood guard. Each one depicted a different species, or perhaps mythological figure, but they all shared the golden plating and the richly jeweled ornamentation. Vines slithered along the nearby trees and archways—not literally, though the constant rustling encouraged that illusion.

The light was dappled with the shadows of leaves. Those shadows played on Cohmac's face as he stepped closer to one of the statues, peering up at the finely carved wings and carapace.

"Do you recognize it?" Orla asked.

Cohmac shook his head. "The style of carving is not unlike the ancient Kubaz. But that system is so distant my first assumption would be that the similarity is a coincidence.

Furthermore, the Kubaz don't have any insect gods, so far as I know."

Orla put her hands on her hips. "Maybe they're not gods. Maybe they're monarchs, or historical leaders."

"Monarchs, perhaps," Cohmac said. "But I doubt they're historical figures. The way they're elevated over the viewers, the grandiose haloes over their heads—see, there are spaces that probably held even larger jewels once upon a time. To me that suggests profound reverence. The deepest respect and adoration. In the long run, history isn't that kind to anybody. But religions are. Myths are. There could be other meanings, too; until we translate this language, I can't offer anything more than an educated guess. Gods would be my bet."

A soft breeze tugged at the edge of Cohmac's robes, played across Orla's cheek. At first Orla simply welcomed that faint touch of coolness. Then she thought, *Guess that's why the vines are rustling. This station has even better ventilation than I'd realized.*

Then Orla felt a delicate shiver of unease. An eerie sensation that only grew with each moment. Cohmac turned to her. "There it is. The shadow. The darkness."

They stood still for a few moments. "We've all felt it now," Orla said. "I might have assumed it was no more than a rogue tree; plants can sometimes be strong in the dark side. But this . . ."

"Is different," Cohmac finished for her.

"It feels deliberate." Orla breathed in and out, tried to center herself in the Force, but such calm was elusive.

By then the darkness was more than a shiver, almost a presence. As if something, or someone, was slowly approaching them. Orla wondered if that could be true. Had a being hidden on this station? Was it not as abandoned as they had supposed?

"I'm checking the corridor," Orla said, hurrying toward the door. From the corner of her eye she saw Cohmac nodding—he'd sensed the same thing—

And then Orla was alone in the howling dark.

She dropped into a crouch before the gale-force winds could knock her down. Cold chilled her to the marrow, and sharp flecks of debris scratched at her skin. Terror clawed at her belly, threatening to drag her into darkness, too. Orla called on the Force to sustain her. Even if she could no longer sense it, the Force was always there.

"Cohmac!" she shouted, not knowing why. "Cohmac, where are you?"

Shards of metal and mineral dug into her hands as she pushed herself up, trying to look around. In the distance, she could make out only collapsed beams of metal—and through them, an ominous glow. Though it was the brightest light she could see, it filled her with nothing but horror. . . .

No more cold. No more darkness. Orla opened her eyes (when had she closed them?) to find herself in the arboretum, near the door, just where she'd been a few seconds before, when the universe made sense.

"Cohmac?" she called, but heard no answer. Rising back

to her feet, she saw him lying among the moss and vines on the floor, either unconscious or in trance, as though prostrate before an unknown god. Orla hurried to his side, and just as she knelt by Cohmac's shoulder, his dark eyes flew open. But his breaths were coming short and shallow, and he stared upward at Orla without seeming to truly see.

"We have to get back to the ship," Orla said gently, unsure whether Cohmac could even hear her. "Let me put my arm beneath your shoulders."

"That wasn't just a vision." Cohmac blinked, then looked up at Orla with complete clarity. "It was a warning."

⚶

Reath had thought they were getting to the easy part. Everybody was safe; everybody needed to share space for a while, so they'd all try to get along, right?

He'd been so wrong.

The first pilots to emerge were humans who looked rough and wanted you to know it. "This place is abandoned, huh?" one of them said, stalking right past Reath's hand outstretched in welcome. "That makes everything on board fair game."

"Wait," Reath began. "Everyone should get a chance at the resources they need."

"Not if they're mine." The guy tugged at the red kerchief around his neck as he smirked at Reath. "Anything that's not bolted down is mine. Anything I can pull loose isn't bolted down. Come on, men. Let's start hunting."

They stalked through the rings, looking for lockers and other storage. Before Reath could decide whether to go after them, another group emerged. These were the Orincans, who appeared to be related to the Gamorreans, only paler and less photogenic. Their captain squealed in outrage at the sight of the humans already plundering the ring, then took off after them.

Reath first went for his comlink. "Master Cohmac, we're dealing with some, ah, unrest among the refugees. If you could come, that would be a big help."

No answer came. Reath drew on the Force, summoned his will, and called out, "You want to stop looting the station and return to this place!"

Nobody listened. He breathed out in frustration. Master Jora was so good at bending people's will with the Force, but it was more an innate skill than one easily taught. Reath might get the knack of it someday, but that wouldn't do any good in the here and now.

Reluctantly, Reath pulled out his lightsaber. Time to lay down the law.

Which he'd never laid down before. But he'd figure it out.

# SEVEN

**A**ffie hadn't realized anything was amiss until she was smack in the middle of it.

"*Duck!*" Reath shouted.

She didn't ask why, didn't turn to look, just dropped to the walkway floor. A metal bar whizzed overhead, slamming into the wall with a reverberating bang. Covering her head, she scurried along until she could push herself behind a barrier of leaves. Maybe it had been a counter once, or a bar. Now, thickly tangled with vines, it had become a hedge. Either way, it would hide her from the looters.

Why hadn't she waited longer to come back down? Too late for regrets.

She was determined to remain low. If she was revealed, they might attack her, seeing her as competition for the few precious goods on the station. Or—if they wanted to gamble on overpowering the *Vessel* (a pretty safe bet) and a quick clearing of the hyperspace lanes, it was possible they'd steal Affie herself. The Republic banned slavery, but she wasn't sure they were in the Republic at the moment. She didn't put it past some of the thugs to make a quick profit by selling her off to someone who'd whisk her over the border.

*So,* she thought, breathing hard, *let's lay low.*

From her vantage point, Affie could peer through the leaves at the fracas. Already the Orincans were ripping through vines on the "ground" level, tearing a hole that would allow them to rummage through anything hidden beneath. Farther up the atrium, two levels above her, the Mizi had dug out something that looked like Amaxine armor. That stuff never rusted or wore out; it was worth thousands. The Orincans would be furious when they saw that their rivals had found such a prize.

Furious enough, probably, to start a fight about it. Affie cast an appraising look upward at the wall. *Scover says that back in the day, older space stations used to magnetically seal their entire hulls. If they did that here, just one blaster bolt could ricochet around this station for minutes. For hours, even.*

The Orincans didn't give a damn about history or anything else besides their own porcine skins. So they wouldn't realize the danger. If a fight broke out, they'd fire off so many bolts that the entire station would turn into a death trap.

Where was Reath? His voice had come from below, but she couldn't see much of the station's airlock ring. Were the other Jedi coming to help him? *Could* they help? Affie had yet to be much impressed by these famed mystical warriors, who as far as she could tell had mostly preached at them before dumping them on an ancient station that was a whole lot of bad luck.

Affie's brief reverie was shattered when heavy booted footsteps began thudding against the floor panels near her. An Orincan? Her glance through the leaves revealed a red-scarved human instead, but one whose greedy, callous smile would've looked at home on an Orincan snout.

"Pricey market out there for little girls," he said in a sing-song. "These ones aren't too old."

Did he mean for her to hear him? Instinct told Affie that he wasn't a slaver; his interest seemed more personal, and even more ominous. Less like she was something he could sell, more like she was something he couldn't afford to buy.

Slowly, slowly, so as not to rustle her clothing or disturb even one leaf, Affie reached for the blaster strapped to her side. It slipped silently free of its holster.

*Yeah, firing into the hull could kill us all,* she thought. *But only if I miss.*

*I won't miss.*

Affie looked through her blaster's sights, aiming them square at the man in the red scarf. If he turned even a fraction of a centimeter in her direction, he'd see her. That is, if he had time to see her before dying, which Affie didn't intend to give him.

But he didn't turn. Instead he began to cackle. "Yes, yes," he called, probably to one of his shipmates, "that one will do nicely!"

He jogged away. Affie felt relieved—more than she should. She'd never killed anyone before and hadn't wanted to begin. *If it's your life on the line,* she scolded herself, *you shouldn't think about that. You shouldn't think about anything but saving your own life.*

Easier said than done.

Then a shriek echoed through the station. Affie couldn't see who had cried out, but she already knew.

They'd taken Nan.

&#8278;

Reath looked around wildly, trying to identify the ringleaders. If he could take out one or two key players, that might well pacify the others.

A voice shattered his concentration. "Reath—help!"

Orla Jareni struggled through the jungle of the exposed atrium, half supporting a staggering Master Cohmac. Anyone on an upper level would have a clear shot. Reath hurried to help them reach the tunnel that led to the airlock ring.

Just as the three of them arrived at the tunnel, Dez Rydan dashed out, lightsaber in his hands, cloak billowing behind him. He went to help support Master Cohmac, but the older Jedi had already begun to rally.

"What happened?" Dez asked.

"He had a collapse. I think we both did," said Orla. "Or we both had—an experience, one I can't easily explain. But it's rooted in the dark side. Of that you can be sure."

The station atrium echoed with shouts, bellows, and the clanging of metal. Master Cohmac nodded quickly as he righted himself. "Orla, are you able to fight?"

Her hand went to the lightsaber at her belt. "Always."

Master Cohmac glanced at Reath, who gave him a quick nod. Then the four of them rushed back into the station. "Orla, take these," Master Cohmac called, pointing at the second level up. "I'll clear the top levels. Dez, head to the far side of the station and see what's happening there. Reath, guard the airlocks."

Reath nodded. Orla and Master Cohmac jumped at the same instant, both of them soaring meters high. Reath didn't watch them any longer than that. Instead he ignited his lightsaber. It had been a while since he'd felt its hum, since its cool green light had bathed him in its glow.

But for someone who considered himself much more scholar than fighter, it felt surprisingly good to have the lightsaber in hand again.

A shriek drew his attention to a struggle taking place near another entrance to the airlock ring. Reath's eyes widened as he saw Nan in the grip of an enormous human man.

Her arms were pinned to her sides, and though she thrashed her head from side to side, it was impossible for her to escape. She looked more furious than frightened, though she had to be terrified.

"Hague!" Nan cried out. "Hague, *help!*"

She had no one she trusted in the whole galaxy to take care of her except one elderly man. Reath didn't doubt that Hague would hobble out there ready to pummel her kidnapper with his cane. Nor did he doubt that Hague would quickly be beaten or killed for his trouble.

Reath ran several steps toward them, then jumped. His leap took him five meters over the grass, through vines that smacked against his limbs, to a point directly in front of Nan and her would-be abductor. Both of them looked equally astonished to see him.

Another human, one wearing a red scarf, swaggered up behind him. "You here to tell us we're not being orderly?" he said in a mocking voice. "No law in these parts yet, little boy. That means we can take as much off this station as we can carry. And we can carry her just fine."

Nan's eyes were wide. "Reath—what are you—" She lost her breath and could only stare at the lightsaber in disbelief.

He ran the scenarios in his head. There weren't many. All of them were more violent than he would prefer.

Reath said evenly, "Put her down and walk away, or I'll be forced to take action."

"What, you think you can take both of us out with your

little twinkle sword?" sneered the thug still clutching Nan in a death grip. "Looks like a toy."

"It's not," Reath said quietly, putting power and intent into his words. *"Put her down and walk away."*

But, like all his other attempts so far at using the Force to change minds, this failed. The red-scarved man swaggered forward, hands on his hips. "Do your worst, little boy."

Never before had Reath been in this position—where he would have to be the first to take action, to do harm. He'd always wondered if he would hesitate. If he'd doubt himself.

When it came to saving a life, however, there could be no hesitation.

Instead Reath said, "I understand prosthetic arms are more advanced than prosthetic legs. More comfortable, too."

No flicker of understanding showed in the man's face, not until the moment after Reath's lightsaber had swept through his arm, severing it at the elbow. A forearm tumbled down onto the ground. The red-scarved man's expression shifted from smugness to disbelief, then crumpled into a grimace as his shocked nerve endings finally broadcast pain.

Immediately the bigger guy dropped Nan and ran into the shadowy jungle surrounding them. Nan put her hand to her mouth as she stared at the abandoned forearm. Reath said, "I have to stand guard at the airlocks. Come with me."

The red-scarved man finally fell to his knees and howled. "What have you done to me?"

Reath holstered his lightsaber. "We'll give you a full medical checkup as soon as the situation calms down."

With that he pulled Nan against his side. He wasn't sure how to balance himself for the leap while carrying someone else, so he recalculated swiftly. "Hang on."

Her arms went around his neck. Reath jumped forward and upward in a sharp arc—until his free hand clutched one of the longest vines. Their momentum and weight did the rest, sending them swinging in a long curve back to the airlock ring.

No sooner had they landed than Nan dashed toward the lock where her ship, and Hague, awaited. Of course she'd want to find her guardian. But she glanced back over her shoulder and called out, "Thanks!"

Reath managed a brief smile for her before he took up his lightsaber again.

◅◈▻

The Orincans leveled their blasters at Cohmac as he leapt onto their deck of the station. *Magnetically sealed?* he wondered of the station. *Possibly.*

The blue blade of his lightsaber ignited, its gleam slicing through the murky dark. As the Orincans fired, he spun his saber, expertly deflecting the beams into the trunks of the larger trees that could bear it, or into some of the boxes and trunks of abandoned cargo. None hit the walls, which was his main objective.

Squealing in consternation, the Orincans beat a hasty retreat. He glanced down just in time to see Orla hold out her lightsaber and ignite it—two blades, shining white, piercing the shadows. The Mizi began backing off immediately. But it was too easy for the looters to escape; the layout of the station meant he and Orla would literally be running in circles trying to pursue them all.

The *Vessel* lacked the military heft to forcibly stop the looters from leaving with their ill-gotten gains. Therefore, stopping the ransacking would have to be accomplished through more than sheer strength. Reason and persuasion hadn't worked, either.

Time for awe.

Cohmac climbed the rungs of the atrium railing. His eyes detected Affie Hollow cleverly concealed behind a greenery-overgrown barrier, but that hardly mattered—except that this girl, too, would finally learn what the Jedi truly were.

He focused his energy and drew upon the Force. Though darkness surrounded him, the sheer vitality of the living things on the station worked on Cohmac like fuel. Strength flooded his body, and ultimate clarity sharpened his mind.

With that, he jumped.

Affie screamed, but the sound flowed past Cohmac, just one more aspect of the illusion-reality around him. Reaching out with the Force, he sensed the atrium floor and balanced himself above it. *Eight meters* above it.

Levitation was a complex art. The more academic Masters

bickered over the reasons why it should be more difficult for Jedi Knights to lift and steady themselves than any other object. Cohmac considered the discussion academic to the point of esoteric; besides, this was a skill that, for him, came naturally.

As he floated in the center of the atrium, he held his lightsaber above his head. Its blue glow flickered against the exposed slivers of metal as though igniting dozens of small flames. He called out, "*Hear me!*"

His voice echoed throughout the atrium, as Cohmac had calculated it would. The sounds of combat slowed, then silenced. Faces of many species stared out, weapons at their sides, slack in astonishment at seeing a human male airborne, held aloft by no power but his own.

Really, it was among the least significant of a Jedi's abilities. But it made people pay attention and earned their respect, which was all Cohmac required at the moment.

"In the name of the Republic, I command you to cease looting and thievery aboard this station *immediately*." Cohmac's resonant voice filled the entire vast space, reaching every antenna and ear. "Within fifteen minutes, every captain of every ship now docked here must have done one of two things: packed up their crew and left, or prepared themselves to peaceably cooperate. You accept the authority of the Republic's laws and stay, or you reject it and leave. It doesn't matter which. But choose one, *now*—or we will be forced to make that choice for you."

Nobody hurried to leave. Instead, many of the groups collected themselves, put down the finds they'd stolen, and began shuffling back toward the airlock level. They'd be ready to negotiate. He and the other Jedi would have a chance to discuss the strange phenomenon emanating from the idols, so strongly linked to the dark side.

But Cohmac didn't fool himself that he'd achieved anything more than a temporary reprieve. As he descended through the air, robe rippling around him, he knew this fragile peace would not last long.

— Twenty-Five Years Earlier —

## PART TWO

Smoke in his nostrils.

Roaring in his ears.

Blood on his tongue.

Last to come clear—faint swirling light, clouded with dust that stung his eyes.

Cohmac sat up amid the wreckage of their craft and took stock of the situation. The ship remained more or less intact, which he knew because the temperature remained constant. Through the viewport he could see the planetoid's surface, salt-crusted, small crystals glittering in the howling winds. They'd made landfall on the slope of a hill, it seemed, because the entire ship tilted perilously to one side. Deep scrapes the ship had left in the surface revealed dark green stone beneath, buried in centimeters of salt.

*I must find Master Simmix*, he thought. That was his most important responsibility—but that didn't mean he could ignore those closer to hand. Next to him, Orla leaned forward, bracing her hands against the pilot's console. Her breaths came shallow and fast. "Orla," Cohmac managed to say. "Are you all right?"

". . . Yes." She sounded as if she wasn't completely sure.

Cohmac reached out with the Force to find the other two passengers. Master Laret Soveral came clear to him almost instantly—she'd moved away from the cockpit, in pain but focused, and yet her spirit was suffused with sorrow.

Where Master Simmix should've been, where his calm powerful centeredness in the Force had *always* been, Cohmac found nothing.

"Master Simmix?" he called, willing himself not to know what the Force had already told him. For the first time in his life, he pushed the Force away, thought of it as a lie. Cohmac got to his feet and walked up the uneven deck toward the back of the ship. "Master?"

Laret Soveral appeared in the doorway, soot staining her face and robes. She was tall for a human female, with striking features and a commanding presence, even at this confusing, difficult moment. Her golden-brown eyes met his evenly. "I'm sorry, Padawan Vitus. Your master is again at one with the Force."

Every tenet of Jedi doctrine proclaimed that Cohmac should feel happy for Master Simmix, who had been freed from the illusion of mortality and the weaknesses of the flesh.

Instead Cohmac felt as though his guts had been torn out by a rancor's claws.

When he shouldered his way past Master Laret, she raised no objection, just let him go. Within a few steps, Cohmac found Master Simmix lying crumpled in one corner. The safety harnesses aboard this shuttle had not been configured for Filithar or any other limbless species; Simmix had laughed about it when they boarded, saying he would take his chances.

*Why didn't I insist?* Master Simmix, always cautious with the lives of others, had sometimes been careless with his own. More than once, Cohmac had had to point that out. Generally it pleased Simmix when he did so; he said he'd outsourced his sense of self-preservation to his apprentice. And yet, this time, this one fatal time, Cohmac had let it go.

*It was my job to remind him of the risks,* Cohmac told himself as he knelt beside his master's scaly green body and reverently closed his eyes. It had not been his decision alone to take the T-1 shuttle, and yet whatever portion of the blame belonged to him would forever be a heavy weight to bear.

✦

"About time something went according to plan," Isamer growled. Before him glowed the readouts that showed the location of the crashed Jedi vessel. He motioned to two of the guards. "You, get out there. If anyone survived, make sure they don't survive much longer."

This, too, had been foreseen by the Hutts. As they'd explained to Isamer, they wanted the Jedi to travel to that area of space, not merely in search of Force-sensitive infants or on solitary journeys of discovery, but as part of a mission. A mission that would fail *terribly.* One that would prove to the people of these worlds that neither the distant Republic nor the Jedi could save them. The old hostility toward the Republic seemed to be weakening. The Hutts wanted it strengthened.

Then, if these outlanders wanted to conduct commerce with the greater galaxy, they would have to go through the Directorate. And, by extension, their new overlords, the Hutts, though Isamer thought less about that aspect of it. Their percentage would be no more than a token, an afterthought. He preferred imagining himself seated among heaped riches, wealthy beyond the dreams of avarice.

All he had to do was ensure that nothing stood in the way of the Hutts' plans for mass enslavement.

In the prisoners' corner, Monarch Cassel ventured, under his breath, "I suppose those are our rescuers."

"*Were* our rescuers," Queen Thandeka replied. "Now they're targets. If they survived the crash at all, that is."

"I've heard the Jedi are very strong." Cassel said, with what sounded like genuine hope. "Perhaps his guards won't be able to destroy them."

Queen Thandeka sighed. The two of them had been huddled together for some time—long enough for her distrust of the E'ronoh ruler to dissipate somewhat. "You're trying to make me feel better."

Cassel shrugged and gave her a sheepish smile. "Not sure we could feel much worse."

Thandeka said nothing. It appeared Cassel couldn't see as far into the future as she could, a blindness she envied.

Because when she projected how this scenario would ultimately play out, every possible track ended with both of them dead.

✺

Orla took Cohmac's arm as they stumbled out into the frigid, salt-sharpened wind. He had only minor injuries and didn't need the physical support—but no doubt she felt contact with another person might help steady him within. The frenzy of grief he felt reverberated through the Force; he could tell that both Orla and Master Laret sensed it. If one of them dreamed of correcting him—*dared* to insist that the Jedi should not feel such sorrow—Cohmac would not be responsible for his actions.

However, at the moment, Master Laret remained focused on their goal. "The caves," she called over the howling gale, gesturing to the vague outline of an entrance farther along the hill. "Let's go."

Together they stumbled through the salt dunes. Cohmac breathed a sigh of relief when their party finally staggered into the cave. Inside, the stone seemed to have been polished—scoured smooth by centuries of salt, so much so that the cave walls almost looked wet as they glimmered in the light of the Jedi's glow rods.

Or maybe not only by salt. As Cohmac's eyes adjusted to the darkness, he recognized carvings in the walls that depicted a large, hooded serpent—not a Filithar, but enough like one that he had to turn his head away. It was as though Master Simmix's portrait had been etched there centuries before to wait for them.

"The kidnappers will raid the wreckage soon," Master Laret said. "I regret leaving Simmix's body behind, but if they find him, they may believe that Simmix traveled alone. If so, that buys us time to find the kidnappers' lair."

Cohmac managed to say, "These carvings—Master Simmix said something about them, about serpents playing a large part in the local lore." He'd been expected to read up on the area's folklore on their journey there. Simmix had urged him to do so. Even though legend and myth were interests of Cohmac's, he'd only skimmed through the reading. They had piloting to do. Fighting to anticipate. What were the chances folklore would come into any of that?

Or so he'd thought. At the moment, with the carved serpent staring down at him, Cohmac was not as sure.

Orla straightened. "The carvings feel important. Like— like the Force is trying to tell us something. Should we turn back?"

Master Laret inclined her head, acknowledging Orla's words without agreeing to them. "To turn back and go elsewhere, we would need somewhere else to go. We have no such place. Our duty is to press forward."

"But if—" Orla said, her voice breaking off as they all heard it. A strange sound from deeper within the caves, almost a rustling—no, too heavy for that—

She and Cohmac tensed. Master Laret, ahead of them, already had her lightsaber in hand and activated it just in time for its blue glow to reveal the enormous white snake, many meters long and more than a meter wide, slithering toward them with its fangs bared.

# EIGHT

**D**ez knew the quiet on the station was fragile, that he was needed to patrol and preserve the calm. Yet he had to remain on the *Vessel* for a few moments, to try to make some sense of what Cohmac Vitus was telling him. He asked, "What do you mean, you were transported?"

Cohmac shook his head. "I do not mean that my literal location in space changed. But my consciousness *was not here*. I was someplace dark and terrifying. Staring down into a terrible abyss. My soul ached with a kind of anguish that could have torn it in two. Why, I cannot say. But the pain was very real."

Dez considered this. "You were investigating the ancient artifacts at the time, weren't you?"

Cohmac nodded. "Throughout the galaxy, there have been legends of objects imbued with the dark side. Of amulets and crystals and even glaciers that contained as much malevolence as any living creature. Some said that the most powerful Sith of old were able to do that—to infuse their own darkness into the objects around them."

"Do you think the artifacts could be marked by the dark side in the same way?" Dez asked.

"Such things are generally no more than legend," Cohmac said cautiously, "but all legend is rooted somewhere in truth. At least one dark side artifact is known to have existed. So we cannot discount the possibility."

"If it's not the idols," Dez reasoned, "then the darkness has to be emanating from the plants aboard the station."

Cohmac made a scoffing sound. "No. I've encountered trees deep in the dark side before; I know what it feels like. The sensations can be powerful, but this was . . . *focused.* Targeted, even. There was intelligence behind it."

Dez frowned. "Intelligence? Without a sentient being behind it?"

"It sounds odd," Cohmac admitted, but he was deep in thought. "But it is possible, especially if—"

"If what?"

Slowly Cohmac said, "If the idols serve as a kind of . . .

warning beacon. If they communicate an intelligent message, namely, that we must stay away from the darkness enclosed within them."

"At the moment, we're very much not staying away from them," Dez pointed out. "What do we do?"

"Nothing. We need someplace for everyone to shelter while the hyperspace lanes are closed. This is the only possibility within the system." Cohmac breathed out heavily, rubbing his temples.

Dez took this in. "So you're saying the dark side is present—"

"And we are trapped here with it," Cohmac finished.

*What can I do?* That was the question Master Jora had trained Dez to think of first. In this case, however, warnings or no warnings, there wasn't much at all he could do about a vague threat of the dark side's presence. If that darkness made itself manifest, then he'd act. Until then, he'd focus on the tangible aspects of their mission.

The memory of Master Jora made Dez realize what should come next. "Take it easy for a few minutes," he said to Cohmac, who inclined his head in concession. "I've got to find Reath."

※※

Reath had spent the majority of his Padawan training immersed in the Archives, but he'd been on rescue missions before. Once he'd helped clear passengers from a badly malfunctioning transport in the Brield system. Another time, he had joined a Jedi team assisting in evacuations from a burning tower in Coruscant itself. The second, in particular, had been difficult, even death-defying. He didn't lack experience.

However, he'd never seen—and was convinced he would never see—any group of people so ungrateful for being rescued as the station refugees were. Even many days into their stay on the Amaxine station, they remained as obstreperous and unpleasant as ever.

"*First* you park us next to Mizi scum!" snarled the Orincan captain. "*Then* you tell us we have to turn over all our food! Who do you think you are?"

A human in a satin-and-fur cloak stroked his goatee as he proclaimed, "Obviously our passengers paid in advance for the deluxe menu, prepared by our famed chefs with premium ingredients, so we couldn't think of depriving them of what they rightfully purchased."

"None of you knows how to share!" retorted Nan, who stood in the middle of them with her arms crossed against her chest. Thanks to her stubborn chin and her diminutive height, she appeared more like a little girl than the young woman she was. The elderly Hague, behind her, kept his hand firmly on her shoulder. "Aren't you ashamed of yourselves?"

The Mizi captain looked down his long nose at her. "No."

"Everyone needs to stay calm," Reath said for what felt like the eightieth time. He stood amid a huddle of most of the passengers, datapad in hand, trying not to show his irritation. (Probably that was why Master Cohmac had stuck him with this task. It was a test of patience.) "We're all in this together, and we don't know for how long. We could get the signal to leave in an hour—or in fifteen months. If you're wasteful or selfish now, there's every chance you're going to regret it, severely."

Silence. They didn't look entirely convinced, Reath thought, but at least they'd stopped arguing for a second.

"Howdy." Leox Gyasi strolled out of the *Vessel*'s airlock door, hands in his pockets, his multicolored beads swaying with each step. "Man, oh, man. Gorgeous in here, ain't it? Spectacular. Like an island getaway, except instead of an ocean we've got open space."

Some of the refugees exchanged glances. This seemed to be a standard reaction to meeting Captain Gyasi.

"Sure could be stranded a lot of worse places than this," Leox mused as he strolled beneath a thick canopy of leaves. He sniffed a yellow flower and grinned. "Coulda been stuck on a desert planet. Or a volcanic one. Or just dead space, alone, sitting around wondering if we'd run out of air before we could ever get away."

Reath reflexively took a deep breath. He wasn't the only one who did.

Leox leaned against a tree, mellow and easy. "See, we can look at this one of two ways. One, we didn't get where we wanted to go as fast as we'd like. That's unlucky. Not really that bad in the scheme of things, but unlucky. Or two, while hundreds or thousands of people died in a terrible disaster, we were delivered to safety—hell, not just safety, but someplace *beautiful*. That's lucky as all get out, don't you think?"

A few people nodded. Nan didn't, but Reath caught the shadow of a smile on her face. Even the Orincans began to shuffle a bit on their feet as they relaxed their usual battle stances.

"So instead of looking at our little bit of unlucky, I say let's celebrate the huge amounts of good luck we've had," Leox said. "We're coming at this from a place of strength. Why not act like it?"

The luxury ship captain paused only briefly before saying, "Honestly, most of our meals could be comfortably halved and still provide the nutrition of a meal. We do have some to share."

Not to be outdone, the Mizi captain chimed in with, "As it happens, we're transporting a shipment of repair parts. Some of them may be of use to those who took damage in hyperspace. Our insurance will cover the losses to our client."

The Orincan captain grunted, which wasn't exactly a friendly sound but suggested she and her people would cooperate.

After that, Reath was able to put together an overall manifest of food and other meaningful supplies fairly quickly. At the end, as everyone strolled away, he turned to Leox, who was still leaning against the tree. "Thanks."

"Don't mention it, kiddo. Sometimes we all need a reminder to focus on the good things in life."

Even a few days before, Reath would've been reluctant to believe that he could learn anything (besides basic ship mechanics) from a person like Leox Gyasi. He was glad to have discovered differently.

As Leox continued his meditative stroll through the greenery, Reath was left alone for the first time since the abortive looting of the Amaxine station. It was an unwelcome solitude. If he didn't have to concentrate on an immediate issue, his mind had time to wander back to the moment he'd faced off with Nan's would-be kidnapper—

The sound of the lightsaber—the heavy thud of the severed limb on the floor—

Reath was startled out of his reverie by rustling in the ferns, which parted to reveal Dez Rydan stepping through. Dez smiled, but Reath knew why he was there even before Dez said, "How are you feeling?"

"Shaken," Reath said. "Not . . . guilty, exactly, but not *not* guilty, either, if that makes sense. I just—I just keep thinking about that moment, and wondering if I could've done something differently so that man would still have his arm."

Dez sat cross-legged on a patch of soil. An 8-T droid laboring nearby scanned him swiftly, must've determined he posed no risk to any roots, and kept on working. "Probably there was something else you could've done," he said. Reath felt it like a lash. But Dez kept speaking. "You don't know what that would've been. Neither do I. In that moment, did you feel like that was necessary in order to rescue Nan?"

"Yes. Otherwise I'd never have done it."

"You know," Dez said, "every couple of years or so, an apprentice gets into trouble for being too aggressive. Using a lightsaber instead of words, resorting to action when diplomacy or negotiation would've better resolved the situation. You wouldn't be brought up on that kind of review, Reath. It was a dangerous moment. The threat was clear. Your response was proportionate to the risk to Nan."

It helped a little to hear Dez say that. But not that much. "I keep thinking about it—replaying it over and over in my head, trying to think of a different way it could have ended."

"Good. It takes strength to question your own actions. Just don't dwell on the past to the point of forgetting the present."

Reath managed a crooked smile. "You're good at this."

"Tell Master Jora that sometime." Dez grinned back. "She won't believe it."

Already Reath's spirits had improved. The weight of what he had done would linger, but only in the ways that would help him learn from the experience. Still, he couldn't stop wondering: "That guy—the one I—how is he?"

Dez replied, "Oh, he'll live. Unless Orla Jareni finishes him off."

"It's a clean severing—right at the joint, so you can move to a prosthetic quickly—and the wound was instantly cauterized," Orla said as she saw the painkillers finally taking full effect on the red-scarved man. "You don't have to worry about infection."

"Infection's not what I'm worried about! I've *lost my arm!*" the man bellowed. Full consciousness had returned, with fury not far behind. "You Jedi are responsible for this—"

"Just as *you* are responsible for the attempted abduction of a young woman." Orla got to her feet, taking care with the small confines of the *Vessel*'s utility bay and making no effort to disguise the contempt in her voice. "You were warned to stop. You could have stopped. But you chose not to, because you thought a Jedi Padawan wouldn't be able to prevent you from stealing the girl. You're reaping the consequences of being very, very wrong about that."

The man knew he was guilty, obviously, but he was unwilling to let go of what he considered the righteousness of his wrath. "Don't get all high-and-mighty with me. Don't the Jedi abduct children, too?"

It took all Orla's training to cast that flash of anger aside. "Families willingly give their Force-sensitive children to the temples, so that they can be trained in the ways of the Jedi. It's their free choice." She took a deep breath in an attempt to calm herself. It only partly worked. "For future reference, when a young girl's screaming for you to let her go? She gets a free choice, too. If you ignore that, then you can't complain about the results. Now, assemble your crew and get your ship away from this station within the hour, or we'll do that for you."

The red-scarved man blanched. "You'd cut us off from air? From food?"

"You've surely recirculated enough air by now to breathe for a few weeks. We won't let you starve. But we also won't allow kidnappers to roam freely." Orla snapped the medpac shut. "In other words, *get out*."

⚜

Once the criminal vessel had detached itself from the station, and an orderly division of goods was underway, Cohmac Vitus felt he could spare a few minutes to center himself.

The ominous darkness aboard the station continued to trouble him—but in order to explore that more fully, he needed his strength in the Force. Meditation was a necessary prelude to action.

Carefully he noted the positions of every other person assigned to the *Vessel*—Reath and Dez on the station with Leox, Orla in the mess, Affie resting in her bunk, Geode apparently in charge of the bridge—before seeking a place of quiet and privacy. He found it in the very back of the ship, in front of a sealed-off cargo container. (Interesting that the *Vessel* crew would apologize so often for the smallness of their makeshift quarters while still reserving so much space for cargo they hadn't even mentioned.) Cohmac laid down his heavy blanket, folded into a kind of meditation mat, then knelt on it.

*I behold the world within myself,* he thought. *I behold the world without myself.*

The mantra had helped soothe him for many years; he liked the balance of it. But it had become too literal, now, to serve as a mantra.

*I am a Jedi. I have always been one. It is my identity, one I have never sought to change.*

*But the Order does not answer the questions that linger within me. The questions only grow over time.*

*Darkness abides upon this station. It is . . . too familiar to me now. But the shape it takes here is different and unsettling. Consciousness without a corporeal being. What created this? How did the dark side take form in this place?*

*How does the dark side take form anywhere? Sometimes I think we, the Jedi, must be somehow to blame. We who refuse to look at the Force in full, to examine the darkness as well as the light.* If the dark side were not so alien to them, Cohmac suspected, they would more readily understand the nature of the idols.

*How can we split the Force in two? How can we justify such an act of violence—and it* is *violence, such a dividing, even the darkness divided from the light.*

Affie gave Leox all the credit for getting their fellow refugees to calm down. But she had to admit, the Jedi were quick to give everyone a common goal—namely penetrating the lower rings of the station. That goal happened to neatly match her own.

They'd accepted her report on the upper rings easily enough, which was fine because her report was true. It was not, however, the whole truth. Affie was keeping the smugglers' code, and her thoughts about it, to herself for the time being.

*It makes zero sense for this to be a regular Byne Guild portal,* she reasoned as she prepared to head down to the lower rings with the rest of the volunteers: Reath, Nan, Dez, and a long-limbed Mizi who, like all Mizi, preferred to be nameless to strangers. *It's out of the way, and it doesn't have any obvious advantages. But what if there's a secret society within the Guild, one that's operating behind Scover's back? They could be skimming off the top, stealing small amounts of cargo or money, falsifying records to hide it from management. The preprogrammed location could've been downloaded from another ship, one that's in on it.*

She didn't have to ask whether Leox was in on it; he would *never.*

As angry as that theory made Affie, it was by far the most plausible she'd come up with. Scover wouldn't hide something like this from her, so somebody had to be hiding things from Scover.

Her chest swelled with pride as she imagined finding

the proof, presenting it to Scover, hearing her say, *Well done, Daughter—*

"All right," said Dez Rydan, bringing her back to the present. The scouting party stood around him near the entrance to the lower ring. They all wore their own versions of utility gear, except for the Jedi, whose workaday garb seemed good for all occasions. "We can't get any specific readings on what might be down there—only that it's not solid metal. If it's storage, there may be items of use to us . . . which will be equally shared among the entire group. As long as everyone understands that, and accepts the risks, let's get started."

"Should you do this?" Reath quietly asked Nan, who barely came up to the Mizi's waist.

"I'm fine," Nan retorted. She showed no signs of trauma from the kidnapping attempt; Affie wasn't sure she could be equally cool under those circumstances. "Besides . . . Hague can't climb. One of us should be here. So it's got to be me."

"You take good care of him," Reath said.

Nan smiled. "He returns the favor."

Enough Flirtation Theater. Affie refocused her attention on the tunnels that led to the lower rings.

Unlike all the other tunnels, these showed signs of damage from their long years of disuse. While the outer structure remained intact, vines and roots from the arboretum had grown down through them, turning what had been clear passageways into thick, thorny mazes deep in shadow. It wasn't anything Affie couldn't have explored on her own; she'd have preferred it that way, in case more of the smugglers' code was written down there. However, the twisty tunnels were ominous enough that she could see the upside of having company along for the trip.

Dez took the lead, lowering himself through the tunnel. Its gravity was on the fritz, which meant the pull was coming from the rings below. Luckily the craggy roots served as a makeshift ladder. Affie gripped on tightly as she lowered herself down.

For a few seconds, she was surrounded by both tree roots and a vast field of stars—a contrast that delighted her in its strangeness. No time to linger and enjoy it, though: the Mizi above her was in a hurry to descend, so much so that he was cutting away vines to clear his path even farther.

She heard the beeps and whines of a droid. Glancing upward, she saw an 8-T scooting along, its treads gripping the outer wall of the tunnel. *Huh,* she thought, *those things are thorough.*

A snap echoed through the tunnel, and Reath made a sound of discomfort. Peering down, Affie could see that his foot had gone straight through a slender root. No big deal.

Or so Affie thought, until the 8-T whirred past her toward Reath, then hit him with an electric shock.

"Ow!" Reath shook his hand as though it stung. "What the—"

The Mizi yelped in pain. Affie looked up to see another 8-T extending pincers toward the Mizi, snapping at his fingers. Farther up the tunnel, at least three more 8-Ts were descending toward them.

She could hardly believe it, but there was no other explanation. "We're being attacked!"

# NINE

"What are they doing?" Affie yelped, trying to swat back one of the 8-Ts. It didn't matter; another two were swarming in to take its place. "I thought these droids were gardeners!"

Reath readjusted his grip on the roots and steadied his balance. "They are. But . . . I guess that means they attack threats to the garden."

"We *did* just cause some damage," Dez pointed out as he swung himself up through the snarl of vines to a place just below Reath. "I can see why they'd feel endangered."

Nan's round cheeks were flushed; both her arms were wrapped around the nearest thick root, but her legs dangled—because the pincers of an 8-T were snapping beneath her feet, keeping her from finding a steady perch. "Are we going to keep talking about droid feelings, or can you stop these stupid things?"

"Stay calm," Reath said.

Which wasn't generally a helpful thing to say, at least not to someone currently hanging by her arms with swarms of attacking robots on the way. But it kept everybody quiet for a moment, giving Reath a chance to think and center himself in the Force.

It also gave the 8-Ts a chance to assemble. Dozens of them were traveling down the tunnel's curved walls, their magnetic treads gripping so well that they might as well have been speeding along a flat surface. Although their dark bodies didn't show up well against the blackness of space, he could see them swarming by the way they blotted out the stars. Their tiny pruning claws, which not that long before had been cute, clicked and clacked ominously. Affie yelped as one of them clipped off the end of her long, braided hair. If those pincers could slice through thick vines or slender tree branches, they'd cut through flesh and bone, too.

Whatever long-ago zealot gardener had programmed these droids had done too good a job.

"Okay," Affie said, huffing as she pulled herself into a more secure position within the labyrinth of vines. "This shouldn't be a problem. You Jedi can fly, right? So just fly us out of here already."

Dez shook his head. "We can't fly. Some of us can levitate—"

"Same difference!" Affie insisted.

"—but it's a complicated thing to do, and difficult under stressful situations," Dez finished, as though she hadn't spoken.

Affie made a face. "So you're telling me you can only fly when you *don't need to*? What good is that, exactly?"

Reath couldn't help thinking she had a point.

Far beneath them, in the lower rings themselves, a strange light flickered—purplish, brilliant. "What was that?" he asked.

"Looks like some kind of an energy field," Dez speculated. "There's *something* interesting down there—whatever it might be."

"Let's figure that out once we're safe from the attack of the killer gardeners—" Affie's words were cut short with a yelp. "*Oww*. This vine has spines or something—it scraped me!"

"We have bigger problems," Nan said, seemingly through gritted teeth, "than a scrape."

Dez said, "Everyone stay calm until I get to Nan, all right?"

The safest place to move was in the direct center of the tunnel, but it was also the place with the fewest roots or vines to balance on. Anywhere safe to stand was also well within the 8-Ts' range.

Dez nimbly climbed past Reath to the place where Nan and the Mizi clung to their feeble handholds. The 8-Ts swarmed closer with each of his steps, but he never paused or even stopped smiling. Reaching out one hand, Dez summoned two of the vines from above, which writhed their way down into his waiting palm. Then he tossed one to the Mizi and bent to gather Nan under his arm. "Follow me with Affie, okay, Reath?"

"Got it!" Reath called back.

Dez nodded to the Mizi, and on an unspoken count between them, they began to climb. The Mizi managed so well that Reath realized Dez was controlling their ascent. It was much easier to use the Force to help boost someone already climbing than to simply levitate them into thin air.

So Reath began working his way toward Affie—but so did the 8-Ts. The full swarm had reached them. Affie winced as the droids crawled like beetles to the bend of the root that provided her fragile hold on the wall.

"I can't believe I'm going to be taken out by severed astromech heads," she said, grabbing for her blaster, "but at least I'm taking a few with me before I—"

"Affie, no!" The idea came to Reath in a rush. "Don't shoot the droids. Shoot the tree roots below us."

"The tree is not my problem!"

"But it *will* be the Aytees' problem! See?"

Understanding dawned. Affie half turned and fired downward, at the lowest root she could possibly target. Her blaster ignited a small fire, which then set some moss ablaze.

Small as the first flames were, it took only those wisps

of smoke to set off the 8-Ts' alarms. The blinking blue lights along their bases turned red and they all rotated as one, swirling to get as close to the tree as possible. As Reath had suspected, protecting the plants from fire took precedence over every other job an 8-T had—including pursuing vandals who'd intruded into the tunnels.

While the droids sprayed small jets of water over the moss, easily dousing the fire, Reath was able to reach Affie, who had already grabbed a vine. He expected her to climb up to the arboretum level without him, but instead she reached out for help, which Reath was glad to give. As she clung to his shoulders, Affie said, slightly winded, "I still think you should've let me shoot one."

"Next time."

Her grip slipped, and he managed to lower her before she fell. Reath expected her to laugh off her clumsiness and to right herself immediately. Instead, Affie staggered sideways, gripping one wrist. "I feel weird. That scrape—from the vine—"

"It hurts that much?" Reath frowned. "Let me see it."

She started to hold out her hand, then slumped against the nearby wall and slid down to the floor. The mark on her wrist was already raised and livid, and streaks spread through it in ominous shades of purple and black.

*Poison.*

Orla paced through the center of the arboretum globe. At the moment, every other being docked at the Amaxine station had somewhere else to be, whether that was their own ships or the station's lower ring. This gave her a chance to study the strange idols they'd found on board.

Unease rippled through her as she approached the statues, that ominous sense of warning emanating from them as surely as light from a flame. Maybe understanding what they were looking at would help determine exactly what this vague warning meant.

She stood face to face with the humanoid queen, the first of the idols to turn up. To Orla's amusement, she realized that they resembled each other somewhat—strong cheekbones, thick brows, proud bearing. However, the stark simplicity of Orla's white robes contrasted with the ornately carved and jeweled raiment of this long-ago ruler.

Although Orla wasn't the scholar Cohmac Vitus was, she had her own gifts to bring to this analysis. Her connection to the Force was instinctive, almost primal; she trusted it to steer her. Sometimes preexisting knowledge stood in the way of discovery—putting boundaries on thought. This, she suspected, might be one of those times. With all his learning, Cohmac had studied these idols already and found only intriguing clues, no truths.

*Let's give instinct a try.*

Orla stared at the dark red jewel that sat topmost in the idol's crown. She let her mind fall into a kind of trance—not full meditation but a deep concentration that allowed random thoughts to rise to the surface. The practice gave the subconscious a chance to be heard.

*A queen. Mighty and defiant.* That much seemed inarguable.

Well. *Mighty* was inarguable. Why had *defiant* come to mind?

*When are we defiant? When we are opposed.*

Orla studied the queen's lifted chin, comparing it to the rest of her bearing. The queen's hands did not hold weapons; instead, a kind of scimitar lay at her feet. She had been forged not with her arms held high in some kind of salute or bearing plundered treasure; her arms remained at her sides, with coiled bracelets around each wrist.

*Bracelets,* Orla asked herself in a flash of insight, *or chains?*

It suddenly seemed so clear to her that she was shocked she hadn't seen it before. The idols didn't represent leaders or gods.

They represented the vanquished, representatives of the forces (civilizations? planets?) who'd been conquered by whoever built the statues.

"So," she muttered, "who the hell were *they*?"

Zeitooine had taught Dez a lot about poisons. The Zeit royalty were made up of treacherous houses, forever attempting to assassinate one another by elaborate means such as powders added to wineglasses or venoms smeared on pillowcases.

Dez recognized the black streaks spreading across Affie's skin even before she'd fully passed out.

"Come on," he said, scooping her up in his arms. "A medpac will take care of this—but we've got to get it right away."

Dez raced for the *Vessel*. Reath ran so fast he passed them, which was good; he could get the medpac ready. Already Affie's skin had turned sallow, and the color had drained from her lips.

"I've got it!" Reath reached the airlock mere seconds before Dez would've run through it with Affie. Instead he kneeled down, bracing the girl. Within moments, Reath dashed back out with a medpac in hand.

Right behind him was Leox Gyasi. "Whoa, whoa, what's wrong with Little Bit?"

"Nothing this won't fix." Dez pressed the antitox booster against her skin; that hiss and click had rarely been more welcome. Sure enough, after only a few moments, the dark streaks on her skin began fading, and Affie's breaths deepened. Leox dropped to his knees in relief and put one hand on Affie's head.

She stirred, opening her eyes. "What was that?"

"A vine scraped you," Dez said. "Apparently it was poisonous."

"Great," Affie muttered. "That's just what we needed on this station on top of everything else. Something poisonous."

"The fun never stops." Leox's grin could've lit up any midnight. "C'mon, girl. Let's get some Jedha tea in you."

Dez let Leox take Affie back into the ship. Reath remained behind with him. "We should tag those vines, maybe."

"I don't see lots of them around, thankfully." Dez stretched his arms above his head, grateful to move freely after the confines of the tunnel. "But yeah, that's not a bad idea."

Reath hesitated as though there was something he wanted to say to Dez—or maybe more like there was something he definitely *didn't* want to say but couldn't help thinking about.

"Hey," Dez said gently. "Out with it."

"Out with what?"

"Out with whatever's been weighing you down since we met up at the spaceport."

Reath leaned against one of the nearby trees, studying Dez with a startlingly adult expression. Or not so startling— Reath was nearly of age, even if Dez still thought of him as the youngling excited to have been chosen by Master Jora. Their friendship had to grow along with Reath, into something more equal and more meaningful.

"I can't believe you chose to come to the frontier," Reath finally said. "Of all the places you could've gone. Even Zeitooine—"

"Zeitooine was endless petty bickering and plotting with next to no action." Dez rubbed his head, warding off the memories of all the headaches that world had caused him. "At least after the first months, once we'd quieted some of the unrest. Once that was over, I didn't do anything of real significance. On the frontier there's a chance to *act*."

"I guess I should be more like you," Reath said. "I know I need to embrace this assignment. Any assignment the Council gives us. But I'm not drawn to action the same way you are."

Dez confessed what he'd hardly admitted to himself: "Sometimes I think I crave action and excitement too much. It can be dangerous, you know."

"So Master Jora says." But Reath didn't sound as though he believed it—he sounded as if he was judging himself, and falling short.

So Dez rose and put a hand on Reath's shoulder. "Listen, the Force is about balance, right? Ideally it's about finding balance within each and every individual Jedi. But that's not the same as finding balance within the Order, which is just as important. We need Knights who crave adventure *and* Knights who don't seek it out. Each individual brings different gifts to the Jedi Order. Our job is to appreciate the value of those gifts, including our own."

Reath gave him a lopsided grin. "Okay. I'll try."

"Good," Dez said, inwardly adding, *I'll try, too.*

"Hey, Dez, I have this one question—"

"Okay. Hit me."

"Did Master Jora ever ask you—do you know why no Jedi can cross the Kyber Arch alone?"

Dez frowned. "No, she never asked me that. And people cross it alone all the time. It's not like some insurmountable challenge, just a meditative practice, like walking a labyrinth."

"I know!" Reath breathed out in frustration. "But Master Jora insists nobody can cross that archway alone, and she wants me to tell her why."

"I've got nothing." Dez shrugged. "All I can tell you is, Master Jora is wiser than both of us put together. If she's given you a riddle to solve, it's worth solving."

Later, once she'd gotten herself cleaned up and freshened up and returned to the cockpit, Affie was disgruntled. "You're *defending* the Aytees?"

"They're gardeners," Leox said, stretched out in his chair, feet propped on the cockpit console. His eyes were closed, as though he could chat and nap at the same time. Maybe he could. "Stewards of the soil. You threatened their very reason for being."

Affie sighed and let it go. Of course the droids were only following their programming. Didn't mean she had to like them.

Besides, she had more important things to tell Leox.

"Listen," she began. "Out there on the station, up in the higher rings—I've found some lines written in code."

"Code?" Leox didn't open his eyes. "Tell me more."

"It looks like some kind of . . . of smugglers' code. Handwritten symbols that give them hints about directions they can travel through hyperspace, that kind of thing."

Leox finally turned his head and looked at her. "Why

would they write that down instead of recording it the usual way?"

"I don't know," Affie said, flexing her still-sore wrist. "They just did."

"That question wasn't rhetorical. Think about it. Hardly anybody actually writes symbols with their hands anymore—not anywhere in the galaxy, so far as I know, at least not on planets advanced enough to have technology. So why are space pilots scribbling important information on the walls?"

It felt good to have the answer even before he was finished with the question. "Because they're skimming stuff off the top, and hiding it from Scover."

Leox sat up straight then, his beads swaying back into place. "Wait. How does Scover come into it?"

"One of the symbols is *this*." Affie pointed to the star shape on her coverall pocket. "It's got to be pilots in the Byne Guild talking to each other, but in a way and in a place my mo—I mean, a place Scover doesn't know about."

He weighed her words for a few long moments. Affie couldn't wait to see him light up with the same astonishment and anger she'd felt. If only Geode were there instead of recrystallizing in his bunk! She wanted her discovery witnessed and confirmed.

But then Leox shook his head. "Not much goes on in the Guild that Scover Byne doesn't know."

"Of course not—but she can't know about this!"

"Why can't she?" Leox's pale blue eyes met Affie's with unaccustomed directness. "The coordinates for this station were preprogrammed into the *Vessel*, as part of the standard nav download every ship gets when joining the Guild. That's not coincidence."

Frustration tugged at Affie's temper. Why couldn't he see this? "These thieves inside the Guild, they could've tampered with the download. Put in the information they'd need to operate behind Scover's back—"

"And share it with every single new ship in the Guild, even if they're not part of this so-called conspiracy?"

Affie folded her arms across her chest. "So how do *you* explain it?"

Leox took several moments before he answered, his voice low and patient. "I know, and you know, that not every Guild haul is what you would call, in the strictest sense, legal. Scover's got plenty to hide from the authorities. This seems like a pretty good place to hide it."

"She wouldn't hide it from *me*!" Affie insisted.

There was no reply. Leox just gazed at her, his expression melancholy and yet kind. It was the kindness that infuriated Affie the most—the idea that she *needed* kindness, that she was some simple gullible fool Scover coddled and humored, instead of a true pilot and Guild official in her own right. So many other pilots looked down on her. Leox never did—or at least he never had, not until that moment.

Without another word, she stalked off the bridge, half hoping Leox would follow her to apologize, but he let her go.

☙❧

Orla Jareni watched Affie storm down the *Vessel*'s main corridor, practically trailing black smoke from her rage. Through the cockpit door, Orla caught a glimpse of Leox watching her go, concern written all over his sun-bronzed face.

*Not a good time for a chat,* she decided.

For the moment, Orla had little else to do. She didn't intend to venture back toward the ancient idols until Cohmac could go with her. Dez was still strategizing a new way to penetrate the lower rings of the station, and Reath was handling things with the fellow refugees—most particularly Nan, it seemed.

Orla still hoped to have a conversation about spacecraft purchasing. Both Affie and Leox appeared to be distracted at the moment. As for Geode—well, a Vintian probably had different needs for a spaceship than a humanoid would. Orla had to put that conversation on hold.

Besides, she and Cohmac had plenty to talk about besides the idols.

Orla found him on the *Vessel*'s "observation deck": a grandly titled meter of corridor that happened to have a small window. Cohmac saw her enter but didn't speak.

"You've got your hood up again," she said. "Never a positive sign."

Generally she got Cohmac to sigh within five minutes. This time she'd had him right off the bat. "I suppose asking for privacy on this ship is futile."

"Oh, I don't know about that. What is futile is expecting old friends not to understand when you're having trouble."

"The many problems on this station—"

"Spare me," she said, not unkindly. "What I'm talking about has been hanging over you since long before the hyperspace disaster."

Cohmac and Orla's bond had formed during their Padawan years because of the Eiram–E'ronoh hostage crisis. The mistakes they'd made then—not being cautious enough about responding to signals, not doing enough research before diving into action—had been redeemed at a terrible price.

Sometimes she reminded herself to see the good that had come from it all. If the mission had turned out any other way, would that part of the galaxy ever have trusted the Republic, much less chosen to join it? Would Starlight Beacon have been built? Orla doubted it.

Still. Neither she nor Cohmac could look back on those events without regrets. That was something Orla understood without having to ask. They'd grown up to be two very different individuals—but their bond endured, and always would.

Orla knew her decisions to become a Wayseeker might separate her from many in the Jedi Order. Not from Cohmac.

"I've never kept secrets from you," he admitted.

"You've *tried*," Orla said. "I just never let you get away with it."

"Don't remind me."

She intended to remind him at regular intervals throughout their lives, but she could drop it for a day. "Are you going to make me interrogate you?"

"Do you have to?" Cohmac's dark eyes searched hers. "Coming back here, on our way to a place so close to E'ronoh and Eiram—finding ourselves imperiled again, having to guess at the dangers that lie ahead—"

"It's a very different situation," Orla hastened to say. The vibrations of that long-ago event were strong enough without delving deeply into it. She wasn't sure she was ready to bear that.

"I sense that there will be further parallels," Cohmac said. "There are . . . other resonances, all around us. Their forms remain unclear, but before this mission is over, we will see them true."

"Got it." No mystic, Orla figured it was time to change the subject, but then she felt it. The same shiver of terrible cold that had seized her before—the same bleak place so far away—

"Cohmac!" she called, but he couldn't hear her. They were both lost in the petrifying vision.

※

Reath strolled along the perimeter of the arboretum level, almost idly, as if he weren't keeping a sharp eye on the Mizi, the Orincans, and some of the others who'd tried looting earlier. (He, personally, would've waited longer to allow everyone to board freely again, but this was not a point on which he felt comfortable challenging a Master.) While Leox had ably calmed them down and the tunnels to the lower rings provided their own deterrents to entry, it seemed possible that a loner from any of the groups might try something. If they took some equipment from the station—Reath honestly didn't care. Anybody who needed spaceship parts badly enough to pilfer centuries-old ones could have them. But if they stole one of the ancient idols, they'd just sell it for the precious metals or jewels without even bothering to study it. *Sacrilege.*

Worst of all would be another kidnapping attempt. Reath again remembered the moment his lightsaber had severed the man's arm, the faint thump through the blade that told him he'd hit and destroyed bone. He shuddered. Dez's kind words had helped, but this wasn't something he could ever totally put behind him. The act of attacking another person with a lightsaber was horrifying, and Reath hoped it would always remain so.

*Let me never forget,* he thought, *that it is another living creature standing opposite my blade.*

He looked up into the dark forest arches within the atrium. . . .

They were gone. Everything was gone. Reath stood alone amid the plants and trees—but not the same ones, or were they just altered somehow?—his lightsaber in his hand, already ignited. Slithering, rustling sounds filled the air on every side, setting him on edge.

Fog, almost steamy in the sudden heat, coiled around him. Reath looked around wildly, trying to understand how the scene had changed. Had he been transported to another part of the station? To another planet? Or had he somehow failed to see the true danger around him all that time?

Ahead of him, he knew, lay the greatest threat of all. Reath didn't understand *how* he knew it, but he was as certain of it as anything else he'd ever known in his life. He shifted his body into battle stance, took a deep breath, and tried to brace himself against the threat he couldn't see.

Then, amid the fog, only steps in front of him, came a sudden streak of blue light. A lightsaber blade.

One that would be used to kill him.

# TEN

**S**tumbling forward through the fog, Reath called out, "Why are you doing this?"

That would fix it. No Jedi would willingly harm another. The other Jedi would come close enough to see Reath, realize that they weren't enemies, and put away his weapon. Reath was so certain of it that his muscles relaxed slightly, ready to declare the emergency a false alarm.

Instead the figure jumped forward at a speed that rendered him (her? it?) nothing but a blur. Reath had no time to focus on his attacker before a booted foot hit him squarely in the chest, knocking him to the ground. He gasped for breath that wouldn't come; he tried to push himself up, only to sink his hands deeply into warm, oozing mud.

A lightsaber's hum made his ears prick and sent a shiver along his skin. It wasn't his own blade—that one had been knocked away from him—so it had to be his opponent's, rising overhead and then slashing down—

And nothing. Reath found himself on all fours on the floor of the space station, surrounded by nothing more ominous than ferns and a couple of contented 8-T droids. His heart pounded with adrenaline, his whole body still on edge for a fight that was no longer happening, or had never happened.

Reath stood up, took a deep breath, and brought his awareness back to his body. Normally he would have called on the Force to center himself, but not now. They were surrounded by darkness—a darkness that sought to terrify and confuse the Jedi.

To judge by the vision Reath had just had, it also sought to turn them against each other.

෴

The tiny communications area had become the place for the Jedi to confer and plan. Orla wished they'd chosen differently—maybe someplace without a low, arched ceiling, someplace she could actually have stood upright. But the *Vessel* offered few options, and at least this way she, Cohmac, and Reath had to huddle together, which she found comforting.

Long-limbed Dez stood in the doorway, which if not comforting was probably more comfortable for him.

"We know the following," she said, counting off points on her long fingers. "Darkness resides within this station. It has a very different 'feel' from the kind normally sensed from plants deep in the dark side. This means we cannot determine its source."

Cohmac nodded. His gaze looked into the middle distance, someplace known but unseen. "We've all sensed that these warnings are emanating from the idols. From their appearance, they are almost certainly not original to the station. Therefore the idols were placed here later for some significant reason. Orla theorizes that they represented conquered peoples, which if true adds another factor for us to consider. Sealing some defeated darkness within these idols—and setting some kind of psychic warning upon that seal—that could explain it. Of course, this is only a possibility."

Orla shrugged. "Let's call it a working hypothesis."

Reath leaned forward, wordlessly asking for permission to speak, which was given. "The Force emanates from *life*. Not from inanimate objects. There are legends of powerful Force artifacts created by the ancient Sith. But the Sith wouldn't have imprisoned darkness, surely. They'd have set it free."

"You assume," Cohmac replied, "that because every such artifact we know of has its origin in the Jedi or the Sith, that only Jedi or Sith could create one. We cannot make such assumptions. Others have possessed that power in the Force."

Orla considered the possibilities. "So what do we do? Continue to ignore their warnings? Because those warnings are intense."

"Ignoring them would be dangerous," Cohmac agreed, steepling his fingers together. "If the idols contain and warn against darkness, then that darkness must be examined. Imprisoned even more thoroughly."

"They're already pretty isolated out here," said Dez from the place in the doorway where he stood. "On a station nobody much travels to, in an obscure corner of space."

"Not necessarily," Cohmac replied. "Affie has indicated that some traders currently use it from time to time. It wouldn't be surprising if this station were soon reclaimed by even more travelers. All the more reason to act."

"I can't see any harm to the station in removing the idols," Orla said. "There's nothing else here but some plants and some gardener droids. So let's test the hypothesis," she said.

"How?" Dez asked.

"One of two ways," Orla said. "Either we try to move and isolate the statues, or we destroy them."

"But we can't destroy them. They're ancient artifacts!" Reath protested. "They're *history*!"

Orla gave him a look. "More to the point, if we destroy something that turns out to be a containment system for the dark side, we wind up setting the darkness loose. So I vote for the first option."

Dez frowned. "There's another possibility, one we haven't even investigated properly yet. What if the darkness that's confusing our minds is linked to whatever's protected by the energy field in the station's lower rings?"

They all exchanged glances. Everyone had thought about this, but apparently with varied conclusions: Reath appeared deeply doubtful, while Cohmac had the look of someone relieved to hear sense for a change. Orla considered herself open to whatever possibility, but not to endless debate. Time to *do* something.

"Then we test that hypothesis, too," she said. "But first you have to figure out how to get down there without being scraped by poisonous vines, and without Aytees . . . *pruning* you to death."

That made everyone chuckle, as Orla had intended. Good. Laughter made people relax and smile. It cast the dark side away and brought them closer to the light.

✦

Reath could hardly have blamed Affie, Nan, and the Mizi if they refused to have anything else to do with the station's lower rings—even if they had managed to pull up the poisonous vines (gently, so as not to disturb the 8-Ts) and cast them harmlessly to the side. However, all three of them rejoined the group to make the next attempt.

"There's got to be something good down there," Nan

reasoned as she rechecked her field utility belt, glancing up just once to smile at Reath. "No way I'm letting you guys have it all."

The Mizi nodded in agreement—the difference being, in Reath's opinion, that Nan was joking with him but the Mizi was completely serious.

Affie was harder to get a read on. Her attention seemed only half-focused on the task at hand. "So what's our plan? We have a plan, right? Better than the last one?"

"Let's say we have a plan to make a plan," Dez began. "Specifically, let's do recon. Do a more thorough survey of this level and see if we can find any potential points of entry besides the main tunnel, and so on—without setting off the Aytees this time."

"That would be preferable," said the Mizi, straight-faced.

It was really the only next step. But Reath couldn't stop himself from wondering whether they couldn't take what they'd learned last time and use it tactically. Master Jora always said, "If you use your defeat to learn the path to victory, it was no defeat at all."

Everyone shifted, about to disperse. Before they'd begun, though, Reath blurted out, "I have an idea. It's either really good or completely ludicrous."

"If it's ludicrous, it's probably great." Affie's enthusiasm had been renewed. "I've learned that working with Leox and Geode."

No doubt. Reath turned to Dez. "The Aytees are

programmed to attack any threats to the plants on this station, right?"

"Sure looks like it." Dez rested his hands on his hips. "What's this about, Reath?"

"Watch." Reath went to one of the smaller plants on the station, a budding yellow flower in a fist-sized round container. Many of them lined the walkways; the containers seemed to operate as makeshift nurseries for the 8-Ts. Gently he eased the container from the soil. As he brushed away some of the dirt, a handful of 8-Ts swiveled to stare at Reath. This behavior was clearly suspect.

Very carefully, he tucked the flower's container into the folds of his robe jacket, then snugly tied the belt around it. His knot was so secure that he could've done an acrobatic flip in the air without bruising a single petal. The 8-Ts stared for another second or so before turning to go about their business.

"There," he said. "They realize this doesn't count as damaging the plants. And if we wear these on our mission—"

"They won't attack us," Nan said. "Because hurting us would mean hurting the flowers!"

Dez grinned, too, and even the Mizi nodded. Affie, however, folded her arms. "So you're saying that we're taking plants as hostages. Using them as body shields."

When she put it that way, it sounded worse. But— "Well, yeah."

"Ludicrous," Affie said. The smile she'd hidden so well before finally shone. "And great."

Within a few minutes, each member of the party was wearing their own flower. The 8-Ts found them more interesting now that they wore plants, but otherwise took no actions as they made their way back to the tunnel and began their descent.

"Now for that energy field." Dez stared at the flickering, purplish light. "Nothing to do but get down there and take a closer look."

"Agreed." Reath started the climb down, followed by the others. To his dismay, the 8-Ts whirred closer and started down the tunnel walls again.

Dez swore under his breath. "Looks like they'll sacrifice a few flowers for the greater good."

"By the greater good, you mean killing us."

"That's what *they* mean by it, I think."

But Dez was wrong. The 8-Ts swarmed along the tunnel walls all the way down to the very edge of the lower ring, extended various tools—and then, in the next instant, the purplish light disappeared.

"The droids turned the energy field off for us," Reath said in wonder. "To make sure we wouldn't fry the plants!"

Dez actually waved at the 8-Ts. "Don't worry," he said, patting the planter that rested against his chest. "We'll bring them back safe and sound."

Were the droids relieved? Plotting revenge? Reath didn't know and couldn't care, not when they'd finally reached the last, most secret part of the Amaxine station.

Once Affie had clambered into the lower rings, she felt vaguely let down. It wasn't all that different from the upper rings—same tilework, same rails—except that it was entirely devoid of plant life, and she didn't yet see any signs of smugglers' code on the walls. Yet.

The ring that welcomed them was very narrow; other curving corridors, yet unexplored, must've made up the rest of the circumference. Without the purple glow of the energy field, the only illumination came from the station above. Still, they had glow rods, so that was enough light to search by.

"So, let's split up," Affie suggested. "Check different passageways on our own." *Could you be any more obvious?* she scolded herself.

But apparently nothing about her suggestion struck Dez or Reath as suspicious. "Sure," Dez said. "Doesn't seem like there's anything too dangerous down here. Might as well cover ground as quickly as possible."

Affie nodded like that was exactly what she'd been thinking.

Finally they broke up, and she was free to delve into one of the passageways by the light of her glow rod. Affie wondered whether she'd find codes, whether the others would, too, and whether they'd be able to make sense of them as quickly as she had.

Sure enough, after the first bend, the first lines of writing appeared. She went right up to them, eager to translate as best she could. Above all, she hoped to find something that would vindicate her mother and prove to Leox that there was a corrupt element at work within the Guild.

"There," she whispered. Her fingers touched the metal just next to the star symbol of the Byne Guild, still stark against the whitish background. This hadn't been written that long before—a decade at most, she'd guess. She tried to follow along, uncertain how to interpret the next few marks, until she came to a small drawing of a bird of prey, beak down, tail feathers up.

Affie stared until the image seemed to be burning into her eyes. She recognized it immediately but refused to believe that it could mean what it so clearly seemed to mean.

*There could be tons of other interpretations,* she told herself. True.

But her parents—her biological parents, the ones she only dimly remembered but still dearly loved—their ship had been named the *Kestrel's Dive.*

Whoever wrote this had been talking about her parents.

That, or it had been written by her parents themselves.

⁂

Reath's journey through another tunnel was shorter, or at least the part he took alone. It was darker down there, so much so that his glow rod seemed weaker—an optical illusion, surely, but a disquieting one. Every one of his footsteps sounded unnaturally loud as he ducked his head under the curved arches of the tunnel's beams.

*If plant life has taken over almost every other part of this station,* Reath wondered, *why did it never come down here? Was that energy field meant to protect what lies down here—or protect us from it?*

His passage and Dez's intertwined after only a few meters, with nothing but a handful of storage lockers and some scribbles on the wall to mark the significance of the spot.

"Looks like we share the same destination," Dez said. "C'mon. Let's check it out."

He felt a quiver of pride. What would his friends say, the ones who so idolized Dez Rydan? There they were, on a mission together! Partners!

Okay, Dez was possibly *too* excited about plunging into the dark unknown, but it was like Dez had said earlier: if some people disliked adventure, some others had to love it.

"Look at this," Dez said. He was gesturing at a circular door ahead. Its hinges were at top and bottom center, suggesting that it rotated to open.

"That's weird. Why build it that way?"

"Could mean something. Could mean nothing." Dez readjusted the planter cradled against his chest, making sure not to crease any of the leaves. "Come on, let's see if anything interesting is on the other side."

Reath reached out with the Force, knowing Dez was doing the same. He sensed no sentience on the other side, no echoes of darkness. "Nothing alive, anyway."

"So it would seem." Dez walked ahead quickly, leaving Reath several paces behind. "Now, is this locked, or—"

The door flipped around, rotating on its central axis hinges so fast that it knocked Dez off his feet, spinning him around to the other side. Reath blinked, suddenly alone. "Whoa. Dez, turn that around." It had actually looked pretty funny; Dez had enough of a sense of humor to appreciate that.

But Dez wasn't laughing. He wasn't speaking. The door didn't flip again.

Vibrations began to shudder through the floor, the walls. Through the thin slits of the doorway, stark white light beamed out so strong that Reath winced and lifted one hand to shield his eyes. "Dez?"

A strange grinding sound—like engines, or some other vast machinery—began. Whatever was happening didn't sound good, and Dez Rydan was trapped in the middle of it.

Dez shouted wordlessly, a sound that betrayed pain. Reath ran toward the door, ignoring the blinding light, and tried to force it open. But the hinges that had swung so easily before refused to budge.

The light flared even brighter, so much so that Reath had to shut his eyes. Through his own eyelids he saw a lacing of fragile veins and capillaries, silhouetted against dull red.

In the next instant, it was dark. The vibration and sound had stopped.

It took Reath a moment to recalibrate. "Dez? Are you okay?"

No reply.

Reath pushed at the door once more without much hope. This time it swung open immediately. The door was surprisingly heavy; the heft of it nearly knocked Reath down, the same as it had done to Dez. He could see into the tunnel— and it was narrow, thickly grooved.

Dez was not inside.

Carefully Reath leaned in to get a better look. Still no Dez, but he glimpsed two helix rings, ancient but still unmistakable. Helix rings were incredible energy boosters, the equivalent of enough pure coaxium to fuel forty or fifty large spaceships; they were seldom used because they generated too much power for almost any non-hyperspace purpose.

They had a tendency to malfunction, especially when older, and created energy surges capable of melting metal, blowing circuits, or—

Or disintegrating a human body, down to the atoms.

# ELEVEN

The first hint came with a wave of panic and sorrow, one so strong it pierced Cohmac's consciousness like a fine silver needle. He stood up in the cockpit, nearly knocking against Geode. "Something's wrong."

"We live in an imperfect universe," said Leox, who was chewing on a stick of something that smelled minty. "So that's a given."

"I mean, something's wrong with our people aboard the station, this moment." Cohmac hurried toward the airlock. Leox was only a few steps behind; all his laid-back torpor had vanished at the first hint that Affie Hollow might be in trouble.

They had only just made it into the leafy glade of the station when they were met by Nan, who was breathing hard and, for some reason, had a potted flower tucked into her pocket. Behind her Cohmac could see the Mizi hurrying toward his own people, and Reath Silas emerging from the vines, his face white. Nan gasped out, "We heard this loud sound—but we didn't see—Reath's the only one who saw—"

"Saw what?" Cohmac resisted the urge to put his hands on the girl's shoulders. It would probably comfort a Padawan, but to Nan it might come across as a threat. "Tell me."

"Dez is gone," Nan whispered.

Gone. What did that mean? He had traveled to another part of the station? Away from the station entirely? None of the docked ships had left—the *Vessel*'s sensors would've picked that up.

Or did she mean . . . ?

Affie was finally emerging from the trees near the tunnel. Leox called to her, "What's happened to Dez?"

"We don't know." Her voice was strangely flat, as though she was in shock, which seemed strange to Cohmac. The young woman hardly knew Dez. "But it's—it's not good."

Finally Reath reached them. He brought his face slowly up to meet Cohmac's eyes. Everything about him radiated misery and grief.

Already, Cohmac knew. *It has happened again. Just as it happened to Master Simmix. The resonances warned me, but I did not see in time. This part of the galaxy has claimed its price.*

Yet he still had to say the words. "Tell me how Dez fell."

The next few minutes were a blur of details that didn't make sense (plants as hostages?), but the gist remained the same.

"Helix rings?" Leox said gravely. "And nothing left inside? That usually means—" He trailed off as he looked sidelong at Cohmac. No wonder. It was a difficult thing to say aloud. But it had to be said.

"Vaporized," Cohmac said. It came out evenly, a logical conclusion, no more. "The likeliest explanation is that Dez Rydan was vaporized instantly."

Affie had finally reached them, and somehow Cohmac had shocked her—as though she had been thinking of something else altogether. Affie said, "You mean he's dead?"

"Yes." Cohmac reached out with the Force, trying to find any scrap of the young Jedi's mind and spirit.

He was answered with nothing but silence.

※※

It took Orla a few minutes to piece together exactly what had happened, getting her information only from the exhausted, shell-shocked Reath and Affie. Cohmac had already walked back through the length of the ship, toward his bunk, declaring his intention to meditate. No doubt he was remembering Master Simmix. Orla had her own grief to bear, but she'd always been able to put emotions aside until there was time to deal with them. Cohmac felt things more deeply, and more immediately. His equilibrium was more difficult to maintain.

Had there been anything to do—any immediate hope—Orla knew that Cohmac wouldn't have retreated; he, like the rest of them, would've done anything to get Dez back.

But there was no such hope. Nothing to do but accept that a courageous, compassionate young man had been killed.

*It would've been better if he'd died in battle,* Orla thought. *Or during a rescue mission. Then his death would at least have had meaning. This? Some malfunctioning equipment on an ancient space station? It's so arbitrary, so unfair.*

So was life.

"All right," Orla said to the assembled group, taking charge in Cohmac's place. "Is everyone else okay? No injuries?"

"No," Reath said, which seemed untrue, given that he had severely bloodshot eyes and a stripe of sunburn along his forehead. But he was upright, moving and talking, so a radiation scan could wait until later. Affie looked like she was in shock, understandably enough. The Mizi had gone back to his own people. Nan seemed completely unaffected, though she wore a saddened expression, probably out of consideration for the feelings of those who'd known Dez longer. *That little thing's sturdier than she looks,* Orla decided. *I wonder what she's seen out here.*

"So nobody needs medical attention," she said. "Okay.

Here's what I need you all to do. Reath, Affie, clean yourselves up and rest for a few minutes. Nan, if you'd be good enough to explain this to the other refugees, it would be appreciated—and don't worry, that bastard with the red scarf is long gone." Nan brightened, then realized her smile was inappropriate and squelched it. "And take these flowers back where they belong, would you? The Aytees are hovering around the edge of the airlock. The last thing we need is an invasion."

"I got that," said Leox, who had been standing quietly at the edge of the group. He carefully took a small planter from Affie, who didn't look up at him once.

"There are no good words to say," Orla began. "We lost a good man and a great Jedi. We'll have to search for answers about what happened, and soon. First we owe him, and ourselves, a little while to reflect on who Dez Rydan was, and to acknowledge his oneness with the Force."

The group broke up awkwardly, shuffling in various directions in silence. Orla put her head in one hand just long enough to take a few breaths.

She couldn't allow herself the same time to reflect she'd granted Cohmac and Reath. Not when she had to figure out what to do with the idols.

Affie took a quick shower in the *Vessel*'s tiny head, waving the wand all over. The process had become strange, as if her body were now foreign to her. It seemed to live in another galaxy entirely, one she no longer inhabited and could only watch from a great, silent distance.

Afterward she knotted her long dark brown hair back into a braid and put on a fresh coverall. Normally this made her feel better, regardless of how she'd felt to begin with. Instead her fingers kept finding the embroidery of the Byne Guild crest, tugging at the threads, but they never came loose.

When she emerged from the head, Leox stood in the hall-way, waiting. "It's free," she said dully.

"Not my immediate concern. I'm more worried about you. Looks like you got run over by a stampede of gundarks."

"I went on a routine search and somebody died," she snapped. "Am I supposed to throw a party?"

"Of course not," he said, maddeningly calm. "But you've got a core of durasteel. It takes more than that to knock you flat."

The Kestrel's Dive. *Who would be writing about the* Kestrel's Dive? Affie kept turning that over in her head. She'd inter-preted other symbols as ships' names before, but she must've misunderstood something, because it had looked to her as if—as if the pilots were writing about their own ships. Which had to be impossible, because otherwise it meant that her parents had been there, on that very station. *They wouldn't plot against Scover. I know they wouldn't. I hardly remember them, but I feel so sure—*

"I'm not going anywhere," Leox said.

"What if I don't have a core of durasteel?" Anger blazed

within Affie, white-hot, infusing her with renewed strength. "What if this is exactly enough to knock me flat? If I'm able to feel compassion for other people?"

Leox held up his hands. "I'm not saying—yeah, it's a hell of a thing, losing Dez. But there's more to it than that, isn't there?"

"No." With that she turned and walked away.

Walking away from Leox, unfortunately, meant walking away from her cabin. It led toward the mess, though. If she grabbed a couple of nutrient bars, that might tide her over for a day or more. She could hide in her bunk, seeing no one, saying nothing. That sounded good.

Affie walked into the mess to find Geode. He had more sense than to interrogate her.

His silent sympathy broke through where no words ever could have. She leaned her head against Geode's side and let the tears come. Patiently he waited with her as she cried, for a dozen reasons and none at all.

⁂

Reath waited until everyone else was preoccupied—by grief, duty, or whatever else—then assembled his equipment pack. He prepared as though for a mountain expedition, with cables and clamps, and double-checked his lightsaber. Nobody noticed him leave the *Vessel* and enter the station.

He had the space to himself, it seemed. After what happened to Dez, nobody from the other refugee ships had any interest in exploring further. The only sounds were the whirring and beeping of droids; the 8-Ts were placidly mulching, as though nothing had happened. To them, he supposed, nothing had.

Reath found the small planter he'd put down earlier and placed it back within his pocket. Then he eased his way into the tunnel, going step by step, mindful of his own slow, steady breathing. *Body and spirit as one,* whispered Master Jora's voice in his memory.

His feet landed on the lower ring with a metallic thud. If anyone else were on the station, they'd have heard him for sure. Reath was grateful he could keep this secret for a while.

He found the exact curve they'd taken before, found the circular door. Opening it again seemed both foolhardy and necessary. Since he knew about the helix rings, he reasoned, he could avoid setting them off.

Then Reath froze as he saw, through the small slits in the door, a faint, flickering light.

This wasn't the burning blaze that had forced his eyes closed when Dez had been . . . lost. It was dimmer, smaller. It was also unfamiliar, unauthorized, and severely suspect. If someone was tampering with Dez's death scene—or if it turned out that this *wasn't* Dez's death scene—

With one hand on his lightsaber, Reath slowly pushed open the door until he heard a bloodcurdling scream. A small figure scrambled back through the tunnel. "Get away from—*Reath?*"

"Nan?" he said. She sat on the floor, heavy with relief that it was only him. "What are you doing down here on your own?"

"Investigating." She pushed her chin forward and folded her arms. "Since everyone else seems like they're ready to write Dez off as dead, when there's no body—"

"No proof, nothing!" Relief eased him, and he sat down beside her. "I thought I was the only one who wasn't ready to accept it."

Nan measured him with a look and apparently found him more interesting than before. "Okay. So at least some of you Jedi can think for yourselves."

Reath didn't think there was any shortage of that, really, but there would be time later to talk to her about the traditions of dissent within the Order. "What have you found so far?"

"Just got here, really. Where should we start?"

"We move forward through the tunnels, watching out for the rings, and see if we can find evidence of what this area was used for. Knowing its purpose might give us some answers. Maybe Dez was transported somewhere else, or taken farther down to an even lower level than we've found yet."

"That's more or less what I was thinking." Nan got to her feet; she seemed to have been studying the rings' fastenings at the floor level, but to no avail. "Let's move."

The tunnels stretched into what seemed like an infinite darkness. Reath kept his glow rod steady, as did Nan, but the sound of their footsteps echoing into the unknown got undeniably creepy after a while.

To break the silence, he said, "How did you come to be Hague's ward? If it's upsetting—"

"A person's growing up without their parents, and you wonder *if* it's upsetting?" But Nan seemed more amused than offended.

"Sorry. I realize that parents are important, but Jedi are raised in the temples together from early childhood. They take most of us in when we're only toddlers, and that's all we've ever known. So I don't assume people come from families. Maybe I should."

Nan shrugged. Her long ponytail fell over one shoulder, framing her round face as though the shadows that surrounded them had draped themselves over her. She'd carried the blue streaks in her hair through to the ends. "It's okay. My parents died well. They did their duty."

Had they been military? Reath decided the subject was too sensitive to pry for more information.

"That was about two years ago," she continued. "Hague was already a family friend. He may only be in charge of a small ship these days, but once he was a brilliant commander. When he offered to foster me, I thought, great. This way I'll get to learn from the best."

"Your parents probably would've liked that part," Reath offered. "Right?"

"Yeah. They would've *loved* that part. My dad always said Hague was as good a strategist as he'd ever known."

*Definitely military,* Reath decided. He wondered whether their home planet was a strongly militaristic one, or whether Nan and Hague were part of a smaller subculture. The sociological ramifications would be ripe for study . . . if that were the kind of thing he still got to do. Which it wasn't.

Another turn in the tunnel brought their glow rods to bear on a second door, this one far larger than the first. No slits or windows, just black, forbidding metal. They exchanged glances, then hurried forward to investigate.

"Control panel," he murmured as he checked it out. Patterns of interlocking circles suggested functions, which let him hazard a guess. "Unfamiliar configuration, but this looks more like it's for maintenance, rather than primary programming."

"I agree," Nan said. "It's not what you'd call user-friendly."

While Reath couldn't read the unusual symbols etched on the panel, the lack of colorful sections or a larger screen definitely suggested that it wasn't for general use. It was a place for service workers to double-check settings, that kind of thing. This indicated that people wouldn't normally travel through the tunnels on foot.

What drew his attention next was the thick plating around the edges of the door. "Does that look like an airlock to you?"

"One hundred percent." Nan took a deep breath. "On the

other side of that door is the void. You can feel the chill in the air."

It was true. Reath had already begun shivering. "To me this looks like it was once a launching station for smaller transit pods. The rings probably powered the pods to leave the station. Their own engines would kick in once they'd cleared the airlocks."

Nan hugged herself. "And Dez got in without a starship— but the tunnels launched him anyway."

The hope had been to prove that the rings hadn't instantly disintegrated Dez. Now Reath had to pray that they had. The alternative was that Dez had been flung forward at bone-crushing speed and then ejected into the vacuum of space. He knew from research that death took longer in outer space than most people realized—up to fifteen seconds to lose consciousness. Not a long period in any absolute measure, but an excruciating amount of time to suffer the hopelessness of mortal terror. And if Dez hadn't been able to exhale, then he would've endured the oxygen expanding within his lungs until they ruptured.

Reath closed his eyes. All he could do was bear a kind of witness to that suffering.

"Are we done here?" Nan said, very quietly.

"Yeah. We're done."

As they emerged from the tunnels, Reath heard the sounds of—celebration?

That sounded so *wrong* right then. He and Nan shared a look, and he could see that her consternation matched his own. The two of them hurried toward the airlocks, where the Orincans and the Mizi were chuckling and clapping hands on one another's backs. Leox stood nearby, his expression more solemn, but not unhappy.

"What's going on?" Reath asked.

"Looks like our time on this depository of strangeness is coming to an end," Leox said. "The galaxy at large just got a communique from the Chancellor of the Republic."

Nan lit up. "Is hyperspace cleared? We can travel again?"

"Travel's still limited." Leox sighed. "But there's an open channel to Coruscant. The senior Jedi have decided it's time to go back home."

— *Twenty-Five Years Earlier* —

## PART THREE

Cohmac's lightsaber flew from his belt to his hand, igniting the second he touched it—

Which was very nearly too late. The giant white serpent slithered toward them at incredible speed, a fine spray of salt marking its way like the wake of a ship. Its mouth opened wide, revealing three huge fangs and a throat already rippling in anticipation of prey.

As soon as his blue blade illuminated, it was joined by another—Master Laret's—and two white ones. Cohmac had wondered whether it was really necessary to have a two-bladed lightsaber, whether maybe Orla wasn't just showing off.

Faced with the serpent's fangs, however, he could see the appeal of an extra blade.

In the very second the serpent struck, all three Jedi attacked at once—Cohmac from one side, Master Laret from another, and Orla from top and bottom simultaneously. The serpent had no chance; it was dead almost within the same second. However, its weight and momentum sent it barreling forward, knocking Cohmac and Orla onto their backs before it skidded to a permanent halt with its head at the very mouth of the cave.

"Okay," Orla said, panting, as she clambered to her feet

and they all switched off their lightsabers. "Rule one. Don't ignore the local myths if those myths are trying to warn you." She pointed toward the carving of the serpent.

Cohmac nodded. He felt foolish, and angry with himself for having let his master down. "Master Simmix assigned me the legends reading for a reason. I thought they were merely stories. Background that might inform us a little. So I didn't pay enough attention." The stories had indeed spoken of serpents a long-ago goddess had banished to the planets' moons. Why hadn't he reflected on the fact that most legends were rooted in some truth?

It didn't matter that much, really. The serpent was dead and no longer a threat. His mistake had not cost them. Yet Cohmac remained haunted. Probably that was because he couldn't help seeing the faint resemblance between this creature and the Filithar. Most specifically, to Master Simmix.

Some masters were stern and severe. Some were remote. Some continually challenged their Padawans to defend every opinion, every action, every thought. All approaches could be successful in molding excellent Jedi Knights. Yet Cohmac had always been grateful for a master who was kind.

Now Simmix was gone, and they'd left his body behind as though it were nothing.

*It is nothing,* Cohmac reminded himself. *Crude matter. Master Simmix is one with the Force.*

Those thoughts helped. But only so much. He was left with the hard knowledge that he'd ignored Master Simmix about the legends. That he'd carelessly neglected his duty to keep his master safe.

That he'd gotten his master killed.

All the while, Master Laret's head had been bowed and her eyes shut. She was renowned for her ability to find paths with the Force, and it appeared she'd done so again when she said, "The caves form a network beneath the planetoid's surface. It is logical to assume that the Directorate has hidden the hostages somewhere within this network, and the Force tells me they are not far away."

"Then let's go," said Orla.

Already Master Laret had closed her eyes and was reaching out through the Force to see if any other giant serpents, or other similarly unfriendly wildlife, might be lurking within the tunnels. Cohmac did the same.

*Nothing close,* he thought. *But that's not the same as "nothing."*

※

The next time Isamer sent minions to prepare a hideout, he'd make sure he sent people with some sense of comfort. Yes, the caves were all but impregnable to anyone who didn't have in-depth surveys on hand. (Which Isamer did, and he'd wiped many droid memories to ensure no one outside the Directorate could say the same.) But it was cold down there, dark and cramped, and the fool humans who'd chosen that spot hadn't considered that the top of the cave came too low for the comfort of a Lasat. Isamer was tired of being hunched over, tired of the weary hostages huddled in one corner, tired of waiting for this operation to end.

Already the governments of E'ronoh and Eiram had taken the first inevitable steps: offering ransom for their stolen royalty, ineptly investigating the kidnapping and following the false trails Isamer had left for them, making clumsy public appeals for calm that had only panicked their citizens more— and asking for the help of the Jedi.

As the Hutts had explained, the greater activity between the Republic and that area of space made it inevitable that some planet or other would turn to the Jedi in a crisis. By creating a crisis at the right time and place, Isamer and the Directorate could ensure that the Jedi rescue mission would fail horribly. Both rescuers and hostages would, by the end, be very messily dead. The Jedi Order would mourn its lost Knights, these planets and all their neighbors would realize neither the Republic nor the Jedi could help them.

Then nothing would stand in the way of the enslavers' bounties. Planets would instead turn on other planets, on their own subcultures or nondominant sentient species, offering up people to enslave in the hopes it would keep them from being enslaved themselves. Fear would triumph. And Isamer would profit.

One of the guards barged into the inner chamber, salt dusting his cloak; in the corner, both Thandeka and Cassel flinched. "Lord Isamer," the guard said, "in the ship we found the dead body of the Jedi."

Too easy. Isamer narrowed his golden eyes. "How many Jedi did you find?"

"Just . . . just the one, Lord Isamer, a Filithar, no one else was with—"

"Fool!" Isamer growled. "They would not have sent only one Jedi on this mission."

The lieutenant pleaded, "But we saw no tracks, no signs that anyone escaped."

"You did not see them because the Jedi are cleverer than you. They know how to conceal themselves. Others *must* have survived and escaped. Find them and eliminate them, now!"

The guard scurried out. Isamer, in a fouler temper than before, coiled in his chair and stroked his claws over the hilt of his blaster. He hoped they'd get to the end of this soon, because he was in the mood to slaughter someone. Anyone. A glorious battle with a Jedi would be preferable, but merely executing the hostages would do.

If it weren't for the Jedi's vaunted mental abilities— the potential that they might've sensed the absence of the hostages—Isamer would've killed them already.

In the corner, Thandeka's eyes met Cassel's in mutual dread. Cassel whispered, "I hope the Jedi find us soon."

"You put more faith in the Republic and their wizards than I do," Thandeka said.

"That's funny." It was the first time there had been any edge in his voice, any hint that their worlds were enemies. "Seeing as how Eiram's the one that begged for their help."

"I doubt it." Surely Dima would've had more pride, Thandeka thought . . . then imagined she were the one safely at home while Dima was in danger. Thandeka would've stopped at nothing to get her queen back. She would've pleaded for help from any who might give it, even the Republic. Even the Jedi. Still, pride made her add, "You can't know that."

Cassel sighed, the spark of animosity already extinguished. "No, I suppose I can't. It's just strange to think of turning to the Republic when we've always guarded against them, well, swallowing us whole."

"Maybe we shouldn't have thought of it like that." She leaned back against the wall and wished for painkiller to treat her throbbing head. "Maybe we should've thought about having someone to turn to in times of crisis. About not standing alone."

"Our two worlds have always stood apart from each other," Cassel pointed out, but he sounded thoughtful. Well, thoughtful for him, anyway. "Not even the history books know why. It's just tradition. That's not actually a very good reason to do anything, is it?"

Thandeka looked at Isamer, and at the heavy blaster holstered on his side. "It doesn't seem like it at the moment." Anything that would've kept them out of this situation— even friendship with E'ronoh—would've been better than sitting there with her wrists bound, waiting to die.

Orla had thought Cohmac and Master Laret were probably being paranoid about the threat of more snakes. How many giant serpents could eke out an existence on a nearly dead rock in space?

Answer: at least five so far.

Fangs slashed down at Orla, backed as she was against the cave wall. Nearby the vibrating hum of Master Laret and Cohmac's lightsabers told her they were fighting off the fourth of the serpents that had attacked them so far, but number five there was all hers. Unfortunately, she was wedged in a place that didn't allow her to strike. But it didn't allow the serpent to reach her, either—by a few centimeters—so she'd take it.

"It doesn't make any sense for you to be here," she muttered at the snake. "How does a carnivorous species manage to live on a moon with almost no other animal life?"

Enough of that. She knew she had a bad habit of looking only at what was logical and sensible, which obscured the fact that the galaxy was neither.

Orla centered herself in the Force as best she could. Breath in, breath out.

Then, as the serpent lunged open-mouthed toward her again, she jabbed her lightsaber straight forward—burying it in the roof of the serpent's mouth.

It howl-hissed, a ghastly sound. Through the Force she felt the creature's pain and knew a moment of pity for it, a mere beast that had only been hunting for food.

*I'm sorry,* she thought. *But "food" is not something I ever intend to be.*

When the serpent collapsed, dead, Orla could see Cohmac and Master Laret standing over another dead snake. Cohmac was breathing hard, and even Master Laret looked slightly ruffled.

"We're clear for now," Orla said. "Right?"

"I believe so," replied Master Laret. Her expression reflected none of the immense relief Orla felt at the thought of no more snakes. Instead, grave and thoughtful, she moved closer to her Padawan.

By now, Orla knew what that meant. "What did I do?" she whispered. "I only acted in self-defense."

"You made no mistakes." Generally warm and empathetic, Master Laret always tried to reassure her apprentice—but she also always found other things Orla needed to work on. *Always.* "Yet today you have repeatedly failed to call upon your full training in combat against nonsapient beings."

*I followed my instincts,* Orla wanted to say. *I stayed alive. I won!*

Instead she nodded. "I'll remember next time."

Master Laret gave her a rare grin. "Let's just hope the 'next time' is more than five minutes from now, hmm?"

"Definitely," Orla agreed.

Inside, however, she couldn't stop thinking, *If the Force speaks to me through my instincts . . . why can't I listen?*

# TWELVE

A few short days before, the news that they could safely travel again at last might've been cause for celebration. Orla would've splurged for a couple of bottles of Toniray wine at their destination— or whatever local vintage they could get—and been the one who got the party started.

Instead she felt nothing. Or, rather, so many emotions were snarled inside her that she couldn't tell them from each other and was left numb.

"We have unfinished business on this station," she said to Leox and Geode as she stood in the cockpit with them. From their vantage point, they could see little but an extremely close-up view of the airlock facings; only at the very highest corner could Orla glimpse a sliver of stars. "Including business that can't really be finished, ever."

"It's tough knowing you have to leave a man behind." Leox shook his head as he took a thoughtful drag on his spice stick. (Orla would've objected to the bitter smoke if it hadn't seemed so petty compared to their other concerns.) "But staying won't change anything. Besides, I'd think you all would consider yourselves well shed of the place, since it's tainted with the dark side—that's what you call it, right?"

Orla nodded. "The thing is, we need to take the darkness with us when we leave, if we can."

Leox and Geode shared a glance—or at least, Leox glanced at Geode. Orla still found Geode's moods tricky to read. "Let me get this straight," Leox said. "You have identified a source of primordial evil in the universe, so instead of heading to the farthest corner of the galaxy possible, you want to *bring it on board.*"

"If we can contain the darkness in a way that allows us to transport it, it'll be completely safe. If not, we won't be able get it on board to begin with." *Assuming that it's not already,* she thought but didn't say. That was a risk none of them had any control over, and besides—the minute you suggested someone might be under an evil influence, they often began to behave like they were. The *Vessel's* crew was better off not worrying about it.

Leox weighed that, then nodded. "Then work that dark magic."

"It's light magic."

"Either way."

Reath had done multiple research assignments on Force-influenced artifacts, which he really hadn't expected to pay off so soon in his career as a Jedi. It just went to show you that research and footnotes and all the other bookish stuff some Padawans scoffed at were actually *very important*.

Master Cohmac, who as an archivist no doubt agreed with him, was the real expert in these matters. But he apparently wanted to see, yet again, how much responsibility the mission's Padawan could handle. So Master Cohmac sat in the corner, as stoic as any of the idols, while Reath took over the explanations.

"The Jedi elders have identified three main kinds of Force artifacts," he said to the assembled group in the comm area. "There are artifacts that contain certain memories or even personalities of past Force users. There are artifacts that enhance a Jedi's ability to use the Force. And then there are artifacts that hinder or confound that ability—Force dampeners, you could call them."

It was hard to tell if Master Cohmac was really listening; his expression was inscrutable. However, Orla Jareni was listening raptly, and Leox and Affie, watching from different doorways, were at least hearing him out.

Reath began, "These artifacts show up in legends more often than in real life—"

"We're not ignoring legends," Orla interjected. Her eyes met Master Cohmac's, as if they were in on some kind of secret that apprentices were not yet senior enough to know. Reath might've thought it was a shared joke, if Master Cohmac had smiled.

Best to simply keep going. "So," Reath continued, "it looks like the statues were placed on this station some centuries after it was first built. Our best guess is that those statues are of the first type—Force containers. If so, they were put here specifically to contain the dark side. Somehow darkness took hold here; maybe that's why the Amaxine station was abandoned to begin with. Or maybe it was abandoned first, so people thought this would be a safe place for the idols. Whatever powers the statues are meant to contain, they keep it in check—mostly. Not completely. Which is why most of us have had those weird visions."

Orla nodded. "Makes sense to me. The Force has been warning us to deal with this or else. What are our next steps?"

Master Cohmac finally spoke. "The statues should be removed from this station. If their containment is failing, then the darkness they hold could break free at any time. Since it looks like this station is already in use by smugglers from time to time"—he nodded toward Affie, who for some reason winced—"that could prove extremely dangerous."

Leox raised his hand. "How do we keep it from being extremely dangerous to *us*, is my question."

"A binding exercise," said Master Cohmac. "The three of us should be able to summon the necessary power. I'll teach those who need to learn the ritual's particulars."

"I already know it." Reath could hardly contain his delight. Always going for extra credit had paid off again. "It came up during one of my past projects."

Master Cohmac put one hand on his shoulder. "Then you already comprehend how dangerous it is. Your bravery is an example to us all."

The risks, which had previously been theoretical, stood out more sharply to Reath. But he didn't quail. Learning was most powerful when it was made real. He was ready.

After Reath's briefing, Orla was finally able to catch a moment alone with Cohmac.

"What's wrong with you?" The question was half concern, half exasperation. "It's one thing to be moody, another to turn your duties over to an apprentice who isn't even your own. Losing Dez is tragic and difficult, but you barely knew him—or is there a connection there I'm unaware of?"

"I barely knew him," Cohmac acknowledged. His face was

impassive, but his dark eyes bored into Orla's, reflecting the challenge back at her. "And yet I knew him enough to under-stand that he was full of life and vigor, that he was always willing to help those around him, that he ought to have had decades more. So when I think of his . . . meaningless, useless death—only one in the wake of the countless deaths caused by this hyperspace disaster—I grow angry."

Orla nodded. "Of course. We all have to overcome our anger—"

"Why? Why should I overcome it? If I cannot feel anger over the loss of such a life, then I cannot feel anything at all. The Order asks us to excise the deepest parts of ourselves— and for what? So that a young man might die unmourned?"

That stopped Orla short. For all her disagreements with the current direction of the Jedi leadership, she never doubted the fundamentals of their teachings. "So that we may not fall into the path of darkness," she said to Cohmac as gently as she could manage. "There is no emotion so justified or noble that it cannot lead to madness, if not kept in proper proportion."

*This is also about Master Simmix,* Orla realized. Cohmac's master had been dead a quarter of a century, and yet the loss still marked him.

"You've carried that burden a long time," Orla said, speaking as gently as she could. "You realize you didn't do anything that wrong, back then? And we all shared in those mistakes, not just you."

Cohmac shook his head. "I have come to realize that it was not my mistakes that scarred me then. I dwelled upon them because the Order would not allow me to grieve. My sorrow had no other outlet. And this, they tell us, is the proper Jedi way."

She wondered if she should probe more deeply, but that would only prolong Cohmac's brooding over an incident he should've put behind him decades before.

*Or is that an excuse?* Orla asked herself. *A reason to avoid examining the flaws of a friend too closely?*

By the time she had questioned her own motives, however, the moment to speak had passed. "You've always found this part of the path easier than I have," Cohmac said. With that, he returned to his preparations for the binding exercise.

Self-doubt flickered in Orla's mind. *Am I leaving to become a Wayseeker because it's truly the Force's will? Or am I merely pushing myself away from other people?*

❦

Leox and Geode were tasked with readying a storage area aboard the *Vessel*, which for some reason Leox seemed to consider a very tricky procedure, one that should only be handled by professionals. ("We've got it. Don't worry your heads about it. No need to even come back here till we're done. *Trust me.*")

Master Cohmac led the others into the center of the arboretum, where the four idols they'd found had all been taken. The vast star field of space twinkled through the translucent hexagonal tiles that formed the primary sphere. There, the station's ventilation caught in the whorls of its rings in such a way that it echoed the sound of the sea within a shell, a distant, granular moan. Reath's skin prickled with adrenaline, his body reacting to the vision he'd experienced before and might again. He wondered if the other Jedi were similarly affected—was this only his own fear or the mere presence of darkness instilling dread?

No, it wasn't only him. The shadows under Master Cohmac's eyes had deepened, and his shoulders were tensed as though he expected to be hit. Orla's breath was so measured that she had to be working through an exercise to calm and center the body, but she held her hands out as if pushing back the dark.

Finally they all stood in the very center of the sphere. The four idols surrounded them, forming a kind of compass: Reath decided that the crowned insect was north, the human south, the amphibian west, and the bird east. In the light, the faceted jewels shimmered in shades of rust, cobalt, and gold. Plant leaves framed each idol so thickly that both the pedestals and the walls were almost hidden. He felt alien there, as though the plants were the true inhabitants.

Master Cohmac closed his eyes, reaching out with the Force so intently that Reath could sense it—the slightest push on his concentration, the outlines of a consciousness not his own. He said, "The four statues seem to be connected. We must contain them all within a Force binding, or the bonds will be broken."

"Got it," said Orla. "Let's begin."

The Jedi stood in a circle, each facing outward. Reath gazed at the warrior queen, the human with her breastplate and crown, until he sensed the moment had come to close his eyes.

"Together," Master Cohmac intoned, "our minds form the nucleus of all energy in this room. We are the center point. The axis. The core. Feel that."

Reath concentrated until he *could* feel it, physically, a kind of warm glow that encompassed them all.

"Push the walls of the core outward. Expand the sphere. Allow your mind to fill that space."

It was as real a sensation as any Reath had experienced, the forward drift that made his entire body sway. The power they held increased exponentially as their minds began to link, and the glowing core they had created filled almost the entire space, stopping just short of the idols.

There, he felt . . . coldness. Stillness—not peace, but the inertia of the grave.

Master Cohmac said, "Now, all of us, as one . . . claim the idols."

Their minds reached out as one, pushing the boundaries of their sphere through the entire room and beyond it. Something undefined within the idols snapped; Reath imagined he could hear it, a quick clean break. Still, darkness swirled around them, but in a very different, more diffuse way than it had before. The Force binding seemed to be in place.

He opened his eyes to see the other Jedi breathing hard and collecting themselves, just like him. As they turned in toward each other, Master Cohmac smiled. "The good news is, these idols are successfully bound," he said.

Reath asked, "What's the bad news?"

Orla answered him. "Now we've got to carry the things back to the *Vessel*. And they're heavy."

They were. But Reath had rarely carried such a burden with so light a heart.

⚜

Affie didn't bother watching whatever weird magic ceremony the Republic monks were tinkering with. Instead, she busied herself getting visual records of every line of smugglers' code.

As she ran the scanner along the walls, she couldn't help trying to interpret more of the symbols. The two rings separated by an asterisk of jagged lines—was that a journey, maybe one interrupted by something disastrous? Surely one of the main functions of the codes must be to warn other pilots of risks.

*It's not* all *about cheating Scover,* Affie told herself, a bleak kind of joke.

There, again, came the star symbol of the Byne Guild.

She increased the resolution to make sure these scans were the sharpest and best of the bunch.

And then—

Affie scowled as she saw a drawing of what appeared to be a being's head, one with a high ridge in the middle. Like a Bivall's head.

Scover Byne was a Bivall.

*They're conspiring against her. Not just stealing—they're after* her, *specifically.*

Affie's eyes focused again on the two rings with the jagged asterisk in the middle. Could that be an explosion? A hint at a future expedition that might be sabotaged?

"Thank the spirits we're leaving this place soon," she muttered as she quickly finished making records. There was no telling how far the plot had already gone.

※

Leox Gyasi had seen some strange things in his day. Enough that he tried not to use the word *strange* too often. To the prepared mind, no element of the galaxy should seem alien; they were all the same star stuff, merely taking different shapes from time to time.

And yet . . .

"There's just something unsettling about having cursed idols aboard again," Leox said. He was alone with Geode, who knew about their last cursed-idol incident and had never reported it to Scover Byne. (Little Bit was precious to him, but you couldn't blame a girl for wanting to talk about things with her momma. Luckily, this had been before her time.) "They're bad luck, as you and I have ample reason to know. Gives me the willies."

Geode was made of more stoic stuff. However, Leox could tell he didn't like it, either. Last time, they'd taken the wrong idols to the wrong planet, on behalf of a Rodian who turned out to be very much the wrong client. The intent, so far as Leox could reconstruct it after the fact, was for the Rodian to be worshipped as an idol-dominating god by the fearful populace.

The populace had had other ideas.

Leaning against the nearest console, Leox studied the insect-shaped idol, the one with pincers and wings. "I mean, I didn't mind the chanting or the incense. The sacrifices were okay since they were just flowers. And, man, that plinth they carved in your honor? Looked just like you. Could've been your twin."

Geode didn't even have to mention the rather less successful mosaic portraying Leox's descent from their celestial starcraft. Wasn't like Leox could ever forget it, no matter how hard he tried.

"It's not good for the spirit, being worshipped. Corrodes you from the inside out." Leox shook his head. "Which is the real curse of these kinds of things, if you ask me. We got out of there not one moment too soon. At least the Jedi are packing these away instead of trying to use them for all the wrong reasons."

That Rodian had wound up fleeing the planet as fast as he could, and in another ship, since Leox had had about enough of his foolishness by that point. Leox and Geode had remained only as long as was decent before leaving the people with a gentle moral code of kindness. Probably those fellows had come to their senses within a few months, once they'd gotten used to having their most sacred ancient objects back on their world and gone back to using its original name.

At any rate, he hoped so. Otherwise, there was now a planet called Leoxo, and if Affie ever found out, he'd never hear the end of it.

◈

"So I guess this is it," Nan said.

Reath stood with her near the airlocks. The *Vessel* was already at the point of departure. "You're leaving soon, too?"

"We're actually going to finish some repairs first. Remember the state you found us in?"

"Right," he said, wincing at his own forgetfulness. "Do you need anything? Supplies, or assistance—"

"Nope, we're good," Nan insisted. "We have everything we need. Including time, now, thanks to you."

Their eyes met. Reath had wanted to say goodbye and had thought Nan might, too. However, as he looked down at her—clearly struggling to find the right words, unwilling to meet his eyes—he realized that their brief time as companions might've meant more to her than it had to him. That the way he'd acted might've come across as romantic interest, at least for anyone leading a more normal life. People on the frontier didn't yet understand the Jedi, which meant they didn't understand the limits on those relationships. Too late, Reath comprehended that he should've been more careful.

But there was no need to be unkind. He said, "It was a pleasure getting to know you, Nan. I doubt our paths will cross again, but I wish you well."

"Paths will cross," she repeated absently, then straightened. She met his eyes steadily, as though making a vow. "You saved me from being kidnapped. That means you're responsible for returning me to my people. I don't take that lightly."

"Any Jedi would've done the same."

"It wasn't 'any Jedi.' It was you, and I will tell them so." Nan looked into his eyes with great solemnity for a long moment—then smiled, her cheerful self once more. "Thanks for telling me so much about the Republic and the Jedi. The galaxy is changing, and you helped me understand it."

Reath felt happy to have done so, but also happy to eventually report this to Master Jora. Then she would understand that he wasn't just rejecting the people of the frontier out of hand, which meant his reasons for wanting to return to Coruscant were *completely objective.* "Glad to be of service."

They parted ways at last. He glanced back over his shoulder once to see her go—the same moment she'd turned to look at him. When their eyes met, Nan raised one hand in farewell.

*I'll see her again,* Reath thought. He knew it as surely as he knew anything. The Force declared it.

# THIRTEEN

"This hyperspace lane might've been cleared for transit, but that doesn't make it smooth sailing." Leox shook his head as he studied the nav coordinates. "Geode, can you triangulate the vortices . . . except, look here, it's already done. Should've known you'd be one step ahead of me."

Geode had the good manners not to rub it in, for which Leox was grateful. His moods had been on edge of late, and he was not a man whose temperament reached the edge very often. He was no Force user, but he did not doubt that the universe had spiritual dimensions, and on this station, those dimensions were seriously out of whack. Call it the dark side, call it whatever: Leox would be glad to see the back of it.

Of course, they'd be flying off with idols that took up the last sliver of storage the *Vessel* had without revealing compartments the Republic never needed to know about. The Jedi said they had it under control.

Not that he took the Jedi's word for *everything*. But the Force—that was their wheelhouse. Besides, the spiritual dimensions of the galaxy weren't warning him about his cargo hold. They were warning him about the station. All the more reason to get out.

"How long until our departure?" Cohmac Vitus asked from the cockpit entrance.

"Just waiting for our copilot," Leox said.

Even as he said it, Affie shouldered past Cohmac and stomped onto the bridge, making the Jedi raise one eyebrow. The glance he gave Leox clearly meant something along the lines of, *Adolescents—what can you do?*

Affie's problems were a whole lot more complicated than that. A whole lot more valid. But none of that was Cohmac's business.

Leox said only, "Tell everyone to get themselves strapped in. We're out of here in five."

Once the Jedi had departed, he returned to his seat. Affie kept her gaze fixed on her controls, not acknowledging her fellow crew members. Geode hadn't dared start a conversation with her, and Leox couldn't blame the guy. He didn't intend to start one, either.

Not because he was afraid of Affie's temper—though that was a very reasonable thing to fear—but because any conversation was going to loop back to her asking the wrong questions, and him holding back the answers she wasn't ready to hear.

The coordinates were set. "Detaching from airlock in five," he announced.

Affie nodded. "Five, four, three . . ."

On the mark, she turned the lever that released the clamps; a heavy metallic thud echoed through the *Vessel*, the sound of their freedom. As the engines powered up, Leox brought the ship's nose around, bringing back their usual view of the stars. It was a relief to see open space again. Leox was uneasy with containment on planets or stations, and only felt at home with a ship at his command.

Often, Affie teased him about that—"We're taking off at last, you can breathe again!"—but that day she stuck to the bare minimum. "Preparing for hyperspace jump."

"That water's still gonna be a little choppy," Leox muttered. "Geode's linked the routes up as smoothly as possible, but that's not the same thing as actually being smooth. You ready?"

Her only reply was, "Jumping in five."

Leox grabbed the handle, took a deep breath, and made the leap. Space stretched into infinity, every star a comet for one brief instant. Then hyperspace surrounded them, blue again (but dark, violet-tinged, not at all right) and shimmering, almost alive.

And angry.

He'd been speaking metaphorically earlier, but the chop was very real as the first of Geode's programmed jumps kicked in. The *Vessel* bucked under them like a blurrg having a bad day, and Leox stayed in his seat only by clutching the arms.

"Whoa." Affie was surprised enough to speak to him normally. "What happened out there?"

"Something even worse than we knew," he said. "Soon we're gonna find out what."

Orla considered herself a good traveler—adaptable, flexible, inventive—and had counted this among the reasons she'd make a good Wayseeker. (Not that such considerations were truly significant, in terms of deciding how best to follow the Force, but she had to go over every factor before making such an enormous decision.)

So it was discouraging to realize she could still experience motion sickness.

"It's like we flew into an asteroid field," she said to Cohmac. They stood together in the cargo hold with the idols, ensuring that the holds they'd placed would remain strong.

"We haven't, have we?"

"No, we're in hyperspace. But hyperspace itself is a little rocky right now." Orla hesitated. "How is that even possible?"

"Not sure," Cohmac said. "As I understand it, there's still

quite a lot of interstellar debris from the *Legacy Run* that needs to be accounted for. Probes sent from Coruscant have given the crew—in particular, Geode, I suppose—enough information to stitch together a makeshift route home for us, which involves several patchwork jumps merged by the navicomputer. Normally there are no intermediate jumps, so this feels like hitting bumps in the road."

Orla sighed. "In other words, it's safe, but not comfortable."

"Exactly," Cohmac said. "It almost makes me wish I'd paid more attention in supraliminal topography class, back in the day."

"Aren't archivists supposed to be interested in *all* subjects?"

"In theory." Once in a very great while—like now—Cohmac Vitus had a wicked smile.

Reath was making the trip in his quarters, where Orla had suggested he get started on assembling a report for Master Jora Malli. They'd leaned on their Padawan heavily throughout this journey; he deserved some rest and privacy. She knew he was also saddened by Dez's death, especially because of the bond they shared from having the same master. It was not the Jedi way to mourn, but sadness was a thing to be worked through, not denied. Particularly for an apprentice facing his first real experience of grief, it could be difficult.

*Better grief,* Orla told herself, *than anger.* She gave Cohmac a sidelong glance. Her old friend seemed appropriately calm and focused again. Yet whatever underlying storm had fueled that anger—it still raged beneath the surface. Orla knew that much. But she'd pried enough. The rest was Cohmac's to work out on his own.

The floor shuddered under their feet; the idols trembled. "If one of these falls and breaks," Orla said, "what would you say are the chances that whatever's trapped inside gets free?"

Cohmac shook his head slowly. "Let's hope we don't find out."

⚜

No path to the *Vessel* was straightforward. Affie's had been odder than most.

Affie Hollow had been fourteen years old and eager to make her mark on the Guild. Her foster mother, Scover Byne herself, had thought it a good idea to begin teaching the girl their trade. Already the Byne Guild had grown almost past Scover's ability to personally control. A loyal, bright, capable daughter would be the ideal second-in-command—once she had experience outside piloting simulators, out in the real worlds.

So when Affie's tour of Guild ships had begun, she'd brimmed with excitement, practically setting off sparks the first time she stepped onto a bridge without her mother by her side. Those sparks had been dampened the minute she looked at the other crew members' faces. The kindest words she could come up with for their attitude were "not impressed."

No reason for them to be. Affie knew she was young and

untrained, more a nuisance than a help. But wasn't that the whole point of training? To make someone useful?

For a few months she bounced from ship to ship, never rejected (she was Scover's daughter, after all) but never accepted, either. A couple of the pilots grudgingly taught her basic skills. That was as good as it got. Once Affie had overheard a navigator grumbling, "My job's plotting courses, not teaching little snot-nosed brats." This was deeply unfair and gave her a complex that led to her carrying around kerchiefs for months.

Then she was sent to the smallest ship yet, the *Vessel*.

Geode was the first individual Affie had felt truly welcomed by in far too long; him, she trusted immediately. Leox Gyasi had been another story. He smelled like spice, and he talked about "the deeper spiritual dimensions of the cosmos," and he wore open-necked shirts with lots of beads like he didn't even *care* if that was impractical for long-haul flights. (Thanks to Scover's influence, Affie cared a great deal about practicality.) The *Vessel* was tiny, and not particularly noteworthy, so she wasn't sure how much of the goings-on would apply to other ships.

But she had to learn about the entire Guild, not just the main ships. She resigned herself to the journey.

To her surprise, her first trip on the *Vessel* taught her more than all her other journeys combined. Leox talked her through every step; Geode let her observe him whenever she wanted, as much as she wanted. Nobody looked down on her because of her age or inexperience. They let her learn by doing.

Scover was nonplussed when, at the end of that journey, Affie asked to travel with the *Vessel* again. She'd tilted her birdlike blue head as she said, "I had thought you might wish to try one of the larger passenger transports, such as the *Legacy Run*, perhaps."

The *Legacy Run* was the biggest, best thing going in terms of transports, trusted to only the finest captains, and Affie wavered for a second, but no longer. "I'll stick with the *Vessel* if it's okay with you."

Scover didn't like it, but she okayed it.

As they finalized preparations for their next takeoff, Affie came up with what she hoped was a tactful question. "Why do you think Scover assigned me here in the first place?"

"Because I'm safe for you," Leox said.

"What does that mean?"

"It means that I have been born blessedly free of the passionate fevers that seize so many beings." He leaned back in the pilot's seat; apparently he'd modified it to serve as a recliner, when he wished. "I possess no desire to reproduce, nor—and more to the point—any desire to perform the actions of reproduction with no generative goal in mind."

Affie worked through this. "You mean you . . . don't have sex." Her cheeks flushed hot; she wasn't a *child*, but she wasn't used to talking about this with grown people.

However, for Leox, she might as well have been discussing the weather. "I've tried it out. Not an unpleasant practice, to be sure. But in my case it's not an imperative, for which I've always been grateful. Seems to free up the mind, insofar as I can judge the minds of other beings. Certainly frees up a whole lot of time. And I relish the knowledge that I am the ultimate fulfillment of my ancestral line, the point to which all their striving led." After a pause he added, "Well, me and my sister. Until she has kids. In which case, the grand cycle turns anew."

"But—our pilots are good people, not criminals or smugglers or—nobody would—"

Leox held up a hand. "Even good people bring their paramours aboard their ships from time to time, and in close quarters, no telling what a young person might see. But here it's just me and Geode, and he won't go into his next mating smelt for another, what, nine years or so?" Geode didn't contradict him. "Like I said, here, you're safe. You're also on duty. So how about you get cracking and show me you can steer this boat out of atmosphere?"

For the first time, Affie flew a real ship. Their course wavered a little, but she managed it. Leox neither overpraised her nor criticized her, saying only, "You'll know to check for atmospheric turbulence next time. Geode's going to set courses from here."

It had been that simple. Leox accepted her as crew and expected her to keep up. Affie always had. Over the next two years and change, they'd developed more than a working rapport. If she had a best friend, it was Leox.

Which was why she couldn't stay mad at him forever.

Geode had evened out their path somewhat, to the point where they had only a mildly bumpy ride. Affie ventured, "I hope Scover's there to meet us." It was easier to say that than, *I hope Scover's still alive.*

Leox understood without her saying it. "I'm sure your momma's just fine." He acted like nothing had gone wrong between them at all. Maybe for him, nothing had. "Except for worrying about you, that is."

This was trickier, but she wanted to say it. "I'm going to report everything I found on the station. Scover will know how to interpret it."

"No doubt."

He said it easily enough, but . . . did Leox look worried? He never looked worried. Ever. Except now.

Affie refused to think of reasons why he wouldn't want her to report a smuggling operation. She focused on keeping the ship steady and put everything else out of mind.

— *Journey to the Amaxine Station, by Reath Silas* —
## REPORT CONCLUSION

*The reasons you gave for accepting a frontier assignment have been fulfilled, master. I've encountered situations more unpredictable than anything that could've happened in the Archives. I've used my knowledge in real conflicts, not just through simulations. I've gained* information about unknown cultures, though Master Cohmac says we still have a lot to learn about the idols and whatever darkness is trapped within them. I've gotten out of the Archives for a while. And I've met forms of life I never knew existed; while I can't say I've managed to communicate with Geode, I sense him through the Force more. A little more. I think.

Since I've already accomplished all that, why remain on the frontier?

Please, just consider, master. Not only did the hyperspace disaster trap both of us in separate parts of the galaxy, separating us for days, but this mission also cost Dez Rydan his life. I know you feel his loss even more than I do. Dez had more experience, more skill, more— well, almost more everything than me. More than almost anyone. He still died, because there are threats out here we don't know about. We don't even know enough to guess what they are, or when we'll encounter them. How can we study the deepest secrets of the Force, achieve higher levels of meditation, if we're too busy fighting to stay alive? How can I put my knowledge to use when the frontier doesn't call upon most of that knowledge?

You know I'm no coward, Master Jora. I've never failed to do what was necessary and right. But being on the frontier isn't necessary. At least, not for us.

If thinking about the Kyber Arch was supposed to clarify things for me, well, it hasn't. Jedi can and do cross it alone. Maybe that was just a puzzle you gave me to distract me from the upheaval of leaving Coruscant.

I'm never going to turn this in for you to read. This is just about *working through things in my head. There's no convincing you to change your mind—I know that if I know anything.*

*But is it so bad if I hope you'll change your mind on your own?*

᠅

Reath turned from his holocam when he felt the subtle shift in vibration that meant their hyperspace journey would end soon. To the cam he said, "Delete all," then got to his feet.

When he reached the jump seats, Orla Jareni was already settling in and adjusting their belts. From the bridge, Leox called, "Should we secure those idols? Last thing I need is evil spirits messing up my landing."

"They're steady." Orla spoke with such confidence that Reath almost quit worrying about the idols himself. That flutter of darkness they inspired had gone mute, which was a relief. No more creepy warning visions, which was even better. It seemed their containment ritual had worked perfectly.

(Just one more advanced task he'd already accomplished and didn't have to seek out on the frontier! Just one more thing that was important to study, and to write up for future generations of Jedi!)

Master Cohmac joined them only seconds before the announcement came. "We're receiving a distress signal," Leox called. "Traffic's still shut down all over the place. Nobody else is going to reach them soon—"

"Go," Master Cohmac commanded. "We're ready to help."

Reath readied himself. Was someone stranded, like they'd

been not long before? That would be a fairly simple thing to fix, if so.

"We're about to drop out of hyperspace!" Affie said. "Hang on!"

Reath grabbed his harness. Almost as soon as he'd closed his hands, the ship rocked once before settling into the familiar subluminous drag of realspace.

He unclipped his harness in the second before Leox muttered, "By the *gods*."

"What?" Orla called. "What is it?"

"You'd better see this for yourselves." He sounded breathless and yet somber. "I don't have the words."

The Jedi dashed to the bridge.

It wasn't that unusual for a ship to run into trouble on its journey, to drop out of hyperspace to deal with whatever issue it was before continuing on. No doubt that was what had happened to strand a ship so deep in empty space, in the billion-kilometer stretch of nothing between various star systems.

What was unusual was to be almost arm's reach from a ship on the point of destruction.

It appeared to be a personnel carrier, though it was hard to tell, crumpled and carbon-scored as its hull was. Not the carbon scoring that meant combat, with the streaks of weapon hits, but the more ominous kind, the expanding black blotches that indicated out-of-control fires within the ship. The upper areas of the ship, including the bridge, had already burned away. Probably that meant nobody was in charge of evacuations that needed to happen immediately. Reath couldn't spot as much as one escape pod being fired.

He was preparing even before Orla said, "Okay, Leox, bring us to their airlock and prepare for docking."

Affie gaped. "You want us to hook ourselves up to the *ship on fire?*"

"People inside are in trouble," Reath said. "Nobody else is around. So it's our job to get them out."

# FOURTEEN

The carrier *Journeyman* had left Cerea ferrying three hundred souls, through a hyperspace lane that had been thought to be clear. But it had been opened prematurely. Space debris crashed into the *Journeyman*, turning it from a comfortable passenger ship to a self-contained hell.

Cohmac ran through the smoke-filled corridors of the *Journeyman*, inhaling only through the breathmask firmly clenched in his mouth. The haze stung his eyes, blurring them, but he relied less on sight than on hearing, and on the guidance of the Force, to find his way to the main loading bay.

When he ran into it, he found—as he had expected—more than two hundred people huddled together, gasping through masks or ventilators, or coughing desperately for breath. Although they were mostly Cereans, he spotted Ogemites, Sarkans, humans, and a handful of Wookiees among the crowd.

Recognition of his golden Jedi robes was immediate. The crowd surged toward Cohmac, surrounding him with a hundred cries: "There's no way out of here!" "The pod doors aren't where they're supposed to be!" "We can't get to the other launching bay!" "I can't breathe!" "We're trapped!" Their frenzy verged dangerously close to panic. When a group of people so large gave way to panic, the result was a mob. No one could save a mob.

Cohmac removed his breathmask to shout above the din. "Take me to the pod doors!"

The crowd parted for him, creating a path that showed the way. He saw instantly that internal blast shielding, intended to bolster the ship against just such disasters, had become stuck in place. If it didn't lift, no one could reach the escape pods.

With one great leap, Cohmac soared above the throng to pounce on a service platform near the top of the blast shield. It took no time to see the problem: a bent metal beam lodged in the shield's workings. He ignited his lightsaber and plunged the blade deep into the beam. Almost immediately it began to melt. Waves of heat emanated from it, only kept from scorching Cohmac's skin through the sheer power of the Force.

"Move clear below!" he shouted. But the crowd had steadied enough to have understood his plan and anticipated the need. Already they were edging back, leaving a wide semi-circle of empty space.

Just in time, too. The beam broke in two, falling to the bay floor with a tremendous clang that hurt Cohmac's ears. Even as the sound echoed, the blast shield began tracking upward, clearing the way to the escape pods.

Cohmac realized he might need to exit via one of the pods himself. Already the corridor he'd arrived through blazed bright with fire. He dropped soundlessly to the floor and joined the evacuating horde, who had already gone from frenzied to steadied by urgent purpose. As he did so, he picked up his comlink. "The main pods will launch soon. Were all other passengers killed in the collision?"

Affie's voice came through. "*A few people were stuck on the higher decks. Orla got most of them out, and Reath's supposed to be returning to the ship with the last one—if he can make it.*"

She didn't have to explain the rest. The *Vessel* couldn't remain close to the *Journeyman* much longer, because the *Journeyman* would soon explode.

Rescuing a tiny child from a burning ship sounded heroic in the most classical sense. The reality was less dignified.

"Ow. *Ow.*" Reath winced as he tried to readjust the squirming, hairy infant in his arms. "It's okay, Wookiee baby. Hang on, Wookiee baby."

But that was the whole problem—the little Wookiee *was*

hanging on, as all its arboreal instincts demanded in a time of danger, by hooking its claws into the nearest object. Unfortunately, the nearest object was Reath.

Also, even an infant Wookiee was large and heavy. Reath could handle the weight, but it made unwieldy going as he ducked under damaged beams and tried to dodge smoldering debris on the deck.

The Wookiee whined pitifully, and Reath tried to pet its head. "Don't be scared, little Wookiee ba—*gahh!*"

As the back of his scalp stung, he saw that the Wookiee had apparently tried to pet his head in return, and in so doing had ripped away Reath's Padawan braid at the roots. *Great,* he thought, *I have to grow that back, assuming we get out of here at all.* At least this had the effect of calming the baby, who promptly put its new acquisition in its mouth.

Reath coughed. The smoke was getting to him. When he'd picked up the little Wookiee, it had been flailing with fright. One of those flails had knocked away his breathmask. At least they didn't have far to go.

*Please let the corridor still be clear, please please please—*

He skidded to a halt. The corridor that led to the *Vessel's* airlock was on fire.

Quickly Reath considered his options. Getting to another escape pod in time was unlikely. He could look for another, more roundabout way to the airlock, but even if one existed, there was no guarantee he'd find it fast enough to save their lives.

The only chance was something he'd never done before—never even tried—but a sense of sureness swept through him, telling him that this power was his to command.

Balancing the baby Wookiee on one hip, Reath freed one hand, stretched it out, and closed his eyes. With all the might of the Force, he concentrated on the flames, on the molecular movement of the heat itself until his consciousness intertwined with it.

Then he pushed outward with all his strength.

With a great roar, the fire rushed out through the holes in the ceiling, clearing the corridor entirely of flames and smoke for one brief moment. That moment was long enough for Reath to dash through with the Wookiee, leaping through the airlock into the *Vessel*.

As soon as his feet had hit the deck, before the fire could blaze back, the airlock spiraled shut. *"You took your own sweet time,"* Leox drawled over the comm. *"Hang on!"*

There was no time to make it to the safety harnesses. Reath simply gripped the furry child in his arms and ducked to the floor.

The *Vessel* banked sharply left, sending him rolling into the nearest wall. Although the Wookiee child howled in protest, it didn't relax its grip as their ship accelerated and flew away. Only seconds later, the shock wave of the explosion rolled through them, making the whole ship tremble—but they were safe.

Orla appeared in the doorway. "And who have we here?"

Despite her sharp features and forbiddingly pristine appearance, Orla must have somehow come across as maternal to the baby, who immediately crawled to her and clamped its arms around her leg. She reached low to scratch its head as Reath got to his feet. "Too young to speak," he said. "We'll have to hope the *Journeyman*'s manifest can be found."

"I'll take care of him for a bit," Orla promised. Reath was more than halfway to the bridge before he heard her say to the Wookiee, "*What* do you have in your mouth?"

When he walked onto the bridge, he was able to view the full scene for himself. Where the *Journeyman* had once been was just a blackened, skeletal ruin. At least that wreckage was haloed by a ring of escape pods, each blinking a signal for pickup. "Do we need to retrieve them?" Reath asked.

Leox shook his head. "A Republic transport's already signaled they're on the way to tow 'em to Coruscant. Oughta be here within the hour. They'll be a lot better equipped to handle that number of people. No way they'd all fit aboard, unless we agreed to get a whole lot closer than I, personally, am comfortable with. Probably not even then."

Affie looked up at Reath and laughed. "You need a shower. Or a polishing. Something."

"Bet I've got soot all over me," Reath said, realizing his robes were completely ash-stained, except for a clear baby-Wookiee shape on his chest. How had Orla also boarded the ship and remained immaculate? Someday he'd learn her secret. "I can't wait to get to Coruscant. Specifically, to the Temple baths."

Over comms came Master Cohmac's voice. *"We have two parents here—they were separated from their very young child—"*

"Are they Wookiees?" Reath asked.

Master Cohmac responded, *"Yes. Their child has mottled-gray fur."*

"Then you can tell them the baby's safe and sound on the *Vessel*." Reath allowed himself a grin.

*"Thank the Force,"* said Master Cohmac. *"We've seen enough of death."*

Reath's smile faded as he thought again of Dez, lost in a flash, forever.

Upon arriving on Coruscant, it would've been acceptable for Cohmac to go immediately to the baths and don his ceremonial garb—or at least to wash his face clean of soot. Instead, he sought an immediate audience with the Council. Somewhat to his surprise, it was granted.

When he walked into the room, he saw a trio of Masters waiting for him, as much of the Council as could be assembled on such short notice. He knelt—an old-fashioned gesture of respect among the Jedi, but one that felt right to him.

"Master Vitus," said Master Adampo, a Yarkoran with magnificent whiskers. "We are pleased to know that you have returned safely, despite the many dangers of the hyperspace disaster. Early reports indicate that you and your ship were instrumental in the rescue of the *Journeyman* passengers." In his voice was the unspoken question: *So why are you here?*

"While stranded on the Amaxine station, we suffered a loss," Cohmac said. "I regret to inform the Council that Jedi Knight Dez Rydan was killed."

Dismay, then pain, revealed themselves on their faces. Master Adampo asked, "Was this due to the hyperspace damage?"

Cohmac summarized, as succinctly as he could, the myriad strange factors that had led to Dez's fatal accident: the ancient station, the idols imprisoning the dark side, the labyrinthine lower rings that had hidden the helix rings until too late. It all sounded very dry and official and correct. Even a droid might've spoken with more emotion. This was, of course, as it should be.

Yet the voice inside his head—the one he tried not to listen to, the one that spoke more and more often—demanded, *Why should it be a virtue to hide your feelings? To pretend that they don't exist?*

Master Rosason, a human woman of advanced years, nodded as he finished. "We await further report on the idols, as well. You have all performed your duty admirably under difficult conditions. Rydan's loss is a blow to the entire Order."

These were phrases that came before farewell.

*You have no more emotion for him than that?* Cohmac wanted

to say. *A young man goes to his death and it's no more than a line in a report?*

He curbed his anger. Tried to remember exactly what it was Orla had said to him aboard the *Vessel* about moderation. But Cohmac's memory, usually excellent, could no longer find the words.

Coruscant transport logs were incredibly thorough and, to Affie's surprise, totally open for public perusal. That gave her a chance to dig into realms of information that would normally be closed to her. Even the Byne Guild's mother ship didn't have so much data.

If only she could've contacted Scover directly! But Scover often kept quiet about which ships she was traveling on when, and preferred to keep it that way. Affie knew to respect her mother's discretion, even when it kept her in such wretched suspense.

Leox took a seat beside her as she stopped scrolling through and pointed at the screen. "Look at this," she said. "There's three Guild ships here, so they made it out of hyperspace okay—"

"And there's the *Rushlight Equinox*." Leox laughed and clapped his hands with real enthusiasm. "Can't wait to talk to Vishla about whatever her crew got up to while hyperspace was down, though I doubt they've got any stories that compare to ours."

"I hope not," Affie said. "Someone got *killed*."

"Makes it a tragic mission, I admit, but there is a certain anecdotal value."

Affie would've scolded him if she hadn't known Leox actually did care about what had happened to Dez. Besides, Geode was already giving him the death glare. No point in piling on.

Plus she still had so much information to scroll through. So many ships. So many courses registered. Coruscant was one of the few places the Guild's ships could've sought safe refuge from the disaster—assuming they'd made it through. Nowhere could she find the mother ship of the Guild.

"Look at this," Leox finally said, focusing the screen on one particular packet of data. "Three more Byne Guild ships cleared dock here yesterday."

"But not Scover's."

"You're not looking hard enough. See here?" His jeweled ring sparkled as he tapped the screen. The words there read: *Rerouted, Sealed Under Express Guild Authority.*

Only one person had the right to designate something as "Express Guild Authority," and that was Scover Byne herself.

"She's here on Coruscant." Affie started to grin, then to laugh, even though tears were welling in her eyes. "Scover made it."

"Told ya," Leox said, hugging her around the shoulders. She was pretty sure he'd told her no such thing, but who cared? Her mother was alive.

The hyperspace disaster had called on all Jedi in one way or another; everyone was involved with rescue, resolution, or analysis. With all the busy activity on every level of the Temple, getting a corridor closed was—as Orla's créche-minder used to say—a job of work. However, nothing cleared people out of the way faster than announcing, "Dark side coming through!"

Not that she actually yelled that out loud. She *wanted* to. But the bare facts had been enough to get the Jedi Council to clear the area fast, which meant she had no excuse, and nothing to distract her from the eerie task ahead.

First, aboard the *Vessel*, they carefully transferred each of the idols to an antigravity floater. Then Orla led their procession from ship to station. Her job was to make sure no one accidentally blundered into the "closed" area, while the other Masters followed behind to keep the most careful watch on the idols.

Dozens of people stood in side corridors, not so much watching as waiting for their pathway to be cleared. However, as Orla led the statues forward, the restive onlookers would hush and go still, until the only sounds were their footsteps and the low hum of the floaters. Even those few civilian guests who couldn't sense the Force would be struck by the ornate carvings and the sinister cast of each idol's face.

As for those who *could* sense the Force? The protective hold they'd placed on the idols back at the station remained strong; there was no immediate danger. But the hold itself prickled uneasily at the edges of Orla's consciousness. It was rather like the feeling of knowing, without turning around, that someone has entered a room that was supposed to be locked.

They were, in fact, about to enter a place that had been effectively locked for a long time—one kept apart from the Temple at large, hidden from the Jedi themselves: the Shrine in the Depths.

Currently, the shrine on the very lowest levels of the Temple was covered by a meditation area, which had been hastily disassembled upon the *Vessel*'s arrival on Coruscant. Orla's heartbeat quickened as they slowly walked through the large, darkened room, over what remained of the floor, until they reached the square dark pit at the center. Stairs had been carved in the stone long before, long enough for the edges to have been blunted. So long before, in fact, that Jedi had not been there at all.

Few people knew that the Jedi Temple had been built atop a Sith shrine.

A vergeance in the Force existed there—a nexus of power and energy that could be put to many uses, both worthy and wicked. Vergeances rose of their own accord; they could not be created, only discovered. In the far distant past of the Old

Republic, back during the ancient Sith Empire, Sith and Jedi had often warred for control of these vergeances. The Sith had held this one first.

*Maybe,* Orla thought, *the idols are coming home.*

She was being melodramatic. The Jedi had controlled this vergeance for thousands of years—first through their own shrine, then through the construction of the Temple.

Still, it was the Sith who had carved the steps.

Orla led the way down, holding up the hem of her white robes as she entered the darkened shrine. They were underground, and she could feel the damp coolness that forever permeated the space. The air even smelled of dirt.

Relics and other objects strongly imbued with the dark side of the Force were taken there for purification. There, Orla would work with some of the great Masters to strip the dark energy from the idols in that safe, sacred space, where it could sink into the vergeance, dissipate into the cosmic Force, and again be made whole.

Orla sighed as she thought, *In theory, anyway. Reality might be a whole lot more dangerous.*

◆

Reath took his Wookiee charge to the spacedock infirmary, to reunite it (her, as it turned out) with her parents. This infirmary only handled less critical health concerns: vaccinations, minor injuries, the occasional quarantine from travel. At least, that was the plan.

Nothing after the hyperspace disaster had gone according to plan. That was made clearer than ever to Reath when a medical droid whirred through the infirmary doors, giving him a look at what might as well have been a war zone. After the first burst of shock, he heard the ecstatic growls of two Wookiee parents coming to retrieve their daughter.

He submitted to thanks, hugging, and even some grooming before leaving the reunited family happy together. As soon as he had, he hurried toward the doors to figure out how he could help.

Every flat surface of the infirmary—beds, counters, floors—was almost entirely covered with the wounded from the *Journeyman* explosion. While those on the floor seemed to have more minor injuries, like broken limbs or lacerations, some of the ones in the beds were hooked up to multiple monitors and regulators. The constant whirrs and beeps could not drown out the moans. While a couple of organic physicians were hurrying from person to person, both they and the handful of med droids were clearly overworked.

"Why aren't they in hospitals?" he muttered.

Although he was speaking mostly to himself, a hovering pill droid nearby replied, "All hospitals are at capacity in the aftermath of the hyperspace disaster. Every medical facility must operate at full strength."

*Or beyond it,* he thought, taking in the incredible overcrowding. Reath saw a woman lying on the floor looking up at him, and knelt by her side. "What can I do for you?"

Mostly, people wanted water. A lot of them also wanted painkillers, which the med droids begrudgingly allowed him to access. At first Reath wondered whether he ought to be dispensing those so freely—but this was an emergency, and he'd worry about the recommendations later. Above all, he realized, they wanted someone to pay attention to them and reassure them that everything would be all right.

Usually he could do that. But sometimes they asked questions he couldn't answer. "Did anyone else from our transport get out?" "We were taking vaccines to Crothy—has anybody reached them? Have they been able to contain the fever at all?"

*Thank the Force that we made it through hyperspace in one piece,* Reath realized. *Though it wasn't all Force. Some of that was thanks to Leox, Affie, and Geode. Or the Force was working through them, I guess. Still—I didn't appreciate how fortunate we were.*

He'd looked too much at the negatives of their situation, not the positives. He ought to have been more like Leox, grateful for the good instead of complaining about the bad.

And if it was true about the accident, maybe it was true about his rejection of this assignment, too.

A med droid wheeled up to him. "Your condition is acceptable?"

"I'm fine. Just here to help." A terrible thought came to Reath then, one he ought to have considered before. It was just so unimaginable—so impossible— "Do you have access to medical records from Starlight Beacon?"

"Yes, data is updating every half day."

"In their infirmary—was there a patient there called Jora Malli? A member of the Jedi Council, the new head of the Jedi delegation on Starlight. Master Jora Malli. Was she injured after the hyperspace disaster?"

The droid tilted its oval head. "Master Jora Malli was never brought to the Starlight infirmary." Reath smiled for the brief moment it took the droid to add, "She was killed in battle against the Nihil."

He couldn't have heard that correctly. (He'd heard just fine.) It couldn't be true. (Of course it could.) Or the droid was wrong. (Droids pulled their information straight from central processing.)

"Dead?" Reath repeated in a small voice.

"Jora Malli was declared lost in action by Jedi Master Sskeer," the droid said. "Is there any further information I can provide?"

Reath knew Sskeer. They'd met when the Trandoshan had been assigned as Master Jora's aide on Starlight. If Sskeer said it was true, then . . . then it was true. He swallowed hard. "No. That's all. Thank you."

As the droid rolled away, Reath leaned against the nearest wall. Breath wouldn't enter his lungs. His eyes wouldn't focus. His ears refused to make sense of the sounds surrounding him. He was nothing but his pulse and breath and the horrible knowledge that Master Jora was gone.

## FIFTEEN

The Padawans' training area was all but deserted that time of day. Other apprentices would be preparing for missions or dining with their masters. Reath, who had no assignment and no master, went there because he had no place else to go.

They'd already reassigned his quarters. Already! It wasn't like one room in the Padawans' dorm was greatly different from the others, and the room he'd been assigned as a temporary measure was a lot more luxurious, actually—the sort of place usually occupied by a visiting Master from another temple. But his old room had been near the hall that led to the Archives. Its small window looked out on the sunrise, or what of it could be seen through the thick cityscape. Most important, it was *home*. Familiarity was what Reath needed more than anything else. Instead he had a finely woven bedspread and a grand vista that looked out on the Galactic Senate, and to him it might as well have been a blank durasteel wall. So he planned to remain in the practice area until he was so tired he could no longer grieve, or even think, and return to his temporary quarters once it was no more than a place to collapse.

He donned a helmet with a blast shield and tipped the shield down over his eyes. With one flick of a finger, Reath ignited his lightsaber; at the very edges of his shield, he could see the faintest green glow. Its hum was familiar in his ears and hand. "Sparring droid," he called, "activate at level five."

He heard the whirring of the sparring droid's treads. While no droid could fully replicate the experience of dueling a sentient opponent, they could test reflexes and aim. Reath sometimes felt he hadn't sparred against them enough; time to rectify that.

Finding center was difficult. If he had lost only Dez—or only Master Jora—no. Each of their deaths had shaken him deeply, crumbling the very foundation of his life. To have lost them *both* . . .

But they would want him to become a good Jedi. A great one. Reath intended to earn that in their honor.

*Reach out with your feelings,* whispered Master Jora's voice in his mind. The pain that sliced through him nearly distracted him from the concentration of energy within the sparring droid—

But not quite. Reath swung his saber up, parrying the blast. Ducked low to avoid the spinning bar that had dispersed just enough air for him to hear. Deflected two more blasts, leapt to his feet, and struck. His lightsaber slashed into the droid, igniting a rain of sparks that he could just glimpse at his feet.

When Reath pulled off his helmet, he looked at the droid. He'd very nearly hacked off its head. They were designed to take damage, but maybe not quite *this* much damage.

"Well done, sir," said the droid's dangling head in a surprisingly deep voice. "I would advise your next practice begin at no lower than a level seven setting."

"Got it. Sorry about, um, your neck."

"It can be repaired. But I must see to it immediately." The droid carefully supported its head in one of its clawlike hands as it turned to wheel out of the room again.

Once again he was alone with his thoughts, the last place he wanted to be.

*I can't stop thinking about Master Jora,* he thought. *Maybe that's what I'm called to do.*

So Reath went down to one of the many meditation chambers within the Temple. While some meditation spaces were small and cozy, others had soaring ceilings and vast open space. This was the latter. And stretching the length of the cavernous white chamber, arching over it all, stood the Kyber Arch.

He stepped silently through the room, taking care not to disturb the half dozen Jedi who sat on various benches or cushions, deep within their trances. While most meditation areas were nearer the center of the temple, this one, nearer the top, actually had windows looking out on Coruscant. At a certain hour in the early morning, sunlight hit the Kyber Arch at just the right angle to dazzle the whole room with rainbows. Reath had missed that hour. Now the arch simply looked dark and jagged, like something that might've been made out of plain old rock.

He went to the base of the path—nearly two meters thick, at that point—and grasped firm handholds. The kyber crystals were cool against his palms. Reath took a deep breath, found his first foothold, and began to scale the arch.

At first the ascent was so easy he could've imagined himself on a climber in the younglings' playroom. As he moved higher, however, the arch narrowed. His footing became trickier to find. Reath climbed without fear; even if he was too shocked to catch his own fall, one of the other Jedi in the room would do so. Still, the task called for dexterity. For concentration. While Reath was doing this, he could think of nothing else.

At last he reached the very top. There, the crystals were fused together in a curve hardly ten centimeters wide. Reath walked steadily across it, then pivoted to begin finding his way back down. By this time, however, his concentration was far less sure.

*I did it, Master Jora. I crossed the Kyber Arch alone. It's possible. It's not even difficult. So why did you—what did you mean by—*

He jumped the final meter to the floor. Frustration welled up in him again, combined with the grief he wasn't supposed to feel, and he somehow felt farther from the Force than before. Probably he should find the nearest cushion and try to meditate, but that kind of serenity seemed out of reach. Before he could think of anything else that might serve as a distraction—some gymnastics, maybe?—his comlink buzzed. He hurried out of the meditation chamber to answer. "Silas here."

*"Padawan Silas,"* said Master Adampo, of the Council. *"We are glad to have reached you."*

He could think of only one reason the Jedi Council would want to talk. "Have I been assigned to a new master?" As much as it hurt to think of replacing Master Jora, there was nothing else for him to do. Unless, maybe, the many problems on their mission had led the Council to decide that Reath had no business training to become a Jedi at all. . . .

*"Not yet. We'll discuss this with you soon."*

"Then—"

*"Communications packets from Starlight Beacon have arrived,"* said Master Adampo. *"They include new and potentially critical*

*information about the sector. As one of the few Jedi to have returned from that sector, your insights may be significant."*

"Send me the location and I'll be right there, master," he said. "Thank you."

Surely Master Cohmac would be more useful in the briefing, not to mention Orla Jareni—but then Reath realized that they would soon be busy with the idols. A shiver went through him as he imagined those things in the very heart of the Temple. Although he'd helped set up the Force containment, it made perfect sense that more experienced Jedi would handle the rest.

Just reporting on what they'd encountered over there, still parsecs away from Starlight Beacon, on the far side of the sector? Sure, Reath could handle that, even if it came down to saying "Mostly we saw a bunch of plants." It would keep him busy, and that was all he wanted.

As big and confusing as Coruscant was—very, and very—spaceports were spaceports everywhere. Affie Hollow hurried through the Central Senatorial Hangar, counting off all the similarities with a huge grin.

Droids directing huge cargo loads? Check. Pilots wearing their flashiest jackets and talking smack at each other? Check. Some ancient freighter that hardly seemed like it could remain in one piece, much less fly into space? Check. A huddled group of travelers hauling too many bags and trying to figure out which was their transport? Check. (In this case, a group of Trandoshans, growling in their confusion.)

At least one huge, top-of-the-line freighter, gleaming as though it had just been polished?

That wasn't something you could find in any old spacedock. But Affie had just located Byne Guild number one-seventy-one, the *Spiderspun*.

She ran up the ramp, long braid streaming behind her. A couple of the crew droids chirped or called to her as she went, but she couldn't stop. Not yet. She just waved and kept running.

The *Spiderspun* was too new for Affie to have many fond memories of it, or very many memories at all. Yet already it felt like Scover's ship: clean down to the tiniest rivet, precisely calibrated, smelling of cleanser rather than grease. Affie was probably tracking in grime. But she knew Scover wouldn't mind.

Finally she ran onto the bridge. A few crew members remained at work even in dock, partly for security reasons, partly because equipment function could never be perfect enough. In the center of it all stood a Bivall woman, her ridged head cocked as she studied the readouts, until she heard the footsteps and turned. At the sight of Affie, Scover Byne smiled. "There you are."

Affie wrapped her arms around Scover, hugging her as tightly as she dared. Scover hugged back—not as tightly, because Bivalls didn't let themselves get carried away about much. Still, it was a hug.

"I'm so glad you're all right," Affie said. "When we heard about the hyperspace disaster—what happened to the *Legacy Run*—"

"My travels had concluded by that time." Scover studied Affie's face. "I trust you did not let your fears distract you."

"No. Leox got me to see reason pretty quickly, so I was able to keep working." Affie pretended not to notice the small crinkle on Scover's brow at the mention of Leox Gyasi. Scover just didn't *get* Leox. A lot of people didn't. Despite their recent disagreements, Affie wanted to stick up for him whenever possible. Eventually Scover would realize what a great pilot he truly was. "That doesn't mean I'm not glad to see you."

"As I am glad to see you. We had no confirmation of the *Vessel*'s safe location." Scover's voice was cool, but she combed stray strands of Affie's hair away from her face as she spoke. "You could have delivered neither of your cargoes under these conditions. Let Captain Gyasi know it will not be counted against him in the Guild metrics."

"I will."

"But—" Scover paused slyly. "May I take it that one of your cargoes went undiscovered by the other?"

Affie pieced that together. "*Oh.* No worries. Our secret remains safe in temperature-controlled storage."

Even Scover had to smile at that. "We have some days before the hyperspace lanes will be fully opened again. Shall we use some of this time to explore Coruscant together?"

"Absolutely." Affie basked in the attention from her foster mother; as the busy manager of a shipping guild, Scover could rarely devote her full attention to Affie or to anyone. Now, however, they'd have a chance to spend quality time together.

And a chance for Affie to finally ask Scover some serious questions.

Within the heart of the Temple of Coruscant, in the Shrine in the Depths, the idols seemed to glow. Their burnished surfaces caught the candledroids' light, and the jewels' color brightened against the dusky gold. Cohmac stood amid them, trying to understand their nature and their secret histories.

*What darkness is contained within these idols?*

When he reached out with the Force, he could sense nothing but the shield he, Orla, and Reath had conjured. It held strong and steady as an energy field, so distinct Cohmac imagined he could visualize the bubble around the idols, even put his finger on the exact place where the barrier ended. This was an illusion—the way a living being's mind tried to make sense of the formless, unknowable boundaries of the Force. But it was an illusion that served a purpose. It made the barrier more real in their minds, which in turn made them better able to confront the powers imprisoned within.

Orla stood by his side, as did a few experts in Jedi arcana.

The Council had chosen a handful of other Jedi to join them for the group meditation, each one a Master, each one possessing unique knowledge and abilities that could help. Poreht La, a Lasat, was an expert on ancient techniques. The human archivist Tia Mirabel had learned more about Force-imbued objects than anyone else in the Order. And Lurmen Giktoo Nelmo's power spoke for itself.

Had Master Yoda been present, undoubtedly he would have led the team. But they would have to manage as best they could without him.

"Are we ready?" Master Giktoo said, smoothing her fur. The other Jedi drew closer, forming a ring around the idols. Cohmac forced himself to have no future, no past—no questions, no anger, no doubts—to exist in nothing but the present as Giktoo continued, "Let us begin."

⚜

Affie made her first attempt while they were eating at one of the stranger local establishments, a place with checkered floors, shiny red seats, and waiter droids that rolled around on impractical wheels. "Did you read our report? About the Amaxine station?"

"I have not had time to review all materials about your journey yet," said Scover, which was not the same thing as *no*. "How is your arm? Captain Gyasi should not have forced you to be the one taking on a hazardous mission."

"I *volunteered* to go down in the tunnels. Leox couldn't

have stopped me. Anyway, my arm is fine. See?" Affie flashed her all-but-healed wrist.

"Now, try some of this," Scover insisted, holding out a small dish of something called *barafuraha*—though Affie had heard most people ordering it as just *baha*. It was apparently a great favorite on Coruscant, but . . .

"It's made of ice," Affie said. "Who wants to eat ice?"

"We made it once in a while, in my family. We came from the Core originally, you know. And *baha* is pleasing to most sentients' palates."

Scover had used the casual name for something, which Scover never did, so she actually must like the stuff a lot. Affie cautiously took a spoonful, winced as the shock of cold hit her mouth, then opened her eyes. "Oh, this is *amazing.*"

"The cold is actually part of the enjoyment, as I trust you now recognize."

"Okay, okay, I admit it. I was wrong. Get me more."

Scover smiled, and the moment for pressing questions had passed. Only after finishing her second dish of *baha* did Affie wonder if that distraction had been intentional.

Her opening for the second attempt came as they toured a holographic shipyard. The sales droid tottered along, bringing up images of new freighters, all of them faster and safer than any before but astonishingly affordable, according to its patter.

"As you can see, it does not sacrifice style for function." The droid enlarged the holo from a whole-ship view that would've fit in Affie's outstretched arms to a life-size image of the bridge. Holographic shimmer masked the shipyard in translucent models of seats, controls, and even a faux star field ahead. "If you would wish to see the crew quarters—"

"Send me the specifications for future study," Scover said. Many people might've snapped at a droid, especially one using hard-sell tactics. But Scover remained polite with everyone at every time. It was a trait Affie both greatly admired and hadn't yet mastered.

"Right away, madam. I'll include packets on our special upgrades, as well." The droid rolled away to transfer the full data packet, leaving them alone amid the holographic image of a ship that did not yet exist.

"Buying freighters in bulk?" Affie began. "*Republic* freighters? Are we really doing that well?"

Scover always preened a bit when she got to talk about her ever-increasing profit margins. "We have seen a substantial increase in business lately. Yes, the *Legacy Run* disaster has caused delays, but these are temporary. Many people wish to move cargo soon, rather than after the Republic expansion, for various reasons with which we need not concern ourselves."

"You're sure of all our pilots' loyalty, then," Affie said. "Cargo isn't, uh, coming in short?"

That got Scover's full attention. "Do you have knowledge of dishonesty within the Guild? Is this about Leox Gyasi?"

"*No.* Leox is clean, totally. It's just—" The story spilled out of Affie then: the Amaxine station, the lines of strange code, the symbols of the Byne Guild, and the fact that an otherwise empty system had its coordinates preprogrammed within the *Vessel*'s navigational computer. Scover listened with keen, silent interest, saying nothing until Affie finally took a pause long enough for it to seem plausible that she was done.

"This is not evidence of a corrupt wing within the Guild," Scover said. "Such written code is occasionally used by pilots in locations where standard messages would be difficult to deliver. The practice is mostly archaic by now, but it lingers in certain locations, including the Amaxine station." Her explanation was as impersonal as any a droid would've offered. That was how Scover always talked, and usually it wouldn't have struck Affie as odd.

But this felt . . . *off.*

"I'm glad nobody's trying to cheat you," Affie said, genuinely relieved. "Still—that station is dangerous, Scover. The helix rings, the poisonous plants, even the little gardener droids attack you, and that's not even getting into all that dark side stuff." Maybe that was nothing but Jedi mumbo jumbo, but given the terrible luck they'd had on the station, Affie was beginning to wonder if they were on to something. "Our pilots shouldn't be using it."

"It is their free choice," Scover said, "to use the station as they see fit, or not. I do not dictate methods to pilots who prove their capability."

Which was true. Affie had always thought it showed

remarkable open-mindedness; like most Bivalls, Scover valued rules, definitions, precision. The fact that she gave her pilots freedom meant she could see things from multiple points of view.

For the first time, Affie realized—it also meant that sometimes Scover didn't have to ask questions that might have difficult answers.

"It is only a way station," Scover said. "You are still shaken by the experience and so giving it undue importance in your mind. With time you will gain greater perspective. Put it out of your mind for now." She smiled. "Would you like to get some buttersweet puffs? I know they are your favorites."

Affie managed to smile. "Sure. Sounds great."

But she couldn't forget what Scover had unwittingly told her, by denying something she had not been asked to deny:

The Amaxine station, whatever else it might be, was much more to the Byne Guild than a way station.

⚜

As isolated as Reath had been before, he wished he were alone again.

He sat at the edge of the briefing, saying nothing, and yet he might as well have been bathed in a spotlight. The other Jedi kept a respectful distance, so markedly aware of his bereavement that they magnified it. Reath felt as though he had to simultaneously show the full weight of his sorrow and hold it together.

*No one here is judging you,* he reminded himself. This wasn't yet another exercise he could practice to the point of mastering. He'd always prided himself on his ability to excel, but no longer. Who cared? Why had he ever thought that was worth caring about?

He and Dez had attended a briefing together in that room once, perhaps three years before. What had it been about? Raiding parties harassing Kashyyyk? Reath couldn't recall. All he could think of was the easy way Dez had sprawled in his chair, confident in his new Knighthood, while Reath had wondered whether he'd ever feel that brash, that assured of his future.

Dez's future had ended in the middle of nowhere, for no reason at all.

Master Adampo walked to the front of the chamber, and the crowd went still. Gratitude swept through Reath. Once the lecture began he could finally escape the echo chamber of his thoughts for a while.

"Today we must examine an enemy element that has caused great trouble on the frontier—a marauder group known as the Nihil," said Adampo as the room fell dark. "Although the Republic had already identified the Nihil as a significant threat to settlements and shipping, it has now been established that the group certainly caused the *Legacy Run* disaster."

Reath sat upright as murmurs of dismay filled the room. If the Nihil were capable of that, what else could they do?

That didn't matter as much as what they'd already done, not to Reath.

If not for the *Legacy Run* disaster and the subsequent conflict with the Nihil, Master Jora would still be alive.

It was as though the rage descended on him—he wouldn't have believed he had the capacity for that kind of hate in him. *They killed my master,* whispered an unfamiliar, undeniable voice in his head. *The Nihil murdered her.* His entire body tensed until he nearly shook.

*Turn away from hatred. This is the dark side,* whispered a more familiar voice  not his own, but Master Jora's. It was only Reath's memory of her, but that was a lifeline to the light.

Slowly he exhaled. Banishing all the tension was impossible, but he resolved to direct that energy toward learning more about these raiders who had caused so much harm, and not only to Master Jora.

"Therefore the group requires more in-depth study than has been conducted of late," Adampo continued. "The Nihil's origins are mysterious; they comprise numerous species from widely disparate worlds. However, we have no solid count on the species included or of the proportions represented, due to their masked faces." Adampo brought up the first holo, an image of a fearsome Nihil warrior with a huge breathmask strapped to his head, storming some hapless ship. The Nihil wore blue battle stripes painted from his hairline down to his chest, over the mask itself. Reath was reminded, bizarrely but affectionately, of the blue streaks in Nan's hair.

Maybe he *had* become too fond of her.

"Nihil ships are uniquely dangerous because they can join together or separate into smaller sections," continued Adampo. "Therefore no opponent can be sure whether he will be facing a storm of small fighters or a massive dreadnought. The ships are generally constructed from pieces of other vessels, like this."

Another holo filled the space, this one showing a pieced-together patchwork spacecraft—one that was far too familiar.

Reath's eyes widened as he realized, *That looks like Nan and Hague's ship.*

*Looks* exactly *like it.*

Their vagueness about where they came from. The violent deaths of Nan's parents. The carbon scoring on the plates of their ship. The blue streaks in Nan's hair.

He whispered, "They're Nihil."

## SIXTEEN

A luxury hotel on Coruscant made the "luxury" of other planets look like rags and ashes. In the Alisandre Hotel, rooms were situated at the highest levels of the highest buildings, complete with personal landing decks, bath pools, and servitor droids dispensing the finest wines, meals, and desserts. Affic, who spent the majority of her days in her tiny, bare-bones bunk on the *Vessel*, spent a solid five minutes running her hands over the silky sheets of her utterly enormous bed.

"The beds are required to be this size," pointed out Scover as the servitor droids put away her things. "Although they are extremely large by the standards of most humanoid species, nothing smaller than this would feel luxurious to a Gigoran, or even be sufficient for a Trodatome."

Affie flopped back into a nest of pillows, relishing the unaccustomed softness. "Okay, you're not impressed. So why bother staying in a place like this at all?" Scover's home was nice but hardly grandiose, and she was always careful with money.

"Important industrialists and politicians stay in such hotels, particularly here in the Federal District," Scover replied. "These may be our future clients. I will be able to set up multiple meetings in the club levels below."

"Leave it to you to find the perfect excuse."

It wasn't an excuse—it was Scover's real reason, as Affie knew—but it sounded enough like teasing that it made Scover smile and ruffle her foster daughter's hair.

Convinced of Affie's contentment, Scover thought little of leaving an hour later to begin working on some of those meetings. Affie lay still in the balcony's antigravity hammock for several minutes afterward, pretending to watch the clouds drifting by just above eye level. Almost idly, she reached out with one hand and swatted the control that would put all the servitor droids into dormant mode.

The moment their mesh eyes went dark, she jumped up. Heart thumping, she dashed across the suite to the wardrobe where Scover's things were stored.

*I may be the worst daughter ever,* Affie thought as she picked up one of Scover's infopads. *I ought to trust her. I shouldn't poke around in her stuff.* The entire time she was thinking this, her fingers were deftly typing in one of the top-level passcodes, one Scover had shared without a second thought.

As soon as the full memory capacity of the tablet was open to her, Affie input the sector codes of the Amaxine station, the same ones that had been preprogrammed into the *Vessel.* (She had them memorized; after several days of seeing them glowing on the *Vessel*'s dash, they were practically seared onto her brain.) She held her breath for the instant it took for more information to scroll across the screen. Certain phrases jumped out as though written in crimson:

Transport Hub/CONFIDENTIAL

Revelation to Competing Guilds Punishable by Expulsion

Incentives Include Double Bonuses/Forgiveness of Ship Purchase Price Interest/Shortened Indentures

"Indentures?" Affie whispered. "The Byne Guild . . . uses *indentured workers?*"

She tried to navigate further into the "transport hub" part of the records, but those were closed even to her passcode. They must be for Scover's eyes only.

In her mind, Affie pictured the long lines of smugglers'

code—especially the small, downturned bird of prey. Quickly she tapped in *Kestrel's Dive.*

This information wasn't protected by any layers of security; Affie could've pulled it up with no passcode at all. That was how little Scover felt she had to hide.

But as Affie read on, her hands began to shake, and she wished that she'd never opened the tablet at all.

＊＊＊

"Many people of various species dye their hair or fur—"

"I'm telling you," Reath insisted, "*they were Nihil.*"

There was a time—in fact, his entire life up until the past three minutes—when Reath would never have dreamed that he might stand up in the middle of a briefing by a member of the Jedi Council and announce that he had important information. But there he was. Later, he'd be embarrassed. For the moment, he was busy trying to convince several skeptical Masters, the remains of the briefing crowd, that the Jedi had already encountered the Republic's newest, deadliest enemy in the form of a young girl and an elderly man.

A protocol droid piped up. "Requested transmission from the *Vessel* incoming, masters."

*Thank the Force Leox was on the ship to get the message, instead of lolling around in some spice den,* Reath thought. *Or . . . could Geode have sent it?*

Before he could wonder about a rock's ability to handle intership communications, the images were projected on-screen. He pointed at Nan and Hague's ship. "Look. See? It's definitely Nihil design."

"The Nihil cannot be the only ones who make ships out of component parts," reasoned Master Rosason. "Especially not on the frontier, where shipyards and supplies are more difficult to find. However—the similarities *are* striking."

"And there's carbon scoring," said Master Adampo, pointing it out before Reath had to. "Proof that it's seen relatively recent battle, although on its own, it hardly looks like a ship that would pick a fight."

"Exactly." Reath focused on details that had eluded him before. How had he not seen it? "This join, right here? It's a weird version of an airlock, but if it were customized to work with other ships rather than with a station—"

"Yes, I've seen similar on holos of other Nihil ships." Master Rosason closed her eyes with an expression Reath found hard to read, then realized was relief. "Even if they were only two, you were very fortunate they decided not to pursue aggressive action on the station. We might have lost more than one soul. As it is, it would appear we escaped very lightly."

This was going to be the hard part. "Um. About that."

Master Adampo's fur stood on end. "You don't mean—do you think the Nihil had something to do with Dez Rydan's death?"

"No," Reath said. "I don't see how they could have." Nan had been no closer to Dez than Reath had been. "But while we were marooned there, Nan and I had several conversations about, well, the Jedi. And the Republic. And Starlight Beacon. Plus future shipments to the area." He wanted to somehow travel back in time and shake his former self, so easily flattered and persuaded. Nan had tricked him into betraying the Order at the very moment when, many systems away, Master Jora was dying. "I thought she was just curious. I wanted to represent us well to a new area of the galaxy. Now I realize she was . . . pumping me for information. Which she got."

He had expected dark, disapproving stares as the first, and probably lightest, aspect of his punishment. Instead, the Council members only looked resigned. Master Rosason said, "I wouldn't have suspected them, either, especially with as little information about the Nihil as you had. And you couldn't have given away any classified material."

"It's still useful information the Nihil didn't have but now do," Reath said. "It's my fault. And I want to set it right, if I can."

The Masters exchanged befuddled looks. "What do you mean?" Master Adampo said.

"Hague and Nan had to stay behind at the Amaxine station. They were still finishing repairs, thanks to help we gave them." Chagrin brought a flush to Reath's face, but he didn't slow down. "She said it would take a while for them to finish. Maybe Nan was lying, but at the time, I didn't suspect anything, so she didn't have any reason to deceive me. Deceive me even more, I mean."

"You wish to confront them," said Master Rosason. "To what purpose?"

Reath couldn't believe it wasn't obvious. "They're Nihil! They learned intel about us; we could learn about them! We could hold someone accountable for what happened to the *Legacy Run*! We might even be able to make an arrest, if their ship can be connected to any of the attacks."

"They're only two people," Master Adampo pointed out.

"They're on the Amaxine station," Reath said. "In other words, the place where the idols were put to contain the dark side. To me that suggests there's something interesting about the station—something about its history we haven't learned yet. Potentially something powerful. If so, I don't think we should leave it for the Nihil to find."

Rosason tilted her head. "All valid points. But they are also hypothetical points. I do not know that at this time of crisis, we can afford to send Jedi away to investigate a mere hypothesis."

The frustration was burning within Reath. "So you want to just let them go?"

Master Rosason put her hand on his shoulder so gently that he was reminded of Master Jora. As he swallowed hard, she said, "If you had learned their identities while still on the Amaxine station, yes, you would've been right to take them into custody if possible. But at this point it would mean sending people we need through hazardous hyperspace lanes to a dangerous station, only in the hopes that Nan wasn't lying to you and their ship has not yet departed. It's too much risk for too little reward."

Maybe that made sense. All Reath knew was that he couldn't accept it. "May I put in a formal request to travel back on my own?"

"You may," Master Adampo said, "but it'll probably be denied."

Master Rosason added, "You have lost your master, and your friend. You need new purpose, constructive action you can take, and you need it quickly."

"This isn't about me and my feelings," he insisted, then questioned it. "It isn't *only* about that, anyway."

"If it were that simple, we'd let you go," said Master Adampo. "But it is a complicated time, and a complex situation."

He spoke so kindly. They all did. It just made Reath more determined to put in that formal request. And if he was denied . . .

He might have to find out just how far he was willing to deviate from the Council's orders.

᠅

Leox relaxed in the *Vessel*'s mess, wreathed in honeyed smoke and feeling pretty fine. The Guild had been fair about their delay and had even kicked in a little hazard pay. That was thin on the ground in the Byne Guild; he suspected he had

Affie to thank. At any rate he was not a man to spurn lar-
gesse purely because of its rarity. The next day he might stroll
into one of those fancy Coruscant shops, get himself a new
pair of boots—Geode might desire a good polishing—

This pleasant train of thought was interrupted by a small
voice. "Leox?"

He looked up to see Affie standing in the doorway. She
had on the exact same coverall as before but had let her hair
down. That one small change couldn't account for how much
younger she looked. How much smaller. "What's the matter,
Little Bit?"

Her failure to object to her nickname worried him more
than anything else. Affie plopped down in the other chair
so they sat opposite each other across the narrow mess table.
Instead of answering his question, she said, "Where's Geode?"

"Hittin' the clubs. The gods only know what time he'll be
back. Someday that guy's gonna have to slow down."

"I don't know how he does it," Affie said, but the shared
joke brought no smile to her face.

Leox leaned back and folded his hands behind his head.
"Looks like I might get a whole lot farther by answering questions instead of asking 'em."

It took her a few moments to begin, and she didn't start
with a question. "The Byne Guild doesn't just hire people. It
indentures them."

"Correct."

"You knew?" She gaped at him. "Why didn't you ever tell me?"

"At first," he admitted, "I figured you had to be in on that little secret, what with being Scover's prize pup and all. Then I realized you had a sweeter view of the world, still, and I didn't want to be the one to take it away. Shame any of us has to lose it."

Affie put her head down on the table. He didn't push or pry, just took another drag and let her work it through.

Indentured servitude sometimes got made out to look better than it was, because it wasn't as bad as slavery. Not even close. However, it also wasn't as good as freedom. Indentures came about when people desperate for employment met employers who wanted workers who couldn't talk back. Even ship owners fell prey to it, when they wound up with more repair and fuel bills than cargo—not an uncommon risk for smaller craft. People sold their labor and freedom of movement for a set period of time, usually no fewer than seven years; Leox had heard of indentures that lasted three whole decades. There were a few legal limits on what indentured servants could be forced to do in guilds that wanted to work with the Republic—they couldn't be required to risk their own lives, for instance—but that still left indentured people trapped for years in the misery of unceasing, unrewarded labor. The Hutts, not surprisingly, built industries of such practice.

"I looked up my parents' ship," Affie finally said. "The

*Kestrel's Dive*. That's how I found out they were indentured to—to Scover."

Getting that out had cost her. Leox reached into the nearby coolbox and grabbed her a bottle of water. She took it without comment.

"You were right about the smugglers' code," she continued. "It wasn't some group trying to cheat Scover out of money. It's just proof that Byne Guild people use the Amaxine station. They almost have to. She offers bonuses and benefits if they'll take the risks, including knocking a few years off their inden tures. I'm pretty sure that's the reason why my parents"—Affie gulped back a sob—"why they took the *Kestrel's Dive* to that station. And why they died there."

"*That's* where they died?"

"I found it in her records," she said dully. "Marked *confidential*. Just a few hours ago. Apparently some traders try tapping into the helix rings to boost their engines." When done correctly, that maneuver could send a ship on a journey using only one-tenth the usual fuel. That would seriously amp up profit margins. But done incorrectly—and it was a hard thing to do right—it could blow a ship to smithereens. From the look on Affie's face, her parents must have made that mistake.

"Oh, man." Leox shook his head. "I'm so sorry you had to find out like that. Sorry you had to find out at all."

"No," she said fiercely. "Not that. I hate the knowledge, but—I'm glad I know."

"You just have to get used to carrying that weight."

She nodded. He clinked his own water bottle against hers, and for a while there was nothing to do but take it in.

※

The breaking of deep trance felt to Orla like surfacing from black waters, breath and light pouring over her. Although her eyes had been open, she had not been seeing her surroundings—or really anything—only connecting herself more profoundly to the other Jedi in the circle.

They all exchanged glances as they turned toward each other, their movements in perfect sync. Orla still retained control of her own mind and body—they had not pooled consciousnesses completely—but they had reached a state of harmony that allowed them to mirror not only motions but also thought and intent. This would give them the best possible chance of combating whatever evil was about to be set free.

As one, they raised their hands, perceived anew the warm intensity of the Force containment—and extinguished it.

The Shrine in the Depths did not fall dark, but everything suddenly seemed dimmer—no, she realized, just cooler. Even if the "warmth" of the containment had been an illusion, illusions had their own strength.

What she didn't understand was that the chamber now seemed to be . . . empty. Nothing more. The only emanations of the Force came from her fellow Jedi.

"Did it dissipate into the vergeance already?" Orla asked.

Confusion was weakening their shared bond. "Or is it still present? Lying in wait?"

"Nothing's here." Giktoo's eyes widened as she took this in. "Nothing is trapped here. Nothing ever was."

"That's impossible," said Master Mirabel. "We shared your memories of the Amaxine station. The darkness you sensed there—that raw power—it was very real."

"And what about the warnings we received?" Orla interjected. "The visions?"

"I fear we may have misinterpreted the warnings." Cohmac walked up to the jeweled insect idol. "Perhaps these were not used to contain the dark side. I think instead they were used to . . . to dampen it. To hold it in place. That's why the containment exercises have been so difficult to execute. We were overlapping with their original purposes, ultimately undoing them."

"Explain in really simple terms for those of us not fluent in Ancient Force Archaeology," Orla said.

"These statues weren't holding the dark side within themselves. They were holding the dark side on the Amaxine station—keeping it imprisoned there, attempting to warn us of it." Cohmac put one hand to his chest as the import of his own words sunk in. "So when we removed the statues—"

"We didn't remove the darkness," Orla finished. "We set it free."

*— Twenty-Five Years Earlier —*

## PART FOUR

To Orla's deep gratitude, they had entered an area of the caves without any serpents. Master Laret led the way, glow rod in hand. Orla and Cohmac followed several steps after. At first Orla had believed her master insisted on keeping some distance between them in case any serpents attacked from behind.

Now that she had been able to better center herself, though, Orla knew as well as Master Laret did that no predators lurked nearby. Instead, the two apprentices were being given space so they could talk freely.

"I'm sorry about Master Simmix," Orla said.

Cohmac nodded. His gaze remained unfocused. "We're not supposed to mourn," he said. "He's one with the Force."

She answered exactly as she was supposed to: "But we can regret his loss—" Cohmac cut her off with a gesture.

"It's ridiculous." He readjusted his robes, restless, ill at ease. "They command that master and apprentice spend years together, working as a partnership, as close as any family could possibly be, and then they expect us not to become attached. I never thought about it before—I never had to—but now I can't escape how unfair it is. Worse than unfair. It's *wrong*."

His words struck an unfamiliar chord within Orla. Master Laret wasn't necessarily completely orthodox in her methods, but never had she or anyone else come out and said that the Jedi might be completely wrong about something. About *anything*.

If only someone had spoken up before. Orla might not have felt so completely alone.

For years she'd been aware that she was most deeply connected with the Force at times and in ways that went contrary to Master Laret's teachings. Orla wanted to follow her master's teachings— Laret Soveral was the perfect model of a Jedi, in Orla's opinion—but her own experience of the Force was not the same.

*It will be,* she told herself stubbornly. *You'll be more like Master Laret if you just keep trying. Cohmac's hurting because he lost his own master, but there's no reason to let his pain drag you away from Jedi teachings.*

*Trust your master. Trust the Order. Trust that someday it will all be clear to you, as clear as rainwater.*

⚜

When Orla fell silent, Cohmac at first wondered if she condemned him—but no. Sympathy still radiated from her.

Probably she was only trying to guide him along the proper path. As Master Simmix had once said, "You can disagree with the Council, but it matters *how* you disagree."

Broadcasting the anger he felt was foolish. It solved nothing and reflected poorly on his master's training. If Cohmac could not grieve, he at least intended to stand as an example of Master Simmix's faithful duty to the Jedi.

Besides, anger was distracting, and this was not a time to get distracted.

Master Laret stopped walking and held up one hand, cautioning them. More serpents? Cohmac tensed and listened for the telltale rustle of scales on stone.

Nothing. Master Laret was staring upward.

In a low voice, she said, "I believe we are beneath the kidnappers' lair."

"Beneath?" Orla kept her voice down, too, despite her obvious puzzlement. "But these caves aren't that deep—"

"We've traveled beneath a larger rock formation. There's more room above us than before. Which means more caves." Master Laret turned back to the Padawans, her expression grave. "Without any schematics, we can't be certain—but I believe we'll find a connection between this cave and theirs. At least some passageway. The air currents suggest it."

Cohmac realized there *was* a slight breeze. "So, we're going in?"

"We're getting closer," Master Laret corrected him. "We don't go in until we know where the hostages are, whether they are alive, and how to keep them safe. Our job here isn't to fight the kidnappers. It's to save the hostages."

It was good, before a skirmish, to remember that any

armed action was only a means to an end. Cohmac nodded, determined to serve well in Simmix's honor.

"You know," Thandeka muttered, "we might not even be in this position if E'ronoh had been willing to negotiate with Eiram."

Cassel had slightly long front teeth, round eyes, and a flatly upturned nose that made him resemble a bright blue voorpak. "I thought it was Eiram that wouldn't negotiate with E'ronoh."

Their two planets had been at odds for so long that no cooperation was seen as possible, and so none was sought.

How long had it been since anyone had even tried? Sometimes it felt as though Eiram defined itself not by its own merits but simply as those who stood against E'ronoh. She was beginning to suspect E'ronoh had done the same thing in reverse. Did anyone even truly recall the reasons for all this hate? Were those reasons still valid in the present day?

*I'll ask Dima,* Thandeka thought before remembering that she would almost certainly never see her wife again.

"Besides, why wouldn't we be in this position?" Cassel said. "These criminals—they weren't a part of any trade talks between Eiram and E'ronoh, I'm sure—"

"No. But if we'd made trade deals with the Republic before, the scum of the galaxy wouldn't be trying to edge their way in now. And the main reason we've never imagined dealing with the Republic is because we've never even learned to deal with each other." For so long, they'd been proud of their independence. But at what point did pride become mere stubbornness? At what point did independence become willful ignorance?

Wherever that point was, Thandeka suspected both their planets had passed it a long time before.

Cassel's face fell, but he tried to smile for her. He seemed to be a kind man. "At least our kidnappers aren't having any fun, either. To judge by the big furry fellow's scowl, he's having nearly as bad a day as we are."

Thandeka simply smiled back. It was kinder than mentioning that the angrier their captors became, the more likely they were to wind up dead.

# SEVENTEEN

**W**hat do they do *with a leftover Padawan?* Reath had been pondering this question since a few hours after he'd learned of Master Jora's death, as soon as he'd recovered from the extreme shock. It stood to reason that he'd be chosen by another master eventually, but when and how?

(It was a measure of the peace and prosperity of the Republic that Reath had never known an apprentice in the same situation.)

When he'd been summoned to another meeting of the Council, he'd assumed that it was about the Nihil he had identified on the Amaxine station. Reath was working hard to think of them that way, as the Nihil, instead of Nan and Hague. Ferocious warriors instead of refugees. Resetting his thinking, excising the kindness he'd felt toward them, might help him handle some of the intense shame he felt for betraying knowledge to an enemy—to the enemy who had killed Master Jora, no less. They had made a fool of him once but never would again.

The Council rarely concerned itself with individual Padawans. So probably they sought yet more information about the Nihil or wanted to chastise Reath for his carelessness. Maybe both.

Instead, as he knelt before them, Master Adampo said, "We wish to speak with you about your new master."

"Has someone already chosen me?" Reath couldn't imagine who. All the Masters he knew well had apprentices of their own—except, of course, those who had been with him on the Amaxine station, but surely one of them would've spoken to him first.

Master Rosason said, "No. You have suffered bereavement, and you alone can tell us the correct moment to resume your training."

Reath hadn't thought about when he'd like to start training again. Padawans didn't get to make many huge decisions on their own, as a general rule, and his first reaction to this one was to wish it away. Choice felt like a burden. His grief for Master Jora was already heavy enough.

"Given the extraordinary circumstances," continued

Master Rosason, "we also welcome your input as to what sort of assignment would be most beneficial to you in future."

"What do you mean?"

Master Adampo held out his hands, an expansive gesture. "Some in your situation might request a frontier assignment, in order to fulfill your late master's wishes. However, others might ask for more time on Coruscant or one of the other Core Worlds, so that your working relationship with a new master can begin on more familiar ground. There are benefits and drawbacks to each option, and to other options we haven't discussed here. It's up to you to research, reflect, and give us an answer."

*I don't have to go to the frontier after all,* Reath thought.

Only a few weeks before, that would've been cause for celebration. But his freedom had been bought at too high a price.

His disquiet must've been apparent to the entire Council, because Master Rosason gently said, "You need not choose now. In fact, you should not; not enough time has passed for you to make an informed choice. We only wished to make you aware that this choice is yours."

Reath thanked them and got out of the Council chambers as fast as he decently could. At least if the Masters had given him this responsibility, they'd allowed him the time to think things through. When he tried imagining his future, he could only picture one thing: going back to the Amaxine station to confront Nan and Hague—and arrest them if possible. To set right the one big mistake he'd ever made in his life.

And that was the one future that couldn't happen.

Could it?

※※

Affie had bluffed her way through the previous night, eating dinner with Scover and spending the night in her vast, luxurious hotel suite. As soft as the bed was, she'd hardly slept. Instead she lay for hours calling upon the few memories she had of her parents:

Riding in the cockpit of the *Kestrel's Dive* on her mother's lap, amazed at the beautiful nebula they were traveling through.

Paddling in the pools of Wrea, her father keeping one hand beneath her belly as she learned to swim.

Coming to them after a nightmare and falling asleep between them, feeling safe from any harm.

*They wanted to be free while I was still young. The only way to do that was to take on Scover's dangerous assignments. So they did. And they died.*

The wrongness of it galled her, as did the knowledge that there was no way to set any of it right. Her mother and father were gone, just like poor Dez Rydan.

Was there really nothing she could do?

At dawn, she made some highly nonspecific inquiries

in information bases, trying to discover whether anything Scover was doing counted as illegal. Probably not, she figured, given how the Byne Guild thrived throughout numerous systems. However, it turned out that the Republic had much more stringent rules about what indentured people could be required to do. Scover wasn't forcing anyone, but the Republic laws were thorough, indicating that overly hazardous "incentives" could be found to constitute a requirement in the legal sense.

But the penalties were harsh. Jail time? Dissolution of any shipping company found to engage in those practices? Affie tried to imagine her life without the Byne Guild and failed.

*We give good work to a lot of people,* she rationalized, *like Leox and Geode. Most of our pilots are free. How could I force them back into being independents?*

It was hard work being an independent pilot, at least one who operated within the law. But it was also an easier question for Affie to ask herself than, *Could I ever put Scover in jail?*

There had to be another way to stop Scover from endangering her pilots. Affie racked her brain until she realized there was one thing she could do—if she had the guts to do it.

That morning, she scarfed down her breakfast and made her excuses to Scover, who waved her off absently; several of the hoped-for meetings had already been scheduled. That left

Affie free to return to the spacedock, walk onto the *Vessel*'s bridge, and announce, "We have to go back to the Amaxine station."

Geode was speechless. Leox turned so slowly his beads didn't even sway, and said, "Why exactly do we have to do that?"

"Other Guild pilots are using that station," she said. "Indentured people, and anybody else who's broke and desperate enough to risk their lives just for one of Scover's bonuses."

"Which is a terrible thing." Leox studied her carefully. "It's also a risk they accept. That bonus alone tells any pilot looking at it that there might be no coming back."

"She doesn't offer those runs to the pilots who are genuinely free to turn them down. Only people who are desperate. That's why none of us ever knew about the station before."

"Right, because it's a terrible place to be. And we would be going back there to do what exactly?" Leox asked.

"To get records," she said. "To make a case. If anyone took all this to the Republic authorities, and they actually listened—and it seems like they do—well, Scover would be in big trouble."

Leox folded his arms across his chest. "That's an understatement. Something like that would earn her jail time. Could even lead to the dissolution of the Guild. Are you ready for that?"

Affie couldn't answer that question yet. Maybe she didn't have to answer it ever. "If I show this to Scover, she'll realize she has to back down. That she has to stop using that station, and any other hazardous locales she sends indentured people to."

"You think Scover will accept that?" Leox looked doubtful. "She's not a lady who accepts many limitations."

Once, that had been what Affie admired the most about her. "She'll have to accept it. Besides, even if she won't listen to anyone else, she might listen to me."

"She might at that," Leox said. He still seemed doubtful. "We need to be prepared, though. The Orincans might've stuck around, and they probably won't be as welcoming when we don't have the Jedi at our side. I mean, the *Vessel*'s got gunnery enough to defend herself, but no more. Nor can we openly purchase a major upgrade in armaments without attracting undue attention from the authorities." Nobody cared if they powered up in preparation to return to an ancient Amaxine station, probably—but Affie understood that the authorities absolutely, positively could not go snooping in the "secret" cargo container. "We'd want more personal weapons, as well."

"That one, we can do something about. I bet there are black market weapons for sale somewhere on Coruscant." Elation swelled within Affie's heart until she felt as if it shone from her like sunbeams. "Geode, you know some—let's say, *interesting* characters. Somebody who might sell a little on the side? Maybe even a thermal detonator or two?"

Geode's knowing look spoke volumes.

Slowly Leox began to smile. "All right, then. Let's get incendiary."

⁂

The millennia-old history of the Jedi meant that there was protocol or precedent for virtually every possible situation a member of the Order could wind up in.

But not for making any mistake as utterly enormous as this.

Orla knew the Council would've put it more elegantly than that. She preferred her own version. There was no point in trying to hide from unpleasant truths, in her opinion, and the unpleasant truth here was that they'd screwed up royally.

Not everyone could accept failure so easily, which Cohmac Vitus was currently demonstrating. Anger roiled around him as tangible as storm clouds. "It *felt like* the kind of binding used with artifacts of that era. Nearly identical."

"No one faults you, Master Vitus," said Giktoo, and maybe she meant it. "It can be hard to differentiate the various forms of Force-bound objects. The only error here was in performing the protective ritual at the very end of your stay on the Amaxine station."

Orla bit back her frustration as she realized Giktoo was right. "If we'd hung around even another day or two, we'd have recognized what we'd done. The darkness aboard the station would've manifested itself."

"Your caution was understandable," Poreht La insisted.

"You did not wish to expose yourselves and the crew of your vessel to darker powers. I cannot say you made the wrong choice."

"We released something deep in the dark side." A throb at Orla's temples presaged a headache. "That feels like the wrong choice to me."

"But what could it have been?" Cohmac said, talking more to himself than to the others in the room. "There was *nothing else* alive on that station, save for plants. And what I sensed was far more complex than anything I've ever picked up from plants strong in darkness."

"Another reason the mistake was understandable," said Tia. The only word Orla could fully take in was *mistake.*

"The warnings," Orla said. "The visions we had on the station. They weren't telling us to reckon with the darkness trapped within the idols. They were telling us the idols should be left *completely alone.*" Frustration grated at her. It was the way of the Force to speak in images and instincts, but Orla wished it could just *be precise* once in a while.

Cohmac took a deep breath, visibly attempting to center himself. Control usually came so easily to him—the struggles he'd spoken of must've run even deeper than Orla had realized. "What's past is past. What matters is the present. What are we going to do about the Amaxine station?"

Orla hadn't had time to ask herself what came next, but the answer seemed instantly clear. "We have to return. We have to replace the seals we broke, and make them even stronger than before, if we can." That would be tough. The previous seal had lasted for centuries, before they came along and ruined it. But Orla was determined to try.

Even though the Masters all nodded, Tia said, "Not yet."

"What are we waiting for?" Orla said. "For someone else to get hurt or killed? That station's still in use by smugglers and free traders. Even if they're engaging in illegal activity, that's no excuse for exposing them to that kind of danger."

It was Cohmac who answered her, though it was to the others he spoke. "Transit to that area is still hazardous. Most of the Jedi close by are assigned to Starlight Beacon, and are busy handling the fallout there. You do not have the Masters to spare."

"We don't need Masters," Orla insisted. "We took that seal down on our own; we can put it back, too."

"You would be unnecessarily endangering yourselves," Poreht La said. "We've lost too many courageous Jedi in this disaster to take such risks. Yes, this must be done. The Council will soon establish a party to go to the Amaxine station. Just not yet. For now"—he gestured at the idols—"these should be removed to a safer location, and the shrine sealed once again."

"Of course. I will take charge of it personally." Cohmac accepted so easily that Orla felt she couldn't object without coming across like a crank. As they left the chamber, Orla's head was pounding. She was determined to talk with Cohmac and see if she couldn't win him over. If both of them presented a united front, the Council might actually listen.

Instead, almost as soon as the doors had closed, Cohmac turned to her and spoke under his breath. "You will notice that they didn't actually *forbid* us to go."

"They didn't, did they?" Orla's head felt better already.

"On our first mission together, we made a mistake," Cohmac said. "Now we have made another. But this one, at least, we can put right—and I intend to do it."

⚜

Acceptance, even resignation, was a skill the Jedi were meant to master. All their skills and all their authority could not set every situation right. The Order might call on them to do things and go places they would not have chosen. Any great Jedi could accept this swiftly and even painlessly.

It was a skill Reath was still working on, with little success.

Since he had no assigned tasks at the moment, and no master to assign any, he was responsible for filling his own time. Memories of Master Jora and Dez pricked him from every side. Everything he'd done or learned during the past few years was tied to one or both of the people he'd lost. Concentration was impossible. Instead, he'd taken himself to his favorite place, the only sure source of comfort he knew.

In the vast Archive chambers, Reath sat inside his old comfortable carrel with one of the texts he'd neglected in recent years—one that retold the fairy tales and legends of the Core Worlds. These figures were all familiar from songs and rhymes taught to children, even within the temples; some of them were even rooted in fact, like Good Princess Chaia of Alderaan or the Ithorian pirate Bluebrow.

Like the Amaxine warriors.

He scrolled through the images of the Amaxines' armor, ships, and weapons, most of them artistic representations found in ancient art. But there were real artifacts pictured, too. As Reath studied the images, he saw patterns with endless circles—looped together, sequenced, enclosing each other—whether etched in metal or painted on vessels.

*No wonder they built a spherical station with rings around it,* he thought. *Circles meant something to them. Maybe some of the legends will explain why.*

Before he could scroll any further, however, another person edged into his carrel. "Hey," Reath said. "This one's taken—Master Cohmac?"

"Good afternoon, Reath." Master Cohmac wore the hood of his gold cloak up, which wasn't unusual for him but at the moment seemed somewhat . . . furtive. His voice was lowered, too, though that was the rule in the Archives. "I saw that you requested to return to the Amaxine station."

"I, uh, yeah." Reath sat up straight and brushed his brown hair back from his face. "For all the good it did. You saw about Nan and Hague, too, right?"

"Correct." Master Cohmac didn't seem nearly interested enough in the fact that they'd been bamboozled by the Nihil.

"Also, we have discovered that the darkness we encountered on the Amaxine station was not bound within the idols at all. They served as suppressors, and as sentries. By removing the idols, we set that darkness free. This cannot be allowed to stand."

It took Reath a moment to process that. "Wait. We weren't supposed to move the idols?"

Master Cohmac winced, as though in pain. "So it would appear. It is important that the idols be returned to the station, and that the darkness is again suppressed."

It was flattering to be asked for help with the binding ritual, which was surely what this was about, but Reath felt it only fair to explain that he had a completely different agenda. "I asked for permission to go back to the station to seize Hague and Nan. They refused and said they couldn't spare anybody, even a Padawan. Did the Council reverse their decision because of the idols?"

"No. That decision is final. However, nobody has been *forbidden* to travel to the Amaxine station. You and I are both currently at liberty, as is Orla Jareni, who shares our concerns. My personal stipend would cover the hire of a ship—preferably the *Vessel*, as they can make an informed choice about the dangers inherent in traveling there."

"So you're suggesting we . . . go rogue? Oppose the Council?"

"The Council has not explicitly forbidden this. Nor would I describe it as a rogue action." Master Cohmac turned out to have a very sly smile. "I prefer to think of it as 'showing initiative.'"

Every single second Reath had spent on the Amaxine station had been proof that adventures were not for him. At *all*.

But he couldn't leave a task unfinished.

He whispered, "Do we have to come up with a cover story?"

"No. We do not lie. We simply *go*."

"What do we need to bring?" Reath tried to think of special devices that might help them capture the Nihil.

Master Cohmac, however, was clearly thinking more about the darkness they would again encounter. "We need the idols."

That had been mentioned before, but only now did Reath see the full implications. "We're *stealing* them?" *Okay, cool to spend more time with historical artifacts, not cool that we have to somehow get them out of the Temple without being noticed.*

"They are the only objects that we know to be powerful enough to counter that darkness. So, we take up burglary."

Reath hesitated before saying, "You made a *joke*."

"It has been known to occur," Master Cohmac said, straight-faced. "The Council tasked me with removing the idols from their place in the Temple and finding a more suitable location for them. It just so happens that the most suitable location is back on the Amaxine station."

Smiling for a change felt good. But Reath's grin was

short-lived. "It's just us? Nan and Hague didn't look like deadly warriors, but I'd bet anything they've got weaponry aboard that ship."

"No doubt you are correct." Master Cohmac became even graver than usual. "Be aware, Padawan Silas, that the journey we are undertaking is extremely dangerous. If—no, *when* we run into trouble, we will not be able to call upon the Jedi Order or the Republic for help. What we do here, we do alone. Consider this carefully before you accept."

"I realized that part from the beginning," Reath said. "I'm in."

Affie was double-checking the landing gear of the *Vessel* when she heard footsteps behind her. *Scover,* she thought, and her gut dropped.

Instead, it turned out to be Reath Silas and Cohmac Vitus, both of them wearing their cloaks with the hoods up like it was windy and rainy instead of a totally beautiful day. Cohmac seemed serene, but Reath's eyes darted from side to side in a manner she could only call sneaky.

"Ms. Hollow," said Cohmac, "we wish to hire the *Vessel* again. Privately, this time. For another trip to the Amaxine station—if you would consider such a thing."

"More than consider it." Affie wiped her greasy hands on a rag as she got to her feet. "We'd take that charter in an instant. Problem is, somebody else already hired us."

Reath's shoulders sagged. Even Cohmac looked disappointed. "May I ask how long that customer's journey will take?"

"Ask our passenger." She pointed to the gangway, where Orla Jareni had just stepped out to collect the last of their things.

Orla grinned. "I'm sorry, Affie—did I not mention that the others would be coming with me?"

"No, you did not." Affie did some quick calculations of risk in her head, but ultimately simply waved at the others in welcome.

Cohmac raised an eyebrow. "Were there any problems removing the idols?"

"Not one bit," Orla said. "Everyone assumed I was taking them to a research facility. I just never happened to mention which one. As long as we research them a bit on the way, I say the *Vessel*'s as good a facility as any."

After that, all three Jedi huddled together at the nearest docking arch in the spaceport, discussing their plans in hushed tones. Affie watched them from the cockpit, standing between Leox and Geode.

"Should we tell them we were going there anyway?" Affie asked. "And reduce their fee?"

Leox shook his head. "Man needs bread."

# EIGHTEEN

The *Vessel* slipped away from Coruscant without incident, just one of the thousands of spacecraft leaving the planet every day. Sometimes, Leox mused, it was good to be just a single drop in the water, a single grain of sand on the shore.

Traveling back was easier than it had been the first time. The hyperspace lane, while still bumpy, was a whole lot clearer. Leox felt free to leave Affie and Geode in charge of the bridge. Besides, those two needed some catch-up time.

He meandered to the mess, hoping they'd picked up some more of that fancy caf—you really could tell the difference, with the good stuff—only to run into Orla Jareni looking madder than a Grindalid at noon.

"We need to have a talk," she said, hands on her hips.

*This does not sound favorable,* Leox thought. "On what subject shall we converse?"

"I accidentally entered your port cargo bay instead of the starboard one you'd refitted as my cabin." Her dark witchy eyes narrowed. "Which means, I know what you're hauling."

Granted, this was not how Leox had hoped the subject would be raised. In point of fact, he'd hoped it would never be raised at all. Still, if explanations were due, might as well get them over with. "Ma'am, I assure you, that spice is perfectly legal."

"Legal, in that it's actually legal?" Orla demanded. "Or legal as in, the laws of the Republic haven't quite caught up to that sector yet?"

"Entirely legal. Absolutely. One hundred and one percent."

"There's no such thing as one hundred and one percent."

Leox shrugged, the expansive and liquid gesture of a man at ease, the sort of man who might put others at ease, too. "A figure of speech. But there's absolutely no reason to object to that spice."

Orla's eyebrow remained raised in an extremely skeptical arch. "No reason, huh?"

He played his best card. "It's *medicinal.*"

"Riiiiiiiight." She sighed. "There isn't anything we can do about it now. And I think you're too smart to lie outright about it being legal—at least, in the most limited sense. So I guess we'll have to let it go."

"That, and I'm the only pilot you'll find who's willing to take a job involving killer gardening robots, poisonous vines, winsome young ladies who turn out to be Nihil warriors, and some mysterious element of the dark side that you, personally, set free."

After a pause, she admitted, "That too."

It turned out to be a much quicker trip when they were heading directly to the Amaxine station, not finding it as an emergency stop. Within the hour, Affie announced, "Everybody strap in. We're dropping out of hyperspace soon."

Reath strapped in. From the moment Master Cohmac had come to him in the Archives, he'd been keyed up— energized by purpose. However, he had to center himself. If he was going to confront Nan and Hague, he needed to do so with the utmost control.

*They're dangerous warriors,* he told himself. *They probably have weapons that you didn't discover before. You have to be ready for them.*

All true, and yet when he thought about Nan and Hague, he still saw a sweet young woman with a round face and shining dark hair, and an elderly man who used a cane to walk.

Their story might be more complex. Could they be under the control of the Nihil, serving the group against their will?

From some of the briefings, Reath remembered that the Nihil were famous for threatening certain planetary authorities, forcing them to turn a blind eye to their marauding or pay enormous ransoms. If the Nihil could intimidate an entire world's government, they could easily force two vulnerable people into doing their bidding.

*Maybe we've come here to arrest them,* Reath realized. *Or maybe we've come here to set them free.*

"Dropping out of hyperspace in five!" Leox shouted over the creaking of the jittery *Vessel.* "Four! Three!"

Reath grabbed the straps of his safety harness, as did the other Jedi.

"Two! And *one!*"

The *Vessel* shuddered, then shifted into the smooth rush of normal flight. Every one of the Jedi breathed out in relief. Wryly, Cohmac Vitus said, "The easy part is over."

From the bridge, Leox called, "You can say that again."

The others exchanged glances. Reath was the one who asked, "Why do you say that?"

"I say that," Leox replied, "because we've got a full Nihil Storm on the other side of that station, and it's carrying enough firepower to turn us back to stardust."

※

Affie had heard of the Nihil. Had seen holos and on-screen images of their warships, their poison gas attacks, and the horrific damage they left behind. They'd destroyed Guild ships—not many, but enough for her to be aware of the devastating losses of life.

None of it had prepared her for the sheer terror of seeing one of their massive warships with her own eyes.

Like Nan and Hague's ship, it was a patchwork of other ship sections and parts, different metals and shapes and aesthetics all savagely jammed together. But the Nihil warship wasn't simply bigger; it was infinitely more dangerous. Weaponry ports riddled the hull from every crevice and angle. There was no safe approach to one of these ships, and no outgunning it. Combine that with the knowledge that the warship could split apart into component ships and suddenly surround them—

Affie didn't want to think about that anymore.

Leox reacted instantly, slapping the controls that would take the engines down to their lowest active setting and turn off all unnecessary systems. Even the running lights went dark. The interior of the *Vessel* might as well have been illuminated by candles.

"They'll still see us," Affie said. Her hands remained frozen on the console.

"But it'll take 'em longer, and that gives us time to do this."

Leox used the smallest bit of thrust to tilt their course down and sideways—just behind a bit of random space detritus, an asteroid so tiny it was barely bigger than the *Vessel*. "Let's tether that."

Already Affie had realized what he was aiming at. "Got it."

She activated a magnetic tether towline, hoping the asteroid's makeup contained enough metal for it to work. A small vibration signaled that it had. Affie exhaled in relief as they floated along, shielded by an asteroid that would obscure them from the Nihil's view. If they scanned the area, they'd just think the asteroid was a little bit bigger and a whole lot more metallic. Any life signs would probably be written off as mynocks.

By this point, the Jedi had crowded around the door of the bridge. Cohmac spoke first: "Well done."

"But we can't stay here forever," added Orla. "Do we wait until they've left to go to the station?"

"We can't." Reath's eyes were wide at the size of the Nihil ship, but he sounded determined. "When the Nihil leave, they'll take Nan and Hague with them, and we'll learn nothing."

Cohmac folded his hands together. "The repercussions could be yet worse. Whatever darkness is aboard that station—depending on the form it takes, the Nihil could potentially claim it for their own."

"The Nihil aren't hooked up to the station itself yet," Leox mused. "Just Hague and Nan. The ion trails indicate they've been here for a few hours at least. Right now, they're just orbiting."

"Why haven't they docked?" Affie asked.

Leox shrugged. "My guess is they've seen readings like these." He tapped the console. Only then did Affie spy the readings that suggested more gigantic solar flares might be coming. Not immediately . . . but too soon for comfort. Leox continued, "Most likely the Nihil want to stay flexible. Leave their options open in case they need to skedaddle."

Cohmac Vitus folded his hands together. "That suggests the Nihil either do not have top-of-the-line sensors that would allow them to be more precise about solar flares, or that their docking procedure takes more time than most ships would. It would be excellent if we could discover which—though, of course, that is not our priority at this time."

The Jedi had remained calm enough to think through the fuller implications of the Nihil's actions. Affie was unwillingly impressed.

As the Nihil ship continued its slow arc around the Amaxine station, codes started rolling from the navigational station. Leox grinned. "Aw, yeah. I see what you're thinking, Geode. Now *that's* a plan."

Affie got it, too, but she couldn't be as enthusiastic. "This is insanely dangerous."

"Yeah," Leox said. "But it's gonna be cool as hell."

They wouldn't be able to use their engines; if they powered them up enough to accelerate as fast as they'd need to, the Nihil would spot the energy surge in an instant. But if they expelled some spare fuel, that would push the ship forward to the Amaxine station. The speed would be adequate—if and only if they managed the maneuver with split-second timing.

With anyone else but Leox and Geode, Affie would've assumed this tactic was a death sentence. As it was, she strapped on her safety harness and got ready.

Once the Nihil ship orbited to the far side of the Amaxine station, both spacecraft were briefly invisible to each other. The *Vessel* dropped its tether, maneuvered at half power around the asteroid and—

"Light her up," Leox said.

Affie hit the emergency fuel eject. Instantly the *Vessel* zoomed forward. Geode's coordinates kept them aimed squarely at their target. Still, even knowing exactly what was happening, Affie couldn't help holding her breath.

At the last instant before collision would've become inevitable, Leox fired the engines just enough to work against the remaining propulsion of their fuel dump. That brought the ship to a near standstill, turning the slightest bit until—

"There," he murmured. "We're in orbit, just like the Nihil. Same speed. We can't see them, but they can't see us, which is the main thing."

"Great work," said Orla Jareni, but her expression was rueful. "However, I'd argue that the main thing is—we somehow have to board a space station without docking. Any ideas on how we're going to manage *that*?"

As it turned out, there was always a way. Not necessarily a *safe* way. But none of them had come back to the Amaxine station to play it safe.

Orla adjusted her exosuit, pleased to have one that actually fit. Reath and Affie did, as well, but Cohmac had to make do with one that was far too large. Normally that would create an unacceptable risk of puncture, but this was an urgent situation, and at least they weren't traveling far.

A large case sat near Affie's feet, one she seemed intent on taking with them. "What's that?"

"Oh, just—" Affie hesitated. "It's something I need to make records of the smugglers' code on the station. I want to figure that out."

Reath shook his head. "Affie, there are Nihil on that station. Not to mention the vines and the Aytees. It's too dangerous to go there only for research." Then, to himself, he muttered, "I can't believe I just insulted research."

"I don't work for the Jedi," Affie snapped back. "I mean, I do as the *Vessel's* copilot, but once we get where we're going? I'm on my own. Which means I'm boarding the Amaxine station whether you guys do or not."

"Can't argue with that," Orla said. In truth, she wanted to argue, but the girl had a point. They lacked any way of stopping her other than physical force, which was the last thing any of them needed. Besides, Geode stood behind Affie, glowering as if daring anyone to oppose his friend's will. "Come on, everyone. Let's get moving."

Minutes later, all four members of the landing party were assembled at the airlock. On the count, Leox released the pressure valves. Metal plates spiraled open, exposing them to the frigid void of space. Gravity released them so they bobbed weightlessly within the hatch. Instead of hearing the usual hiss of lock meeting lock, Orla was instantly enveloped in total silence.

Several meters below their feet lay the scrolling surface of the Amaxine station.

"*We should be coming up on the airlocks within forty-five seconds,*" said Cohmac, via helmet comms. "*On my count.*"

Synchronization was essential. Orla readied her handheld thruster and got into position with the rest.

Cohmac's deep voice came through the comms: "*Three—two—*one."

Orla fired the thruster, allowing its momentum to push her forward, out of the *Vessel*'s airlock and toward the station's surface. She had her magnetic clamps ready even before her feet made contact. Instantly she latched on. *Got it.*

Everyone else managed it, too, with varying degrees of grace. Then they all edged together toward the nearby airlock. Reath was the one who grabbed the manual handle from the outside and spun it to *open*. As the doors slid wide, they all maneuvered their way into the airlock.

*Now,* Orla thought, *for the tricky part.*

On cue, the *Vessel* released its cargo bay doors. Out drifted its contents: the idols, tethered together with basic cargo cords. For one moment they floated free in zero G, and Orla could imagine them flying: the insect, the bird, the queen, the amphibian.

But they could not be allowed to go far. She lifted her hand at the same moment Cohmac and Reath did; as one, they reached out with the Force, bringing the idols closer. The four golden shapes floated nearer and nearer, until the Jedi were able to maneuver them within the airlock, as well. She pushed them to one side—she didn't want those things overhead when the gravity came back on—managing it just before the doors shut again.

For an instant they floated in total darkness. Then lights came on, gravity tugged at them again, and the telltale hiss of air grew louder and louder. The idols landed with an enormous thud. As atmosphere continued filling the space, Cohmac said, *"Well done, everyone. We made it."*

Orla grinned, but couldn't help adding, *"And now, for our reward—mortal danger."*

The station doors slid open, revealing the jungle.

Cohmac removed his helmet as soon as he could. The warm, almost steamy air of the station surrounded him, along with the familiar smells of soil and flowers. An 8-T rolled by, paused, apparently concluded he represented no threat to weeding, and continued on its way.

He began stripping off his exosuit, relieved to be rid of its shapeless, unwieldy bulk. Their eventual escape might be quicker if they kept the suits on—but that would make all their tasks more difficult to perform, forcing them to stay on the Amaxine station longer. Every moment they remained was another moment the Nihil could become aware of their presence.

"I'm heading to the storage facilities in the upper rings," announced Affie, who'd already shaken off the exosuit and stood there in her Guild coverall. "You guys do whatever you need to do. I won't let them see me. Should be ready to go within ten minutes or so."

"We may well take longer," Cohmac warned. "Be careful."

Affie nodded, then hurried off through the greenery to whatever task she'd set herself.

The Jedi were alone. As they set to work moving the idols back into a central location near the stone seat, Orla said, "Do you feel it?"

"Oh, yes." Cohmac could sense the darkness pressing in on him from every direction, as if trying to compress his body down to bone. "It's as if the darkness knows the idols have returned."

"That energy—it can't fall into the hands of the Nihil," Reath said quietly.

Cohmac held up a cautionary hand. "Do not reveal your

presence if you can possibly help it." There was no knowing exactly where the two Nihil were on the station, or what they might be doing. "But seek out any evidence of their activities since we departed. We must know what their plans have been before we can know how to counter them."

Reath nodded as he set aside his exosuit helmet. "Nan was sneaking around in the lower tunnels. That's probably where I should start."

Cohmac nodded. He didn't like letting an apprentice go into such a hazardous situation alone, but he and Orla would have to give all their power to the effort that lay ahead. Reath could be shielded from that danger, but no others.

"The visions we had before," Orla said, frowning. "There's something about them—"

"What?" Cohmac had taken them as no more than nightmares generated by the nearness of so much negative energy.

"Something familiar, when it wasn't before." Orla paused, then shook her head. "I can't explain it yet."

"Whatever answers we can get, we need soon." With that Cohmac walked into the station, Orla at his side, readying himself for whatever came.

☙❧

*How did these tunnels get even darker?*

Nothing could be blacker than black, but it seemed to Reath this particular blackness had really, really tried. He made his way forward very slowly, setting each foot down silently. The beam from his glow rod illuminated only the thinnest sliver of the curving walls around him.

Before long he found the circular hatch where Dez had died, which led to the path he and Nan had traveled down before. At that time, Reath had been looking for answers about Dez. He no longer trusted Nan's explanation for why she'd been there. What had she *really* been after? Whatever it was, he'd probably kept her from it.

Time to figure it out. Hague and Nan had clearly had a secret agenda throughout their stay on the station, and Reath didn't intend to let it slip by him again. If he managed to confront and arrest them, he intended to hold them responsible for *everything* they'd done.

Cautiously, Reath spun the hatch open and eased his way through, reminding himself, *Be careful about the helix rings—*

*I don't actually see the helix rings—*

*Since when is this tunnel white inside?*

The hatch slammed shut.

Reath wheeled around and tried to push it open again, but no. Through the thin slits of the door, he saw no light or movement; nobody was out there. Whatever had happened with the hatch was automatic. But an automated system could kill him as surely as any being's malice.

Even worse than the locked door was the realization that the tunnel he'd entered was no longer a tunnel. It was much smaller—pale inside, almost like some kind of a cell—

Everything shifted, vibrated, *changed*. Reath was thrown backward as light suddenly filled the tiny space, and he found himself in a room that had to be intended for a prisoner. The small seat molded in the back, the thin windows . . .

Reath's eyes widened. He saw that not all the light surrounding him was coming from within the pod. Some came from outside—and it was the unmistakable electric blue of hyperspace.

*This isn't for a prisoner,* he realized. *It's for a passenger.*

*Where the hell am I going?*

*And how am I ever going to get back?*

# NINETEEN

A deep shudder-shiver within the station froze Affie where she stood. *What was that?*

She moved to the nearest corner, wedged her back into it, and kept her blaster at the ready. Her instinct told her that what she'd heard wasn't the work of the Jedi, the Nihil, or even the 8-Ts—that it had been mechanical movement deep within the workings of the station itself.

An airlock being blown? No, if that were it, they'd already be fatally depressurizing. The Nihil warship docking with the Amaxine station? Affie wasn't even sure that was possible. She hoped not, anyway. If that happened, it would take many, many more Jedi to save them than they had on hand.

The sound was vaguely familiar to her. It took Affie a few seconds to place it before she realized she'd heard something very like that when Dez Rydan was killed.

Had Reath blown himself up? She hoped not—she'd become fonder of him than she'd expected to. It turned out even arrogant citified guys could prove to be decent people.

Maybe he was dead. Maybe he wasn't. There was nothing Affie could do about it either way. After a few seconds, when no other sounds emerged from the station, she resumed her progress through the dark chambers. She made her way through the thick curtains of vines that dangled down, brushing against her from every direction.

In the far distance, she saw movement, too high from the ground to be an 8-T, too far from the central chamber to be one of the Jedi. Affie ducked low as she took a careful look and recognized Nan.

Instead of the colorful dress she'd worn earlier, Nan wore a coverall as simple and utilitarian as Affie's own, and bandoliers and a belt strapped with at least three times as much weaponry as Affie was carrying. Nan's arms were bared, revealing tattoos—not pictures, but some kind of writing, too small to be read from that distance. To Affie, it seemed like a lot of tattoos for someone so young. Maybe that was common among the Nihil.

But she'd worry about getting more intel on the Nihil later. For now, Affie only needed to know that Nan and Hague hadn't discovered their presence, and to judge by Nan's nonchalant stroll, they hadn't. That meant the Jedi were free to do whatever they were doing.

And Affie was free to get the proof she needed to make Scover back down.

⁂

"This is bad," Reath repeated to himself as he slumped into the seat of the hyperspace pod. "This is very, very bad. This is what happens when you don't have access to research materials."

He trusted in his ability as a Jedi, and in the ways of the Force. His lightsaber remained at his side. So Reath could prepare himself to deal with whatever came.

But preparing himself included accurately assessing the situation he'd found himself in, which was in fact *extremely terrible*.

"I am in a hyperspace pod," Reath said out loud. The rounded interior of the pod caught sounds and shaped them strangely. "No navicomputer on board that I can see, and besides, this has to be too small to have a hyperdrive of its own. I think . . . I think this has to be some kind of one-way transit vehicle, the human-sized equivalent of a probe droid."

He tried very hard not to dwell on the words *one-way*. Panic couldn't help him, while analysis . . . probably wasn't going to help much, either, but it was at least worth trying.

"I don't know where I'm going, what I'll find there, or how to get back. Okay. That more or less sums it up."

Hyperspace journeys could last anywhere from a few minutes to several weeks. Without any way of knowing how long this one would be, Reath began to be concerned about the lack of food, water, and an evac tube. But no sooner had he noticed that than the pod suddenly jolted out of hyperspace. He blinked as he stared at the thin windows in the hatch, the ones that had just blinked from electric blue to black night. A star field lay beyond. Had the pod deposited him in the middle of nowhere?

The one sensor within the pod began to blink, and Reath felt the rumbling that could mean only one thing: a tractor beam.

"At least I'm going *someplace*," he said, taking his light saber from his belt. Whatever came next, he intended to be ready.

The pod tilted as it began descending through an atmosphere. Clouds didn't vary that much planet to planet—assuming they were water vapor and not methane, which Reath profoundly hoped to be the case. He wasn't going to be able to tell much on the way down; investigation would have to wait for the planet's surface.

The tractor beam pulled the pod down inexorably, but in a controlled descent. Reath felt no more than a small thud as the pod settled into . . . something.

He looked through the thin hatch windows and saw nothing but greenery: trees, bushes, a sort of marshy landscape. In fact, he recognized the vines from the station; some seeds must've made the same journey in the past. This strongly suggested that the atmosphere was breathable by humans. Nobody was waiting to kill him, either, which was always a good sign.

Reath pushed the hatch door open and stepped outside. Thick clouds filtered, but didn't conceal, a white sun's light. The air was warm and damp, and it smelled like loamy soil, salt water, and thick green marsh plants. Wet ground had to be nearby. However, the pod had come to rest on a spar of rockier land.

A spar that must have been chosen, very long before, as the base for this hyperspace pod.

As Reath stepped farther back from the pod, he got a better look at the mechanism. The small, almost spherical pod he'd been in was only part of the whole—the "cabin," as it were, at the head. Behind it stretched the rest of the mechanism, long and slender, what he had to assume was the hyperdrive. Another such pod, identical to the one he'd traveled in, rested farther along the sinuous track. *It curves through the tunnels,* he realized. *It's an ancient, fully automated mechanism. There must be multiple pods still within the Amaxine station. People step inside a pod, and it travels to predetermined coordinates.*

*So where have these coordinates taken me?*

He paid attention to his immediate surroundings first. He recognized the circular motifs of the Amaxines in the landing platform, which coiled around, clearly setting up the hyperspace pods for their return trip. Helix rings hung in place there, too, which meant there was probably power and fuel enough for more than one voyage. Reath had to hope so; otherwise, this was his new planet of residence. Although moss had grown over some of the central hub—the controls?—all the equipment appeared to be in working condition.

Which meant he probably had a way to get back to the Amaxine station. He just had to figure it out.

Then he heard rustling in the leaves, in the reeds. Reath whirled around, lightsaber in hand, to see . . . nothing. Just trees. Just plants.

Yet as he stood there, he could feel an oppressive weight settling over him—the presence of the dark side, powerful, acute, and focused. Someone was approaching him with ill intent, seemingly from every direction at once.

It occurred to Reath that he could make a run for the pod controls. This technology appeared to be highly automated; he might be able to launch a return trip to the Amaxine station within only a few minutes. Another pod had been waiting for no telling how long. That meant he had two chances to get himself out of there, to return to the others and the important mission at hand.

But the Force told him he had to stay. That whatever was on the planet—dangerous as it might be—was of critical significance. That he could learn something he and all the Jedi badly needed to know. The secrets of the Amaxine station would not remain on the station; they would expand far past their old boundaries, into the galaxy at large. The Jedi had to be ready.

Reath took a deep breath, settled into defense stance, and ignited his blade.

❖

Cohmac's research into Force artifacts and lore had taught him that the containment of the dark side usually took one of a very few forms: the echo of a Sith or other servant of darkness; a specific memory of an atrocity, usually the remembrance of those who had committed it; or a more amorphous, unfocused energy.

What he felt now—on the unbound, unprotected Amaxine station—was something entirely different. As impossible as it was, or ought to be, this was *consciousness*. Sapience. Individual will . . .

No. The will of multiple individuals, every single one possessed of murderous intent.

"Did you ever hear of the clay warriors of Zardossa Stix?" Cohmac murmured as the two Jedi moved deeper into the forested glade in the center of the station.

Orla said, "Sure. The ancient statues of a fallen army. The Zardossan legends claimed that the statues were the only things keeping the warriors dead—that if they were ever destroyed, the army would spring back to life. Now I'm asking myself why you'd bring that up at this particular moment, and none of the answers are good."

"I think these idols," said Cohmac, "may have been holding back a sort of army, or some other dangerous group."

Orla stopped in the middle of the glade and held out her arms. "I'm not seeing any army."

"But you can sense one," Cohmac said as the impressions became more tangible. His stance shifted from merely alert to battle ready. "Reach out with your feelings."

"I feel *something*," Orla replied, "and I sense its malice. Still, we made a pretty thorough search of this station. Are you telling me we somehow managed to miss an entire military force?"

Then they heard the first footstep.

Both Jedi whirled around until they stood back to back, a single fighting unit. They ignited their lightsabers in the same instant, two white beams from Orla's double-bladed saber and Cohmac's lone blue beam shining into the murky patches among the vines.

The rustling grew louder with every heartbeat, yet the more Cohmac heard, the less he understood. None of the approaching enemies wore boots; nor could he hear any telltale clicks of metal hinting at weaponry. And the sound was off, somehow, unmistakable and yet strange. . . .

He saw a tree sway toward their clearing, as if pushed. Then it came closer and he realized it wasn't a tree at all.

The creature that stood before them was two meters tall, gnarled and hulking. It possessed nothing as central as a trunk; instead it seemed to be a slithering mass of thorned vine tentacles, many of them plated in bark-like armor. There did seem to be a kind of "head," one antlered with thorns and possessed of a wide, grinning mouth like the trap of a carnivorous plant, designed to snap shut on its prey. Coming up behind it were at least a dozen more of the same species, all of them enormous. Cohmac realized these things had blended in perfectly with the thickly overgrown greenery within the Amaxine station, but earlier, the creatures had been still.

Dormant.

Until the Jedi had set them free.

"Finally," their leader said in a low, rumbling voice. "Some meat."

***

"Stop hiding," Reath called to his unseen foe. "Show yourselves."

The vines around the pod launcher swayed. Branches rustled. Still, Reath saw nothing but plants. . . .

His eyes widened as he took in the incredibly huge forms approaching him, crawling toward him on dozens of vines, or tentacles. If anything they looked like swamp matter compressed together, plated with bark, then studded with thorns. Only one detail clashed with their arboreal appearance: in their ... stems? stalks? ... they held blasters that looked both extremely old and extremely lethal.

The enemy hadn't been hiding *in* the plants. Somehow they *were* plants.

"Whoa," he said. The researcher in him had overtaken the warrior. "That's amazing. You guys are botanical rather than animal, but you're sentient?"

They all looked at each other, apparently nonplussed. Whatever reaction they'd been expecting, it wasn't that.

Reath had already collected himself, but he sensed that keeping the enemy off guard was a smart strategy. His initial response had done that pretty well, so he'd stick with it.

Slightly lowering his saber (while keeping it at the ready), he said, "Your mouths look a little like flytraps. Is that what they are? Or is that the kind of creature you evolved from? Do you have histories that go back that far? I hope I'm not being rude. Just—wow. I've never met a species like you."

"It speaks more than the other one," said one of the swamp beings to the others. "But it too has forgotten the name of the Drengir."

"Never heard of the Drengir before," Reath said truthfully. He was only guessing that was the name of their species, but since none of them contradicted him, it must've been an accurate guess. "Or anything remotely like you. There are sentient plants in the galaxy, sure, but they tend to be rooted in place. Literally rooted. Not you guys."

None of them looked at him even once. One Drengir said, "I think it is younger than the other."

The Drengir leader snarled, "All meat looks alike to me."

*Meat* was really not a descriptor Reath wanted to hear applied to himself. He plowed on as though nobody had spoken, mentally taking the tally the entire time. "I'm a human. My name's Reath Silas. Coming here was an accident, so if I'm intruding, uh, very sorry about that." *Seven Drengir in the party. Two keep their weapons at their sides and may be noncombatants. Vulnerable spots uncertain, but watch for the thorns.*

"If it is younger, then it is even less likely to have information than the one we have," the Drengir leader continued. "It will not know how this relay works. Pieces of foolish meat tumble out of the pods and we learn nothing. But two visitors means we have confirmed—our landing space remains intact. We can again find our brethren. And we can stop asking questions of our prize. At last we can eat it."

Nobody was talking to Reath, but he thought he should weigh in, if only to get past being called meat. Could they not hear him? Or understand him? Their accents were strong, more like the way people had talked centuries before. Still, he'd try. "Probably those other *people* didn't mean to come here any more than I did," he guessed. "We thought that was Amaxine technology—"

"The Amaxines!" All the Drengir made a snap-rustling sound that must have been their version of laughter. *So,* Reath thought, *they can hear me. They just think I'm not worth talking to.*

The Drengir leader continued, "One of our first great conquests. They built this relay to make war on us, attempting to take our planet as they had many others. Instead, we defeated and devoured them." Even this comment was more of a pep talk to his fellow Drengir than a statement directed at Reath. "We made their station our own. From there we planned to wreak havoc on many worlds. But then our people fell silent. None of them returned in either glory or defeat."

*We haven't seen your people on the station,* Reath wanted to say—but was stopped by two realizations.

First, they *had* seen Drengir on the station. Now that he looked at them, he recognized the curl of their thorns, the particular dark yellowish-green of some stems. The Drengir had been there the whole time, silent and still. Were *they* the darkness that had been held in check by the ancient idols?

Second, only a few moments before, the Drengir leader had said another person had recently come through in a hyperspace pod. How recently?

"Who else has come to your planet via the pods?" Reath asked, tightening his grip on his saber.

"This one is fresh," said one of the Drengir, still ignoring Reath. "Not like the wilted one with sap running from his head. Maybe it can answer more questions."

Reath ignored the implied threat of interrogation. He realized who the other human who'd gone there had to be. "Bring him here," he said, calling on the Force to shape their wills. *"Bring Dez Rydan to me."*

The last cogent, coherent thought in Dez Rydan's brain had been: *That hatch is going to hit me square in the face.*

Pain had smashed into his forehead, jolting through his entire body like electricity, the agony of it reaching his gut, his fingers, his feet. Everything after that had been dark for a long while, and silent, but not painless. The agony was the only sensation left to him, and his only desire was for it to stop. If it stopped because he died, that seemed fair. As long as it stopped.

There came a time when he was turned over and forced to see sunlight; his head throbbed so badly at the sensory input that he'd vomited. Something had lashed him cruelly across the back as punishment. A whip? A vine? Dez didn't know and didn't care. He only wanted his head to stop hurting.

As the days went on, he should've either felt better or died. Instead, although he could feel the swelling in his face and neck going down, Dez remained in a terrible kind of stasis. Was he being poisoned? They pricked him with thorns, after which he would feel sleepy and nauseated. His eyes refused to focus, but whether that was because of his injury or what was being done to him, he couldn't tell. The Drengir kept asking him questions, but he couldn't understand exactly what they wanted to know. He wasn't even sure Drengir was the right name. If he could've explained things to them, he would have. But the world swirled around him, sickening and blurry, beyond his comprehension.

Dez suspected they had caged him, as unnecessary as that was. Branches encased him on every side. He couldn't have stood up if he wanted to. He didn't want to.

One of the Drengir approached; by then he knew the scent of them and associated it with pain. But even as he braced himself, the Drengir whispered, "There is more meat here."

Maybe. Dez wasn't totally sure what he'd said. It didn't make any sense, but nothing else did, either.

"We wish to see what your people think you can do with these." Between the branches, Dez could see the Drengir dangling what they'd taken from him when he first arrived unconscious: his lightsaber. "Kill him, and we will let you go free."

"The lightsaber is not—is not the tool of a murderer." Dez coughed. He couldn't even stand up; how could they expect him to fight? He had no idea who or what was here—a pirate? A smuggler? Leox Gyasi? It didn't matter. He refused to slay another sentient being for the Drengir's amusement. "Let him go free instead. Kill *me*." Then, at last, it would be over.

"That tells us nothing," the Drengir said. He was speaking to himself as much as to Dez. "We wish to see more than that."

Another thorn pierced Dez's flesh, and he cried out in

pain—but in the very next heartbeat, the pain vanished. He sensed that it wasn't gone, only masked, but that alone felt like reason to live.

Whatever had been injected into him had other effects, too. His heart beat too fast, and his muscles began to tighten and shake. *Adrenaline*, whispered some part of his brain that was still functioning but was all too far away.

"Fight and the pain stops," the Drengir said. Through his blurry vision, Dez saw the door of the cage swing open. "Fight and be free."

His mind no longer mattered. Dez was nothing but his body, nothing but anger and desperation and a wild chemical frenzy. He clutched for his lightsaber, and the Drengir let him take it. Instantly Dez swung the lightsaber in a long, low arc, slicing straight through the Drengir, which fell in two pieces to the ground.

Was that what he was supposed to do? He'd killed something; would they set him free now?

Each part of the Drengir twitched. Then twitched again. Then began to grow tendrils. Dez's vision doubled, trebled, then doubled again as the tendrils reached toward each other. They grew fast and thick, splicing the Drengir back together until he stood intact.

"Very good," said the Drengir. "Now we will take you to the new intruder, and you will do that again."

# TWENTY

Using the Force to shape another's will came instinctively to some Jedi. The teachers even had problems, occasionally, with younglings who'd gotten the hang of it but didn't yet understand not to play with others' minds. For other Jedi, however, it was a trick that could take years or even decades to master.

Reath was in the latter category. So when one of the Drengir returned to the clearing, dragging a human figure behind it, Reath was at first even more astonished than pleased. *I actually did it?*

Any thoughts of his own accomplishment vanished the

second he recognized the man being pulled forward. Reath had known who it had to be, but his face split in a smile as he yelled, *"Dez!"*

Dez didn't call back. His gaze was unfocused, his breaths came too quickly, and his face was flushed. Reath's grin faded as he saw the purple swelling around one of Dez's eyes, and that his black hair was matted with blood. Worse than Dez's appearance was that of the Drengir, whose flytrap mouths were smiling.

At least they'd let go of Dez, who stood there staring dully at the transport pods. He didn't seem capable of understanding that they meant escape, freedom, home. Either because of his head injury or what the Drengir had done to him—maybe both—he was in a deeply altered state of consciousness.

But Reath had to get through to Dez somehow. He tried, "Dez? Come on. Let's go."

No response. The Drengir had begun laughing, an eerie rustling sound.

*Maybe my mind trick didn't work after all,* Reath thought. *Or maybe it only worked because they already intended to bring Dez to me. Because they wanted me to see him. But why?*

Still, Dez hadn't moved. Maybe a gesture would be easier to understand. Reath held out his hand to Dez.

Finally, Dez took a step toward Reath and the transport pods. The Drengir made no move to stop him. Reath knew that could only mean bad news. Just a few minutes in these creatures' company had taught him that they weren't the type to let their victims walk away.

"This one?" Dez said, slurring his words.

"Yes," said the Drengir leader. "That one. Kill him, and go free."

Reath had no time to process what he'd just heard because even in that instant, Dez was leaping toward him, lightsaber blazing.

"Who are you?" Cohmac demanded.

The plant creatures ignored him. In the heart of the Amaxine station, they surrounded the Jedi. They always had, Cohmac realized.

He also recognized the oppressive weight settling over them, not so different from the uncanny sensation that came before a groundquake or cyclone. The dark side held power there, power that had been unleashed.

"Your ancestors were imprisoned here," said Cohmac. "Ages ago. They were held in place by the idols. Am I correct?" Even with his lightsaber in hand and facing down enemies, he wished to remain a scholar.

That the plants heard, or at least didn't bother pretending not to hear. The plant creatures made a hissing sound of pure contempt. "Not our ancestors. *We* were imprisoned here. A simple trick, we see now—but we did not see then. It will not be so easy to capture the Drengir again."

Hadn't the idols been in place for centuries? But Cohmac vaguely remembered that some forms of plant life could go dormant in hostile environmental conditions, "sleeping" for months, years, or even longer. These beings known as the Drengir must have similar capabilities. In any other situation, it might have been fascinating.

"They are the descendants of the ones who put us here," snarled another of the Drengir. "Look at their weapons, the ones that glow. They are the same."

Jedi trapped the Drengir there? Before Cohmac could open his mouth to speak of it, the Drengir leader said, "Not the same. The other weapons were red."

Orla and Cohmac exchanged quick glances. They each knew what that could mean.

*Sith.*

A shiver crawled up Cohmac's back as he realized that the Drengir must have fought, and been captured by, the ancient Sith. If the Drengir were deep enough in the dark side to have presented a challenge to the Sith themselves . . .

Then the Drengir leader said, with a widening grin, "Time to eat."

Cohmac responded to the motion before he'd even truly seen it, a slash-flash of movement at the corner of his eye. His lightsaber blade sliced through what he could only call a whip of thorns, as thick around as a human's forearm. It flopped to the floor, then kept thrashing, bending, almost slithering.

But there was no more time to analyze what it was or what had happened, because the Drengir were upon them.

Cohmac reached out with the Force, working to sense his opponents' moves before they made them, which gave him time to dodge one of their whips. For her part, Orla leapt up over them in a wide arc, flipping head over heels to land behind the Drengir leader. Both blades of her lightsaber sparked as they pierced the creature's trunk with two rotating slashes, bright white spears emerging through its bark skin.

Instead of collapsing, the Drengir laughed. It pulled forward, free of the saber, and turned around to slash its thorn whip at Orla. Cohmac realized that the trunk was already healing itself—growing new tissue to replace what had been lost.

*Damn and damn,* Cohmac thought. *How do you kill an enemy who can't be injured?*

The situation wasn't quite as dire as that, as she proved an instant later when she severed the lower tentacles of a Drengir, who collapsed, alive and conscious but unable to regenerate quickly enough to get back into the fight. *Those tentacles must be critical to their balance,* Cohmac reasoned. At least they knew one vulnerability to strike at.

But even those injures were only temporary. More and more Drengir emerged from the vines, revealing that the Jedi were not fighting a mere armed group—but, yes, an army.

Dez's ears rang. His head ached. The thing in front of him held a fiery saber like his own and kept shouting something Dez couldn't understand. Only one word made sense: his name.

He didn't want to hear his name anymore. He didn't want to hear anything anymore. Dez simply wanted to make everything stop. They said if he killed this thing, it would.

With all his might, he brought his lightsaber down on the other. They crashed together, sending a vibration through his hands and arms. His opponent stumbled backward. Through the rush of blood in his ears, Dez heard the Drengir laughing. He wanted that to stop, too.

For an instant he was able to focus on his opponent—someone young. Someone vaguely familiar. A voice called, "Dez, why are you doing this?"

It made no difference. The opponent had to die.

❈

On her belly, Affie crawled between the layers of storage bins, in search of more of the code. She'd recorded a fair bit of it, but she felt like she needed absolutely everything written on the Amaxine station to prove her case.

And maybe, just maybe, she'd find something else about her family . . . even something her parents wrote themselves. . . .

She startled at more sounds below. This wasn't the loud grinding from before—not nearly as thunderous as that—but still counted as what Leox would term "a ruckus." Thuds from things or people hitting the floor, the hum of lightsabers, and for some reason a whole lot of rustling from the plants . . .

Affie grabbed her comlink. "Leox, come in."

*"Something the matter, Little Bit?"*

She had bigger problems to deal with than that stupid nickname. "The Jedi are making a whole lot of noise down in the central chamber. No idea why, but they are. If I can hear it all the way up here, I guarantee you Nan and Hague can hear it, too."

*"Hang on just a sec, let me check something—"* Leox went silent for a moment, then quietly muttered a rude word he'd never spoken near her before. *"Yep, the Nihil know they're not alone."*

Affie's hand tightened around the comlink. "How can you tell?"

*"I can tell because they're no longer orbiting the station. The warship's assumed a locked position. Which means we have to stop orbiting, too, or else they're going to see us in about . . . two minutes."*

"Get out of here," she said. Maybe it was wrong, making a decision like that without the Jedi's input—but there was no time to waste, and the Jedi were the ones who had caused this problem in the first place. "You and Geode. Just go. Save yourselves."

*"Calm down. All we have to do is slam on the brakes. Maybe we can even link up to one of the airlocks, make ourselves available to help you guys if the situation gets worse."*

"Good," Affie said. The crashing and yelling from below grew louder. "Because I'm pretty sure it's going to."

※

Lightsaber dueling was widely considered the coolest class at the Jedi Temple. (Reath preferred Ancient History, but he was in an extremely small minority.) All the emphasis on dueling obscured one simple truth: this was a situation a Jedi would almost certainly never encounter even once in a lifetime of service. Only other Jedi carried lightsabers; Jedi did not fight each other in the field or anywhere else, for that matter. Ergo, dueling was effectively useless except as exercise.

So Reath had argued, and he still felt like he was right in principle. At the moment, however, dueling practice was the only thing keeping him alive.

Dez Rydan, wild-eyed, went at Reath again and again, relentless. His obvious injuries hadn't sapped his strength; if anything, Dez was going berserk with adrenaline, almost incapable of rational thought. It was like approaching an injured animal—you could try to take care of it, but it would only snap and claw at you.

*Parry. Position two. Twist and parry. Block high, block low, position four.* Reath's body knew the stances and drills so well that he could defend himself without conscious thought. But that was all he could do—defend himself and prolong the fight.

The only other option was maiming or killing Dez Rydan.

"Cut him with the blade that burns," growled one of the watching Drengir, all of whom seemed highly entertained. "Cook the meat for us."

Reath wasn't sure which one of them the Drengir was speaking to, but he didn't like that instruction either way.

*I have to wake Dez up,* he thought. *Make him hear me, if he even can. How am I supposed to get through to him?*

Then Reath remembered another voice saying, when he'd been complaining about the frontier assignment, "How am I ever going to get through to you?"

"Master Jora," Reath said. "Remember her? Our master?"

Dez hardly seemed to understand what Reath was saying. So Reath reached out with the Force, filling his mind with memories of Jora Malli: her warm smile, her surprisingly deep laughter, her insatiable cravings for Bilbringi food—

And then the knowledge that she was dead, far away, never to be seen again—

Reath had managed to create a connection with Dez's mind just in time to flood it with grief and pain. Dez pulled back and brought up his lightsaber for another blow. Sooner or later, he was going to hit harder than Reath could parry.

Dez stopped mid-movement, as though frozen. His expression remained glazed, but in his eyes there was some evidence that he was at least trying to make sense of what Reath was saying.

Sweat slicked Reath's skin. The air was thick with

moisture and the smells of soil, sap, and mold. He stood there in defense stance, keeping his eyes locked with Dez's, not knowing how long the respite would last.

Reath attempted to reach out with the Force, to connect with Dez that way, but immediately he stopped. Dez's mind was almost unrecognizably disordered—frenzied. Even if a connection could be forged through such chaos, it was as likely to disrupt Reath as it was to stabilize Dez. The risk was too great.

He'd have to reach Dez another way.

Carefully, Reath said, "Think about Master Jora. Just imagine her voice. I know you can hear it, inside your head, if you'll listen. She'd tell you to stop fighting and let me take you home."

At first it seemed as though Dez hadn't even heard him. But then he lowered his lightsaber—only a few centimeters, but it was enough to give Reath a chance.

It wasn't honorable to hit an opponent when he was down. Usually. This was one of the exceptions. Reath swung his blade sharply upward to collide with Dez's almost at the base. With Dez wobbly and dazed, his grip on his lightsaber gave way. It spun upward, and Reath caught it with his free hand.

He placed himself between Dez and the Drengir, blades crossed. Even through the glare, Reath could see the fury on their twisted faces.

To Dez he said only, "Come on. Let's go home."

"And to think," Orla panted, "some people—say gardening—is a—relaxing hobby!"

Cohmac didn't laugh at her joke. Not that he ever laughed much. And no doubt he was distracted by trying to keep his head from being chopped off by the Drengir's thorny whips.

One of those whips had scraped Orla's calf earlier in the fight. It had been only a glancing blow, but it was enough to make her leg ache from toe to hip. Swelling had already stiffened her ankle and was beginning to do the same to her knee. Poisonous thorns, she figured.

A Drengir lunged at her, but Orla flung herself backward, half jumping, half levitating, until she was clear of the fight. Not that she intended to leave Cohmac alone in it for long, but they could fight better as a unit once she had some perspective on what they were dealing with.

As she came back down, her sore foot made contact, not with the floor, but with something curved and unfixed. Orla landed hard on all fours and glared backward at the 8-T that had had the nerve to be in her way. The droid took no notice, simply kept on pruning back branches.

Pruning.

With shears specially designed to slice through plants.

Orla's mind whirled with possibilities. *The Aytees attack anything they perceive as a threat to the plants. They're not attacking us at the moment, which means they don't consider the Drengir to be plants under their care.*

*Which means there has to be some way to sic the Aytees on the Drengir.*

She turned and pounced on the 8-T's dome; it whistled once in consternation but otherwise kept to its task. No obvious interface presented itself. If she was going to use the droids, she would have to work with their existing programming.

Orla clambered to her feet, ignoring the stab of pain in her ankle. From her vantage point she could see that Cohmac was pinned near one of the central arches. Overhead curved one of the bowers, so thickly enveloped in vines that the metal was almost invisible.

This was one of those rare moments when a blaster would've been more useful than a lightsaber. Orla reminded herself to carry one in future, then summoned the strength to leap even farther up than before—again half levitating—soaring all the way up to the bower. At the topmost point, she swung her lightsaber, severing the bower's connection to the ceiling. As the metal sagged and she began her descent, she yelled, "Look out above!" Her friend would need no more than that to understand what she'd set into motion.

Orla controlled her fall as best she could, but even her soft landing sent more pain jolting through her entire leg. The poison had continued to spread. *Antitox,* she thought. *As soon as possible. Just not yet.*

Entangled as it was in vines, the bower fell in stages—each stem unraveling only so far, then pausing, until the weight forced it to go farther still. It wobbled from side to side, which got the attention of the 8-Ts. Orla limped back toward the thick of the fray. As she'd anticipated, Cohmac had figured out her plan; he'd edged backward until he was well clear of the bower's ultimate resting place. The Drengir, believing their enemies to be in retreat, had moved into prime position. Orla rejoined Cohmac, each of them parrying blows from the thorn whips with their sabers in a whir of light. Every sweep of a saber sent the tips of thorns spraying around the station, like deadly poison darts.

The bower finally tumbled to the floor with a thud. It clocked one of the Drengir, but that was just a side bene-fit. The Drengir were covered with the vines and trapped as surely as though they'd been caught in a net. That wouldn't last long, of course, before they got out. Orla *wanted* them to get out—or, rather, she wanted them to try.

"Cut yourselves free!" yelled the Drengir leader. One of his spiky hands slashed through a vine with a spray of sap. The other Drengir followed suit, shredding the vines with all their might.

And that was when the 8-Ts stepped in.

They swarmed the Drengir. First a handful, then a dozen, then more droids from all over the station were rolling across floors and down walls, pruning shears clicking. Soon the Drengir began to howl in protest as those shears found their targets. The Drengir would have no trouble destroying the 8-Ts once they were free—but that would take them a while.

"Good thinking," Cohmac said to Orla. "This is our chance."

"Couldn't agree more."

Orla let the battle fall away from her memory, the tension from her body. She inhaled deeply, inhabiting only the moment. From the depths of her mind, she called upon the Force to answer.

As she opened her perception further, she became more able to sense Cohmac beside her, doing the same thing. His courage rallied her own. With renewed determination, she traced the outlines of darkness, formed it in the shape of a sphere, felt Cohmac's effort doubling her own. Then she centered that energy within the idols, squaring the circle—

A burst of brilliant greenish light lit up the entire station for a moment. Orla's first impulse was that something had gone wrong with the inner illumination, or worse, that internal systems were beginning to explode. Then she realized the light had been only in her mind's eye, her consciousness attempting to make sense of the pure power of the Force.

In that instant, the fight between the Drengir and the 8-Ts ended. Once again the Drengir blended into the murk of the jungle. Orla could almost have lost them. The 8-Ts whirled in brief confusion, then got back to the important work of gardening.

Would this hold the Drengir in place?

"That's the seal," she said, almost in a daze. "It's working."

"Hopefully forever, but at least for a short while." Already Cohmac had fully recovered and had once again pulled up the hood of his robe in preparation for travel. "That gives us time to escape and reconnect with Reath. I hope Affie has finished with the code."

"If she hasn't, we'll make Leox and Geode call her back." Orla pushed up the sleeves of her spotless white robe. "Let's move."

They hustled toward the door that would lead to the airlock ring. Sensing their approach, the door slid open, revealing the darkened space. But in the middle of that area stood a slender, stooped figure. As Orla's eyes adjusted to the light, she recognized who had found them.

"I'm afraid I have to ask you to stay right here," said Hague, leveling his blaster straight at them.

*— Twenty-Five Years Earlier —*

## PART FIVE

Cohmac and Orla crept along behind Master Laret through the cave tunnels. They were getting closer to the kidnappers' lair—they all could sense that—but pinpointing their precise location was proving difficult. The problem was compounded by the reality that choosing the wrong path to the hostages could lead them straight into armed guards, or explosive booby traps.

Orla brought up the rear, where it was darkest. Her own faint silhouette was only one of the many shadows surrounding them. They were, at this point, too close to risk activating their lightsabers or even using their glow rods at any but the lowest setting.

She didn't doubt Master Laret. Finding pathways through the Force was a known gift of hers. More important, Master Laret's judgment was invariably, inarguably *correct*. It wasn't a matter of slavishly following the Order's dictates—Laret Soveral made up her own mind, no matter what, as Orla had learned when trying in vain to sway her judgment. But in making decisions, her master always had some rule in mind, whether it be ethical, legalistic, or otherwise. All those rules urged them to keep doing what they were doing, namely, searching for the royal hostages.

Orla, however, always felt the urge to follow her instincts

first, rules be damned. At the moment, her instincts were telling her to stop.

Just to stop. Not to search. Not even to reach out with her feelings. To stop and wait for a sign that would tell them more.

*You're scared,* she told herself, resolutely gripping the hilt of her lightsaber. *Don't give into fear. That's all this is.*

Monarch Cassel whispered, "I've been thinking."

*That must be a first,* Thandeka said to herself, then felt guilty. On Eiram, the jokes about Cassel's intelligence, or lack thereof, were common . . . and perhaps not completely wrong. But after hours physically bound to him, she'd learned whatever the man lacked in cleverness, he made up for in kindness. "What about?"

Cassel glanced over at Isamer before answering. The Lasat was too busy stuffing his face with barely cooked meat to pay any attention to their mumblings. Reassured, Cassel said, "He keeps sending his guards out to look for the Jedi, so the Jedi must be fairly close to us."

"It's a possibility," Thandeka said. She wouldn't extend her hopes any further than that. Thandeka had resigned herself to death hours before—at least, mostly. The one part she couldn't fully accept was never seeing her wife again. "Why do you mention it?"

"I was thinking that we could do something to get their

attention," Cassel said, his Pantoran face flushing dark blue. "Shout at the top of our voices, something like that."

"We're surrounded by solid rock. I don't think shouting will do us much good." Then Thandeka considered it. The particulars of Cassel's suggestion might not be useful, but the basic idea . . .

She looked around the miserable lair with fresh eyes. Before, she'd only been searching for a means of escape (none) or the weapons that would likely be used for her execution (blasters). This time, Thandeka looked for communications equipment. Nothing in there would broadcast a signal off-world, or even to the surface. But if the Jedi had come close enough to their location, then maybe she could reach them.

One of the handheld comm devices used by the Lasat's guards sat atop a nearby crate. Thandeka nodded toward it. Cassel stared at her in consternation, but then his jaw dropped as he caught on.

She glanced back at their captor. Isamer was still gulping down his food, oblivious to anything else. They had a brief chance.

Together she and Cassel wriggled a few centimeters to the left, just far enough for her toes to touch that crate. Thandeka thumped it as hard as she could. The comlink tumbled down, landing on the soft edge of her robe, which muffled the sound of its fall. (Not that Isamer was likely to hear it over his growling and smacking.) Using her foot, she pulled the comm unit back toward them.

Cassel and Thandeka's eyes met in shared glee. Still, getting the comm unit was one thing—effectively using it was another.

The cuffs on her hands made it difficult to grab the comm unit, but she managed it. There was no question of bringing it to her mouth so she might whisper a message; anything she could say loudly enough to be heard at that distance would immediately alert Isamer.

Different kinds of messages could be sent over comms, though, not just voices. Various codes and signals—none of which Thandeka knew—but her message didn't need to make sense. She only needed the Jedi to detect something, *anything*, coming from their location.

With her thumb, Thandeka hit a switch, closed her eyes, and thought, *They say the Jedi can do anything.*

*We shall see.*

❖

Orla's comlink began to vibrate against her hip. Confused, she picked it up and saw no message, heard no words. Signal bursts were sometimes used to send codes, but this was just one long burst—static, basically.

Still, it was being sent from very close by, closer than any ship could possibly be.

*The kidnappers would communicate with each other intelligibly,* Orla reasoned. *So this is either a malfunction, or a botched attempt at reaching us.*

Either way, it had given her a means of tracing the signal's location.

Relief washed through Orla. She hated nothing so much as the feeling of being trapped, and wandering around in that maze had felt too much like imprisonment.

But now they could escape.

# TWENTY-ONE

Keeping both lightsabers crossed in front of him, Reath began backing toward the transport pod. With his shoulder he was able to nudge Dez along, but not quickly.

Reath would have strongly preferred to move quickly, because the Drengir continued to close in around them. However, his obvious plan of escape seemed not to concern them, which meant there was some serious flaw Reath hadn't thought through yet.

*If it's that big a problem, I'll find out about it soon enough,* he told himself.

He wanted to get them talking, both to learn what he could and so they'd finally stop referring to him as meat. "So," he said, "are the Drengir from this world and some of you traveled to the station? Or did you settle this planet by leaving the station on one of the hyperspace pods?" To Reath, the pods looked like an automated relay, but he wanted the Drengir to confirm that.

What he said interested them, he could tell—but they still didn't acknowledge him. One of them said, "Others of our kind remain on the station. It has seen them."

The Drengir leader hissed, which seemed to be their version of a thoughtful sound. "Then they were not killed. Only dormant. If they are dormant, they can be freed."

"Can we do it without falling dormant ourselves?" asked another Drengir. "Why should we risk ourselves for the weak?"

In response, the Drengir leader lashed out with his thorn whip, forcing the speaker to crouch submissively. "We do not risk ourselves for the weak. We risk ourselves to learn if we can again use the pods. If so, we can resume our hunt. At last we will find fresh meat."

"Okay, so, that's just one mention of 'meat' too many, and we're going to go now," Reath said, nudging the tottering Dez more strongly toward the first pod.

"We will be able to hunt!" A Drengir pointed a moldy green finger at Dez. "This one has told us that nothing holds us back any longer."

*When did Dez start giving Drengir pep talks?* But by then Reath understood that Dez wasn't himself and hadn't been since almost the moment of his transport. He'd obviously sustained a serious head injury, but that had been only the start of his problems. The Force alone knew what Dez might've been drugged with or interrogated about.

He faced the Drengir evenly as he kept edging Dez farther and farther back. They'd almost reached the launch mechanism.

"Once the Amaxines were our enemies," said the Drengir leader to those who surrounded him. His followers all rustled in apparent agreement. "They built this structure to better fight us. Then we found it, and used it to fight them. They abandoned the station, left it to us. Our victory!"

The Drengir all shouted with the memory of that glory. Based on what Reath had studied about the Amaxines, any victory against them would've been hard-won. All he cared about was that the howling celebration had given him the moment of distraction he needed to elbow Dez through the pod door. Dez stumbled and landed on his hands and knees; Reath winced, but told himself that at least that would be the last of Dez Rydan's suffering.

One of the Drengir motioned toward them. "Let them go to the station. We will follow."

"Follow . . ." Reath's voice trailed off. There were two transit pods in the launcher, and he'd worked them around to one while not noticing Drengir already boarding the other.

Summoning his courage, he said, "Fine. Follow us. We have friends aboard the station."

They acknowledged him again—but with braying, rustling laughter that sent shivers along Reath's spine. "This station will be ours, and our conquest of the galaxy can resume."

Reath imagined the thick greenery throughout the Amaxine station. Drengir could've been—*must've* been in stasis the entire time, hidden in plain sight. The darkness surrounding them hadn't been the shadow of something long dead, but of something that could awaken again.

"Gotta go," Reath said. "Thanks for the stimulating conversation."

The Drengir's laughter filled his ears until he, too, was in the transport pod. Extinguishing the lightsabers, Reath dropped them, pulled the hatch door shut, and hit the one control on the panel. Immediately the workings began their strange whine-hum.

"Where are we?" Dez managed to say. He remained on his hands and knees. "I don't understand where we are."

Reath helped Dez into the one seat, crouching by him to keep him steady. "It doesn't matter, because we're not staying," he said gently. "We're going home."

*And the Drengir will be right behind us.*

Hague's blaster fired.

As though in slow motion, Cohmac saw Orla's raised hand and felt her pushing back through the Force.

The energy bolt crackled in the air—not frozen in place but moving forward slowly enough that the Jedi were able to easily step around it. As soon as it was behind them, Orla let it go. It crashed into the wall with a spray of sparks that briefly illuminated Hague's astonished face.

"Why do you attack us?" Cohmac demanded. "We have done you no harm."

Orla added, "We *helped* you."

"Yes, you did. But you did that as much for yourselves as for me, didn't you?" Hague retained some remnant of the avuncular warmth he'd shown when they all first met after the *Legacy Run* disaster, but the blaster he held told the true story. "It suited your vanity to be the great and wise, saving the poor and helpless. But the Nihil are poor no longer, and we have *never* been helpless."

And there it was—Hague's anger, no longer masked. In him it was not a sudden flame of temper but a deeply banked, volcanic heat that roiled on and on. Nor was his anger purely for himself; this was something he bore for his people. Cohmac wondered who the Nihil were—where they must have come from—to carry such wrath as their birthright.

He said only, "None of that answers the question. Why do you attack us?"

"We were the only ones stranded here—but misfortune fell on our entire Cloud."

Hague spoke as though they should know what "Cloud" referred to. *Probably a subset of the Nihil,* Cohmac reasoned.

Meanwhile, Hague continued, "What should have been a moment of supreme triumph is instead indignity. When we are asked for our trawl, we will have almost nothing to offer, and they might cast us out." A gleam came into his eyes. "But if we offer them the lives of the Jedi—and the secrets of this space station—those will make up for everything. Now that the rest of our Cloud is here, we can finally act."

Hague lifted his blaster and fired—not at the Jedi but at the shield doors behind them. They slid shut with a heavy bang, sealing them in. Cohmac and Orla exchanged glances that revealed they'd each looked for an exit and found none.

"Your sorcery cannot save you," Hague said. But he appeared somewhat shaken.

"We don't need sorcery," Orla shot back. She always did let herself be baited a little too quickly. "We have lightsabers."

Hague no longer wanted to engage with them; Cohmac could not tell whether the man was intimidated or merely moving on. Hague's head turned as he spoke into a small comlink pinned to the lapel of his jacket: "Intruders aboard the station are confirmed. Two Jedi. Possibly others, as movement in the transport areas of the station has also been detected."

*Transport areas?* Cohmac filed that away for later reference—assuming there was a later.

From Hague's comlink came a harsh voice: *"Send a team to investigate the transport areas and clear them. Hold the Jedi. Another team will join for the extermination."*

⁂

Affie didn't want to leave her mission unfinished. But the Jedi were already in trouble. That meant Leox and Geode might be, too. While she hadn't been able to identify every strange sound ricocheting through the station in the past few hours, the last loud bangs had definitely been blaster fire striking metal. She wanted her friends to leave the station alive, which meant putting her mission aside for a while.

At least they'd rearmed themselves, as Leox had suggested. She put one hand on the lone thermal detonator in her bag, just to reassure herself it was there. It would be better not to fight at all, but if the Nihil had started a fight, Affie wanted to know she could end it.

A barely audible thump seemed to be coming from the airlock ring. Affie hesitated—get to the fight or head to the airlock, where apparently the *Vessel* had just docked? They'd have better odds in a fight if Leox and Geode were with them. The airlock ring it was.

Bag scraping along the wall behind her, Affie made her way around the corner, into a corridor that opened up into the main arboretum. So far as she could see, nothing had changed; the idols were back more or less where they'd been before and the 8-Ts were gardening as usual. But some of the greenery down there—trees and logs and such—had it *moved*? Since when did plants wander?

Affie gave herself permission to keep going and ask questions later.

She continued down the long spiral walkway into the path that traced the circumference of the airlock ring, where, apparently, the *Vessel* had *not* docked. Instead, several dark-clad figures were emerging from what had to be a massive ship. As Affie's eyes adjusted, she could make out the blue streaks painted into their hair and across the ghoulish breath-masks they wore.

Those masks were all too familiar.

"The Nihil," she whispered. Their huge warship had docked with the station after all. They were invading the station en masse. What chance did she and her friends have?

None . . . unless she stopped the war party from boarding.

Affie didn't see the Jedi below her. For their sakes, she hoped they weren't too close by. No time to check. She took the thermal detonator from her bag. Its heft felt strange in her hand, unfamiliar and frightening; Affie knew how dangerous a weapon it was. She'd never actually used one before.

But she'd brought it to save her friends, and that's what she intended to do. Affie set its timer to ten seconds and then hurled it straight toward the airlock connected with the Nihil ship.

Dropping to the walkway floor, she had just enough time to cover her head before the explosion.

*BOOM!* The shock wave hit her, a physical impact that knocked her onto her side. Even though her arms had been over her ears, she was momentarily deafened to anything but a high-pitched static sound. Blinking, Affie stared up at air thick with swirling dust and small scorched pieces of what might have been fabric, armor, or skin.

Nausea gripped her. Affie'd had to defend herself and her ship before, but actually killing multiple people—even if they were Nihil—

Then she felt, rather than heard, feet marching up the metal steps of the walkway.

Someone had survived the blast, and that someone was coming directly toward her.

* * *

*Me and my big mouth,* Orla thought, not for the first time, when she realized the Nihil freighter was docking with the station only fifty meters down that arc of the airlock corridor, past the nearest arch. *I bragged about our having lightsabers, and what happens? More enemies than the three of us could ever cut down.*

Probably this was the Force teaching her about humility. Orla *hated* humility.

Her consternation lasted only as long as it took her to turn toward their oncoming attackers, because at that moment, something detonated with a mighty roar. The flash-bang of the explosion sent Hague staggering backward, and even the Jedi rocked on their feet. At least some of the Nihil fell, but through the roiling black smoke just beyond the arch, other warriors continued rushing toward them, ignoring their fallen comrades.

Had a Nihil weapon gone off accidentally? Was this ancient station finally starting to break down after all the mayhem of the past several days?

*Doesn't matter,* Orla figured. *You caught a break. Use it.*

She launched herself toward Hague, who had righted himself—but only just. Orla landed almost at his feet, as if she were kneeling before him. Maybe he thought she was about to surrender. Instead she ignited her double-bladed saber— blades parallel, handle still locked—and slashed upward to slice his blaster rifle into three parts. Plasma sparks sprayed around them as Orla snapped her saber handle open so the two blades shone from either end.

Hague winced, but his anger was greater than his cau- tion. With the smoldering piece of the blaster rifle still in his hands, he swung down at Orla's head. She managed to dodge, then leapt backward several meters to get a better look at the unfolding conflict.

Cohmac faced the archway, blocking fire with his light- saber at such speed that Orla could hardly make out the blade; he seemed to be holding a swirling shield of brilliant color. Because of that, the Nihil couldn't advance past the archway to infiltrate the station at large.

That wasn't a victory. Only a stalemate. Even if Orla joined him, two Jedi could only hold that many armed warriors at bay for so long.

She looked around and saw, embedded within the various arches of the outer ring, what looked like emergency doors, probably put there in case of atmospheric breach. Their structure appeared compromised by both the explosion and time; the centuries-old frame was showing strain and even fine patterns of small holes. They wouldn't keep anything airtight any longer. But that didn't mean the doors couldn't be put to use.

She'd need the manual controls, which she spotted near the ceiling. A small service ladder provided a way for Orla to get up there without spending the energy to jump directly; from the looks of things, she needed to reserve her strength. The ladder was close enough to one of the controls for her to reach. Unfortunately, it was also high enough to make her a perfect target for the blasters of the Nihil. Reigniting her saber, she spun its two white blades to create a kind of shield, like a shimmering circle, that deflected the blaster fire. To judge by the yelps and curses she heard, the fire was ricocheting straight back at the Nihil. With her free hand, she reached for the controls—they were just past the tips of her fingers—but it took only the slightest tug with the Force to pull them free.

The walls began to shudder. She cried, "Look out below!"

With a mighty crash, the long-dormant emergency doors shot out and slammed shut. They created a three-meter-tall wall that nearly blocked the entire length and width of the ring; a few holes betrayed time and damage, but they weren't easily breached. The barrier was hardly impregnable, since the Nihil could go around the long way, but it would slow them down. Maybe it would also make them think twice before escalating the conflict.

Sliding down the ladder got Orla back to the floor before the dust had settled. Cohmac stood there panting, only just beginning to lower his lightsaber, and gave her the shadow of a smile. "You always were excellent at improvisation."

"It's my specialty." Orla put one hand on his shoulder. "Are you all right?"

Cohmac held up a hand as he coughed. "Fine. I inhaled a few particulates. Nothing a kolto rinse can't fix."

Next they needed to come up with a plan to not only keep the Nihil out of the station at large but also drive them away completely. Or so Orla thought, before she heard the scream. "Who's that?" she said. "Not one of the Nihil—"

"It's Affie," Cohmac said, his face falling. "She's in trouble."

Orla finished for him. "And I just trapped her on the other side."

The electric-blue swirl of hyperspace visible through the transport pod windows might've been comforting if Reath hadn't known the Drengir were seeing it, too.

*At least there's no debris on this path,* he told himself. It wasn't much of a bright side.

Dez slumped on his shoulder, weak but conscious—more or less. He murmured, "Are they gone?"

"The Drengir? They're gone for now." Reath checked Dez's eyes, saw that they were bloodshot and his pupils slightly dilated. His condition hadn't improved, but at least it hadn't gotten worse, either. "They might catch up to us at the station, but we'll have the others there to help us. Master Cohmac will be there, remember? Orla Jareni, too. Plus the crew of the *Vessel*—remember them? Leox and Affie and the rock guy?"

With a shake of his head, Dez seemed to wake himself up a little more. "We'll have help."

"Right. Exactly." Probably this wasn't a good time to mention that Hague and Nan had turned out to be Nihil. It was definitely *not* the time to get deeper into Master Jora's death. It was possible Dez didn't even remember that she was gone; if so, Reath envied him. Anyway, they already had enough to deal with, especially given that the Drengir were absolutely, positively going to catch up to them at the station.

*Homicidal warrior plants,* he thought. *Never read a single thing about those. Just one more thing I need to write up for the Archives.*

With a subtle shimmy, the transport pod slipped out of hyperspace. Pressing his face to the hatch, Reath caught a glimpse of the station ahead, which they were approaching at high speed. Were the return mechanisms working as well as the launchers had been?

"Well," he murmured to himself, "we're about to find out."

Once again, a tractor beam took hold of the pod. Reath exhaled in relief as they slowed; at least they had a chance of landing alive. Then, through the skinny windows of the hatch, he glimpsed something alongside the station's equatorial ring—was it a ship? If so, it was a whole lot larger than the *Vessel*. But then the angle shifted, the station dropped out of view, and he wasn't certain he'd seen anything at all.

Darkness swallowed them as the pod entered the launch tube. In only seconds, it came to a stop. Immediately Reath shoved the hatch open.

"C'mon," he said, tugging Dez's arm around his shoulders so he could tow him back to safety. "Let's go. One foot in front of the other." It wasn't clear whether Dez understood any of that, but he stumbled along.

They made their way into the tunnels of the lower ring. In the darkness, their labyrinthine twisting had never been more confusing. Reath had just determined the way out when he heard what he recognized as a transport pod docking. The Drengir had arrived.

He did his best to hurry, but that was a mistake; Dez got tangled up in his own steps and tumbled to the floor. Reath leaned over him, grabbing Dez's robes in his hands. "You've got to get up—you've got to—"

Dez stared up at him slackly. He was in no shape to climb up through the treacherous tunnel that led to the main part of the station, even if the 8-Ts didn't attack—and there was no guarantee of that. Although Reath had the strength and the ability in the Force to bring Dez up with him, he wouldn't be able to do so quickly enough to escape the pursuing Drengir.

He refused to leave Dez—even though that meant they were trapped.

# TWENTY-TWO

**M**ove, move, move! Affie pushed herself onto her feet, desperate to run away. In what direction, she couldn't tell; the world had turned to smoke and ash, almost devoid of light. But she had to get out of there before the Nihil found her.

She braced herself against the walkway rail, trying to catch her breath—then gasped as a gloved hand grabbed her hair.

"It has to be her!" One of the Nihil dragged her close to him. His many-tubed breathmask had the greasy sheen of an oil slick. Through the visor Affie met his narrowed eyes. "She threw the explosive—she may have more!"

He was rabid with fury, which was probably why he didn't think to check her for a blaster right away. His hand shifted to the place at her holster the moment after she'd drawn. Affie shoved the muzzle into his gut, hard, hoping it would hurt.

"Let me go," she said. Her voice was scratchy from all the cinders in the air. "Now."

Instead he hurled her sideways, violently. Affie hit the railing hard, lost her balance, and tipped over.

She screamed as she fell, certain she'd plummet onto metal and dash her brains out. Instead, she landed on some other Nihil, sending all of them sprawling. The landing still hurt, but Affie ignored her injuries as she tried to escape from the tangle of arms and legs and weapons below her. But the Nihil were recovering even faster than she was, and when one of them seized her forearm she realized she'd lost her grip on her blaster in the fall. She was surrounded by helmeted figures, all of them angry, all of them armed, and there wasn't a single thing she could do about it.

At that moment, through the sooty smoke came a swirling circle of brilliant white light shining in the darkness. Panels of heavy metal slammed across the tunnel with a thud, and then three rays of light shone out—one blue, two white.

*Lightsabers,* Affie realized. She just hoped the Nihil recognized them, too.

They must have, because her attackers instantly released her and stormed toward the Jedi. Affie ducked down to avoid getting clobbered by their weapons, but once she was down, she realized how hard it was to catch her breath. The smoke was getting to her.

Her comlink buzzed. "*Affie?*" She'd almost never been gladder to hear Leox's voice. "*We just picked up some serious shock waves—*"

"I threw the thermal detonator at the Nihil," she said. She was crawling across the floor, down low where the air was cooler and marginally clearer. Inhaling had gotten a lot easier.

"*An understandable impulse, even if I might express some quibbles with its strategic value. Can you get back to the ship?*"

"I don't think so. Besides, I'm not done yet." Affie felt her bag; while a few devices had rolled free during her tumble from the walkway, she still had the majority of what she needed to take the records she sought.

"*The hell you aren't.*" It was so weird hearing Leox sound stern. "*The Nihil change our whole strategy, in that our only strategy is now 'Get the heck outta here.' We need you on board.*"

They didn't need her. Leox was just worried because the situation had become more dangerous. Maybe Affie should've been concerned, as well, especially since the Jedi and the Nihil were battling furiously only meters away, the frenzy of it not entirely obscured by smoke.

But her parents would've been frightened, too. Frightened for their own lives, frightened about what would become of their little girl. Scover had taken their choices away. Affie intended to make sure everybody had a choice from that moment on.

"Hold down the ship," she said. "I'll be back soon." And she shut off her comlink before Leox could say one more word.

⚜

Reath couldn't center himself. If he could, maybe he'd be able to levitate Dez, ease him out of the tunnels into the station at large, and get him to the rest of the Jedi. Maybe he'd be able to levitate his own body, save them both. But he was too scattered to do it, the adrenaline in his blood at war with his better instincts.

"When you cannot achieve balance within yourself," Master Jora had said, "simply lean toward the light and do your best. There's no point in reacting to a lack of calm in a way that makes you even less calm."

"Okay," Reath muttered as he balanced Dez against him, Dez's arm around his shoulders. "For light and life. Here we go."

"What did you say?" Dez looked over at him groggily.

"Keep walking forward, all right? We'll try climbing up through the roots in a few minutes. Maybe you can hang on to my neck." Reath managed a smile. He wanted to reassure Dez, though there was very little that was reassuring about their current situation. But when he thought about what Dez must've endured over the past several days—delirious, in pain, surrounded by creatures who tortured him for information he wasn't even in a state to give them—it was impossible not to want to give some comfort.

All thoughts of comfort fled when Reath heard the tell-tale thuds of the Drengir pod settling into its base.

*In just a minute, they'll be loose. Coming after us.*

*So I won't give them a minute.*

"Stay here," Reath said unnecessarily, allowing Dez to slump onto the floor. Then he ran toward the Drengir pod.

The Force led him to their hatch, which they would open at any second; already he could see green frond-like hands grappling with the handle. Reath held out his hand and mentally pushed the Drengir away from the door. They went toppling backward. That was the easy part.

He closed his eyes and reached out again with his feelings. This time he wrapped his mind not around the Drengir but around the pod itself. Its shape became real to him, tactile, almost as if he were holding it in his palm.

Finally he pushed the entire pod backward down the launch tunnel. It felt as though he were physically shoving pure heavy metal backward, straining every muscle in his body—but he managed to move it a couple of meters. That would be enough, if his plan worked at all.

Despite the thick hatch door, Reath could hear the Drengir emerging from their pod, simply crawling out into the tunnel. They were heading for the hatch, coming to confront him—

Brilliant white light flashed in the tunnel, and howls of

pain echoed for just one instant. Then the tunnel fell dark; all was silent.

Lightsaber in one hand, Reath used the other to swing the hatch door open. Instantly he was greeted by the scent of charred plants—slightly pleasant, actually, like woodsmoke or fragrant herbs.

By the glow of the saber, he could see limp, blackened leafy scraps on the bottom of the tunnel, smoldering just over the helix rings. Their energy had destroyed the Drengir in a split second. There was a sense of rightness in knowing that the rings had spared Dez, instead killing the ones who had tortured him.

*There is no rightness in slaying an enemy,* Master Jora scolded within Reath's mind. *Killing is never true victory. At best it is the knowledge that you have done what you must.*

"I've done what I must, master," he whispered. It seemed possible that perhaps, in the cosmic Force, she could hear.

⚹

"Affie?" Orla cried out. She couldn't see the girl in all that mess; she could barely see her own lightsaber in front of her face. Deep within she sensed that the girl remained alive, but she couldn't yet spare the mental energy to search any farther.

Not until she'd driven back the Nihil.

Orla faced off against two Nihil warriors, one for each of her blades. They bore energized polearms that could parry a lightsaber's thrust—but it cost them, every time. They slashed at her, their attack savage but uncoordinated. She let the Force flow through her, sensing all their moves the instant before they were made, her saber moving almost of its own accord to block each one. They were shifted back with each strike, not far, maybe not even enough for them to notice, but enough for Orla to know she was the master of the situation.

Next to her, Cohmac was extinguishing his lightsaber. Before Orla could even consciously wonder why, Cohmac reached out with the Force toward a metal beam lying on the floor, dragging it toward the Nihil. It never entirely rose into the air, but he didn't need it to; as it was, the beam swept under the Nihil, knocking them off their feet and sending blaster bolts flying in random directions.

But one of those directions might be the place where Affie Hollow was trying to hide. . . .

Almost as one, the Nihil turned and ran away from the Jedi, back toward the airlock ring. The movement was too coordinated to be a simple flight or surrender; it was a strategic retreat. The Nihil would regroup and attack again, stronger than before. All the more reason to wrap up their business on this Force-forsaken station and leave.

Cohmac gestured after the Nihil. "They will return with more firepower."

"Undoubtedly," Orla said. "Do you see Affie?"

"No. The girl has moved deeper into the station." Cohmac gazed into the middle distance. "We must find her, and Reath, and remove them as soon as possible."

Orla nodded. "We know Reath's in the tunnels. Cohmac, why don't you head down there while I search for Affie?" He ran toward the nearest access point for the lower rings, which would have to serve as a yes.

Already Orla sensed that Affie was missing on purpose. She was trying to do something she thought the Jedi shouldn't know about. Orla didn't know what it was and didn't care. She just had to get Affie and get out before the Nihil attacked again.

※※

Dez swayed on his feet, leaning against Reath as they walked through a jungle.

*It's the arboretum of the Amaxine station,* he told himself. The farther away from the Drengir he went, the more Dez could remember. But he could still feel the toxins in his blood, making his body and thoughts sluggish, and everything remained dreamlike and surreal.

In the center of the arboretum, he could dimly make out shapes that he recognized as the Drengir. *They're here, too. They're everywhere. I can't get away.*

Before panic seized him, however, Reath murmured, "It's all right. We brought the idols back to imprison the dark side again. They must have trapped the Drengir, because look— they can't get away."

Dez realized the Drengir weren't moving. Once again the four idols stood sentry, watching over them all. That helped the fear, though the burning strangeness in his blood continued muddying his mind.

"Do you think that would stop the Drengir from ever using this station again?" Reath said. "The power of the idols? Because we can't let them take possession of this place. It's too dangerous."

Dez managed to say, "Am I supposed to actually come up with an answer? Or are you just trying to get me to talk?"

"The second one. You're doing better!" Reath grinned.

Dez might've smiled back, except that then he saw a figure approaching them from the darkness. Fear spiked within him, crushing and complete—until his blurry vision cleared enough for him to make out the person's face. "Master Cohmac?"

Cohmac hurried toward them, eyes wide with wonder. "How is this possible?"

"The lower rings are a transport area," Reath said. That made sense, Dez thought. They'd been in hyperspace. Hadn't they? His head still hurt. "They're outfitted with automated hyperspace pods. Dez wasn't killed; he was sent from here to the home planet of these evil plant guys called—"

"The Drengir," Cohmac finished. "We've made their acquaintance. By the Force, Dez, what did they do to you?"

*How bad do I look?* Dez thought. *Probably I don't want to know.*

"They were interrogating him," Reath said quietly. "They drugged him with something, sent him out of his mind for a while. But I don't think he's critically injured. We just have to get him off this station."

"Easier said than done. The Nihil have boarded. They may suspect the transport capacities of this station."

"Oh, no." Reath's eyes widened. "Right now the controls are programmed for the Drengir homeworld—at least, I guess it's their homeworld. Maybe it's just a planet some of them live on—never mind. Those controls could be reprogrammed to direct the transit pods anywhere. To Republic shipyards, to frontier planets, even to Coruscant itself."

"They are only pods—" Cohmac began.

Reath said, "It only takes one or two agents to take down a security shield, or provide reports on defense capabilities. I'd bet anything this is how the Amaxines got intel on their targets before they struck."

"Or carried explosive devices to detonate only after they were gone. All the more reason to stop the Nihil," Cohmac said. "Let's get Dez to the *Vessel*, if we can. And take it from there."

The words were getting away from Dez. He couldn't focus for more than a few moments at a time, on more than one or two things at once. He was with his friends again; he was in danger. That much he understood. The rest would be up to his fellow Jedi.

Aboard the *Vessel*, Geode was the lone element of calm as Leox paced around the bridge.

"There's about eighty other ways we can stop Scover Byne

from sending indentures to this station," Leox said. His beads swayed across the bared expanse of his chest as he walked. "But no. Little Bit's gotta perform cryptanalysis—and yeah, I know, she's outgrown that nickname, it no longer describes her myriad complexities as an individual, so spare me, all right?"

Geode spared him, which was about the only break Leox figured he'd get all day.

"We now have only a very roundabout pathway from the center of the station to the ship, and I suspect Affie is unaware of this important fact." Leox breathed out in frustration. By then the Nihil knew another ship had docked, but they either hadn't found the *Vessel* yet or were distracted by other concerns. For the moment—for a very brief moment—this ship remained the one safe place around, and it was the one place Affie couldn't get to. "She's not going to be able to come back to us. Which means we're gonna have to be the ones who get to her."

Leox Gyasi was not a warlike man, but he was one who believed in the power of preparation. He went to the painted, carved trunk he kept on one side of the bridge, opened it up, and dug around beneath the shirts and incense for a second before he pulled out a blaster. It had been a long while since he'd shot anyone, but he remembered how it was done. If anyone got between Affie and safety, pulling that trigger wouldn't be hard.

He turned to face Geode, who looked on in solemn silence.

"Guard the ship," Leox said. "Stay at the controls. And don't even think about coming after us unless the situation gets a hell of a lot worse. Not sure exactly how that would even be possible—but fate has a way of showing us how, doesn't it?"

Which was when the readings on the console began to spike in ominous ways. Solar flares—coming in hard, and soon—extreme enough that they might cause damage even to ships hidden behind the station. Which would mean penetrating the *Vessel*, and everyone within it, and vaporizing them instantly.

And there wasn't a damned thing Leox could do about it.

He refused to worry about things he couldn't change. Time to concentrate on what he could.

With a final nod of farewell, Leox headed for the airlock, toward Affie.

Reath, Dez, and Master Cohmac reached what had once been the closest entrance to the airlock ring and was now a mass of twisted metal. An abandoned Nihil weapon lay on the floor; it took Reath a moment to realize the Nihil lay there, too, half-hidden and crushed by the fallen beams. The man's helmet had been ripped off in the collapse, revealing a human face that was utterly ordinary except in its slack paleness.

"Who *are* they?" Reath whispered. "Why do they want us all dead?"

"According to the limited information we have so far,

the Nihil are generally more interested in capturing wealth than in slaughter." Master Cohmac readjusted Dez against his shoulder, all the while looking around them and analyzing the scenario. "However, they won't hesitate to kill when it serves their purposes, as it very often does. If they want to claim this station as their own, use it the way the Amaxines did, as an advance scouting point for their attacks—"

"Then killing us serves their purposes," Reath finished. The way to the ship was all but blocked by the wreckage of what appeared to be some kind of blast doors or emergency airlock. "We'll have to find our way through this mess."

No sooner had he finished speaking than someone hoisted himself through an opening in the wreckage and landed on their side. Leox Gyasi had removed his beads and carried a blaster, which Reath found unexpectedly jarring. Apparently he'd overheard them, because Leox grinned and said, "*That's the way through this mess. You're welcome.*" Then he brightened. "*Dez!* Good to see you, my friend! Looks like you've got a story to tell."

Though Dez was patently in no shape to tell his story or any other, he managed a crooked smile.

Master Cohmac was less amused. "Captain Gyasi, your courage is commendable, but your prudence is lacking. You are safest aboard the ship—"

"For one, while Affie's in danger on this station, my own safety doesn't mean a damn thing," Leox said. "For two, we've got more solar flares coming in any second now, intense ones, so I'm not sure any of us is particularly safe anywhere in this system."

Reath thought fast. "The station's shields. Can we strengthen them? Then we could expand them to protect the ships."

"Perhaps," Master Cohmac said. "But finding the controls, much less interpreting them—"

"They'll be in the lower levels," Reath interjected. Had he really just interrupted a *Jedi Master*? But this was too important, and they had little time. "I've learned my way around down there, and I think the controls are starting to make sense to me. Maybe I can boost the shields."

Leox nodded. "Sounds like a plan, kid. Good luck down there." With that he jogged off in search of Affie Hollow.

Master Cohmac wasn't as easily convinced. "I should be the one to—"

"Please, master. I'm the one who has experience with Amaxine tech." Reath's experience primarily consisted of being shot into hyperspace against his will, but it was still more than anyone else in their party possessed. "This task should be mine. Besides, Dez needs you right now."

His plea might not have worked, if it weren't for Dez's knees buckling at that very moment. Master Cohmac caught him, then shook his head. "Very well, Reath. May the Force be with you."

Reath smiled, turned, and dashed back toward the central arboretum, and the passage that would lead him down to the lower rings.

With the 8-Ts no doubt distracted by all the other mayhem aboard the Amaxine station, reaching the lower levels was easier than it had been. At this point, Reath was grateful for any break they got. Once he reached the main controls, he was able to bring up the station schematics fairly easily—and from there, it was merely a matter of touching the screen. The low hum of power surged through the station, including the shields.

Reath *hoped* it included the shields, anyway. They'd find out one way or another. With any luck, it wouldn't be the way that involved being burnt to a crisp by solar flares.

He'd done all he could do, and all that was left was to get back to the ship as fast as possible.

As he hurried back along what remained of the corridor, the scent of smoke thick in the air, he caught sight of more Nihil corpses, more abandoned Nihil weapons. A lightsaber was by far the best weapon to have in battle, but it struck Reath that a blaster could come in handy. One lay far enough away from any of the Nihil bodies for him not to feel like a grave robber, so he knelt to retrieve it. Just before his hand closed over the grip, someone said, "Don't move."

Reath froze—except for his eyes, which looked up to see Nan standing there, her blaster aimed directly at him.

# TWENTY-THREE

The strangest part was that Nan looked so very much the same. Despite the fact that she wore a coverall instead of her colorful patchwork dress, that her bared arms turned out to be thick with tattoos, and that the blue streaks in her hair were matched by lines painted down her face, no great transformation had taken place. Her behavior before hadn't been a disguise, Reath decided, just another facet of her personality. She was both Nihil warrior and lonely young girl.

Which side of her would win out?

The only reason Reath didn't assume it would be the

Nihil warrior was the simple fact that she'd gotten the jump on him, yet he remained alive.

No point in bothering with preliminaries. "Everything you told me was true, wasn't it?" he asked. "The wreck, your parents, all of it. You just left out the part about being rescued by the Nihil."

"Close, but not quite," Nan said. Her face was blank, unreadable. Her grip on her blaster remained steady. "Our family joined the Nihil together. They offered us the chance for a better life than we could ever have had otherwise. My mother and father were proud of their choice. *I'm* proud of their choice. When they died in a raid, I was taken in by Hague. By then I knew I'd always be small—that I'd have to learn how to fight smarter, since I'd never be stronger. That I'd need strategic skills. Who better to teach that than a man who can no longer fight with his body and has to use his brain?"

The sureness in her voice—the clarity of absolute conviction—unnerved Reath. He was used to hearing Padawans speak that way, or Coruscant Patrol starfighter cadets. It hadn't occurred to him that anyone could still believe in violence as a creed, at least not by taking such pride in it. While he'd known such mindsets weren't just artifacts from history, this was his first encounter with one. He longed to talk about this with her in depth, to understand the Nihil on their own brutal terms.

Getting into a philosophical discussion with a zealot was

probably a mistake, though, especially when the zealot was holding a weapon on you.

"Makes sense." Reath adjusted his stance slightly, as though moving his weight from one leg to another, hoping she wouldn't realize he was triangulating their positions versus the nearest exit. "I can tell you're a great strategist already. You got enough information out of me."

The self-deprecating joke was meant to get Nan off her guard. It didn't work. "I can't claim any credit for that. You were overflowing with explanations, because that was your job, right? To tell the desperate frontier folk how glorious their lives will be now that the Jedi have come?"

"I don't remember promising anyone glory," he pointed out.

Nan shrugged, like, *Fair enough.* "You can stop looking for your escape route. I don't intend to kill you."

"Your blaster aim suggests otherwise."

"You could deflect any shots," she said, nodding toward the lightsaber he still hadn't drawn from his belt. "Hand to hand versus a Jedi? Useless. That's one more thing you taught me. When I kill a Jedi, it'll be with my ship."

Reath considered this. "You could've killed me when my back was turned. You didn't."

"No. I haven't forgotten that you saved me from being kidnapped. You returned me to my fleet. That earns you one chance to walk away." Nan's finger massaged the trigger of her blaster. "*One.*"

*Thanks,* Reath nearly replied, before deciding he really

shouldn't have to thank anyone for not blowing him to pieces. "Did you enjoy it? Pretending to be helpless?"

"It's loathsome. I don't intend to make a habit of it."

"I can respect that."

"You *will* respect us," Nan said. "In time, you will bow before the Nihil."

* * *

"And here I thought this station was as screwed up as it could possibly be before we even docked," Leox muttered to himself as he stepped over smoldering wreckage from the explosion. Affie had done a number on the place, that was for sure.

The main thing was to make sure the Nihil didn't do a number on her.

Sounds echoed from farther down the corridor— footsteps, something else. Leox figured that was the Nihil; the Jedi moved as quiet as tooka cats. Quickly he ducked behind the nearest large piece of debris—a couple of beams that formed a nice solid barrier between him and any marauding warriors. *Always good to put something between yourself and negative energy,* he thought. *Especially* armed *negative energy.*

Despite his lackadaisical habits and disheveled appearance, Leox Gyasi had a sharp mind when he cared to employ it. With near-eidetic precision, he called to mind the layout of the station as they'd previously mapped it, then overlaid Affie's plan for scouting the code. From there it was relatively simple to figure out how far along in the upper rings she would've gone before the Jedi found themselves in trouble, and therefore where she would've headed back to after the explosion's aftermath.

This, naturally, would require Leox to somehow get past both the Nihil and the idol-controlled area that contained the Drengir.

But he wouldn't have had it any other way. How was he supposed to give Affie a proper guilt trip later if it wasn't difficult as hell to get her out?

Grinning, Leox waited for his opening, then darted into the station's inner darkness.

A voice rang through the station. "Nihil, you are summoned!"

Reath turned, startled; Nan bit her lower lip, then said, "If you want to walk away from this alive, I suggest you do so now. The others are coming. I owe you something, but they don't."

*The Nihil wouldn't consider themselves bound by a kindness to one of their own,* he thought, filing that away for future reference. "Got it."

He dashed for the nearest doorway, not bothering to glance behind him. If Nan hadn't shot him in the face, she wouldn't shoot him in the back.

As soon as Reath had made it to safe cover, however, he ducked and angled himself to see inside the central globe chamber as best he could. Nan stood exactly where he'd left her, but she wasn't looking after him. Her attention was all for the other Nihil.

They didn't wear uniforms, exactly, though there was a sameness to their garb: dark, padded, covered in strips or panels of safety material that would be impervious to water, maybe to fire, as well. Their telltale helmets and breathmasks hung around their necks or from utility belts, which suggested a gas attack wasn't imminent. As far as Reath could read their expressions, they seemed neither exultant nor discouraged. That suggested his fellow Jedi remained alive . . . but the Nihil still felt they could accomplish their goals.

"Cloud," said this Nihil group's leader, a Trandoshan male, "we have a way to prove ourselves to the Tempest Runner."

Grins and a few cheers answered this. *They seem to use weather imagery, storm imagery,* Reath reasoned.

"This station gives us the power to reach any place in the galaxy within moments," said the leader. "Only our people, not our ships—but our people can make the way ready for the attacks to come. Take down shields, create distractions, send homing beacons . . . anything and *everything* we need to become the dominant power in this part of the galaxy."

"No!" shouted someone in the back. "In the entire galaxy!"

This won more cheers, and the leader smiled. "We thought we would not be able to make up for failure to enter the action. But when we reveal this station—and reveal that by taking it, we have humiliated the *Jedi*?—we'll be in his favor. The best raids, the best position within the Tempest . . . all of it will be ours."

*The Drengir believe they can use this station to wreak havoc across the galaxy,* Reath thought. *The Nihil believe they can, too.*

*Which means if anybody's going to hold this station, it has to be the Republic—*

*But maybe nobody should hold it at all.*

※

Almost at the moment Cohmac would've given up all hope of finding a clear path, a glint of illumination revealed just enough space clear of debris for him to bring Dez through to the docking ring.

Dez tried to make it through on his own, but his movements were still slow, uncoordinated. Cohmac had to help him every centimeter of the way, practically dragging him at the end. What had the Drengir done to him? What toxic effects did their poisons have? Was Dez recovering—or was a slower-acting substance working its way through his system, tearing him down?

"Here we are, see?" Cohmac adjusted Dez so he could look ahead, into the entrance of the *Vessel*. "Back where we belong."

"The Drengir . . ."

"No, no," Cohmac said, hoping Dez could truly understand. "They are gone now. They can hurt you no longer."

As he hustled them toward the *Vessel*'s airlock, a large

shadow in the distance—darker than the other shadows—
caught Cohmac's eye for only an instant. In the next, he
could see nothing there. But it had looked like . . . It couldn't
have been . . .

Cohmac muttered, "Geode?"

The scent of smoke clung to Affie. It seemed to have embedded itself in her clothes, her hair, even her skin. She longed
for that incredible bathtub in Scover's fancy Coruscant hotel
room. . . .

But that was too close to longing for Scover for Affie's
approval. She couldn't think about that as she crawled back
into the guts of the Amaxine station. Her loyalty to Scover
couldn't coexist with her desire to erase the illegal practices
that apparently formed such a large part of the Byne Guild's
prosperity. Her love for her adoptive mother was at war with
her love for the biological mother she'd lost so long before.

*She'll see how much better it is to do without it,* Affie reasoned
as she crawled. *She'll be happier knowing her pilots are safe. I won't
have to turn anything in, just show my proof to her, and she'll back
down. It'll teach her a lesson in the best possible way.*

Next up on Affie's list of places to search was the station's
gravitational matrix. It was located up high—near the very
top of the sphere. Instead of crawling, it was time to climb.

When she found the access tube that led upward, her

heart sank. It was narrow and showed more signs of age than most other areas of the station; just with the beam of her glow rod, she could make out several places where panels were missing, exposing wires. There was no other illumination in the tube, meaning she'd have to make her way upward in the dark. And vines had grown through holes and slits in the walls, curling all around the tube ladder's rungs. That would make it slippery, but Affie told herself the tube was almost too narrow for her to fall. At least the 8-Ts were busy.

She began working her way upward, glow rod tied to her utility belt so the beam would point up; instead of clarifying her path, it swayed back and forth, casting eeric wobbling shadows. The vines on the ladder were even trickier to work around than she'd thought, because the slightest pressure sent sap running down the rungs and across her palms.

And by then she understood that no matter how narrow the tunnel was, she could still plummet all the way down. She'd just be more likely to break a limb along the way.

*Keep going,* she told herself, ignoring the trembling in her muscles as she pulled herself even higher up. *You have to keep going—*

"Affie!"

The echoing voice startled her so badly she nearly lost her grip. Swearing under her breath, Affie steadied herself and pointed the glow rod's beam downward. "Leox, what are you doing here?"

He'd stuck his head through the access hatch, which showed her just how dangerously high up she was. "Getting you off this station immediately."

"I'm not done."

"Doesn't matter anymore. See, the Drengir want this station. The Nihil want this station. Once they find out about it, my guess is the Republic's gonna want this station, too, and if not, they'll blow it to smithereens. Regardless, this place isn't Byne Guild territory anymore. Even if the Republic leaves it intact, there's no way Scover can keep using it. Code or no code, no other pilots are going to be forced through here, not ever."

That should've made Affie feel better, but it didn't. "That's not enough."

"Why?"

She ignored this. "I have to keep going."

"You're not trying to save the other pilots any longer," Leox said. "If that was all this is about, you'd have started down that ladder already. What you're trying to do is save Scover's soul. That's not your job, Affie. Only Scover herself can do that."

Affie leaned her head against the nearest rung of the ladder. Her hands itched; the sap irritated her skin. Leox wasn't wrong about her reasons—she could see that—but turning back still felt so wrong.

"Affie, please." The raw pleading in Leox's voice got to her.

"Your life's not worth one bit less than hers. If you ask me, it's worth a whole lot more. So will you get back down here?"

She held on for one moment longer, envisioning her long-lost parents in this same tube. If they'd had a way out, they would've taken it. They would've wanted her to be safe.

It was for them—not for Leox, not even for herself—that Affie finally began descending toward safety.

Recon around the station had only darkened Orla's take on their chances. She saw no strategic areas to take that would give them an advantage over the Nihil. It took only a few scans to confirm the enormous scale of the Nihil ship; the *Vessel* would stand no chance in a space battle against it. They literally had no option but to run away and hope they weren't seen—and with access to the *Vessel* so limited and hazardous, she wasn't even sure they'd get a chance to run. And where the heck was Affie?

*You need more time,* she told herself. *So you have to buy some, somehow.*

The best way of buying time from an enemy was usually to create a distraction, by making a mess so big that the Nihil would keep themselves busy cleaning it up while the *Vessel* got away from the Amaxine station.

*Exactly how much bigger a mess can I make? The place is already on fire.*

Then it hit Orla. *I take a mess we already cleaned up and make it messy all over again.*

If the Jedi had had so much trouble fighting the Drengir and so much trouble fighting the Nihil, Orla could hardly imagine the trouble they'd have fighting *each other.*

Sometimes bottling up the darkness only made it stronger. Sometimes you had to let it go.

# TWENTY-FOUR

**R**unning through the broad airlock ring of the Amaxine station, Reath thought, *I actually came back to this place of my own free will? I defied orders to do it? Maybe Drengir pollen warps minds.*

Once he'd finally gotten within a couple dozen meters of the *Vessel* without running into any more of the Nihil, he felt encouraged. Better yet was when he caught a flash of white moving amid the shadowy columns of metal—Orla Jareni's telltale robes.

She looked equally relieved to see him. "Thank the Force. I thought the Nihil might've caught up with you," Orla said, putting one hand on his shoulder.

"They did. Or, actually, Nan did. But she said that since I'd returned her to her fleet once, she'd give me one break. So here I am."

"At least one of them has a sense of honor, then." Orla's expression was skeptical. "But I'm not convinced that's a value of the group as a whole."

"Me either," Reath said. He remembered the way Nan's finger had remained firm against her blaster's trigger; she'd wanted to kill him badly enough that letting him go had been hard. It would be a mistake to test her "honor" again. "The Nihil want to use this station as a base of operations for raiding this entire area of space. The Republic has to either hold the Amaxine station as its own property or destroy it."

"I'd gathered as much," said Orla.

Reath tried not to feel disappointed that she'd already reached that conclusion without him. "At least we've got the Drengir taken care of."

"About that." Orla winced. "We're about to set the Drengir free again."

"Wait, what? *Why?*" But Reath instantly realized the only reason that would ever be under consideration. "Is there no other way to sneak off the station without the Nihil seeing us?"

She shook her head. "Not a chance. We have to distract them on a scale that will have every single warrior on that massive ship hurrying onto the station to fight. Otherwise, they'll blow us to pieces as soon as we're free of the airlock."

Reath couldn't suppress a shiver as he thought about facing the Drengir again. This time, at least, he wouldn't be at such a disadvantage: trapped on a world not his own, trying to protect someone injured and unable to defend himself. All they had to do was keep themselves from being killed long enough for the Drengir and the Nihil to collide with each other, at which point the Jedi would fall much farther down each enemy's list of priorities.

But keeping themselves from getting killed that long, with both groups out for their blood—it wouldn't be easy. More than that, a sense of dread was creeping in at the edges of Reath's consciousness. Danger lay ahead, in some way they hadn't yet fully recognized.

"Did you see Cohmac?" Orla said. "He went after you—"

"He found me, and Dez." The astonishment and joy on Orla's face erased Reath's worries, at least for that moment. "There's a transport area beneath the station, which is why the Nihil and Drengir are so interested in the first place. Dez was accidentally sent to the Drengir homeworld—at least, maybe it was their homeworld; there were a lot of them there—he was badly injured, out of it, and I'm positive they interrogated him harshly." What simple words for describing a nightmare. Reath pressed on. "Anyway, Cohmac took Dez back to the *Vessel*. Do you need him to help remove the Force barrier?"

"Dez needs help more right now, and we're already here. So let's see if the two of us can handle it," Orla said. She sounded more confident than he suspected she felt—certainly more confident than *he* felt. Already she was putting away her saber, preparing for the journey back to the arboretum. "Are you ready, Reath?"

It hit him, then, what she was truly asking of him: to go with her into the heart of the storm.

"Yes," he said. "Let's go."

⚜

Affie's hands continued to redden and sting as she and Leox made their way back toward the *Vessel*. "I think that sap is toxic to humans," she said.

"I think you may be right. Hopefully some sort of salve or unguent aboard the ship will set you right. Until then, let's keep moving."

Leox kept hurrying her along, like he thought she remained on the verge of turning back. That annoyed Affie, even though he wasn't entirely wrong. She wasn't going to turn back; she just kept wishing she could.

*I guess I'll have to talk to Scover about it directly,* she thought. *Make her explain exactly what she was thinking and see if—if she actually understands how wrong she's been.*

If she didn't . . . no. Affie wouldn't even imagine that. Scover would get it. She *had* to.

The two of them reached the corridor that encircled the arboretum. In the far distance, she could hear rumblings and marching feet that had to be the Nihil. She tensed as she heard footsteps much closer.

"What the—" Leox stopped, then put his hands on his hips. "Didn't expect to find any friends here."

Affie peered ahead and sighted two of the Jedi coming toward them through the shadows: Orla Jareni in her white robes, which somehow remained spotless, and a rumpled Reath Silas. Probably Affie didn't look so great herself.

Orla ignored Leox's friendly words. "You two need to get back to the *Vessel* immediately. Prepare to leave within ten minutes. If we haven't made it back by then, you're to leave without us."

"Whoa, whoa, whoa." Leox held up both hands. "What's this about? I don't intend to leave anybody behind. It's the kind of thing that reflects poorly on a commercial pilot."

That won him half a smile from Orla. "The only way to distract the Nihil long enough for us to escape the station is to release the Drengir."

"The who now?" Leox said.

"Evil sentient plants." Reath gestured toward those trees that had changed location. "That's what was held in place by the idols. But we have to set them free again, to distract the Nihil."

Affie wasn't sure how deadly a bunch of plants could be, but Reath's battered appearance gave her pause. There were other objections to the Jedi's plan. "If you set these

Drengir free, we'll have two groups trying to kill us instead of just one."

"The hope," Reath said, "is that they'll be too busy trying to kill each other."

"How do you know they won't join forces to turn against us?" she demanded. Nobody had an immediate answer for that, which confirmed Affie's worst suspicions: the Jedi were making this up as they went along.

*Look at the bright side,* she told herself. *If you die, you don't have to confront Scover.*

Orla managed to send Leox and Affie back to the ship before the girl asked any more uncomfortable questions. Maintaining focus was easier when she didn't think of all the many things that could go wrong.

Many, many things.

She and Reath headed back into the arboretum. The shadows of the petrified Drengir chilled her, but more unnerving by far was the sheer power pulsing around the room, cross-angled through the idols, a power that reverberated in her body. Even though Orla had helped put the barrier in place, the enormity of what they'd done struck her anew.

"It's not going to be like dropping a curtain, or opening a gate," Orla murmured to Reath. "It won't be a gentle impact, like before. The re-created barrier is new. More vital. When the barrier drops, the reaction will be intense."

"I sense it, too." Reath braced himself.

She nodded. "Just follow my lead."

Orla reached out with her feelings, making contact with the edge of the barrier. The tension there was almost aware—all but conscious of its duty to hold the Drengir within.

*You are needed no longer,* she sent into the swirl of energy that wasn't quite a mind. *You have done well. But you will do better, now, to let go.*

Next to her, Orla could feel Reath doing something very similar—reaching into the field in his own way, coaxing it to release. But the field was stubborn, hanging on tighter and tighter as they tugged against it.

Orla redoubled her efforts. Her arms shook as she held them out, physically straining to pull back the powers they had unleashed. It felt to her as if the barrier was not falling but expanding, coming closer and closer, until static electricity raced along her skin and stood her hair on end. Sparks zapped through the air, and for one instant she wondered if they would succeed only in paralyzing themselves, too, trapping them with the Drengir—

Then they lost it. The hold they'd had on the energy field slipped away, leaving them both breathing hard.

"We came close," Reath said. "If we try again—"

"No." Orla shook her head. "Two people aren't enough." With that she kneeled amid the debris on the station floor and took up a blaster.

Reath frowned. "What are you going to do?"

"Desecrate history," Orla said. "Sorry about that."

She aimed directly at the idol of the human queen—right between her golden eyes—and fired.

⚜

*The field is woven through the idols,* Reath was thinking. *Destroy one of the idols, and you destroy—*

A wave of energy hit Reath like a tsunami, sending him sprawling backward on the floor, sliding for more than a meter. The electric charge of it tensed every muscle in his body and made him bite down on his tongue hard enough to taste blood.

And the Drengir were free.

The Drengir stood there, shuddering, apparently struck by the same charge that had felled the Jedi. It would take them another second or two to figure out they were free again. That gave the Jedi a few moments to escape. Orla looked dazed, maybe semiconscious, as she struggled to stand. He crawled to her and tugged at her white robes. "Get up. We have to move, *now.*"

As she recovered, so did the Drengir. Frond-like hands pointed in their direction as Reath and Orla clambered to their feet, and already it was time to run.

Running over the arboretum floor was like traversing rocky terrain, covered as it was with vines, debris, and the remnants of 8-T droids destroyed in the explosion. It would've been difficult to make good time even if Reath didn't feel sea-sick and dizzy from the sheer impact of the Force barrier's collapse.

Behind them he heard the eerie rustle-thudding that had to be the sound of the Drengir running. Whatever it was, it was getting louder. And closer.

Ahead of him was the entrance to the equatorial ring—which was no longer empty, but filling with dark-clad, breathmasked, blue-striped warriors.

For the first time, and the last, Reath was relieved to see the Nihil.

One of the Nihil threw a gas missile, probably intending to hit the Jedi. But both Orla and Reath ducked it handily while sucking in deep breaths. A Jedi could last longer without breathing than the average sentient being; that gave them a chance to put distance between them and the toxic gas.

Instead, the gas detonated in the heart of the Drengir—

And they weren't fazed in the slightest.

Gas weapons only worked against beings who breathed the same gases. That didn't include plants.

The creepy rustling laughter of the Drengir grew louder as they bounded forward—passing Orla and Reath completely—in favor of attacking this new enemy. *Looks like the Drengir didn't just wake up hungry,* Reath thought as he kept running. *They woke up ready for a fight.*

For a split second, the Nihil hesitated. That second was

long enough for Reath to recognize that these were raiders, not warriors, and their courage faltered in a conflict where no profit was to be had. But all beings will fight for their lives.

The Nihil shouldered weapons and began firing. Brilliant light from blaster bolts flickered in the darkness as Orla and Reath kept running toward the *Vessel*.

*We have to get out of here,* Reath thought. *Then—do we just leave this station to the Nihil or Drengir?*

*We can't do that.*

*No matter what.*

⚜

Returning to the *Vessel* already felt like surrender. Affie's mood plunged even further when she and Leox reached the airlock ring to find their way almost completely blocked by collapsed, smoldering debris. Ash still fogged the air. She groaned. "Did I do this?"

"Pretty much." Then Leox stopped beside her and studied the wreckage more carefully. "Wait. Maybe you didn't."

The scene around them was obviously the aftermath of the explosive she'd set off, so Leox's reaction caught her off guard. "What do you mean?" she asked.

"Everything's been moved. More debris has been shifted into this area."

That made no sense. "Who would do that?" Affie said. "With all the things happening on this station, who's got time to rearrange the wreckage?"

Leox picked up one of the smaller beams and tossed it aside. In the newly cleared space, Affie was startled to see vines growing—thick and ropey, spiny like cacti. At least half a dozen vines reached along the length of the floor. "They've grown this far in the past several minutes? How is that possible?"

"We don't have a damn clue what the Drengir can do now that they've been set free." Leox folded his arms across his chest. "Looks like the vines are working their way through the entire station as they grow. Not promising."

He had a gift for understatement. Grimacing at the twisted vines, Affie said, "Let's just get to the ship before the vines do."

"We might be too late."

She thought Leox was being fatalistic until they made their way toward the airlock, vines underfoot the whole way—and then rising along the walls of the airlock itself, stems poking through every vent and crevice. Affie dashed onto the *Vessel* and sighed with relief to see the plants hadn't grown on board. That relief lasted only as long as it took her to reach the cockpit, where she saw thick vines reaching across the entire front of the ship.

Leox sat in the pilot's seat and began checking sensors. "Dammit, I told Geode to stick around."

"What could he have done about this?" Affie gestured toward the vines.

"Not a thing. I just wish he were here instead of mixing it up on the station—he never does know when to walk away from a fight." Leox slumped in his chair. "We've got 'em all over us. The Drengir have tied us tight."

Affie tried to imagine how the vines could possibly live in the cold of space. Probably they didn't have to survive for long. Dead vines could bind the *Vessel* in place nearly as strongly as living ones.

"Signal the Jedi," Leox said. "Let them know we have yet another complicating factor to deal with."

Quietly she asked, "How do we get away from here?"

Leox replied in the same tone of voice. "Blast our way out or die tryin'."

As softly as they spoke, they were still audible to Cohmac, who stood not far from the cockpit entrance. He'd meant to talk with them about Dez, to get more information on the scene inside the station, before returning to fight alongside Orla and Reath. Instead, he turned and dashed out of the ship, back into the docking ring.

*What happens between the Nihil and the Drengir at this point is no longer our most immediate concern,* he reasoned as he leapt over the snarl of vines along the deck. *We are responsible for the lives of the* Vessel's *crew, and that of Dez Rydan. Any other complications can be dealt with later.*

*Now, we must escape.*

His pathway through the debris scattered across the station led him closer to the arboretum, where a battle was raging. Before he could even seek Orla and Reath through the Force, they burst from one of the passageways, smelling faintly of toxic chemicals. Their comlinks were blinking at their belts, no doubt with Affie's warning about the vines.

However, they were able to see the problem for themselves. "What now?" Orla said. "Is it some kind of . . . giant Drengir?"

"Uncertain," Cohmac said as Reath kicked at one of the vines. "Undoubtedly the Drengir have created the vines; that's all we know. The vines have already begun to entrap the *Vessel*. We must leave immediately."

Orla fell into step at Cohmac's side while they hurried back. "The good news is, the Drengir and the Nihil are keeping each other busy. If we can get away, I don't think we have to worry about being pursued. How's Dez?"

"All but delirious," Cohmac said. His mind was only half on the present moment as he attempted to consider ways of damaging the vines.

Which was why he didn't notice their party was missing someone until they were already boarding the *Vessel*.

Orla realized it at that same moment. "Wait—where's Reath?"

☸

Reath had swerved away from the others after only a few meters.

He'd watched Cohmac and Orla go, wanting to stay

behind and make absolutely sure that events were unfolding the way they should. If anything went wrong with their plan, he and his friends would need to know right away. But even if everything went right, Reath had an important job to do.

This station couldn't be left for the Nihil and the Drengir to fight over. It had given the Amaxines a tactical advantage, millennia before; it remained capable of enabling a great deal of harm. Maybe the Republic could claim it—but the Republic wasn't coming to this area of the galaxy to conquer by sneak attack.

*We would only be holding it to keep the Drengir or Nihil from taking control,* Reath thought. *Both groups will want it back. It'll stir up needless conflict, cost lives, and for what?*

If the station couldn't be safely held, then it needed to be destroyed.

Not *literally*, at least not now: Reath wasn't carrying anything like the kind of firepower necessary for that. The *Vessel* wasn't, either. But he didn't have to demolish the Amaxine station to end its strategic capability.

All he had to do was launch every single hyperspace pod, at once, empty, and preferably to locations in the middle of dead space.

No doubt, if he'd spoken of his plan, either Orla or Master Cohmac would've insisted on performing the task instead. Reath didn't want anyone else taking a risk.

"Controls are going to be down low," Reath muttered as

he made his way into the central globe. "Not looking forward to going through that tunnel again."

His second descent through the tunnel was as uneventful as the first, though his sense of suspense had gone from ratcheted up to almost unbearable. When he became a full Jedi, maybe he would be able to enter a meditative trance at such times. But he wasn't there yet.

When he found the controls again, he placed his hand on them; they lit up. It took a little experimentation and a lot of faith in the Force to bring up location holos, but Reath finally got them going—tiny circles of light hovering in midair. The language and the notation systems were very old . . . but not unfamiliar to anyone who'd done multiple studies on the ancient Amaxines.

*Research,* he thought with a glimmer of satisfaction. *Don't knock it.*

Reath shifted the coordinates for each of the pods by a measure that should put them near, but not on, any planet to which they'd previously been headed, even for the largest inhabited planets known to science. Space stations and closer space traffic would also be safe. A distant moon or two *might* take a hit—but it was much more likely that the pods would simply appear in empty space and float there until they were smashed by random asteroids or harvested for scrap metal.

Once the coordinates were laid in, he pressed the central control. Instantly the entire lower ring began to vibrate—the power that had jolted through the station when he and Dez left but exponentially greater. Reath was nearly flung to the floor, but he held out his hands, keeping his balance as the pods zipped away to the far corners of the galaxy. The Amaxines' work was undone.

It felt a little sad, spoiling a piece of ancient machinery that had worked so well for so long. But as Reath heard the continued clash of the Nihil and Drengir above, he thought, *Nothing can last forever.*

He clambered up and out of the tunnel, wincing as he realized how much closer the fight had come. They remained oblivious to him thus far, and to the loss of the pods. But Reath had no clear route to the outer ring of the station—to the *Vessel*, or to escape.

Then his comlink buzzed. Trusting the din of battle to cover the sound, he lifted it to his ear and heard Leox: "*I would ask what the hell you're up to, but I'm guessing it has something to do with the jillionty pods I just saw launch from this station.*"

"Good guess," Reath said. "Listen, my way back is blocked right now. I'll try to get to you, but if I can't make it—I trust you guys to leave in time to save yourselves."

"*Noble sacrifices are not currently of any use. We* can't *leave. The Drengir have the* Vessel *tied in, literally. Sent vines to bind us to the station. We're going to try breaking free, but we need to go as soon as possible—the vines are still growing.*"

"What?" Reath had never even considered that the others wouldn't be able to handle the vines on their own. They were just vines, weren't they? But when he thought about how long and thick the roots would have to be to burrow through the station itself, he realized the ship might as well have been bolted in. "Is there any way to stop them?"

*"Not that I know of, other than brute force. If brute force is to be of any avail, it needs to be applied immediately. This is the best chance we're ever going to get."*

It wasn't much of a chance. Reath could hear that in Leox's voice.

If the *Vessel* was going to get away, the people on board would need time to cut away the bindings. Time when neither the Nihil nor the Drengir would or could attack them. The current battle had their enemies distracted, but for how long?

He thought of Dez, injured and helpless—the other Jedi on the mission, who'd tried to lead him in Master Jora's absence—and the crew of the *Vessel*, who had somehow become his friends. They were all in peril, all grasping at their last chance to survive.

Master Jora's voice echoed in his mind again. *Why can no Jedi cross the Kyber Arch alone?* And, finally, Reath knew the answer.

Reath had to save his friends if he could.

Even if the cost was his own life.

## PART SIX

"If we get through this," Cassel said to Thandeka, "at least things will be better from now on."

Thandeka, distracted by her raw, aching wrists and the angry muttering guards near Isamer, took a moment to process what he'd said. "What do you mean? What things?"

He flushed deeper blue again. "I mean, between Eiram and E'ronoh. We can stop all this silly bickering and be allies. Friends, even."

There were more substantive disputes between their two planets; it wasn't merely a matter of "bickering." And friendship took time. But Thandeka had seen the opportunity, too. "We'll open diplomatic relations. Allow some travel back and forth."

Cassel looked more cheerful than Thandeka had yet seen him. "Oh, I *love* diplomatic events. Getting dressed up with the stole and the regalia and all that."

Thandeka couldn't help smiling back at him. "I have to admit, Dima loves any chance for us to wear the crown jewels. Sometimes we fight over the best tiaras."

"Splendid, splendid." Cassel nodded as though everything was already set. "It's good to have something to look forward to, isn't it?"

Thandeka wasn't sure she believed they would outlive the day. But the Jedi were coming—and there was no point in *not* having hope. "Yes. Yes, it is."

Orla crept closer to the cave entrance. By then she and the others could hear movement, even muttering. They had clear passage into the very chamber where the hostages were being held. Master Laret, just ahead of Orla and Cohmac, held herself in battle stance, waiting for the right opportunity.

Tactical training clearly indicated that the ideal moment for action would come when sounds were farthest from the entrance, and that they should enter swiftly, immediately scan for the hostages and the kidnappers, protect the hostages first, and go after the kidnappers second. Their lightsabers would provide cover that allowed them to first defend, then attack.

Yet all Orla's instincts were telling her, *Find the kidnappers and take them out first.*

But tactical training existed for a reason. She decided not to ignore it.

Heavy footsteps headed farther from the door. Master Laret shifted position subtly, but enough to tell the apprentices the moment was at hand. The order was silent but Orla heard it as surely as though her master had shouted:

*Go.*

All three of them burst through the cave entrance at once. Orla's instincts were so strong they seemed almost to be steering her blade—but she held on, maintaining formation as they moved to surround and protect the hostages.

A tall, heavily armed Lasat sprang forward, but not at the Jedi themselves. Most species couldn't have leapt over two humans and an Umbaran in one bound, but a Lasat could, and this one did. Orla realized what was happening too late to jump up and block him, only in time to think, *There's nothing between him and the hostages—*

⚜

Thandeka screamed as Isamer's blaster pointed directly at her. It was the first and only time she'd screamed during her abduction, and despite her mortal terror, she hated that she'd broken, even in the last split second of her life.

Then Cassel flopped toward her, not able to cover her body completely but close. His blue face was only centimeters from hers. Their eyes met.

The blaster bolt fired, deafening and blinding her as though it were the end of the world.

⚜

Master Laret spun around, slashing her lightsaber through the Lasat's midsection in the instant after he'd fired. The two halves, cauterized, fell to the floor, and then there was no sound at all. It was all over within one minute. Orla stared at the wreckage before them—the smoldering walls and crates, the dead bodies on the floor, shot by their own deflected blaster bolts. How could it have ended so quickly?

The next sound she heard was sobbing.

Orla turned to see Monarch Cassel lying on the ground, his robe still smoldering from blaster burn. He was very near death. Queen Thandeka knelt beside him, tears streaming down her face. "You covered me," Thandeka managed to say to Cassel. "You protected me. Why?"

"So—so you could go home—to your queen." Cassel smiled weakly. "Invite the—the next monarch—to . . ."

His voice trailed off. His eyes went blank. Cassel was dead.

The queen leaned down, resting her forehead against Cassel's shoulder, and surrendered to tears. "He gave his life for mine."

"Then he died nobly," said Master Laret, putting one hand on Queen Thandeka's back. "He will be remembered."

Orla's instincts had told her to go after Isamer immediately. Why hadn't she listened to them?

*Because that's not what the Jedi Order says to do,* she reminded herself. It would be many years before she fully reckoned with that moment, and realized that if the Order was telling her to ignore the Force . . . it wasn't the Force that was wrong.

Cohmac watched Queen Thandeka with an emotion so strange it took him a few seconds to recognize it as envy.

She could cry for her loss. He could not even acknowledge his.

*Master Simmix would've told me to bury the grief,* Cohmac told himself. *There's no place for it in the Jedi. No place for it within you.*

So he buried it as deeply as a mine.

One that could wait years before exploding.

A few days later, and half a galaxy away, word of the Directorate's failure reached the Hutts. Reports indicated that not only had Lord Isamer been killed, but the information gathered at the kidnappers' lair had allowed the authorities to track down and arrest nearly every top official in the entire organization. The Directorate was gone.

Which was just what the Hutts had hoped for.

They'd set up a fool's errand. Laid a snare. The Directorate had been fool enough to step in it gladly. Now the only major criminal syndicate in that area of space was no more.

So whenever the Hutts decided to move in—be that one year later, or twenty-five—nothing would stand in their way.

# TWENTY-FIVE

Reath had to buy the others time. But how? Desperately he looked around the chaotic scene surrounding him in the station's central globe. It took only a moment for him to find a possibility.

As he'd noted earlier, one larger, irregularly shaped airlock to the side opened directly onto the arboretum area. He could see the controls only a few meters away. He crawled over to check them out. All signs suggested they were fully operational.

What he was about to do might kill him. But it was the only way to eliminate both the Drengir and Nihil threats to the *Vessel* at once.

Besides, maybe he could make it. *Exhale,* he reminded himself. *Exhale and hang on with all your strength. That's your only chance.*

With that, Reath eliminated the time delay, clutched a nearby service ladder, breathed out hard, and hit VENT.

The airlock slid open, exposing the arboretum to the emptiness of space. Normally the delay would've kept the magnetic containment field in place long enough for anyone present to escape; this time, it flicked out of existence immediately.

Explosive energy grabbed everyone and everything in the center of the station: Nihil, Drengir, droids, plants, debris, heat, air. Shrieks of dismay sounded in the first instant; after that, there wasn't enough air for sound to travel through. It felt as though he were being buffeted by gale-force winds. Reath clung to the service ladder with all his strength, but it felt as though he were being dragged by his feet, his elbows, his hair, every part of his body. Space wanted to claim him.

❧

Vines streamed out of the arboretum like ribbons. Walls that had been covered with plants for centuries were stripped clean. The bodies of Nihil and Drengir pinwheeled past him—limbs flailing, weapons sometimes still firing—and Reath felt regret at being required to spend so many lives. But they had been determined to take the lives of others; that made them forfeit in combat.

Ice crystals began to form in his hair and on his clothes. Reath kept his chest flat, empty of breath, though the strain made his ribs ache. If he inhaled and took in any of the remaining air, the lack of external pressure would cause the gas to expand, rupturing his lungs. *Hang on,* he told himself, *hang on, hang on—the doors will shut soon—*

But not soon enough. The ladder began to shake; the screws holding it to the wall had begun to give. It would tear away at any moment.

Reath was not afraid. Sad, but not afraid. If this was when he became one with the Force again, so be it. At least he had bought his friends some time, and a chance to live. That was more than most deaths earned. He was lucky that his had meaning. Nobody could ask for anything beyond that.

His mind filled with the memory of Master Jora's kindly face. *We'll unite in the Force soon,* he thought.

The ladder gave way. Reath slid across the floor, toward the airlock and open space. He closed his eyes against the void—

And hit something very solid, very hard.

*What the—* Pain echoed through Reath's whole body. But whatever barrier he'd hit wasn't giving way to the vacuum; it was too strong for that. He opened his eyes to discover he could see around the edge of the thing—which showed him the airlock doors finally sliding shut.

The vacuum vanished. Reath tumbled to the ground, gasping for air. It took the station's environmental controls a few more moments to restore oxygen. In those blurry seconds, he looked for what had saved him.

No, not what. *Who.*

"Geode?" Reath gasped.

Geode stood above him, reassuringly calm and steady. And Reath could *feel* that now—a connection to a life-form profoundly alien, and yet as vividly alive as any being he had ever encountered.

Reath's comlink buzzed. *"What just happened?"* Affie's voice rang out. *"The readings we're getting—Reath, are you still out there?"*

He managed to reply in a raspy voice: "Thanks to Geode, yeah. Still here. We're still here. But the Nihil and the Drengir are long gone."

*"You're going to have to explain that later,"* Affie said. *"Hang on. We're coming to get you."*

He flopped back onto the floor and stared up at Geode. "My hero."

Geode made no reply, but Reath knew he understood.

⚜

Vines had begun tracing their way across the cockpit, signaling the complete enclosure of the *Vessel*, when their sensors had lit up red. The ensuing panic about the decompression inside the station had distracted them all. But when Orla and the others finally knew Reath was safe and the station was intact, they turned back to see that the vines had not only stopped growing but had also begun turning black. They'd died when the Drengir did.

After that, getting away from the Amaxine station wouldn't be that difficult. Yes, it took them a long while to cut away all the thick, ropey dead vines entrapping the *Vessel*, but they had time to work, with no Drengir or Nihil to worry about.

(At least some of the Nihil had survived; their ship remained operational. Probably most of the survivors had been on board when Reath blew the airlock, rather than on the station. But there couldn't be that many of them—scans indicated that they'd shut down most areas of their spacecraft and were taking stock of the damage. Orla had no doubt the Nihil would want revenge for this someday, but they knew better than to try to take it that day.)

"Is the station completely emptied out?" Affie asked as Leox and Geode ran final systems checks. "Broken? Useless?"

"Honestly, most of it survived in pretty good shape," said Orla, who had just completed a quick search to check on things. "Several plants had grown outside the arboretum—I imagine they'll find their way back in, with the help of the Aytees that were in outer sections of the station when Reath blew the lock. All the major systems are intact. However, it has no hyperspace pods any longer, all of which were launched away from their return mechanisms, meaning this place has no more tactical value. It's just an arboretum now."

Affie nodded. The girl seemed oddly satisfied by the station's depowering for some reason, but Orla chose not to pry. It was enough to know that they were all alive—even Dez!—all more or less well, and able to go home.

And with more hyperspace lanes being cleared every day, the frontier couldn't elude Orla for much longer. Wild open space beckoned, and she couldn't wait to answer the call.

※

Reath got to take it easy on the trip back to Coruscant. His injuries from the venting maneuver were minor but numerous: scrapes and cuts on his skin from shards of debris, a slight sprain of one hand from gripping the ladder so hard, plus bruises and a blackening eye from his lifesaving collision with Geode. This meant he got propped up in his bunk with hot tea, blankets, and praise for his heroic actions, which was the best painkiller of all.

For the purposes of keeping their eyes on both patients at once, the other Jedi had taken down the barrier between Reath's "room" and Dez's. Unfortunately Dez wasn't doing nearly as well.

Dez lay on his cot, his breath ragged. His golden-tan complexion had turned ashen, and his skin had gone clammy. Despite being bandaged with synthplast skin, the wounds on Dez's arms and legs remained livid and tender.

When Master Cohmac came to check on them, he murmured, "Have you tried a healing, Reath?"

"I tried," Reath said. "Master Jora always said it was worth trying. But I doubt I did much. Not knowing exactly what toxins the Drengir put in his bloodstream—well, that didn't help."

Orla poked her head in. "How is he?"

"He's not getting worse," Reath said. "But he's not getting better, either." It was clear that Dez needed to get a lot better, and fast.

"Pardon the intrusion," said Leox, who was coming through the door with a cloth-wrapped packet in his hands. "I may be able to provide some surcease of our friend's pain."

Orla and Cohmac exchanged glances as Leox went to sit by Dez's head. Then Reath couldn't register their reactions, only his own shock, as Leox pulled out pressed leaves that smelled distinctly, strongly, *unmistakably* of spice.

Leox began pressing the broad, soft leaves to Dez's chest, then wrapped others around his wounds, and finally laid one across his forehead. By the time he'd finished applying them, Dez had already begun to breathe easier.

When the Masters exchanged glances, Leox said, "I *told* you it was medicinal."

Master Cohmac actually smiled. Reath generally didn't think it was a good idea to keep secrets from the Jedi Council . . . but this one time might be the exception. Besides, the Council would be unhappy enough with them already.

It had been just over a day since they'd left Coruscant, but the memories felt far more distant. Reath reflected again on the rules they'd broken to get there, the reaction that would inevitably result. "We'll be disciplined, won't we? For coming here in the first place."

"They may decide what we accomplished here is worth pardoning us," said Master Cohmac. "If they don't, we'll not only be disciplined, but perhaps even thrown out of the Order completely."

Reath blanched. Would his first mission as an independent Jedi be his last?

Then Orla laughed. "Cohmac, take it easy on him, all right? Reath doesn't have the experience to know the difference between what *could* happen and what's likely to." She turned to Reath and said, "Yes, we're in trouble. But I wouldn't worry too much about it."

Orla was seriously underestimating Reath's deep, long-standing relationship with worry. He pulled his blanket firmly up to his shoulders and began mentally composing his own defense.

❦

The *Vessel*'s return to Coruscant ought to have been a relief. They were safe again, unlikely to encounter the Drengir for a long time to come. The Nihil—well, they were still out there, but at least Affie wouldn't have to deal with them for a while.

Yet she felt numb. Directionless.

As she trudged through the tasks associated with docking—lubing up the landing-gear joints, putting in

Guild bank codes for refueling—she kept thinking about the Amaxine station.

Scover couldn't use it for its original purposes anymore. The Jedi had seen to that by making the station known. Undoubtedly some entrepreneurial species or group would take it over and turn it into a standard commercial stop. No more desperate, indentured smugglers would be able to make illegal use of it. Scover's insidious "bonuses" would vanish. Nobody else had to die the way Affie's parents had.

Yet Scover would keep on using indentured pilots. The Amaxine station was far from the only hazardous place in the galaxy. She would keep coercing those pilots under her control to undertake dangerous missions. It would still be the one possibility to pay out of an indenture before old age.

*I thought this would teach her something,* Affie decided. *It wouldn't have. It would've showed her how angry I am, that's all.*

She went to Scover's hotel that night and endured the inevitable scolding.

"Running off like that was very worrying," Scover said over a luxurious dinner on the spacious balcony overlooking the Coruscant city lights. Her even tone suggested no worry at all—but that was how Bivalls were. How Scover was. So Affie had always told herself; she still mostly believed it. "I realized you had to be on the *Vessel*, but I hadn't thought you would leave without telling me goodbye."

"The Jedi wanted to go back in a hurry, and in secret." This was true, if not the whole truth.

"And the customer is always right." Scover nodded. "It's good that you have learned to prioritize pleasing our clients. Profit cannot be maintained otherwise."

Affie couldn't resist saying, "There are more important things than profit."

"Yes," Scover said, "but not many things."

"Our pilots' lives are more important," Affie said. After a pause she added, "Don't you agree?"

Scover seemed unbothered. "That is a determination the pilots must make for themselves. We all balance risk and reward, Affie."

"People don't usually risk their lives for rewards. They usually risk them to escape something terrible."

"Plenty of people risk their lives for rewards." Scover continued sampling the Chandrilan delicacies heaped on their dining table. "Racer pilots, for instance. Mmmm, have some of the *baha*. I remember that you loved it."

Affie obediently took a dish of the *baha*. But even its cool sweetness couldn't penetrate the fog of depression. She might as well have been eating plain crushed ice.

"There, now." The small smile on Scover's face widened just a little. "You appreciate good things, Affie. You must appreciate that you receive these things because of the Byne Guild's prosperity. Someday, two or three decades from now, I will retire, and all this will become yours. But I must know I'd be leaving my Guild in the right hands. You understand it all now, don't you?"

"Yes," Affie said. "I understand it all."

That night, Affie considered returning to the *Vessel* to sleep. But the view from the balcony soothed her—the constant low hum of activity turning into white noise, tranquil in its way. She needed soothing. Her brain was racing.

Long after Scover had gone to bed, Affie sat up late, her brown hair ruffled by the breezes. She looked up at Coruscant's strange, starless sky and wondered whether she could keep silent. If she did, Scover would continue to give her more and more authority within the Guild. Affie might gain the ability to free indentures earlier, at far lower prices. When Scover died or retired, Affie would inherit it all—wealth and power almost beyond imagining, if their Republic expansion plans came to fruition. Then she could end indentures in the Guild and protect everyone.

When that day came, years and years later. Decades. The better part of a human lifetime.

Yes, Affie could wait. But the indentured pilots couldn't.

Reath stood at the center of the Jedi Council among his friends.

On one hand, it was amazing to realize that these full, adult Jedi Masters—Cohmac Vitus and Orla Jareni—considered him friends. To reflect that they looked on him as more than an apprentice, more of a partner in their endeavors.

On the other hand, he was uncomfortably aware that this

friendship might have to continue outside the Jedi Order. They had all either ignored or directly defied the commands they'd been given (except for Dez, of course, who was finally resting well among the Temple's medics).

For the time being, all he could do was stand at his full height, express deference to the Council, and hope for the best.

"You are each aware, of course," said Master Adampo, "the dangers when Jedi go rogue. Even Wayseekers have protocols to follow. The abilities we possess, the skills we have learned to wield—these cannot be used in the pursuit of selfish concerns. If they are not employed in the service of others, they are employed wrongly. That is why the Order exists, to ensure that our abilities do not corrupt us, but instead enrich the galaxy and the Force itself."

Reath caught a fleeting expression on Orla's face, one that suggested she didn't agree with every element of that speech. He was relieved that she (uncharacteristically) decided not to share those thoughts with the Council. That was probably more for his benefit, and the others', than for herself.

"However," Master Adampo continued, "while your reasons may have been unofficial, they were not selfish. In fact, they were selfless in the extreme. Jareni and Vitus hoped to contain entities deeply connected to the dark side. And Padawan Silas knew he could gain more information on enemies of the Republic on the frontier. The risks you assumed were great. All of you nearly lost your lives. Yet you managed to take a valuable strategic resource away from enemies of the Republic. More than that, you saved Dez Rydan, whom we had all believed lost."

Master Rosason added, more sternly, "Given that this is not common behavior for any of you, and the importance of the results you achieved—the Council votes against discipline at this time. But be aware: future rogue actions will be judged far more harshly."

"In other words," said Master Adampo, "don't make a habit of it. We are adjourned."

Reath's shoulders sagged with relief. The other Jedi were less surprised than he was—maybe they had enough experience to tell how far they could push the Council. That was experience Reath had no intention of gaining. From then on, he was following every rule more faithfully than ever before.

As they all turned for the door, however, Master Adampo said, "Padawan Silas, if you could remain for a few moments?"

*Oh, no. They're going to punish me after all.* Despite the sinking feeling in his gut, Reath turned back to the Council and stood tall before them. From the corner of his eye, he caught a sympathetic glance from Orla, but the others had been dismissed and had to leave. Reath was on his own.

Master Adampo said, "Padawan Silas, you have not yet answered us."

"No, sir. Ah, what was the question again, sir?"

"We're not discussing this hearing, but our previous conversation with you. Are you ready to begin training again?"

Reath remembered, as though recalling a dream, that the Council had put his future in his own hands. Where would he go? What path would he walk?

"It's up to you, Silas," said Master Adampo. "What comes next?"

# TWENTY-SIX

Affie was used to "government offices" that were official in name only. They operated out of someone's ship, or the back of a cantina. Instead of laws and regulations, most people obeyed the customs of a region, or the whims of some local potentate.

The Republic ran things differently. She'd been told that before, but the truth of it didn't fully hit her until she walked into the offices that regulated shipping. Every step she took in her shabby boots echoed off the polished stone floors; the high ceiling was held aloft by columns too thick for her to put her arms around. Every piece of equipment she saw gleamed with cleanliness, as though each had been put in place only the day before. Affie had timed her visit for just after opening—mostly because she couldn't stand to hang around for Scover to return from her breakfast meeting, but partly because she thought most people wouldn't be up that early. Instead the place was bustling, yet orderly.

She found the pristine environment more intimidating than welcoming. The files she'd downloaded onto the datapad in her bag glowed with imagined heat, like they'd burn their way through the canvas. More than once, Affie thought of simply walking back out the way she'd come.

But she stayed put long enough for her name to be called.

Affie was ushered into a small room with a Twi'lek minor official. Despite the fact that Affie was a seventeen-year-old girl, the Twi'lek seemed to be taking her seriously. If he'd laughed her off, that would've given her an excuse—

But she was sick of excuses.

"You wish to make a report?" the Twi'lek asked.

"Yes." Taking a deep breath, Affie pulled the datapad from her bag and handed it over. She'd thought it would feel better once there was no turning back. It didn't. She plunged ahead anyway. "I'm reporting the abuse of indentures in the Byne Guild."

※

At first, Reath waited for an invitation. None came. Finally, three days after Dez's release from the hospital, Reath decided not to wait any longer.

When he pushed the door chimes, at first he received no response. The autofunctions had said Dez Rydan was home and awake, but that wasn't the same as accepting guests. He could be tired. Still recovering. Reath was already turning to go when the door unsealed.

It slid open to reveal Dez's quarters. Reath knew these were normally messier than the average Jedi's quarters, by a power of about ten, but even Dez could only make so much mess within his first few hours out of medical care. He sat on a meditation cushion in the center of the room, a casual robe wrapped loosely around him. He'd regained the weight he had lost, and to judge by what Reath could see, there wouldn't even be any scars.

"You look good," he said, smiling as he walked into the room and the door slid shut behind him. "Lots better than the last time I saw you."

"I can imagine." Dez ran one hand through his thick black hair. "I definitely *feel* better. It would be difficult to feel worse."

"Maybe this wouldn't be helpful to you," Reath ventured. "But for me—I'm going to have a vigil for Master Jora. Her body was lost, so we can't have a pyre. Still, I'm going to light a fire and keep watch. Would you want to join me?"

"I can't," Dez said. His voice sounded remote; he didn't quite meet Reath's eyes. "Tomorrow I'm leaving for one of the contemplation worlds. I'm taking the Barash Vow."

The Barash Vow was an extreme commitment to gaining

ultimate communion with the Force. Those who took the vow spent years—sometimes even decades—in deep meditation, and in solitude. It was the last path Reath would ever have foreseen for Dez.

"But why?" Reath asked. "The Barash Vow—it's taken by Jedi who've made terrible mistakes. You didn't! You haven't broken your connection to the Force."

"No," Dez said. "That was broken by the Drengir. The healers have pieced it back together again, but it's . . . shaky. The cracks are showing. It won't hold, not unless I commit myself with all my strength to renewing it."

"But—" Reath's voice cracked. "Is that the life you really want?"

Slowly Dez nodded. "You have to understand, the Drengir are *profoundly* connected to the dark side. The days I spent as their prisoner were days that damaged and tested my connection to the Force. I don't know that I passed the test. Without you, I might have become their creature—a mindless servant of darkness. That is, if they hadn't eaten me first."

"You passed the test," Reath insisted. "You're still you."

"Yes, I am. But there are ways in which that's not a good thing. I've always wanted . . . action, excitement. I've wanted that a little too much. Jedi aren't meant to please themselves. We're meant to serve. Service doesn't mean only doing what you want to do. It means listening to the Force. And I'd stopped listening." Dez shook his head. "I know what I have to do."

"I understand," Reath said. "I've been thinking about that, too." His resistance to the frontier assignment—that had been all about what he wanted. Not about service. Honoring Master Jora with a fire and vigil meant nothing if he didn't honor everything she'd taught him. By taking the assignment on Starlight, she'd been trying to teach him what service really meant.

*I'm learning, master,* he thought.

Dez seemed to recognize the impact his words had had on Reath. "What will you do next?"

"I think—" Reath paused, then nodded. "I think I just figured that out."

By midday, at the spaceport, Republic officials were busily cataloging every Byne Guild ship and interviewing every Byne Guild pilot. As far as Affie could tell, they'd started within minutes of her report to the authorities. She'd assumed it would take the Republic days or weeks to act—time that might've given Scover a chance to travel back to the frontier. She had more influence there, and the Republic less; she could've remained free.

Instead, officials had arrested Scover right away. Affie had forced herself to watch the arrest footage from the hotel (which had made it available to her, as Scover's guest). Scover had remained calm and quiet the entire time she was being cuffed and led away.

That calm might shatter when she learned Affie was the one who had reported her, which was news Affie intended to deliver herself. This would be the toughest encounter of Affie's life, but it was one she could not turn away from. Scover had raised her, cared for her, even loved her. She deserved the chance to ask how her foster daughter could've done this to her.

And Affie deserved the chance to explain why.

She stood awkwardly in front of the *Vessel*, watching the activity throughout the spaceport. The worst part wasn't the guilt or the uncertainty; it was knowing her entire future was being shaped by forces outside her control, and having absolutely nothing she could do about it.

Footsteps on the boarding ramp made her turn. Leox was strolling out alongside the human Republic official checking the *Vessel*. The official nodded her head as she checked off items on a datapad. "No irregularities here, so I can clear this ship for takeoff."

"Most kind of you," Leox said, "but at the moment we have no place to go."

"Take whatever work you want." The Republic official obviously saw herself as their savior, or at least the bearer of very good tidings. "According to Republic law, upon the dissolution of an illegal shipping concern, all ships are considered the individual property of their senior officers. Which means the *Vessel* is now yours, Captain Gyasi."

Leox shook his head. "Not so fast. If you're jotting all this down for the annals of the Republic, be sure you get it right. I'm not the senior officer assigned to the *Vessel*. That'd be Affie Hollow, standing over there."

When he pointed at her, Affie managed to close her mouth so she wouldn't be goggling at them like a fool. "*Me?*"

"Official Guild representative trumps the captain every time." With a shrug, Leox was handing over ownership of the thing he loved most in the world—the thing he could've claimed for his own in a heartbeat. Although Scover had showered a few fine things on Affie over the years, she had never received a more generous gift.

The Republic official seemed willing to take Leox's word for it. To Affie she said, "Will you be changing the designation of the ship?"

"No," Affie said, a grin spreading across her face. "This is the *Vessel*, always and forever. And Leox Gyasi remains her captain. He just . . . works for me."

Leox was smiling, too, as he shook his head. "What have I got myself into?"

As the Republic official went on her way, Affie hugged Leox with all her strength. "I want it all to remain the same. Just like it was before, except this time we're in it just for ourselves. On our own."

"Works for me, Little Bit—and I can call you that again, because you've become my boss, which means the nickname has become ironic."

Was she going to fight him on that? Maybe later, Affie decided. "All three of us—wait. Where's Geode?"

In the spaceship depot, Orla looked from the sample holo she'd been given to the actual item: the new ship that would be hers. Almost pyramidal in structure, with three engines, a pointed prow, and an equally angular stern, the ship had a sharpness to it—like a dart or a shard of glass. Like Orla herself. The vessel gleamed against the stark blackness of the depot, its pearlescent hull as beautiful as any jewel.

The sales droid whirred up to her. "If you wish to enter the ship—"

"Oh, yes. Yes, I do."

Orla stepped within her new ship almost with reverence. During the hyperspace disaster, and the events on the Amaxine station, she'd wondered whether she was being selfish by declaring herself a Wayseeker and setting out on her own. Now that it was all over, however, she found herself newly certain of her choice. The galaxy was bigger and stranger than any one being could ever know. There was a place for the Jedi Order to operate within it—and places for other Jedi to discover on their own. Serving the Order was important, but she could never give it the best of herself unless she knew herself, her instincts, and the Force more truly. She'd never felt more ready for the journey to begin.

"She's beautiful," Orla said, running her hand along the sleek pilot's chair. "A work of art. Pass my compliments on to the designers."

The sales droid's lights blinked with pride. "Does that mean you'll take it?"

"After a little haggling on the price." Orla shrugged. "What can I say? I'm in love with it, but that's one hell of a markup."

The haggling didn't last too long; Orla's suggested price was fair, and the droid clearly had a sales quota to meet. Within the hour, Orla had put her thumbprint to every document and obtained all the passcodes for her new ship.

"The *Lightseeker*," she said. "I'm calling her the *Lightseeker*."

"Duly registered," replied the sales droid. "Shall I report that she travels with a crew complement of one?"

"Yes—unless I can convince my navigator friend to join me?"

Geode stood nearby, his silence his only reply. He'd been willing to look over ships with her, but Orla already knew his loyalty was to Leox, Affie, and the *Vessel*.

Besides, this was a path she needed to walk alone.

"Maybe next time," she said, patting Geode on the side, already dreaming of the voyages to come.

Once she was alone on the bridge of her ship (her ship!), she sent a message to Cohmac. When his face appeared on the screen, Orla scooted over so he could see more of the *Lightseeker* than of her. "What do you think?"

"Beautiful." Cohmac's smile didn't reach his eyes. "I am truly happy for you, Orla. The Force has called you, and you have answered."

"I've been fighting my instincts my entire career," Orla admitted. "Forcing myself to follow a path that wasn't mine. I want to serve the Order, and the galaxy, but I can't do that if I'm living a lie."

She thought again of that long-ago day when they'd rescued one hostage but lost another, all because she'd put what was "right and proper" ahead of what the Force told her. Orla wouldn't make that mistake again.

Cohmac nodded. "I envy you the surety of your convictions, Orla."

The anger he'd felt after Dez's supposed death—the echoes of the death of his master and of the hostage, so long before—had taken a toll on Cohmac, a deeper one than Orla had realized. She said, "Are you all right? Do you need to do some wayseeking of your own?"

"No. I need the Order now, more than ever. But I need something else, too. A new direction—a focus. That, only time can provide."

Orla wasn't positive that the Order was what Cohmac required. But she couldn't give him those answers. That would be up to the Force.

"May the Force be with you, old friend." She raised one hand as he did, a mutual salute of farewell.

❋

Reath entered the Jedi Temple's meditation center with some trepidation. It was impolite to disturb others' trances.

However, by chance, Master Cohmac was in the room alone, sitting in midair.

That couldn't be easy. No doubt this was a profoundly deep meditation. Reath wondered whether he should tiptoe out again and was on the verge of doing so before Master Cohmac said, without opening his eyes, "What is it, Reath?"

"I was hoping to speak with you," he said. Which was obvious. But at least Master Cohmac didn't point that out.

Instead he descended to the ground and walked with Reath to a gathering area just outside, one where a carved fountain bubbled. "How can I help you, Reath? I assume it is urgent."

"I didn't want to interrupt you," Reath said, "but I saw that you had put in to leave on one of the next transports to the frontier, to take up your original assignment. Since I didn't know when that would be, exactly, I figured the smart thing to do was find you right away."

Master Cohmac cocked his head. "Yet you still have not told me why."

He wasn't sure how to phrase what came next. "I wanted to ask—just ask, no pressure, no hurt feelings if you say no—"

"Ask me."

It came out in a rush: "Would you consider taking me on as your apprentice?"

Master Cohmac stared, as though he had never dreamed of such a thing. Probably he hadn't. But it wasn't such a strange request, was it?

Maybe Reath hadn't made himself clear enough. "During our adventures on the Amaxine station, I came to have a great respect for you. In many ways you're not a typical Jedi—but I think, maybe, I need to expand my idea of what a Jedi can be. Of the kind of Jedi *I* can be. Training with you would teach me so much, and I want to learn. If you're willing to take me, that is." After a moment's hesitation he dared to add, "Returning to the frontier is what Master Jora would've wanted for me. We're both heading out there. I thought we might go together." Master Cohmac still looked nonplussed. Reath decided to offer a tactful out. "If this isn't the right time, I understand."

"It is . . . an interesting time," Master Cohmac said. He began to pace slowly along the courtyard, and Reath fell into step beside him. "I have heard Jora Malli described as the kindest and wisest of teachers," he said. "It's difficult to imagine picking up where she left off. But what she had to give you and what I have to give are two very different things."

Reath brightened. This sounded promising. "Yes, exactly. I mean, yes, sir."

"You've shown initiative in coming to me, and in wanting your training to proceed along a new path. Now I must show courage and be open with you." Master Cohmac stopped in place and met Reath's eyes. "I have had doubts, these past weeks, about whether the ways prescribed by the Jedi Council are invariably the best course to follow."

Had he heard that right? He couldn't have. "Sir?"

Master Cohmac sighed. "The darkness is as much a part of the Force as the light. The Order thinks it can bisect the Force so neatly—as though the primal living energy of all existence were a thing to be sliced and served."

Reath took a moment to consider this. "Doesn't that separation keep us safe?"

"Does it?" Master Cohmac said. "Or does the divide only make the darkness darker, more dangerous, than it ever would have been in a state of nature?"

"I don't know," Reath admitted. He hadn't thought abstract philosophy would be a major part of training—but it seemed it would be with Master Cohmac. At least, it would be if he took Reath on. "I only know that our work is good work. That we save lives, end conflict, and bring peace."

Master Cohmac smiled at him. "You are sure of your path, Reath Silas. Never let anything shake you from it."

"I only thought I was sure before," Reath confessed. "But before I left for the frontier, Master Jora asked me a question. She said when I knew the answer, I'd know why we needed to leave Coruscant. She asked why no Jedi can cross the Kyber Arch alone. Now I understand. No one crosses it alone because the arch itself wouldn't exist without all the Jedi Knights that have gone before. Both the ones who fell in battle and the ones who built the arch for others to remember. I was giving the Order only as much of me as I wanted to give. It was all about *me*. Not about *us*. From now on, I'm putting *us* first."

"Jora Malli was a wise woman," said Master Cohmac. "I doubt I could match the profundity of her teachings."

That sounded suspiciously like goodbye. "So," Reath began, "are we—"

"I still have much to learn," Master Cohmac said. That sounded even more like a no until he added, "And there is no better way to learn than to teach. You will be my first Padawan, Reath, and perhaps my greatest instructor in the Force."

※

Weeks later, Starlight Beacon officially went online. Its beams shone out through the galaxy, bright as any supernova, in a wordless message of the Republic's promise of guidance, protection, and prosperity.

As the beams were illuminated, applause rang out aboard the station from the many parties present: the senior Jedi Avar Kriss, Elzar Mann, and Stellan Gios; other Jedi such as Sskeer and Burryaga; Republic officials; various diplomats; and delegations from nearby worlds—

And one Padawan who'd made the last choice he would ever have expected just a few short weeks before.

Reath Silas clapped along with the rest. For a moment he wished Master Jora were there to celebrate with them—to stand in a position of honor up on the dais. She had wanted this for Reath, this place on the frontier where anything and everything could happen but nothing could be taken for granted. At long last, he recognized the value of what she had wished to give him, and he had resolved not to refuse his late master's final gift.

No, he didn't care for adventures. They were dangerous, messy, and best avoided; the Amaxine station had proved that beyond any doubt. Reath still preferred for adventures to remain in stories, where they belonged.

But someone had to live the stories before they could be told. Someone had to tell the tales. Maybe Reath was meant to be one of the tellers. All he knew was that he was ready to serve the means of the Force, whatever or wherever—they might be.

There had been various speeches and performances throughout the ceremony, and those would continue for some time to come. The next, however, seemed to draw special attention—an older woman with vivid silver streaks in her black hair was ascending the dais to cheers and applause. Her sumptuous cloak and glittering coronet testified to her royal status even before it was announced, "To address the crowd, Queen Thandeka of Eiram!"

The queen lifted her chin, and the entire crowd fell silent. She was the wife of the ruler of a nearby planet, as Reath understood it, but something about her presence gave her a greater authority.

"We welcome the Republic," she said, her voice ringing out over the crowd. "Twenty-five years ago, we had sealed ourselves off from the rest of the galaxy. We didn't trust the

Republic, or the Jedi, or even each other. All that changed when the Jedi came to rescue me, and the late Monarch Cassel of E'ronoh gave his life for mine." She bowed her head slightly when she said Cassel's name. "After that, our worlds began to listen to each other more. We dared to learn more about the galaxy beyond our narrow confines. We learned that independence is an illusion—that no one truly stands alone. We regained the courage to trust, without which we could never have moved forward. To trust is to hope, to believe in a better future and believe that others will work with us to make it possible."

Many people clapped. Reath joined them.

"It is in memory of Monarch Cassel, and of the Jedi Master who died on our rescue mission, that the decision was made to place Starlight Beacon so close to the planetoid where the crisis took place," Queen Thandeka continued. "We celebrate their memory here, today and forever."

More applause, and the queen descended from the dais as a choir assembled to perform. Reath, never a music lover, was relieved when his new master began steering them away from the center of the ceremony. "What comes next?" Reath asked.

Master Cohmac, beside him, continued applauding. "I believe what follows is the grand feast."

"Good. I'm *starving*."

That made Master Cohmac laugh, which Reath considered a good sign.

After the musical performance, as they began walking

with the crowds toward the banquet, Reath said, "What happens after this, master?"

"Anything could happen," said Master Cohmac. "And that is the joy of it."

⁂

Half a galaxy away . . .

Nan knelt before the leader of the Nihil. *The* leader—the Eye—Marchion Ro, a figure so high above her she'd never have presumed to dream of any meeting. She would've prostrated herself before him; never had she felt so unworthy of her stripes. But her emotions were less important than communicating the facts.

"My guardian, Hague, was killed by the Jedi's trick," she said. "Along with so many of the others. I only survived because I had returned to the lower tunnels to make sure they were clear of other Drengir."

Marchion Ro nodded; the light shimmered dully on his metallic gray skin. "You are not to blame," he said. "Their deaths are the responsibility of the Jedi. And the Jedi will pay."

The anger in his voice restored Nan, gave fuel to the vengeful flame inside her. And yet she had to caution him. "I fear the Jedi are very powerful. They have abilities unlike anything we've ever encountered before."

Marchion Ro merely smiled. "You are wise to fear the Jedi and the Republic. But they should fear us in return. For the Nihil will be the destruction of the Jedi."

READ ON FOR A SNEAK PEEK AT ANOTHER
EXCITING HIGH REPUBLIC ADVENTURE,
COMING IN SUMMER 2021!

# OUT OF
# THE SHADOWS

JUSTINA IRELAND

**S**ylvestri Yarrow looked at the balance sheet before her and tried not to scream. Why hadn't anyone warned her how expensive it was to own a ship? Between the rising cost of fuel and the Nihil threat forcing them to alter their routes, she and her crew were barely scraping by. Once the shipment of gnostra berry wine—the most lucrative cargo they'd had in *months*—was delivered, there would still be a slight shortfall from their last fuel pickup in Port Haileap. Not to mention the bill they still owed on Batuu. At this rate she was going to be in debt to half of the galaxy.

And she *still* hadn't paid her taxes from the last couple of hauls.

Syl leaned back in her seat in the cockpit of the *Switchback*, her pride and current frustration, and watched the peaceful blue of hyperspace stream by. The cockpit was dark enough that she could clearly see her own reflection in the glass, and the dark-skinned face that looked back at her was long past worried. It was positively distraught, and if her copilot, Neeto, saw her he would know things were bad. Syl took a deep breath, closed her eyes, and forced herself to think.

There had to be an answer. Longer routes? Hauling passengers? Doubling fees, which were already higher than they had been a year ago? What was the magical equation that would make shipping profitable, especially in a time when the Nihil—space pirates without any sense of honor or self-preservation—plagued the shipping lanes?

Syl didn't know, and trying to puzzle it out was giving her a headache.

"Em-Two," she said, opening her eyes and turning toward the droid sitting in the copilot's seat. "I think we might be in trouble."

The droid turned its head with a shrieking sound, and Syl winced. "And we need to quit buying you that cheap oil." She grabbed the nearby oil can and went to work on the droid's joints. At over two hundred years old, M-227 was the oldest droid Syl had ever met. Like the *Switchback*, he had been part of Syl's inheritance when her mother was killed by Nihil raiders and one of the few things Syl could call her own. She should have traded him away, but she couldn't bring herself to sell the droid. He was like family. He reminded her there had once been better times.

Just a few months ago, in fact. It was a time that Syl had started thinking of as *before*. Before the Nihil had destroyed a good portion of Valo and killed hundreds of thousands of people. Before the Republic had realized they were a threat. Syl's mother, Chancey Yarrow, had known the Nihil were dangerous from the beginning. She'd joined with a number of other shippers to demand that the frontier planets align and try to nullify the threat. But it hadn't done much good.

It hadn't stopped Chancey from losing her life to the raiders, either.

Syl dashed sudden tears from her eyes.

"Please. Do not worry," M-227 said in his stilted voice. His speech box hadn't been updated in years, just one more task that Syl had been putting off until she had some extra funds.

"Too late," Syl whispered, mostly to herself. She rested her head in her hands and took a deep breath, running her fingers through her dark, frizzy curls until they stood even farther out from her head. Syl loved the *Switchback*. She loved flying through the darkness of space and jumping into the cool blue of hyperspace. She enjoyed meeting new people and going to places that seemed impossibly strange and exciting. And most of all, she loved that no one questioned her about any of it. She had far more independence than so many other eighteen-year-olds in the galaxy.

But at this rate she wasn't going to be able to feed herself, let alone repair the finicky hyperdrive or improve the engines the way she'd wanted to.

The *Switchback* came out of hyperspace with a bump, and every single proximity alarm began to blare all at once.

"I leave for one minute and things go sideways," Neeto Janajana said, strolling down the corridor from the crew mess. The Sullustan did not run, just stretched out his legs a bit more. Syl sometimes wondered if he knew the meaning of "hurry up" or if that was just something he didn't believe in, like minding his own business.

"I didn't do anything. We just got kicked out of hyperspace. This seems to be a bit early," Syl said, looking at the readouts. She put the balance sheet to the side. No need for Neeto to know they were not just broke, but hemorrhaging credits. He might seem unflappable, but the threat of indenture could get a rise out of anyone, and he'd been down that road once before.

M-227 stood with a screeching of metal, and Neeto sat down in the copilot's seat, taking the droid's place. He frowned, the ridges around his large black eyes narrowing a bit. "Well, it wasn't debris. Otherwise you and I would be having this conversation with a lot less oxygen."

Syl nodded. "Running diagnostics right now to see what happened."

"Good idea. Although I will say this feels a bit too familiar."

Syl agreed. When they'd lost her mother there had been a bit of strangeness before the attack: weird readouts, alarms, and then the sudden appearance of ships bearing down on them. But surely it couldn't be the Nihil? M-227 had planned a route that avoided any sector that had ever had any reported sightings of the marauders. It should have been safe.

Syl pushed her worries aside and began to run the diagnostic on the hyperdrive as the ship drifted. It was standard procedure. It wasn't common for a ship to get knocked out of hyperspace, but with the *Switchback*'s sketchy hyperdrive it happened occasionally. And just like that, Syl was worrying about credits all over again.

"This is wrong," Neeto said, dragging Syl from her despair spiral. "Did you see this? It looks like we somehow circled back to the Berenge system. Nothing out here but a dead star and a whole bunch of nothing."

Syl blinked as a number of ships appeared on her readout. "How—nonononono. Not again."

Neeto looked out the viewscreen. "Is that . . . ?" he asked, voice low.

She and Neeto exchanged a look, and a chill ran down her spine. "Nihil," she said.

Neeto nodded. "Sure enough. They must have discovered a way to kick ships out of hyperspace without damaging them. But I am not about to sit around and ask them for the recipe."

Syl nodded, all of her worry now focused on the ships bearing down on them. "Let's get out of here."

"Already on it," Neeto said, flipping switches.

The *Switchback* powered up and moved around, away from the approaching ships and back toward the spot where they'd been ejected from hyperspace.

"I can't find a single beacon," Neeto said.

"Can we jump without a destination?" Syl asked, trying to cycle the navicomputer so that it could calibrate the path. It was a rhetorical question. She knew the answer; she just didn't much like it.

"It's not a good idea, but it's preferable to whatever our friends on the approach have planned. And yes, I know. But it's a risk we have to take."

Syl grimaced. "I was afraid you were going to say that."

"All right, hold on," Neeto said, rerouting all of the ship's power to the hyperdrive to help them jump just that much faster. Any other ship would have been caught by surprise by such an attack, but Syl and Neeto had tangled with the Nihil before. They knew this dance.

That was, of course, when the engine blew.

The sound of the ship shutting down, of every component losing power, left a cold lump of dread in Syl's middle. "Oh no. Not now."

Neeto grimaced. "I'm guessing that the coaxium regulator

couldn't wait to be replaced, after all," he said, not a hint of fear or stress entering his voice. The only sign that he was not having a great day was the extra line that had appeared between his large, liquid eyes.

"We're spine fish in a barrel," Neeto said. "We have to evacuate."

"No," Syl said. Her fear hadn't lessened at all, but she straightened just a bit.

"Yes. The Nihil want the ship, which we do not have time to fix. If we run we can maybe save our lives. I doubt they'd notice an escape pod. Em-Two-Two-Seven? Tell Syl our odds of survival if we evacuate now. Before they get to us."

M-227 turned creakily. "Evacuation is best."

"No," Syl said, hunching over in her seat. She wrapped her arms around herself, suddenly chilled at the idea of leaving the *Switchback*. "This is all I have, Neeto. And you know running is not my style. If the Nihil want my ship, then they can take it from me. Betty and I can handle them." Syl reached down and pulled the modified blaster rifle from its holster under the control panel. It had been a joke when her mother had first given her the rifle, naming it after her childhood doll. But the name had stuck, and Syl and Betty were a lethal combo. She'd never missed a shot with the snub-barreled blaster rifle, and it had only been because of the gas the Nihil used that she hadn't stopped the marauders who'd boarded their ship the day her mother was killed.

Neeto sighed. "Syl."

"A captain doesn't quit their ship, no matter how bleak things get." Syl blinked away hot tears and turned back to Neeto. "This is all I have left."

Neeto stood and pointed through the cockpit's window, to the ships approaching. "How many people do you think have died just like your mother? We have to tell someone what is happening out here. Do you think the Republic or the Jedi know that the Nihil can now kick ships out of hyperspace? They've already killed so many, but this means that not even hyperspace is safe. We have to let someone on Coruscant know. Otherwise, how will we keep other haulers safe?"

Syl blinked, and M-227 began to move toward the escape pod like a very old man, each movement punctuated by a squeal of rusty hinges. Syl knew they were right, but in this moment she couldn't help herself. She didn't want to do the smart thing. She wanted her heart to stop breaking.

"The *Switchback* is my home," Syl said.

"It's my home, too," Neeto said, his voice clogged with emotion. "And I promise you we will get it back. But first, we have to survive."

Syl nodded and reluctantly stood, sliding Betty into the backpack holster she wore. And then she ran to the escape pod with Neeto and M-227, fleeing for her life, giving up one of the last things she had left of her mother.

They made it to the escape pod just as the sounds of the Nihil breaching the air lock reverberated through the ship. As they launched out into the darkness of space, Syl's thoughts were only for the *Switchback*.

She would do everything in her power to get her ship back.

Either that, or she would extract its price in Nihil blood.